THE WHITE SEA

THE WHITE SEA

An Alex Mavros Mystery

Paul Johnston

CRÈME de la CRIME

This first world edition published 2014
in Great Britain and in the USA by
Crème de la Crime, an imprint of
SEVERN HOUSE PUBLISHERS LTD of
19 Cedar Road, Sutton, Surrey, England, SM2 5DA.

British Library Cataloguing in Publication Data

Johnston, Paul, 1957– author.
   The white sea.
   1. Mavros, Alex (Fictitious character)–Fiction.
   2. Kidnapping–Fiction. 3. Private investigators–
   Greece–Fiction. 4. Suspense fiction.
   I. Title
   823.9'2-dc23

ISBN-13: 978-1-78029-067-6 (cased)

All Severn House titles are printed on acid-free paper.

Severn House Publishers support the Forest Stewardship Council™ [FSC™],
the leading international forest certification organisation. All our titles that
are printed on FSC certified paper carry the FSC logo.

MIX
Paper from
responsible sources
FSC   FSC® C013056
www.fsc.org

Typeset by Palimpsest Book Production Ltd.,
Falkirk, Stirlingshire, Scotland.
Printed and bound in Great Britain by
TJ International, Padstow, Cornwall

To Rob Wilson
in memory of Jane, who loved Greece

AUTHOR'S NOTE

Aspects of Modern Greek

1) Masculine names ending in -os, -as, and -is lose the final -s in the vocative case: 'Mavros, Kostas and Babis are laughing'; but 'Laugh, Mavro, Kosta and Babi!' Some names (e.g. Stephanos) retain the older form -e (Stephane) in the vocative.

2) The consonant transliterated as 'dh' (e.g. Alexandhras, Haralambidhis) is pronounced 'th' as in English 'these'.

3) Feminine surnames differ from their male equivalents – Kostas Gatsos, but Evi Gatsou; Vangelis Myronis, but Eirini Myroni.

PROLOGUE

The night of the raid was calm. The sea was running almost silently and the sweet scent from the night flower blossom rose up to the star-spattered darkness.

September in Lesvos was usually warm and welcoming, although many of the island's tourists had left. In 2010 the mornings had a bite to them and the atmosphere wasn't pleasant. More than meteorological conditions were in play. Greece's economy was in free fall and, because of a rapid increase in sovereign debt, the government had been forced to get out the begging bowl. Funds were provided under an agreement with the International Monetary Fund, European Central Bank and the other member countries of the Euro zone, but the cost was high. Salaries and pensions in the oversized public sector were slashed, jobs in the private sector fell away like leaves, and a package of new taxes was applied. Autumn was coming early for anyone who hadn't moved funds abroad.

Kostas Gatsos had no worries on that front. Less than five per cent of his wealth was in Greece. He might have been eighty-three, but his mind was sharper than the business end of a swordfish. He laid his manicured fingers on the smooth marble that topped the wall and stretched the arthritic joints. As he looked across the wide terrace of his villa outside Molyvos on the island's northwest point, he thought of the many triumphs in his life. Over the darkening straight lay the Turkish coast. His parents had come from a Greek village to the east of Constantinople – none of his employees, Greek or otherwise, was allowed to refer to the city by its modern name – and had been driven out in the exchange of populations that followed the over-ambitious Greek campaign in Asia Minor in the early 1920s. He'd been born in a basement in Mytilene, the capital of Lesvos, only a few months after his parents had managed to get out of a pestilential refugee camp. Although he grew up in a shack in a new suburb of Athens and spent his working life all over the world – New York, London, Geneva – he still regarded the island as home. His second wife, Tatiana, long divorced and dead from liver failure, once asked him why, given his miserable early life there.

'Because being looked down on by the locals was better than being bayoneted by the Turks,' he said, glaring at her and then smiling crookedly. 'Besides, I'm worth more than the whole island hundreds of times over. I like playing king.'

Gatsos emptied the glass of fifty-year-old malt whisky and lit a cigarette. Both had been banned by his doctors, but they could go fuck themselves. He knew his body better than anyone else. He was captain of it as well as his soul – he had come across Henley's poem 'Invictus' when he was buying his first ships in the 50s. People were surprised by his interest in Victorian poetry, but he liked its often overblown emotional display. It inspired him; for twenty years he had been admiral of one of the largest fleets globally: tankers, bulk carriers, refrigerated ships, bulk and gas carriers, and more recently container ships. He hadn't been convinced of the capacity for growth in the latter market, but he invested in time. His six high-capacity vessels had maintained impressive charter rates ever since they went into service.

He was the last of the great Greek pirates, as less successful shipowners called them: Onassis, Niarchos, Latsis – he had outlived and ultimately outearned them all. He had also outmanouevred and outthought them more often than they had him. One of the most important lessons he'd learned was that you had to move on quickly from every defeat, taking all you could from it. It had been a great life, bringing him wealth that even his accountants struggled to count, not least because he had different bean-counters covering his multifarious operations across the world. That wealth had brought him two of the most beautiful and desirable women as wives, as well as dozens of short-term lovers, though they cost him plenty; an art collection that even the Russian oligarchs envied (and that was only the works he had bought legally); eleven residences across the world; and the private numbers of every important global player, from kings and queens to presidents to industrialists to Hollywood moguls – he had backed several successful if mindless films. Konstandinos Gatsos did not believe in cultivating the masses' capacity for thought.

He went into the dining room, where his son Pavlos was waiting, nervous and serious-faced as ever. Gatsos had been disappointed by both of his children – the male slow-witted and the female wanton – but he had hopes for a couple of the grandchildren, Loukas and Evi: they were in the Piraeus office and rising fast.

'What is it?' he demanded.

Pavlos looked down. 'The French finance minister. She's sent our government a list of Greek account holders at one of the Geneva banks.'

'So?'

'We . . .'

'We're on it? Who gives a fuck? Do you seriously imagine the idiots in Athens will come after us?'

'No,' came a voice from the terrace. 'That's why we're doing that.'

Kostas turned, his pure white hair catching the light. 'Who the hell are you? Pavlo, press the button.'

'I wouldn't,' said the man in black combat uniform, raising a silenced pistol. His features were concealed by a balaclava. 'I wouldn't do that either, Mr Kosta.'

The old man stopped. He'd been on his way to remonstrate with the intruder. As he got closer he saw there were two more of them, carrying machine-pistols. He looked round. Pavlos was standing like a tailor's dummy, his lower jaw slack. A fourth figure had appeared at the door that led to the interior of the building.

'Do something, you fool!' Kostas shouted. 'Where is everyone?'

'Unconscious or, in the other case, bleeding from his femoral artery,' said the man with the pistol. 'A large bald man with a scar on his head.'

'Boris,' Pavlos said, his voice faint.

'He displayed excessive zeal. Now, Mr Kosta, you're coming with us.' He grabbed the old man by his right arm.

'What about my son?'

His captor glanced at Pavlos. 'Goodbye,' he said, then shot him through the left eye.

ONE

Mavros didn't notice that October had begun until his mother wished him 'Good month' on the late afternoon of the first. He returned the greeting without looking away from the computer screen.

'Haven't you done enough for today?' Dorothy Cochrane-Mavrou asked, her voice tremulous. She was eighty-five now and although she still took an interest in Persephone and Hecate Publications, the company she had founded and owned outright, she had gradually allowed herself to slip into the background.

'It's the crisis, Mother,' her son said, graying hair on his shoulders. 'If we don't turn the backlist into e-books soon, our cash flow will dwindle even more.'

Dorothy sat down and looked at the photographs of her lost men. Spyros, her husband, a lawyer and high-ranking Communist Party official, had died in 1967, not long before the dictatorship of the colonels began; and Andonis, her oldest child and elder son, who had disappeared while the Junta was still in power, no doubt because he had been a leader of the student resistance. They lived on in her and her other children, but that had never been enough.

'I thought we had let them go,' Mavros said, having swung round silently on the leather office chair. The lines on his face made him look older than forty-eight and his bloodshot eyes suggested he was drinking more than was advisable.

'Of course we have, dear. But you of all people know how hard that is.' Dorothy was referring to her son's long-term lover Niki, who had died under mysterious circumstances five years earlier. He hadn't fully recovered from the loss.

Mavros nodded but didn't meet her gaze.

'Alex, it's been wonderful having you run the business these recent years,' she started.

'But?'

Now it was Dorothy who turned her head away. 'It isn't good for you. There's only one thing you really want to do.'

'That's where you're wrong.' Mavros got up and opened the sliding glass door. Scents from the flowers on the terrace came in, along with the Athenian traffic noise and regular horn blasts. 'After Niki . . . after that, I had no more interest in finding people who'd gone missing. It was because of me that she . . . that whatever happened to her—'

'No, it wasn't,' Dorothy interrupted. 'You can't blame yourself. Or rather, you can't keep blaming yourself. Who knows what was going on in the poor woman's mind? She was never exactly renowned for stable behaviour.'

Mavros turned quickly, his fists clenching. It looked as if he was going to shout at his mother, but he got himself under control. To her surprise, he started to laugh softly.

'No, she wasn't, was she?' He sat down next to Dorothy and allowed her to take his hand.

'We all leave this life,' she said. 'Some too soon, like Spyros and especially Andonis, and some not soon enough. Like me.'

He looked into her eyes, their brown cloudier than it used to be. 'Come on, Mother, you're fine.'

She smiled. 'I'm living from day to day and you know it. That's why you spend every night here.' She nudged him. 'Well, nearly every night.'

It was true. He had agreed with his sister Anna that he would live in Dorothy's large central flat to keep an eye on her. It made sense, given that he was effectively running the company. But he did need the occasional week-day night off, which Dorothy declined to report to Anna on the grounds that she was perfectly capable of looking after herself. The weekends were different: she spent them at her daughter's house in an outer suburb.

'Go and see Yiorgos,' Dorothy said, smiling sweetly. 'I'm not taking no for an answer.'

'But the crisis is killing us. People don't have money to spend on books any more.'

'A problem which won't be noticeably worse by tomorrow morning. Go on, get out of here.'

Mavros kissed her powdered cheek and got up. 'All right. The Fat Man could do with being roused from his sofa.'

'I don't know why you still call him that, dear.'

Mavros shrugged. 'The habit of a lifetime. Besides, the Thin Man hardly cuts it.' Then it struck him that, like his mother, his friend

Yiorgos might not be around for much longer. That sent him off without a skip in his stride.

The Fat Man's house had been burned down during the case that culminated in Niki's death. He had a long struggle before the insurance company paid up, eventually buying a top-floor flat in an apartment block a hundred metres higher up the hill from his old place. It was new, well equipped and too large for his purposes, not least because all his possessions, personal and family, had gone up in smoke. Then, a year ago, he'd had a heart attack and been told that, if he didn't change his diet and take daily exercise, he wouldn't be long for this world.

As Mavros walked round the Lykavittos ring road his phone rang. He scowled when he saw the caller ID and let it go to messaging, not that he intended to retrieve it. He turned down to Neapolis. The area was adjacent to Exarcheia, the hang-out of students and anarchists, and it had gradually become less safe. Not that Mavros cared. Since Niki died, he hadn't cared much about anything. In the past he'd have run up the five sets of stairs, but now he took the lift. His belly had expanded and he took less exercise than the Fat Man.

He hammered on the door and heard flip flops approaching.

'There is a bell, you know,' Yiorgos said. 'I thought the riot police had arrived.'

'Rubbish. You wouldn't have opened the door to them.' Mavros examined the thick steel panels and crossbars. 'And they wouldn't have managed to get in. What have you got to hide?'

The Fat Man tapped his nose. 'Secret party archives.' He'd been a Communist since he was a kid, though he'd let his membership lapse some years back. The comrades wanted a cut of the illegal card games he used to run in his café.

'Yeah, right.' Mavros looked at him. 'Is that the beginnings of a gut I can see under that filthy shirt?'

'Might be,' Yiorgos said, turning towards the large *saloni* that contained little more than an armchair, a sofa and a TV. 'What's it to you?'

'What's it to me? Do you think I want to carry a corner of your coffin?'

'Don't worry, that's all arranged. I'm getting cremated in Bulgaria. Special deal for comrades.'

'Ex-comrades. For God's sake, Yiorgo, you're only sixty-seven.

You've got plenty of time left – if you stay off the . . . what's that?'

The Fat Man was surreptitiously trying to slide a pizza box under the sofa with one foot. 'A friend brought it over last night. I only ate one slice.'

'You haven't got any friends apart from me.'

'Yes, I have.'

'Name one.'

'Angelos.'

'He's in a nursing home.'

'Piss off, smartarse.' Yiorgos patted his slack abdomen. 'I've got to fill this up. I walk around like a becalmed ship under full sail.'

'A striking but completely confusing image.'

'Huh. You're not exactly Mr Six Pack 2010 yourself.'

Mavros shrugged. 'I lead a sedentary life.'

'What does that mean?'

'I'm on my backside all day.'

'Exactly. And you were smoking on the way over here.'

'Just the one. You know I don't do it in front of Mother.'

Mavros's phone went again. The same caller, the same failure to respond.

Yiorgos turned on the TV. 'Who was that?'

'You don't want to know.'

'You're right, I don't.' The Fat Man settled on a channel showing basketball.

'At least cut the volume,' Mavros said. 'What are you doing watching the modern opium of the masses?'

'It's a game of great skill.'

'It is if you're playing. Doesn't take much skill to lie around watching it.'

'Go and stick your head in a bucket. Do you want a beer?'

Mavros got up and went to the kitchen. 'You're not allowed, of course,' he said over his shoulder, but he brought two cans of Amstel back. 'One for each of my kidneys.'

'Fool.' The Fat Man caught his can with one hand. 'See, great skill.'

They drank and abused each other until the match was over.

'Time for your salad?' Mavros asked.

'Already eaten it. Time for souvlaki.' Yiorgos picked up the phone. 'You?'

Mavros shook his head. His mother still cooked and they had eaten a three-course lunch. 'You know what the old woman said to me today? That I should go back to work.'

'She's right.'

'Not you too.'

'No, really, you should. I'd have thought you needed the money these days.'

'I never looked for people to make money.'

The Fat Man caught his eye. 'No, you did it because you had to – because of Andonis, who's the only person you've never found. So why have you given up?'

'What? Looking for my brother?'

'Not necessarily. Realistically it's too long now. The trail's gone colder than the summit of Mount Olympus. But you still have the need to do the job, admit it.'

Mavros got up and walked around the room. 'People don't have only one need, Yiorgo. Maybe I do still want to find people – I'd give my right arm for the slightest trace of Andonis – but I can't be responsible for any more deaths.'

The Fat Man sighed and got to his feet. 'Some time you'll have to realise that Niki's death isn't on you, Alex. She committed suicide when the balance of her mind was all over the place or she was murdered by that fucker, the Son. You aren't guilty in either case.'

Mavros stared at him. 'But I am. I led her into danger. It's as simple as that.'

'So find the murdering bastard and take it out on him.'

'I haven't got it in me any more, Yiorgo. I haven't got the strength.' He headed for the door. 'Are you going to let me out of this fortress?'

'I'll come with you. You need another drink and so do I.'

'You need another drink like a hole in the heart, my friend.'

The Fat Man laughed. 'I can watch you, can't I? Anyway, we might pick up a pair of well-stacked divorcées.'

Mavros shook his head. 'Not unless you change – and I don't just mean your clothes.'

He was sent to hell by two hands with splayed fingers. Then he caught sight of himself in a small mirror by the door. Christ, he looked grim: hair like a derelict's, stubble too long, face like it had recently been ploughed. Not even his trusty left eye – dark blue flecked by brown – would attract women now.

'Caught you,' Yiorgos said.

'Just checking the damage. Not good.'

The Fat Man slapped him on the back. 'The trick is to get them drunk, remember?'

Mavros followed him to the door. He shivered as Niki's vertical body swayed before him as it did at least once a day. This was no kind of life.

His mobile rang again. He turned it off.

'I'm sorry, Mr Thomson, there's nothing left except palliative care. We've done all the surgery we can and your wife refuses more chemotherapy.' The oncologist looked at the file as if it could tell him anything he didn't know.

'So that's it, doc? I just take her home?'

'Until that gets too much for you both and she goes into a hospice. There's no shortage of good ones in Melbourne.' The doctor looked like he'd just left university. His black hair was short, without a hint of grey. Although he was strongly built, his eyelashes were long and curled like a show girl's.

'Any point in homeopathy or Chinese herbs?'

'That's up to you, but I wouldn't waste the money. Raising your wife's or your own hopes will only make things worse in the end.'

Jim Thomson went over the conversation as he sat on the balcony of the Victorian terraced house in Kensington, three miles northwest of central Melbourne. He couldn't get beyond the doctor's last word and his lack of hesitation in using it. He'd been right though. Ivy didn't want any treatment except the morphine drip. She lasted three weeks at home and another five days in the hospice, then slipped away when he was dozing, her hand in his. He didn't know how long she'd been dead when he woke up. There was nothing material left of her except the plastic urn on the mantelpiece.

But he could still smell her in the house, still put his hand where hers had been on plates, glasses, cutlery, pots. And her shape, for all her weight loss, was still imprinted on the mattress they'd slept on for sixteen years. The place and its contents were his now, even though the doctor had been mistaken in describing Ivy as Thomson's wife. They'd lived together for so long that it came to the same thing, but neither of them had felt the need of formalising their relationship. They loved each other. What else mattered?

The house had been bought by Ivy and her first husband back in the 80s, when the abbatoir was still in operation. Timmie got himself killed in an industrial accident that Ivy never talked about, not long before his place of work closed down for good. Jim hadn't known the area then, but it must have been oppressive, especially the stink in the summer. The old yards had been demolished and turned into a housing project. He was glad he didn't live over the killing floors that had run with the blood of countless animals.

Then again he'd never intended to come to a city with so many Greeks. It had been easy to disguise himself – his English was good and his blue eyes didn't smack of the old country. His hair was already a shock of white when he arrived in Australia though he was only forty. He'd been through plenty in his wind- and wave-battered life; he was lucky he had any hair at all. All the cities, the ports . . . The lights, the buildings, the food, the women . . . He should write his memoirs or maybe a novel. He laughed, making a couple of Chinese kids look up at him. He waved to them like the crazy old guy he was. He couldn't write anything. Not because he was illiterate – he'd had a good education, even if it had been prematurely terminated – but because he would have to remember. After nearly forty years of confining the horror to the deepest part of his being, he wasn't going to do that.

But maybe he wouldn't have a choice. Ivy's last wish, whispered to him the day before she died, was that her ashes be spread in the waters off the island her grandparents had come from. She made him swear on their love that'd he do it, said there was a ticket to Athens in his name already paid for. All he had to do was choose a date.

All he had to do. He'd kept his background to himself. So many secrets. Ivy knew he hadn't told her everything, but she didn't mind. She had him to herself and that was enough. He went out to work at the picture-framers where old Kinch had taught him the trade despite his advanced age as an apprentice. That could have brought him into contact with artists and dealers, but he had no interest in that world and kept to the workshop. He rarely went out in the evenings, fearful of hearing Greek in bars or restaurants. It was a strange wind that had blown him to the city with the world's third largest Greek-speaking population, but it was Ivy's home and he never wanted to leave the third woman he loved – in some strange way, despite being on the other side of the world, he felt he was home.

And now he had to go back to the country of his birth. He'd considered reneging on his promise to Ivy and sprinkling her ashes in the Yarra, but that would have been wrong. He still retained a sense of decency. In fact, living with Ivy had turned him into a fully functioning human being. For that he owed her much more than a journey to Greece.

The sun had gone down when Jim Thomson went into the house. He breathed in his lost love and then opened a tinnie. He was thinking about the doctor again. Ivy had come to her end, but his was still ahead, beckoning him like a sultry goddess, one who would not refused; a journey back to his beginning to find what monsters awaited him there.

TWO

Mavros and the Fat Man ate and drank at a taverna on Alexandhras Avenue. It was a dingy place, a continuous stream of cars and buses passing even late in the evening, but the meat was from the owner's farm in Viotia and he knew how to cook it. Yiorgos managed to confine himself to a single beef chop, but disposed of two salads and enough wine to make a tractor tip over. Mavros wasn't far behind, except on the salad count.

'So how about it?'

Mavros raised an eyebrow. 'I know you're meant to take regular exercise, but I didn't think that meant with me.'

'Don't flatter yourself. I might have a girlfriend for all you know.'

'Uh-huh.'

'Why not? Everyone's entitled to a private life.'

Mavros nodded slowly, remembering the times before and after Niki's death when he and his family – as well as the Fat Man – had been forced to take extreme security precautions. Which, in his lover's case, had been for nothing. Fortunately the man who had been a threat had shown no sign of life since then, not that Mavros thought he was dead. It would be just like the Son to taunt him by disappearing for a long time and then making an explosive reappearance.

'You are too, you know,' Yiorgos said, in a low voice. 'One-night-stands are fine, but it's five years since Niki—'

Mavros raised a hand. 'Private means private, yes?'

The Fat Man shrugged. 'Suit yourself. Maybe you've forgotten but I know you've got a great capacity for love.'

'Fuck off,' Mavros said, not entirely in jest. 'When you start giving me relationship counselling, I know the end of the world is nigh.'

After half an hour they went their separate ways. Mavros was panting when he reached the Lykavittos ring-road, the lights from the chapel of St George on the summit shining. He had an exercise-bike in his mother's storage space and it was well past time that he started using it. He reached the junction with Kleomenous Street, the luxury hotel bathed in a soft glow that must have cost more than an entire working class street's lighting. Just before he reached the entrance to number six, a car door opened in front of him.

'What the—'

'Get in. Immediately. Or I'll arrest you.'

'Fuck you.'

A heavily built policeman in uniform got out of the driver's seat, spun him round, attached cuffs to his wrists and pushed him into the back.

'Consider yourself arrested.'

Mavros looked at the besuited figure next to him. 'On what charge?'

'Not answering your mobile phone.'

'Fuck you again.'

'Now you're being childish. How about resisting arrest? For a start.' Brigadier Nikos Kriaras was head of the Athens and Attica organised crime division. He did imperious without even trying. 'Back to HQ,' he ordered.

Mavros tried not to show that sitting with his hands behind his back was uncomfortable. Keeping quiet seemed like a good tactic.

Kriaras wasn't fooled. He'd known his man for fifteen years and knew exactly how to play him. When they arrived at the imposing glass and concrete block at the eastern end of Alexandhras, the driver got out and hauled Mavros to his feet.

'The cells,' Kriaras said, signalling to a uniformed officer to take charge of the vehicle.

Mavros walked along the corridors with his head high, the smell of disinfectant fighting a losing battle with that of human waste. The driver shouldered open a door and pulled the captive to a chair, clipping a chain attached to the floor to the one linking the cuffs.

'Ready, sir.'

The brigadier walked in, ignoring the chair on his side of the table.

'I had a feeling these measures would be necessary.'

'You always were a bully.' Mavros's relations with Kriaras had never been more than functional, but since Niki's death they had ceased completely. The inquest into his lover's death had concluded that she committed suicide, but both Mavros and the brigadier knew there was more to it than that. The former suspected that the Son, the stone killer who had sworn to strike at him, was behind the photo that could have driven Niki to take her own life. Even though the technicians had failed to establish that anyone else had been in their flat, Mavros still thought it was possible the Son had slipped in and murdered her. Kriaras's refusal to investigate further and his earlier links with the Son had led Mavros to break off contact with him.

'When's he coming?' he asked.

'Who?'

'You know who. Is he going to hang me from the ceiling with fish hooks like his old man used to do for the Junta?'

Kriaras gave him a disdainful look. 'I have no idea where the Son is. He has nothing to do with this.'

'Yeah, right.'

'Believe what you want.' The brigadier paused. 'I have a job offer for you.'

'Stick it up your festering ass.'

'A quarter of a million euros up front, the same on conclusion of the case.'

Mavros couldn't stop his jaw dropping.

'I thought that would get your attention.'

'Screw you. Most of the jobs you put my way nearly got me and the people I care for killed. Why do you think I gave up missing persons investigations?'

Kriaras gave him a disdainful look. 'I assumed it was because you lost your nerve.'

Mavros managed not to react to that.

'All right, here's how it's going to be, Alex. All you have to do is talk to your potential employers. If you don't take the job, more fool you. On the other hand, if you refuse to meet them, you're staying here with our large friend for company. Rations, not very much bread and very little water. For as long as it takes.'

It was obvious that someone with a lot of clout was tugging Kriaras's chain. Mavros thought about the money. Not many Greeks had that amount to throw around these days, especially as a down payment for work that might go nowhere. A quarter of a million would keep his mother's company going for a while longer – half of that would suffice. He knew how much that would mean to her. The prospect of unlimited incarceration in the sifling cell didn't bother him unduly – he could be as cussed as Kriaras – but he didn't have the appetite for more posturing.

He raised his shoulders as far as the chain permitted. 'All right, I'll talk to them. Who are they? The Onassis Foundation?'

'Close,' muttered the brigadier.

The floor of Kostas Gatsos's cell was uneven and he could feel that the brick walls were unplastered. There was no light or furniture, and no window frames. He had tried pacing with his arms outstretched and the space seemed to be about seven metres by five. Was he in a storeroom? A basement? An oversized grave?

He had been pushed inside what must have been some weeks ago. Without a watch or a view of the sky, he had no idea of how many days had passed. His captors opened the steel door at the far end from where his stinking mattress lay and left a chunk of bread and a bottle of water, but he had the suspicion they did so at irregular intervals. Were they deliberately disorienting him?

He tried to remember what had happened after Pavlos was shot. He had been rushed through the house to the front door, where a hood was put over his head. He had seen Boris in a pool of blood on the marble of the hall and one of the maids was sprawled in the corner, he hoped only unconscious. A heavy hand had pushed him down to the floor of a vehicle, his shoulders jammed between the front and rear seats. The driver was skilful and the engine smooth. At times he thought they were going uphill, but he couldn't be sure. Then they stopped and he was pulled out. Someone took his right forearm and led him to what he soon realised was a boat, though he had no idea of its size. He could smell the sea from the loose bottom of the hood and hear the roar of a powerful engine. His hands were cuffed behind his back and he was pushed into what he assumed was a cabin. He could only feel about with his head. It seemed he was on a mattress.

'Lie still, old man,' came a coarse voice in heavily accented English. The man who had shot his son spoke Greek. 'Or it's a bullet in the leg.'

He did as he was told with alacrity. He may have been known as the Pit Bull because of his aggressive negotiating, but he knew when he had no room for manoeuvre. He had to use the time to plan, to work out how to talk the savages into letting him go. It would come down to money, these things always did. He wasn't the only shipowner to have been kidnapped and held for ransom. Loukas and Evi would know what to do. They would bring in experts.

The boat was on the water for about four hours, he estimated. He had spent a lot of time at sea over the years. Not on the cargo ships the group owned and operated, but on his yacht, the *Tatiana*, which he'd sold after he'd divorced his second wife, she of that name – he hadn't felt the need to remarry – and even more on his 150 metre motor yacht, the *Golden Arrow*, which he took round the Mediterranean every summer. Prime ministers and film stars, artists and bankers, opera singers and even the occasional royal were his guests. The *Arrow*, a former passenger ferry, had been reconditioned and its interior refurbished by the best Danish designers. Good taste was the by-word. There were no bar seats covered in whale foreskins.

Then the vessel put to sea again, this time moving for only about an hour. After a stop of maybe three hours – he couldn't see his watch – another voyage, this one much longer, maybe twelve hours. And then more stops and starts, till he'd lost count. Where were they? Off the coast of Turkey? Or had they gone west towards the Sporades or south to the Cyclades and Crete? He had no idea and that distressed him. He was used to being in possession of all the relevant facts.

When he called, one of the men took him to the toilet and pulled down his trousers and pants. It was a small cabinet and his feet were against the walls. They put wads of paper in his joined hands, leaving him to wipe himself as best he could. They fed him bread and water, one of them lifting the hood up to his nose and another stuffing bits of bread into his mouth and pressing a water bottle against his lips. That was all he got in his place of imprisonment too – never enough to assuage his raging hunger and thirst. Why were they treating him like this? He was a valuable commodity.

Then the boat reached land again and this time he was taken off, the bottom of the thick hood tightened with a drawstring so he couldn't tell if it was day or night. This time the vehicle he was put in was older, the engine sound much louder. They drove for a long time, the road getting progressively rougher. Between the seats, his head was knocked around and his nose hit the floor hard once. He felt blood pool in the hood and cried out. That earned him a slap on the back of the head.

At last the vehicle stopped and he was dragged out. He was lifted up by a large man and carried over a hundred paces, some of them downstairs. Then the handcuffs were finally unlocked, relief crashing over him.

'Feel that?' said a familiar male voice speaking Greek. He hadn't heard it on the boat. 'It's the barrel of the gun that ended your son's life and it's against the back of your head. I can guarantee the bullet will take your eye out too – after ploughing through your oh-so-smart brain. So don't try anything, Kosta.' The first name was pronounced as if it were a particularly crude insult.

His clothes were removed; the linen Brooks Brothers jacket, the Indian silk shirt, the chinos. And they took the Patek Philippe watch he'd bought after his first major contract – grain from the US east coast to Antwerp. His 700 euro loafers had gone not long after he was taken on board the boat. A rough garment was pulled over his limbs and body.

'What's this?'

'A boiler suit. We know how much regard you have for engineers.'

The words puzzled him. He had never had much interest in the men who tended his vessels' propulsion units. What did the gunman mean?

Then he was pushed into the cell, basement, hole, whatever it was that had been his home for what seemed liked months. The hood was removed as he went and he found himself in total darkness.

'You'll find a bucket to void yourself into, old man,' said his captor. 'I hope you like your own stink.'

Kostas Gatsos reckoned they emptied it every ten meals, but how that related to days he had no idea. He had been fastidious about cleaning himself ever since he started earning. Being left with his excreta, very little paper and no running water was torture. He was sure his captors knew that very well.

Mavros was dropped off outside his mother's place.

'I'll be here at 9 a.m.,' said the beefy driver. 'Don't be late.'

'Don't you ever sleep?'

The officer grinned. 'Not when there are criminals to be nailed to the wall. Oh, and citizens to be protected.' He drove off at speed.

'One of Kriaras's finest,' Mavros muttered, as he went in the street door. There was a camera and a code. They'd been installed when the Son was a threat and were still in operation, though the

private security guards had been dispensed with. Too expensive. A
quarter of a million would change that, though maybe the Son had
been nailed, to use the cop's delicate term. He doubted it.
In the flat he checked that his mother was soundly asleep and
went to his room. It was a mess, like that of a teenager – clothes
all over the floor, books and CDs piled precariously on table top,
chest and shelves, framed posters for exhibitions at the National
Gallery hanging askew. This was his domain, though he knew his
mother looked in when he was away. She was long-suffering enough
not to comment. She just told the cleaner to ignore it, forcing him
to tidy up every few weeks.
He pushed the manuscript of a book he'd been reading off the
bed and lay down, only taking off his leather jacket, boots and jeans
when he was horizontal. Anything to make life more difficult. The
Fat Man had suggested he become a Catholic, so guilty had he
become since Niki's death. As if religion would have helped a
lifelong atheist. He'd almost been tempted to do it to see the look
on his friend's face.
There were five hours before he had to get up, but sleep wouldn't
come. He wallowed in semi-consciousness, wondering how to get
back at Kriaras for his display of force; trying to imagine who could
possibly be offering 250,000 euros up front and failing; then –
inevitably – thinking about Niki. There were no photos of her in
his room, though he had plenty stashed away, and none in his laptop
or phone. It wasn't that he was trying to forget her, rather that she
was always with him. Their relationship had been seriously erratic,
as she was; they'd broken up several times but always got back
together. When she died they were trying for a baby, although she
had gynaecological issues. She'd been worried by that, but she
wasn't depressed. It would have taken more than a photo of Mavros
and his admittedly very attractive female client in Thessaloniki to
have driven her to suicide. He'd spoken to her on the phone not
long before he found her and she sounded fine. No, he was sure
she'd been murdered. The only candidate was the Son. Working
with Kriaras, or at least doing what he wanted, might enable him
to put the squeeze on the brigadier. He was sure the bastard knew
more than he was telling about the professional assassin.
By five in the morning Mavros had convinced himself that taking
the job would be a way of finally laying Niki to rest. He remembered the dull autumn day when her coffin had been lowered into

the grave in the cemetery on the slopes of Mount Imittos. His family had been there, as had the Fat Man – who hated Niki but was doing a good job of looking repentant – and others of his friends. There was no one from Niki's family because she had none; she'd been adopted by a kindly couple who were long dead. She had friends and colleagues from her office – she was a social worker doing what she could to improve the lives of immigrants – and one of them, Maria, was so upset that she nearly jumped into the grave. In one of her better moods, Niki might have raised a smile at that, if only because Maria was an even more committed atheist than Mavros. For some reason, probably linked to her general insecurity, Niki had stipulated a full Orthodox service in her will. At the gathering afterwards the company drank cheap brandy and ate sweet cake. Mavros couldn't get away quickly enough.

At least Nikos Kriaras hadn't had the nerve to show up. Given what Mavros knew about his previous links with the Son, he might have brought about the brigadier's own funeral. In the five years since then, he had moderated his position slightly. The Son was capable of running rings round even as calculating and politically savvy an operator as Kriaras. That didn't mean Mavros trusted him, but the fact was he had come to Mavros offering a case, meaning the balance of power between them had shifted in Mavros's favour.

On that happy if debatable thought he finally fell asleep.

THREE

The colossus was standing by the unmarked car when Mavros appeared.

'You're late,' he said, getting into the driver's seat.

Mavros walked to the front passenger door. 'Unlike you I don't work shifts.'

'Unlike me you can get a slap.'

'Long live police brutality. Where are we going?'

'Wait and see,' the policeman said, as he went down Lykavittos.

'OK, how about this? You got a name?'

'Yes.' There were traces of a smile on the big man's fleshy lips.

Mavros sighed. 'You going to tell me what it is?'

'No.'

'You're required to show me ID if I ask.'

'So ask.'

'Show me your ID, please.'

The driver took one hand off the wheel and took out his wallet.

'Haralambos Haralambidhis,' Mavros read. 'What do I call you?'

'Lieutenant.'

Mavros laughed. 'Lieutenant Haris? Lieutenant Lambis? Lieutenant Babis?'

'Just lieutenant.'

'Don't your colleagues get confused?'

'I don't have any colleagues. I'm the brigadier's special assistant.'

'That must be fun.'

'Can be. Not enough truncheon use for my liking.'

'You're not by any chance a member of an extreme rightwing organisation?'

'No.'

'Just checking. Because if you had been, I'd have had to get out.'

'Be my guest.'

They were now driving at speed down Syngrou Avenue towards the sea.

'You mean you were lying about being a Nazi?'

'I never lie.'

Mavros laughed long and loud. 'That makes you a unique Greek policeman.'

The big man shrugged. 'Could be.'

They turned towards Piraeus on the multi-lane highway, leaving it about two kilometres before the port. The lieutenant pulled up outside a modern building covered in green glass. 'Fifth floor,' he said. 'They're waiting for you.'

'Who?'

'Mr Loukas Gatsos and Ms Evi Gatsou.' He pulled the door shut and drove to the parking area.

Shit, Mavros thought. The Gatsos case. It had been all over the media for the last month. Now he knew why he hadn't been told earlier. There had been no sign of the old shipowner since he'd disappeared from his palatial villa on Lesvos and no ransom demand, at least in public. The police had been busting a collective gut but had got nowhere. What did they expect him to do? He stood in the shade of a palm tree and weighed up his choices. He could walk away without seeing the family members, he could see them and refuse the case, or he could take their money and run into the same cyclopean walls that the cops had. The first option was the most attractive, despite the lure of the cash. He looked towards the hill of Kastella and the sunken roof of the Stadium of Peace and Friendship. There was a train station near it. He took a step . . .

And was grabbed by the left arm.

'Are you Alex Mavros? You are, aren't you? Please, help us. Please.'

He turned and took in an expensively dressed young woman who had been unlucky when the genes that brought about beauty had been allocated. She was much shorter than him, even though she was wearing high heels. What got through his guard was her broad face. Copious tears had made her mascara run and she looked like a bereaved queen from an ancient tragedy.

The one thing that really got to Mavros was a crying woman. He let himself be tugged into the unsightly green building.

Jim Thomson had delayed confirming the date of his flight to Greece. In recent weeks he'd felt becalmed; Ivy's death had left him bobbing aimlessly on the waves like a ship with engine failure. He would only leave the house to buy beer and food, not much of the latter. He could hear people's voices as they walked down the pavement outside the house, but he had no desire for company. His boss at the gallery had rung a couple of times then given up, assuming he would come back when he finished grieving. He was a good man; he'd keep Jim's job open even though he'd have to hire a replacement.

But Jim wasn't grieving – he'd pushed Ivy's death to the back of his mind – and he didn't think he'd be going back to the gallery. The idea of returning to the old country had thrown him out of kilter and brought back memories he hadn't allowed to surface for decades. Now he was living in the past all day and most of every night. He was . . .

. . . back in the water after they'd thrown him from the ship, his wounds initially stinging, but then going numb like the rest of his body in the chill winter Aegean. He was barely conscious after the shock of hitting the dark surface. As he came back up, he saw the lights of the navy transport moving steadily away. There was a half-moon and its light cast a ghostly path on the water. He tried to get his breathing under control and then started swimming slowly, his arms and legs like oars rather than limbs, so disconnected did he feel from them. He made slow progress along the moon path he thought would lead him somewhere, then allowed the waves to carry him into the darkness. Let it go, he heard a voice tell him, give it up. He was about to do that when he recognised the speaker. It was the fucker who had tortured him, the security police animal who'd stuck fish hooks into him and pulled the lines attached to them as if he were a catch being reeled in. The pain . . . he still heard himself screaming . . . telling them everything them wanted to know . . . names, addresses, contacts . . . he didn't care about the Party any more, the student resistance groups could go to hell . . . all he wanted was relief from the pain. Eventually it came, though the wounds in his skin and flesh still throbbed back in the stinking cell.

After days, maybe as many as ten, he could hardly remember who he was, never mind who the people he had worked with were. The torturer had moved on to other victims, no doubt the ones he'd betrayed. He was left to rot until he was taken to the shower and forced to clean himself. The cuts and weals had partially scabbed over and he avoided touching them. Even the dribble of water in the open stall made them smart; but not as much as the hurt in his soul, the agony of failed responsibility. He would never be able to look anyone he knew in the face again . . .

The officer behind the desk was friendly, offered him a cigarette. He ignored it.

'Don't worry, young man. You've been brave. No one has lasted so long against the Father. He's been getting people like you to talk since the Civil War.'

He sat with his head down, the flattery dashing over him like the contents of a cess pit.

'There's one more thing we need you to tell us.'

He might have known. The colonels' specialists never gave up.

The officer with the pencil moustache blew out smoke. 'And I do hope we won't have to send you back to the Father for further . . . persuasion. It's simply this. If we let you go free, will you work for us? You can easily pin leaks of information on other comrades. You'll be paid, of course.'

He suffered moments of indecision. To his shame he gave the idea consideration, so low had he sunk. But he had reached his limit.

'Never,' he said, his voice hoarse.

'Are you sure?'

He kept his head down, eyes to the floor.

'Well, it was worth a try. Don't worry, we won't send you back to him. You're in luck. You're going on holiday. There's a ship leaving for Rhodes tonight. We have a centre for your type there. It's really quite comfortable.'

He hadn't believed the Bureaucrat of Pain even after he was put in a van with blacked out windows, to emerge in what he smelled was a port, presumably Piraeus – he couldn't see because there was a blanket over his head. He was led up a gangway that shifted from side to side and then along metal corridors. The blanket was pulled off and thrown at him when he was shoved into a small room. In the dim light he touched his wounds. Two of them had reopened. He put a finger on each, oblivious to the risk of infection.

No one gave him anything to eat or drink. He fell into a disturbed sleep, hooks and lines looming before him, then the former burrowing into his flesh like malevolent worms. He was woken by the clang of the door.

'On deck for some fresh air,' said the first of a pair of uniformed security policemen.

They dragged him to his feet and led him along a corridor to a steel stairway. Then he was outside, the ship's lights illuminating white-capped waves.

'Commie shit,' said one of his guards, seizing his arms from behind. 'Have a good swim.'

Between them they picked him up and heaved him over the side.

Jim came back to himself, panting and quivering. Gradually the familiar shapes of the living-room's furniture reformed before him. The water . . . He touched his clothes. He was dry, but he had let the past pour back into his life. He didn't think he'd be able to survive seeing the white sea again.

'I'm Evi Gatsou, well, Gatsou-Myroni, but I don't bother with my father's name at work,' the woman said, stopping outside the front door of the green building to wipe her face. 'God, I must look a mess.'

Mavros offered another tissue. 'It must be very difficult for you.'

'You don't know how . . .' She broke off. 'I'm sorry, of course you do. I've read about you.'

He stiffened. 'Courtesy of Brigadier Kriaras.'

'Partly.' She put the used tissues into a waste bin and pushed open the door. 'There's no shortage of information about you on the internet. I'm so sorry about Niki.'

Mavros didn't know whether to be offended or touched by the over-familiarity. The young woman gave the impression of being emotionally gauche. Then again, she was from a shipping family. How to dissemble was drummed into them when they were toddlers.

She led him to the lift and they went up to the fifth floor. People were hunched over desks, talking on the phone or hammering keyboards.

'Your business is going well,' Mavros offered.

'Why do you say that?'

He glanced around. 'In the middle of the crisis, every desk is taken. There can't be many Greek companies who can say that.' He decided to show his teeth. 'Of course, shipping has its own ways of doing business and paying tax. Not much of the latter.'

Evi Gatsou didn't rise to the gibe. 'Come and meet my brother. He's taken over from my grandfather and my father, God rest his soul.'

'My commiserations.' Mavros had forgotten that the missing shipowner's son, Pavlos, had been killed during the abduction.

'Here he is,' Evi said, opening a glass door. 'Louka, this is Alex Mavros.'

The thin man in his late twenties who rose from behind a wide mahogany desk had a distracted air.

'Ah, the private investigator.' He came round and extended a hand.

'Ex-private investigator.'

Loukas stared at his sister.

'Brigadier Kriaras explained we would have to tempt Mr Mavros into taking up his old profession again,' Evi said.

'Please call me Alex. You should know that I've been doing other things for the last five years.'

Loukas led him to a set of armchairs in the corner of the office.

'Good view,' Mavros commented. 'If you can get used to everything being green.'

Evi sat down opposite him and kicked off her shoes with evident relief. 'One of our grandfather's ideas. The Gatsos family brand is all about standing out from the crowd.'

Loukas sniffed and ran a hand over his slicked back black hair. 'We've been standing out a bit too much in the last month.' He looked at Mavros. 'So we have to convince you to take the case. I'd have thought the down payment would have done that. Coffee?'

'No, thanks.' Mavros was as yet unwilling to accept anything from the shipowners. The Fat Man would lambast him if he heard he'd even crossed their threshold. Even lapsed Communists regarded their kind as robber barons who exploited the few Greek seamen they still employed. They were part of the shadowy powers that pulled the strings of marionette politicians and public servants – as was shown by Kriaras acting as their front man.

'What can we do to bend you to our will?' Evi said, with a girlish laugh.

Mavros rubbed his stubble; he'd deliberately not shaved that morning, though he had showered and put on a clean shirt and jeans. The leather jacket and biker boots weren't up for discussion.

'The police have been crawling all over your grandfather's disappearance for a month. What do you expect me to find that they haven't? Plus, kidnapping isn't my speciality.'

'Grandfather's a missing person, isn't he?' Evi said. 'You're very good at finding them. In fact, you've never failed.'

Mavros considered telling them that his brother, Andonis, was the one who'd got away, but decided they weren't entitled to know that.

'Let's start from the beginning.' He raised a hand as Evi let out a squeak of excitement. 'I need to get a feel for the case. When I have, I'll decide whether to take it.' He turned to Loukas. 'I'm not going to take your money and then pretend to work for it.'

The young man caught his gaze. 'Believe me, you wouldn't be allowed to do that.'

Mavros held the look until Loukas broke away.

'Very well, Evi will give you the file we have compiled on our grandfather, as well as the press cuttings and links to other media reports that refer to the kidnapping. I believe the brigadier will allow you to examine the police records.'

Mavros nodded. 'That's all very well, but what I need from you – and other members of the family – is what isn't in any files.'

'What do you mean?' Evi said.

Mavros was aware how tightlipped shipowners were. His decision about taking the case would hinge on how they responded to what he was about to say.

'Some of this the police must have asked. For instance, who were his enemies? And don't bother saying he didn't have any. Had he received any threats? Is there a power struggle going on over the presumably large number of companies he owns? What's the state of his private life?'

Loukas and Evi exchanged glances.

'You're right,' the former said. 'The police did ask most of those questions.' He fell silent.

Mavros sat still, prepared to play the game for as long as it took.

Loukas cracked first. 'We provided the answers we thought were appropriate.'

'And they didn't have the nerve to ask for more details?'

'No.'

'It's very simple. If you even want me to consider taking the case, you need to answer all my questions.'

'But that's ridiculous,' Loukas said, gesticulating while remaining in his chair. 'How do we know that you won't go to our rivals or the press with such sensitive information?'

'Pleasant to meet you,' Mavros said, getting up to leave. He was halfway through the office before Evi caught up with him. Without shoes, she was like an unusually broad child.

'Come back, Alex,' she said. 'Please, we'll give you everything you want.'

Mavros kept going, lifting her off the ground on one arm. 'I don't think so. This'll never work.' He reached the lift and pressed the button with his free hand, then lowered his passenger to the floor.

'I'm begging you, Alex. You must help us.' Evi started to cry again.

The nearest desk workers concentrated on their work even more assiduously. Mavros wondered if they'd seen the owner's grand-daughter in such a state before. Maybe it had been standard since the old man had been taken – or even before.

'I'll pay you the quarter million myself.'

'That isn't the issue.'

'I mean just to consider taking us on as clients.'

Mavros failed to hide his surprise. Loukas might have been stand-offish, but his sister really did seem to be desperate about her grandfather. He felt sympathy for her well up despite his distaste for the hyper-rich.

'What your brother said before about me not being allowed to take liberties – that implies I'll be under scrutiny. I can't accept that.'

'Loukas is always suspicious, it's in his nature.'

And not yours, Mavros wondered.

'I'll sort that out,' she said. 'Will you come back?'

'All right. But you don't have to pay me to do so.'

Evi drew a silk-clad sleeve across her face, damaging both it and the remains of her make-up, then smiled.

Mavros knew he was done for. He felt sorry for her and he wanted to make things better. As the Fat Man said, he was always a sucker for people in need; not that his friend would have included members of a shipowning family in that group.

FOUR

Kostas Gatsos woke when the door was opened.
'Food,' said a gutteral voice. The door was rapidly closed again.

He felt his way over in the dark until he found a bottle of water that was double the size of what he was normally given and then a metal pot. He touched it, then lifted the lid. The smell of meat in sauce filled his nostrils. His fingers located a plastic spoon and he knelt down over the plate like a dog at its bowl. He shovelled the food into his mouth from close range – it was tasty and on a bed of rice. He had only just finished when the door opened again.

'Bring bottle,' came the order.

Kostas went out of the room and was led round a corner. The ceiling light made him blink even though it wasn't very bright. This time his captor was masked and there was no hood for him. Bare feet stinging on the gritty floor, he was led to a double wooden door set into a rough stone wall.

The man in the balaclava knocked three times.

'Come forward,' said a familiar male voice in Greek from the other end of what was like an old storeroom, the walls rising to an arch.

He did as he was told. More lights came on and he saw a table on a platform. Behind it were five figures, the central one in a balaclava and the others in masks that made his stomach churn. He swallowed bile, wishing he hadn't eaten so quickly.

'What is this?' he said, running his gaze over the four figures. All were wearing black, but each had a different, oversized mask. One was a crocodile head, the next that of a bird with a long beak; beyond the man in the balaclava was a figure wearing a gleaming human skull, while the last was an octopus, pink tentacles hanging down like dreadlocks.

Kostas stumbled against the back of a wooden chair. The guard put handcuffs round his wrists, this time not behind his back, and fastened them to a chain mounted on the floor. Kostas was then forced to sit.

'Drink if you will,' said balaclava man.

Kostas sipped from the bottle and put it on the tiled floor.

'The court is in session.'

'Court?'

'The prisoner will be silent until he is addressed,' said the man in the centre. 'Every breach of this rule will result in a fingernail being removed.' He raised a pair of gleaming pliers from the table.

Kostas had to work hard to stop his meal erupting. He drank again.

'Konstandinos Gatsos, son of Emmanouil, you are accused of breaking UN Security Council Resolution 418 of 1977, which mandated an arms embargo against South Africa. Your vessels KEG *Hope*, KEG *Providence* and KEG *Fortitude* transported over three thousand tonnes of small arms and ammunition, air defence and missile systems, and armoured cars. How do you plead?'

'What? Not guilty, of course.'

'Why "of course"?'

'There's no proof of any such activity.'

'There's always proof.' The man in the balaclava turned to his left.

A female voice emanated from the crocodile head. 'Do you remember a Chief Officer Platon Zimas?'

'How can I be expected to remember—' Gatsos broke off as the man in the centre raised the pliers. 'No.'

'Let me refresh your memory.' Crocodile Head pressed keys on a laptop and an image appeared on the wall behind the table. 'Do you recognise yourself in this photograph?'

'I . . . yes.'

'And your son Pavlos?'

'Yes.'

'Who else?'

'A captain and a chief officer.'

'Their names?'

'I don't know.'

The woman turned to her left. 'He's lying.'

The man in the balaclava rang a small hand bell. The guard moved forward.

'Remove a fingernail.' The pliers were tossed to Kostas's captor.

'No, no! I recognise the captain.'

The man in the centre raised a hand. 'His name?'

'Lefteris Kotetsis.'

'Captain of the . . .?' said the crocodile woman.

'KEG *Hope*.'

'And next to him is . . .?'

Kostas eyed the man with the pliers, his fingers twitching. 'Platon Zimas.'

'Thank you. And what did Chief Officer Zimas do?'

'I don't understand. His job, of course.'

'Last chance.'

The man with the pliers stepped closer.

'He . . . he made unauthorised copies of the cargo manifest.'

'Which he intended to pass to the United Nations because he was so appalled by how the arms were being used in South Africa.'

'How do you know that?'

The woman ignored the question. 'Chief Officer Zimas arrived at Athens Airport on March 4th 1985 on a flight from Karachi. He was picked up by a company car and never seen alive again. His body was washed up on a small beach near Lavrio and could only be identified by dental records. The driver said that the dead man had asked to be dropped on the coast road outside Glyfada because, I quote, "he seemed a bit upset and needed some air". The driver also stated that the chief officer took all his luggage from the car, although none of it was subsequently found.' Crocodile Head looked up. 'But you know all that.'

'I . . . the poor man killed himself. That's what the coroner's ruling said.'

The woman stood up, got down from the platform and walked towards Kostas.

'What you don't know is that Platon Zimas, my father, called my mother from Glyfada. He said he was frightened and that people were after him. The phone call was cut short.'

'I know nothing of this. Why didn't your mother tell the police?'

'Because she was terrified. Men came to the apartment. I was only four, but I remember them. You paid her to keep quiet, not that it was very much. She took an overdose when I was fourteen. What do you have to say to that?'

'I'm sorry for your loss. Losses. But this is all speculation. I know nothing about your father's death. And how did you find out about the copies of the manifests?'

'Because he told another officer, who was too scared to talk,' the man in the centre said.

'And you . . . you found this man?'

'We found everything,' the crocodile woman said, turning away.

'Members of the court, what is your judgement?'

'Guilty,' said all four masked people.

'Full sentence is deferred. In the meantime remove all the nails from the prisoner's right hand.'

Kostas Gatsos screamed, and went on screaming till he fainted three minutes later.

Evi Gatsou asked Mavros to wait outside her brother's office. Through the glass he could see her moving her arms as she talked. He wondered about their relationship. Loukas was older though not by much, and 'Kostas Gatsos' was engraved on the door. Wasn't it presumptuous of the grandson to have already taken over the missing man's office? Did he know something he wasn't sharing? But if so, why pay for a fruitless search?

Evi emerged. She'd put her shoes back on and her head reached his abdomen.

'It's all right,' she said. 'I've talked sense into him.'

Mavros followed her in, closing the door.

'I'm sorry, Mr . . . Alex,' Loukas said. 'We really need your help. I considered calling in experts from abroad, but we need a local.' He smiled tightly. 'Especially one with your record.'

'It doesn't concern you that I've been away from work for five years?'

'If you think you can do it, I'm prepared to accept that.' Loukas frowned. 'You'll have to sign a confidentiality agreement.'

Mavros raised his shoulders. 'I always observe client confidentiality. But I do reserve the right to use trusted staff during investigations.' He would need help if he took this case, that much was obvious. 'I take it you're prepared to answer my questions about your grand-father's enemies, private life and business activities, as well as whether he had been threatened.'

Loukas slid a stapled document across the table.

Mavros looked through it and signed. It wasn't the first time rich clients had required him to do so. The potential damages for disclosing classified information were very high.

'This applies even if you don't take the case, of course,' Loukas said, retrieving the document. 'My sister says you won't charge for your initial consultation, but I can't accept that. Our grandfather always said – says – that people should be appropriately reimbursed.'

Mavros was pretty sure that didn't apply to the crews on the family ships, most of whom would be Filipinos or similar these days.

'I'll pay you 1000 euros for your time today.' Loukas opened a drawer, took out two notes and pushed them over the mahogany surface.

Mavros smiled. 'No receipt?'

'I'd hate to go against the canard about tax-evading shipowners.'

'No doubt.' Mavros sat down, which had the effect of bringing Loukas round the table to join him. A minor power play. 'Let's start with threats. Were there any?'

Loukas said, 'no' and Evi, 'yes' at the same time.

'So I'll take that as a . . .?'

'He got threats all the time,' Evi said. 'Always anonymous, in English as well as Greek, both frequently mangled and misspelt.'

Her brother waved a hand dismissively. 'Disaffected crew members, anarchists, nothing serious.'

'Do you employ security personnel?'

'Grandfather had bodyguards, if that's what you mean,' Evi replied.

'No one at senior level?'

'Our lawyers deal with such things – Siatkas and Co. I presume you've heard of them.'

'They have a . . . reputation.'

'Indeed they do. They respond to the messages in the necessary fashion.'

'I'll need copies of all those messages and replies in the six months before Mr Gatsos was seized.' Mavros saw the smile on Evi's lips. 'Or rather, I will if I take the case. How about enemies?'

Loukas laughed. 'He was the last of the great individualists in shipping. Everyone in the business hated him. Not on the surface, of course. He was invited to all the parties and receptions, and everyone smiled like snakes. However, you may be surprised to hear that shipping is basically an honourable business. A man's word still counts for something.'

Mavros caught his eye. 'And what did Mr Gatsos's count for?'

Loukas frowned. 'Plenty. He played hard but fair.'

'I'm going to need records of any deal or intervention that could have caused bad blood. Over the last ten years. These things can fester.'

'All right,' Evi said. 'Regarding Grandfather's private life – he was married and divorced twice. Marguerite, Loukas's grandmother, was American and died in 2008, while Tatiana, my maternal grandmother died in 1997.' She raised her right hand to the corresponding eye.

Loukas said, 'I have a sister, Nana, who's married to an art dealer and lives in New York. Our mother, Myrto, spends most of the year in Paris.'

'Do they have anything to do with Gatsos shipping?' Mavros asked.

Loukas smoothed an eyebrow. 'They both have shares in several of the group's companies and sit on some boards, but neither has any interest other than in collecting their fees and dividends.'

Mavros noted his sharpness of tone.

'Then there's my mother, Eirini,' Evi said.

'Who married a waster by the name of Vangelis Myronis,' Loukas put in. 'He was given various jobs in the group but proved to be both incompetent and venal. Fortunately Aunt Eirini is neither and she keeps him in check.'

Evi glared at him.

'You know I'm only telling the truth,' Loukas said smoothly. 'Do you want to tell Alex about Dinos or shall I?'

Evi lowered her head. 'My brother, Dinos, who's twenty-five, was named Konstandinos after our grandfather. *Pappous* preferred that Loukas be given the name of his older brother, who was killed by the Turks before the family left the village in Turkey.'

Mavros had been surprised that Loukas, the elder grandson, hadn't been named after Kostas in the traditional way.

'Anyway, Dinos is the black goat of the family.'

'He's only in his mid twenties,' Loukas put in, 'but he's already been in rehab seven times. It never works.'

'You've no idea how hard it is to shake off heroin addiction,' Evi said.

Mavros was taking notes. He had the perfect source to confirm these details.

'So there are no power struggles going on in the family companies?'

Loukas glanced at Evi. 'Certainly not. My father was CEO of the group and he reported to our grandfather, the president, on a daily business – sometimes every hour. As for the business in general, despite the crisis we are holding are own. Many of our competitors are not.'

Mavros nodded, wondering if the group's financial standing might have driven its enemies to play dirty. It was clear that the old man still ran things. Then again, his grandson seemed to be coping.

'I'll need a financial breakdown of all the companies in the group.'

Loukas stared at him. 'Are you capable of understanding such a thing? Have you any idea how many companies there are? Let alone the issue of confidentiality.'

'We've already covered the latter. As for understanding it, no, I'm not an accountant. But I have an associate who is.' That was only partly true, but he wanted to see which way the young man would jump.

'It'll take some time to put together.'

Mavros stood up. 'Goodbye to you both.'

'No, wait!' Evi said, reaching out to him.

'I'm not an idiot. You can access up-to-date information about every company on the computer. How else can the group function?'

Evi glared at Loukas.

'Does this mean you're going to take the job?' the acting CEO said.

'I'll get back to you about that by midnight. You understand I have to satisfy myself about the information you give me.' Mavros handed over his card. 'If you don't want to email material, you can send a courier to that address.'

'Persephone and Hecate Publishing,' Loukas read. 'That rings a bell.'

'We've met Alex's mother, Dorothy, at receptions,' Evi said.

Her brother nodded. 'She dresses more acceptably than you do.'

'Keep on giving me reasons to turn you down,' Mavros said, with a grin.

Evi took his arm and they walked to the lift. 'Pay no attention to him. He's on a massive power trip. I sometimes wonder if he really wants *Pappous* to come back.'

Waiting for the lift, Mavros gave that further thought.

'Please help us,' Evi said, clutching his hand.

'Make sure the company information comes through,' he said, enjoying the rare experience of giving orders to the super-rich.

*   *   *

Jim Thomson was in bed but he wasn't asleep. He'd woken from a dream that was more real than anything he'd experienced for decades. Again he checked to see that the sheets were dry. It was quiet in Kensington, though the all-night noise of central Melbourne came across on the wind. But he wasn't in the southern seas, he was back in the Aegean . . .

. . . after he'd been thrown overboard. The lights of the ship had gone and he couldn't see any others wherever he turned. He stopped struggling like a drowning kitten. He was a good swimmer, he'd been in the junior water polo team before he went to university. But the water in the pools had never been as cold as this. Late October nights might still be all right for hardy tourists to skinny dip, but deep water was a different proposition. He looked up at the sky. Orion was sinking in the west, which meant most of the night had gone. When he was young he went out with his uncle in the fishing boat and learnt about the constellations. What he wouldn't have given to be back in the old *Ayia Kyriaki* now . . .

Then he took a heavy blow to his back. He turned and put his hands on the end of what seemed to be a log – the moonlight wasn't bright enough to be sure. He manoeuvred himself along it to the other end. It was buoyant, presumably a hard wood that had resisted saturation. He tried to get on top of it, eventually succeeding when he located a rusted iron strut he could hold on to with his hands. The piece of wood, perhaps a stanchion from a ship, sank a bit but held him above the surface. He kept his feet in the water to stabilise the rudimentary craft.

And then he drifted away, on the cusp between consciousness and the abyss below.

FIVE

'Lieutenant.'

The big cop was leaning against a pillar at the front of the Gatsos building. 'Signed up for the job then, hippy?'

Mavros followed him to the car. 'That's no way to talk to a citizen who's done nothing wrong.'

The policeman got in and started the engine. 'Brigadier Kriaras is going to be very unhappy if you haven't.'

'I'm deciding at midnight.'

'Doing a bit of research first, are you?'

Mavros was impressed by the big man's acuity, if not his driving. 'Do you have to go so fast?'

The officer's foot pressed the accelerator even harder. He wove between lanes skilfully, eyes flicking between windscreen and mirrors.

'Obviously you need as much time as possible to make the right decision.'

Normally that would have put Mavros off the job automatically, but he was too scared to consider that. They were in the centre of Athens in under fifteen minutes.

'How fast can you do it when you turn on the siren?' he said, wiping his forehead.

'Under ten if I run the lights.'

Mavros decided against imagining what kind of chaos that would cause. He opened the door when they arrived outside his mother's building.

'Thanks for the ride.'

'Think nothing of it. I'll be back tomorrow.'

The engine revved and Mavros stepped swiftly away. Back tomorrow?

He went up the stairs, panting by the time he reached the second floor. He had to do something about his fitness. Then again, he had a thousand euros in his wallet. He should go out on the town. No, that would be unprofessional.

'Hello, dear,' said his mother, heading back to the desktop computer after letting him in.

'Are you working?'

'Just answering some messages.'

Mavros looked over her shoulder. 'I thought we weren't going to publish that book.'

'I couldn't resist. It's really very funny. For a change this foreigner who came to live in Greece excoriates the locals.'

'Who's going to buy that?'

Dorothy looked up, her eyes twinkling. 'I should think it'll go down very well in German translation.'

'But we'll have to pay a translator.'

'Bravo, dear, you've finally got the hang of publishing.'

No, I haven't, Mavros thought. The company will go to the feral cats as soon as Mother packs it in.

'You haven't heard from Anna by any chance?'

'I have. She's coming round in half an hour.'

'Good.'

Dorothy peered at him suspiciously. 'You aren't being ironic.'

'No, I want her help.' Mavros and his sister had a loving but fraught relationship. They could manage a day together at most, but then Anna would start picking at her brother's lifestyle – though she'd laid off slightly since he'd been working with Dorothy.

Mavros had a shower and a sandwich, then joined his mother in the *saloni*, where she'd lain down on the sofa.

'Have you overdone it?'

'I'm having a little breather.'

He looked at her. She seemed to have begun to shrink and her limbs were painfully thin. Still, the doctors had been happy enough with her recent tests.

The bell rang. Anna's face showed on the screen by the door and he slid the heavy chain off. She kissed him on the cheek as she came in.

'You're clean,' his sister said, as she walked past him, heels clicking on the marble tiles. 'For a change.' She was wearing a close-fitting pale blue trouser suit and a white blouse, her hair as jet-black as ever, though he was sure she'd been dyeing it for some time.

When he got to the main room, she had already greeted Dorothy and was opening a paper bag.

'You must try this, Mother. It's a Chinese herbal supplement. The experts swear by it.'

Dorothy was always suspicious of her daughter's gifts. 'Who are these experts?'

Mavros let them talk but when the conversation began to flag, he struck.

'What do we know about the Gatsos family, the shipowners?'

Anna, gossip columnist par excellence despite her preference for the job description 'features writer', looked as overjoyed as if she'd been asked to deliver an all-expenses-paid lecture at Harvard.

'They've given me a heap of stories over the years,' she said. 'How long have you got?'

'If I could butt in,' Dorothy said, the edge to her voice suggesting her maternal rights were being trampled over. 'I've known Kostas Gatsos for over thirty years. He even lent the company money at a reasonable rate of interest once. I paid it back, I'm pleased to say. I met his wives, the poor women, his children and his grandchildren – apart from the drop-out.'

'Dinos,' Mavros supplied.

'You're surprisingly well informed,' Anna said. 'For an ex-private investigator.' She exchanged a look with Dorothy.

'Go on, Mother,' he encouraged.

'Kostas was always charming, definitely had an eye for the ladies, even when his wives were alive, but you never really knew what was going on behind that wrinkled face. I could take him for about five minutes – he was quite gallant with me.'

Mavros wondered if he'd ever heard that adjective except on a Victorian TV series.

'Unlike he was with his own women. Marguerite was the first one and . . .' Dorothy broke off, stymied by amnesia.

He shook his head at Anna, who was desperate to come out with the other name.

'It was Russian,' Dorothy continued. 'Though the nearest she'd ever been to Moscow would have been the suburbs of Thessaloniki. She was a fortune hunter if ever there was one.' She smiled. 'Tatiana. I rather doubt that was her real name.'

Anna had her laptop open and was tapping away.

'Yiorgia Tsimba,' she announced.

'Alcoholic,' Dorothy added. 'The story was that Kostas let her do what she wanted with whoever she wanted and she afforded him the same privilege. Their daughter Eirini was pretty much the same, though she wasn't as attractive as Tatiana. Her husband's an awful man – handsome enough in his day but downright sleazy.'

'Vangelis Myronis,' Mavros said.

'That's right, dear.'

'What about Pavlos?'

Anna was following the exchange in bewilderment.

'Nice enough man,' Dorothy said, 'but no spine to him. Kostas was still running the family companies. Terrible that Pavlos was killed so horribly.'

'His wife, Myrto, spends most of her time in Paris, I hear.'

Anna's eyes opened even wider.

'That's right. Little love lost there. She had a fondness for cocaine. I wouldn't be surprised if old Kostas banished her.'

'Apparently you've met two of the grandchildren, Loukas and Evi.'

'Yes, you're right. They were at one of those charity galas. Nice young people. He seemed very sharp. Shame she's such an ugly duckling.'

'Mother!' Anna said, seizing her opportunity. 'That's a very harsh way to describe Evi.'

'You know her too?' Mavros said.

'I interviewed her last year. She owns a donkey sanctuary.'

'Really?' Mavros looked at his sister. 'Any rumours about her not being her father's daughter?'

'Some. But why do you care?'

'I'll tell you in a minute. This Tatiana died over ten years ago. Has Kostas's name been attached to other women since then?'

Dorothy looked away. Sexual shenanigans, as she called them, did not interest her.

'I can give you . . .' Anna moved her finger down the screen. '. . . fourteen names. And that's only the high society ones. It's said –' her voice dropped to a stage whisper – 'that he uses expensive escorts.'

'The old goat,' Dorothy said, eyes still on the photographs of her husband and lost son. Recently she had been looking at them more frequently, as if she were reaching out.

'Could you put together everything you have on the Gatsos family and email me it ASAP?' Mavros said.

'I could,' his sister replied, leaning back in her chair. 'If you tell me why you're interested.'

Mavros laughed. 'It isn't much of a quid pro quo, I suppose. But don't tell a soul. Loukas and Evi – well, Evi mainly, I think – want me to find their grandfather.'

Dorothy's gaze turned back on him. 'You aren't serious, Alex. What will the police say?'

'They have the police in their pocket – at least, that's the way it looks. I'm going to pull that scumbag Kriaras's chain to find out how far he'll go.'

Anna's fingers were moving at speed over the keyboard again. 'So you're a missing persons specialist again.' She glanced at their mother, whose expression was neutral.

'I'm thinking about it. I'll decide by midnight. That's why I need all you've got. Is Nondas around tonight?'

Anna's husband was a financial mover and shaker. In recent months his career had become markedly less secure than it used to be.

'He'd better be. He's cooking dinner.'

Mavros knew that wasn't evidence of his being henpecked. Nondas was a Cretan who loved food, especially that not produced by his wife. He was just the person to run an eye over the Gatsos group's records. He'd have to be sworn to secrecy, though.

'Alex, are you sure you want to do this?' Dorothy asked.

'There are 250,000 very good reasons for taking the job.'

Anna and Dorothy had an eyebrow raising competition, the former winning.

'A quarter of a million? Euros?'

'Well, not *dhrachmes*. And another quarter million if I find him.'

'It's a tidy sum, even with the tax deducted.' Dorothy was fastidious about fiscal matters.

'He'll probably get paid in Switzerland,' Anna said lightly.

'He most certainly will not,' her mother said. 'This country's been ruined by overseas banking and tax evasion.'

Mavros raised his hands. 'Point taken. Even though I may not accept the offer.'

Anna stared at him. 'You'd be crazy not to.'

The street doorbell rang. Mavros admitted a courier, who came up and handed over a slim envelope.

'Give that to Nondas, please,' he said to Anna. 'I'll call him about it.'

'So I'm being kept in the dark,' his sister said sharply.

'Need to know basis only, dearest.'

'That's enough, you two,' their mother said. 'Time for tea.'

Anna and Mavros reverted to childhood mode, the former going to help Dorothy in the kitchen and the latter calling his brother-in-law. Unsurprisingly, Nondas was very interested indeed.

Kostas Gatsos's torn fingertips were painted with antiseptic before he was shut up in his unlighted cell. The pain wouldn't go away and he was unable to do anything except moan until his mouth dried up. He moved through the darkness with his good hand outstretched and found the water bottle. He managed to grip it between his thighs and unscrew the cap. Then he went back to the corner with the mattress and lay down. Eventually he fell into a tormented sleep and found himself in a world of polished steel tools and crates of weapons, from which he emerged drenched in sweat.

The trial. Who could be behind it? Was the woman in the crocodile mask really the daughter of the chief officer? He had only a vague recollection of the event, having left trusted men to silence the fool. They must have allowed the officer to get out in Glyfada, before thinking better of it and picking him up again. Of course, they'd never owned up to him about that. The sailor's head was smashed against the rocks in a deserted inlet and the copies of the manifests recovered. End of story, he had thought.

Apparently not. But why a pretend trial? It wasn't as if he'd done worse things than other shipowners. If people wanted to get at him they would surely demand money, which, given the state of his hand, he'd happily give them; though he would have them tracked down afterwards. The fact that the people were all masked was to his advantage. They didn't want him to see their faces, suggesting he would be freed at some stage in the future. But no – the woman had identified herself.

Kostas tried to ignore the throbbing in his fingers by thinking about who could have organised the kidnap and trial. He was still surprised by the shooting of Pavlos. Would any of his business rivals have gone so far? He didn't think so. Could victims of his activities have got together and hired a professional gang? The man in the middle, the one with the balaclava, was the one who'd shot his son. He seemed to be in control but he wasn't a common villain – he sounded educated beyond the level of the thugs he'd occasionally dealt with and was running the whole ludicrous process knowledgably and, when he chose to, savagely. No, none of his competitors had the balls to set a thing like this up.

But who did that leave? The government? They were spineless cretins panicking about the economy and they wouldn't want to risk the secret donations he provided. The armed forces? He had good relations with the chiefs of the three services; they saw him as a steadfast ally, again because money changed hands. Some far left or anarchist group? They would have abused him verbally and made him read out lengthy statements for broadcasting. No, this was way beyond amateur night performers.

Who, then?

Kostas went over his professional dealings, recalling the people he'd beaten to deals by undercutting their offers – bribery was an essential tool – or ripped off. The latter was par for the course in shipping. If you had tonnage in the right place and there was cargo to be urgently moved, you could charge enormous amounts. The trick was knowing where to have your ships. The more you controlled the better and the better your market information the more clout you had. Would even a rabid Marxist have put him on trial for that?

No, this was personal. He couldn't tell if the dead chief officer's daughter was typical of the masked accusers. There were certain . . . episodes that he hoped would not come to light. If they did, he stood to lose a lot more than his fingernails.

Kostas took refuge in the Victorian poetry that had kept him going in the toughest times. It was his most private secret, which gave additional solace. The other shipowners could play at charity and build their research foundations. He had no need of a mauso-leum. The words of the immortals raised him to their sublime level. Even in this desolate hole, racked by pain, he remembered Tennyson's lotos flowers and fruit:

> Surely, surely, slumber is more sweet than toil, the shore
> Than labour in the deep mid-ocean, wind and wave and oar;
> Oh rest ye, brother mariners, we will not wander more.

Mavros put his laptop in a shoulder bag and took a cab to the Fat Man's. If the call he was about to make went as he hoped, there would be more comings and goings before midnight and he didn't want his mother disturbed. He dialled the number he'd memorised, having been told not to write it down if he wanted to stay a free man.

'Yes?'

'It's me.'

'As in Mavros. What's the matter? Embarrassed by your name?'

'Embarrassed to be calling you, more like, Briga—'

'Be quiet! I hope you're in a secure location.'

'Yes, for a cab it's quite salubrious.'

There was a pause. 'You're calling me from a taxi? Are you out of your mind?'

Mavros smiled. He'd forgotten how enjoyable it was to rile Kriaras. Then he remembered how little he trusted the bastard. 'I need all the files.'

'I presume you're talking about the disappearance of a well known individual?'

'Correct.'

'So you're taking the job?' The brigadier sounded relieved.

'I'll decide by midnight. You'd better get those files round to my friend's place within the hour.'

'The Fat Man's? I'm not letting that Communist lump of lard see confidential material.'

'Who says he's going to see it? There's plenty of other things for him to work on.'

'It goes against the grain to let you have the files too.'

'Up to you. The family in question will be very disappointed.'

'All right. I'll send an officer round.'

'Please can it be the lieutenant? He's got such a sense of humour.'

'You'll soon be laughing out of a different orifice.' The connection was cut.

Mavros frowned as he put his phone away, feeling that Nikos Kriaras had somehow put one over him. He looked out the window. Two figures in rags were leaning into a rubbish bin.

'This is what it's come to,' the driver said. 'People scavenging for food. My grandfather says it reminds him of the war.'

'Does he?' Mavros decided against pointing out that over a quarter of a million Greeks had died during the famines brought about by the Axis occupation. Then again, the current crisis was under a year old.

SIX

Jim Thomson woke up. His body was in Kensington, Victoria, but his mind and spirit were on the pebble beach where he'd found himself all those years ago. The wooden stanchion was beneath him, the water running up his legs. He rolled off and got to his feet, then immediately collapsed. After several attempts he managed to get out of the wet. There was a line of dusty bushes about ten metres away and he took cover in a space between two of them. The sun was up on the other side of a cliff, but it hadn't reached where he was. He struggled out of his sodden clothes, not feeling the numerous small wounds any more. Then the first rays hit the far end of the beach and he staggered to the light. It took some time, but eventually the cold left his body. It was then he realised he was desperate for fresh water. He looked around and followed the stones up a watercourse. He found a pool of water and transferred palm-fulls to his parched mouth. Then he made his way back into the sun, revelling in it like a child on an outing. Pangs of hunger soon struck him. He had spread his clothes out, but they needed longer to dry.

He sat looking across the sea. There was no land in any direction from the beach, only the warm blue sky and high trails of cloud. He couldn't see any boats or larger vessels. Then he heard goat bells. He retreated into cover between the bushes and watched as a line of the animals came down the steep slope, the leader with large horns that curved backwards. He was so desperate for food that he considered braining one of the smaller goats with a rock. As he reached for a suitable weapon, he heard a series of shouts. More goats came down the incline and a figure in a faded dress, army boots and a black anorak appeared, carrying a herdsman's crook.

He pulled his hand back, feeling vulnerable without clothes. Soon he heard steps crunching across the pebbles. He peeked out and watched the woman rapidly shed clothes. As she ran into the water, he took in a well proportioned body and brown hair tied in a scarf. He saw an old knapsack by her clothes and wondered if there was any food in it. He couldn't stop himself running out. Yes! A chunk of bread and an onion. He grabbed them and turned back.

'Hey, what are you doing?' The woman swam quickly back to the shore, seized her stick and came after him. 'Give me that back.'

He had eaten half the bread by the time she reached him. She poked the crook at him, unashamed by her nakedness. Stiff nipples pointed from her heavy breasts. There were drops of seawater all over her skin, as well as in the dense triangle of brown curls below her abdomen.

'Come on, out of there,' she said, hooking him by one ankle and pulling hard.

He yelled as some of the wounds on his leg opened. Then his other ankle was caught and he was dragged fully into the open. He dropped the bread and put a hand over his groin.

'Bit late to be shy, isn't it?' The woman squatted down in front of him, legs closed and breasts flattened against her thighs. 'Who are you?'

He didn't want to say his name: it belonged to the life he'd escaped so fortuitously and, besides, he was ashamed of it.

'Iakovos,' he said, pressing the fingers of his free hand on the blood dripping down his ankle.

She looked at the cuts. 'What happened to you? Lose your boat?'

'I . . .' He clutched at the first idea that made sense. 'I was on a friend's yacht and we . . . we hit heavy seas and I . . . went overboard.'

'And the water dragged you over the rocks.' She turned to her right. 'There are some sharp ones off that point.'

'Yes, there certainly are. Where . . . where am I?'

'Ikaria,' the woman said, with a smile. 'Welcome!'

He realised she was younger than he had first estimated – late twenties, perhaps. The joints of her fingers were thick and her legs were covered in scratches, presumably from the scrub on the slopes. Working on the land took a toll of people's bodies; he knew that from the children of farmers in the Party, who returned from harvest with sunburned arms and necks, and swollen fingers.

'I'm Marigo,' she said, getting up and walking to her clothes. 'They call me "the mad one".'

He knew nothing about the island of Ikaria except that it was isolated and relatively large. He managed to escape attention on Marigo's family farm for months. Her father was incapacitated because he'd accidentally fired into his legs when hunting, resulting in a double amputation, while her mother was a tutting but kindly soul. Her uncle, who was friendly with the drunken police chief, managed to obtain a new ID card for him under the name of Iakovos Kambanis.

He married Marigo and helped her with the goat herding, cheese-making and Easter slaughter. They were very happy.

'What's this about?' the Fat Man demanded, as he opened the door to Mavros.

'Top secret.'

'My favourite.'

Mavros looked at his watch. 'The problem is, we have to get through a load of material by midnight.'

'Or we turn into pumpkins?'

'Yes, like you used to be.'

'Ha. Exactly why is it you go around wearing a semi-inflated life preserver?'

'It's my money-belt.'

'Uh-huh.'

'If I take this job, there's a quarter of a million euros up front and the same at the end if successful.'

Yiorgos gave him a smarmy smile. 'Can I massage your life preserver, great master?'

'No, but you can get my laptop up and running. Anna's sent me a lot of her old articles. Go through them and take a note of anything suggestive – I mean unusual – about the Gatsos family.'

'Whoah!' The Fat Man held up a hand. 'The shipowners?'

'Well, not the poet.'

'I'm not soiling my eyes with anything to do with those blood-suckers. The old fucker who got kidnapped deserves everything that's coming to him. If he's still alive.'

Mavros took the computer from him and booted it up. 'Old Party prejudice, eh?'

'What else? Shipowners are leeches on the body of the people, international thieves and money-launderers, exploiters of the—'

'Workers, I know, I know. These particular ones are also a gift horse that I'm seriously considering looking right in their perfect teeth.'

Yiorgos gave him a sheepish look. '250 grand, half a million even, is a lot of money.'

'Some of which will be headed your way – if you get down to work immediately.'

The Fat Man grabbed the laptop.

There was a long ring at the doorbell.

'I'll get it,' Mavros said, picking up the entry-phone. 'Yes.'

'Police.'

'Oh joy. Fourth floor.' He waited and then opened the apartment door. 'Lieutenant. That *is* a lot of filing. I'll take it.'

'No, you won't.' The big man barged past him, giving the Fat Man a dubious look. 'This is the Communist?'

'He doesn't pay his dues any more,' Mavros said, wrestling the stack of pale blue folders from the cop. 'Good evening.'

'I've got orders. The files don't leave my sight. And no taking notes.' The policeman grinned. 'Until you accept the job offer.'

Now Mavros understood what Kriaras had said at the end of their conversation. Typical, though not completely unreasonable.

'Wait a minute,' Yiorgos said. 'This gorilla's going to sit in my flat until midnight?'

''Fraid so. Why don't you make him a coffee? That should win him over.'

'He can—'

'How do you take it?' Mavros asked.

'*Metrio.*'

'There you go, Yiorgo. I'm sure our guest would appreciate a couple of pieces of your *galaktoboureko* as well.'

'He can—'

'No, he can't,' Mavros said sternly. Eventually the Fat Man complied, muttering as he went to the kitchen. 'So what's your name? Haris, Lambos, Lambis, Lambias, Babis, Babos—'

'Babis, if you must know, but I prefer "lieutenant".'

'You can whistle for that.' Mavros opened the top file. It was a compilation of documents about the crime scene, Kostas Gatsos's villa on Lesvos. At the bottom was the local police's original report, but they had been ordered to do nothing after they had ascertained that the owner was missing and had evacuated the staff. The guard who had been shot in the thigh had died from loss of blood. Kriaras's special operations team had flown in at first light and carried out a detailed search. It wasn't stated anywhere, but obviously a minister or perhaps even the prime minister himself had ordered in the experts.

Yiorgos appeared with the coffee and custard-filled pastries. He looked as disgusted as if he'd been told to serve the former king.

'Thank you,' the officer said, without looking up.

'He's called Babis,' Mavros said, 'but he prefers "lieutenant".'

'Babis, Babis, Babis,' the Fat Man said. 'On second thoughts, I prefer "lieutenant" too. No familiarity.' He went over to the laptop.

'Good coffee,' Babis said. Then he bit into the *galaktoboureko* and his eyelashes fluttered like a teenager's on his first date. 'Christ and the Holy Mother, did you make this? It's the best I ever had.'

'Another satisfied customer,' Mavros said, running his eye down pages at speed.

'Can I charge him?' Yiorgos said.

Mavros ignored that. 'I see you were at the scene.'

The policeman nodded. 'Where the brigadier goes, there go I.'

Mavros glanced at him. 'Was that a paraphrase of Shakespeare?'

'Might have been.'

'Standards at the academy really have gone up. All right, since you're here talk me through this.'

For the first time, the cop looked at sea. 'I haven't been ordered to do that.'

The Fat Man laughed. 'Good little lieutenant, only does what he's told.'

'Never mind him. Call your boss, if you like.' Mavros grinned. 'Or act on your initiative.'

'All right, but the Communist goes.'

The Fat Man stood up, gesticulating wildly. 'This is my home, you can't order—'

'Take the laptop into your bedroom,' Mavros said. 'Please. It'll save a lot of time.'

Yiorgos unplugged the machine and stomped off, the effect diminished by the flapping of his threadbare slippers. The door slammed convincingly though.

'OK, let's have it, Lieutenant Babi.'

The big man stood up as if he was about to give a speech. 'Special ops team arrived at the villa north of Molyvos at 0745 on September 2nd. Local units had sealed off the grounds and surrounding roads. Two bodies were found inside—'

'Pavlos Gatsos in the dining room and Boris Zyvkov in the entrance hall.'

'Correct. A female member of staff was unconscious there too. Seven others were found locked in the wine cellar, along with two security guards. All their mobile phones had been taken.'

'The other guards were Vadim Gudunov and Gleb Tishin. They gave up without a fight.'

'Correct. Witnesses reported four intruders dressed in black combat gear and wearing balaclavas. All armed with pistols and machine-pistols, as well as knives and grenades.'

'The road through the estate is asphalt so there were no tracks.'

'Correct. The same goes for the road from Molyvos to Eftalou. It's likely that some if not all of the intruders – there may have been more than four – arrived by boat at the jetty below the villa.'

Mavros was turning pages. 'And the coast guard at Molyvos has no record of any vessel that was unaccounted for. Please don't say "correct" again.'

The policeman smiled, revealing unusually even teeth. 'That is . . . correct. The straits between Lesvos and Turkey are patrolled around the clock, but no suspicious vessels were identified. The relevant logs have been checked.'

'So I see. As for the crime scene, the technicians picked up traces of earth from the garden and a few fibres from black combat gear, manufacturing source unidentifiable.' Mavros raised a finger.

Babis nodded, smiling.

'Pavlos Gatsos was killed by a single bullet from a 9 x 19 Parabellum cartridge, both of which were found at the scene.'

'Corr—. That's right. The bullet was found in the frame of a painting on the rear wall and the cartridge was on the floor near the French windows.'

'A common round, so no need to bother picking it up. The bullet and cartridge that killed Boris Zyvkov were also located.'

'Ballistics confirmed that there was no record of the weapon in their archive.'

'Did anyone hear gunfire?'

'No external witnesses report that, but the villa is nearly two kilometres from the nearest houses, only one of which was occupied at the time – by an elderly and distinctly deaf woman.'

Mavros went on turning pages. 'So we have a group of operatives that managed to arrive and depart without attracting attention and take out what the report refers to as "experienced security personnel". Plus one of them showed no mercy to Pavlos Gatsos. Surely he would have been worth a ransom.'

The lieutenant rubbed his close-cut hair. 'But there hasn't been a ransom demand.'

'Yet.'

'Statistics show that people taken for ransom are usually killed quickly if a demand isn't made because they're injured, they try to escape or the kidnappers lose their nerve.'

Mavros looked at him. 'These people are professionals. They're waiting for a reason.'

'That's what the brigadier thinks.'

There were files detailing searches made of the neighbouring coastline and the surrounding countryside. 'I see there's a Mount Lepetymnos, 968 metres, not far away. Was the whole of it covered?'

'So the local officers say. There are a lot of trees, I can tell you that much, but not much else.'

'Caves?'

'Does the report mention any?'

Mavros checked. 'No sign of recent occupation.'

'There you go.'

Mavros stretched his arms and sat back in the Fat Man's lumpy sofa. 'The thinking is that they're not on the island any more, is it?'

'Correct. The brigadier thinks they've got Gatsos in Turkey. The police over there are aware of the case, but they're only going through the motions. I don't blame them. It's a big country and we haven't got a clue where the victim might be. If the kidnappers are really professional, they may have even taken him further away. To Russia, for example.'

'True. Apart from the small matter of who organised the kidnap – which you lot have no ideas about – we're left with the question of motive.' Mavros glanced at the files. 'There's nothing in here about that.'

'It would only be speculation.' The officer ran a finger over the empty plate, then licked the tip. 'Do you think there's any more *galaktoboureko*?'

'Maybe.' Mavros looked at his watch. Two hours to go. 'The kitchen's over there. I'm going to see how the Fat . . . Yiorgos is getting on.'

'I'll come with you.'

'He doesn't allow strangers in his bedroom, let alone cops.' Mavros tapped his nose. 'He's embarrassed about the smell.' He opened the door and closed it behind him.

'Is the pig still here?'

'He's eating the rest of your *galaktoboureko*.'

'Ha! There isn't any.'

Mavros looked over his friend's shoulder. 'What have you got?'

'I'll say this for your sister: she's very thorough.' The Fat Man and Anna had a relationship based on mutual disdain. 'Unfortunately, there don't seem to be too many cans of rotten sardines by shipowner standards.'

'What about the grandson Dinos?'

'The dopehead? Just a few references to him going to rehab in the UK. The rest of them seem to be pretty dull, as you'd expect with the soulless, thieving hyper-rich.'

'Onassis had an exciting life.'

'Bought the most expensive women he could find, that's all.'

'I hear Kostas Gatsos was a philanderer too.'

'Your sister hints at that, but she's obviously being careful – hardly surprising when the magazines she writes for are owned by friends of the old tosser.'

'Could there be a cuckolded husband or an outraged father?'

'Several, I'd say, but it'll take time to check that.' Yiorgos had become remarkably proficient on the computer in recent years – he claimed not only because of porn sites – and had picked up a fair amount of English.

'What do you think? Should I go for this?'

'Doesn't sound like you've got anything to lose.'

'I've heard that one before.' Mavros went over to the bed and called his brother-in-law. The Gatsos group's finances were likely to be where the roots of the kidnapping lay.

SEVEN

The door slammed open and the usual figure in the balaclava stood in the light. Kostas Gatsos saw him put down a large chunk of bread and a litre bottle of water. His stomach flipped and he put his good hand over the damaged one. At least three days must have passed. Were they going to hurt him again? He tried to eat but couldn't keep anything down. Even a sip of water was too much. Not much later his captor came back and tossed him a clean but ragged boiler suit to put on.

'No!' Kostas shouted, retreating to the mattress.

The hefty figure shrugged. 'Suit yourself.' He came across the room and grabbed him by the shoulder. 'Come naked. People will enjoy seeing your cock shrivel.'

'Wait!' Kostas grabbed for the garment.

'Fool,' the guard said, propelling him down the passage. Soon he was in front of the masked people again, handcuffed and chained to the floor.

'I protest,' Kostas said. 'You've broken the law by abducting me, let alone shooting my son. You have no right—'

'No,' said the man in the centre. '*You* have no rights. Be thankful we haven't nailed you to a cross to follow these proceedings. Though that can easily be arranged.'

The old man kept quiet.

The man in the balaclava looked at the papers in front of him. 'Kostas Gatsos is accused of arranging the sabotage of the vessel KEG *Homeland*, a 63,000 gross tonne bulk carrier, before its final voyage in March 1986. How does the accused plead?'

'Not fucking guilty.' Kostas yelped as the right side of his head was struck.

'Repeat your plea.'

'Not . . . guilty.'

'Really?' The accuser turned to the figure wearing the bird's head. 'My colleague here has evidence to the contrary.'

The voice that came from the mask was deep and male, speaking Greek. 'Before I start, I would point out to the defendant that I am here as an albatross.' He moved his head to the side to display the long, crossed beak. 'Have you any idea why?'

'Because you like the work of Samuel Taylor Coleridge?'

'That would be the wit that charmed so many society hostesses, I imagine. No, because the albatross flies over the vast expanses of the Pacific Ocean, where the KEG *Homeland* disappeared eight days into a voyage from Hay Point, Queensland, to Fukuyama, Japan. Do you remember the incident?'

'Of course. It was a nightmare. The wrangling with Lloyd's took years.'

'You were concerned only by the question of insurance?'

'Certainly not. The company lost a good captain and crew. We did what we could for their families.'

'I have details of those settlements. The sums involved are hardly high.'

'My lawyers handled that.'

'No doubt. But to return to the question of sabotage. You will recall that there were rumours of foul play after the ship sank.'

'Standard Lloyd's tactics.'

'So you know nothing about the deliberate weakening of the vessel's hull in the centre section?' The speaker raised a hand. 'Remember what happened to your fingernails at the last hearing.'

Kostas swallowed hard, his damaged fingers tingling. 'The last survey showed the ship's hull to be in excellent condition.'

'That was nine months earlier. The ship was in dry dock in South Korea before she returned to Australia.'

'To replace the propeller.'

'According to the reports, yes.' The man in the bird mask lifted a file. 'But that wasn't the only work done, was it? A trio of engineers from Greece also visited the ship to carry out what was described as "routine hull maintenance". In fact, what those men did was install a large quantity of high explosive in the double bottom. I presume you bought the silence of the dry dock operators, as well as that of the engineers.'

'Rubbish.'

'Two of whom have since died.'

'I know nothing of that.'

'Of course not. You are also unaware that the third of those men, currently in the terminal stage of bladder cancer, has sworn an affidavit describing what was done, as well as supplying photographs.' The lights dimmed and an image appeared on the wall behind the platform. 'This is the timing device, a highly sophisticated one for the time. It was activated shortly before the ship left Australia with its cargo, by the man who is now on his death bed – he sailed on the *Homeland* from South Korea to monitor the new propeller's performance and disembarked at Hay Point.'

More images appeared, showing sections of the hull and blocks wrapped in heavy plastic.

'I repeat, I know nothing of this,' Kostas said.

'But it is the case that the Gatsos group was in financial difficulties at the time, is it not? Sinking one of its newest ships provided a useful influx of funds.'

'Except it cost a fortune in interest payments on the loans we had to take out before the insurers eventually paid.'

The albatross picked up another file. 'You also sued the builders of the *Homeland* and received a large settlement.'

'Again, after a considerable delay.'

'So you deny all knowledge of the sabotage, despite the affidavit.'

'The ramblings of a dying man.'

The man in the centre stood up. 'You took a big risk. What if there had been any survivors? What if there had been other ships in the vicinity?'

'Shipping is all about risk.'

'Your bravado is admirable,' said the man with the albatross head. 'But in this case misplaced.' Another image appeared on the wall. It was a photograph of Kostas Gatsos with three men in a taverna. Glasses were being raised.

'The engineers in question with you on their return to Greece.' A button was clicked. 'This is the reverse of the photograph. You can see the date it was developed printed clearly. April 29th 1986.'

'It's a fake. I never meet engineers.'

'You did on this occasion.' The accuser sat down.

'I think we can come to a verdict,' said the man in the centre.

All pronounced the defendant guilty. Kostas sat trembling, waiting for the pliers to reappear, but they didn't.

'Take him back to his hole,' the man in the centre ordered. 'And remove his right ear.'

'This is gold dust,' Nondas Chaniotakis said, over the phone. 'Did the Gatsos family really give you it?'

'Yes,' Mavros replied, 'but you can't use anything. You promised.'

'Don't worry, I'm not into shipping. They're all thieving bastards and I don't trust them a centimetre. Besides, the CD-ROM is copy protected and there's a limit to how much I can note down.'

'This from a card-carrying capitalist.'

'Besides, this stuff doesn't tell the whole story. They'd never give that to outsiders. What it does is point to how complex their operations are. There are hundreds of companies, some of them owning only one ship – most of those are registered in Panama or Liberia, of course. That's interesting enough, not least because of references that I'm pretty sure are to off-shore banks and other tax havens.'

'What a surprise. Anything else?'

'Yes!' Nondas sounded like a boy with a new ball. 'For a start, they're in bed with plenty of dodgy regimes – in the Middle East, Africa, the Far East . . .'

'Again, hardly a bolt from the deep blue sea.'

'But get this, Alex. They're also doing business with Arab countries *and* with the Israelis.'

Mavros immediately thought of his last case. What he had thought was a search for a Holocaust victim turned into something much more complex – and lethal. 'I suppose that's also standard in their world.'

'The relevant people will have two passports, sure. But here's the real cracker. Gatsos group shares aren't only owned by family members and carefully selected investors. They've got Colombians on board too.'

Mavros's heart missed a beat. 'What kind of Colombians?'

'That's what I've been trying to find out. Nothing's visible on the surface, but I know how to read between the lines. There are two Colombian-registered companies in the group and they're not one-ship concerns. There's an arms manufacturer and a logging company. I've got no idea if they're clean, but I'm harbouring doubts.'

'Any names I can use?'

'With caution, I'd recommend. There's Laura Moreno – she's the CEO of Colarmco – and Santiago Rojas, if that's how you pronounce it. He runs Maderera Jaguar, a big logging company. I haven't had time to check them out.'

'Don't bother. I need that CD-ROM back by midnight. I'll send a courier.'

'I'll bring it over, Alex. I could do with getting out of the house.'

Mavros gave him the address and rang off, wondering what Anna had said or done.

'What was that about Colombians?' the Fat Man said, looking up. 'Only there's a photo of Pavlos Gatsos with a spectacular Colombian woman. Hang on . . .'

Mavros went over. An article dated August 12th 2009 came up on the screen. It was his sister's usual summer round-up of high society comings and goings. There was a group on the deck of a large motor-yacht.

'"Kostas, Pavlos and Loukas Gatsos with Laura Moreno, a Colombian beauty whose sultry looks they clearly approve of." Christ, I hope Anna doesn't write the captions.'

'Bet she does.'

Mavros ran his eye down the text, but there was no mention of what Ms Moreno did for a living. She certainly was stunning, her black hair long and shiny, her cheekbones pronounced and the glory of her figure brought out by a well cut dark red dress.

'Keep this to yourself,' he said to Yiorgos, wishing he hadn't mentioned the Colombian connection aloud. Was Loukas assuming he didn't have the financial knowledge to go below the surface of the group's affairs, or did he have nothing to hide? The magazine photo suggested the latter – the Gatsos family could easily have had it pulled if they wanted.

He wondered if Nikos Kriaras knew about it. He didn't openly move in such exalted circles, but he had a deep knowledge of the people who ran the country from behind the scenes. There was one thing he was sure of: Colombians or their hired help could easily have pulled off the kidnap of Kostas and the murder of Pavlos.

It was after eleven.

'What do you think then?' he asked the Fat Man. 'Should I take the job and its tainted lucre?'

'Why not? Looks like we're going to be able to dig up all kinds of shit about these tossers.'

Mavros twisted Yiorgos's ear. 'You do want a cut of the lucre, don't you?'

'I'll give it straight to the Party.'

'Of course you will.'

There was a knock on the door.

'It's me, the lieutenant. Can I come in?'

'No!' the Fat Man yelled.

'Only I think I may have broken your TV control.'

'Useless fucking cops,' Yiorgos said, looking up at Mavros. 'Go and tell him to pay for a new one, will you?'

'With pleasure.' As Mavros walked out, it occurred to him that the cop might have been listening at the door and was using the broken zapper to distract them.

Dawn's faint red fingers came through Jim Thomson's window. He had opened the curtains earlier. The beginning of the day had been his favourite time since his years in Eastern Samar. But they too had begun with water and another immersion in the night sea . . .

If only he could have stayed on Ikaria with Marigo, looking out across the waves every day as he worked the land or minded the goats, but never getting into the water, not even when August's burning sun drenched his clothes in sweat. No, he was never tempted, but he would watch his wife gambol in the sea like a child, sleek as a dolphin. She stopped going in when her belly swelled. He tried to make her do less work, but her parents were ailing and even then she had more stamina than him. His wounds had healed, leaving small raised scars on his forearms and lower legs. They heard on the radio that the dictatorship had fallen after a lunatic attempt to overturn the government in Cyprus that resulted in Turkish invasion and the loss of the eastern part of the island. He never felt the urge to join up as many young men across Greece did. He no longer had any interest in his country or its tarnished ideals. The return of democracy was a good thing, but he had no faith that it would benefit ordinary people. Occasionally he considered getting in touch with his family. They would have been grieving for him since he'd been taken, tantalised by his disappearance, as would the comrades. He couldn't do it. The torture and shame that he'd been broken had erased their faces from his memory, even those of his parents and siblings. That was the old life and it had nearly destroyed him. He had a different future now with Marigo and the first of many children.

But she died in childbirth, even though they got her to the health centre in the town as quickly as they could. The doctor was inexperienced and bungled the emergency Caesarean. The baby was a boy. He held its sticky still body for a few moments, kissed Marigo on the forehead – he couldn't get the salt from her sweat from his mouth for weeks – and, three weeks later, joined the crew of a cargo ship in Piraeus; one of Marigo's cousins went to sea every winter and managed to fix his papers with the union. He started as an assistant cook, learning on the job, and found he had an aptitude for the work, even when the ship was plunging up and down like a horse crossing a river in spate. After three years he was put in charge of the galley, then gradually worked his way up to larger ships.

The last of which was the KEG *Homeland*. He was completely in command of his job now, instructing his junior how to produce the quality dishes required when management or customers visited, though still doing more of the daily hands-on work than he needed to. It soothed him, kept his mind off the lives he'd left behind, both his own and those of others. Marigo . . . he could hardly see her any more, as if she had been swallowed up by the darkness he'd brought with him to her island. He had flashes of her – leaping naked from the sea, shuddering as they climaxed, screaming in fear before the anaesthetic put her under forever.

At night he would go to the stern and smoke, looking down at the wash of water from the propeller. Many times he was close to going over the rail, but the thought of immersion in the salt element put him off. Besides, there were plenty of knives in the galley. Except that, by the time he got there, the impulse had left him and he was back to being the grim-faced, unfeeling creature he had become. The crew called him *to teras* – the beast – but only behind his back. They were frightened of him and, besides, they liked his food.

When the *Homeland*'s spine broke, he was in his cabin, only half asleep. The alarms started to blare. He was on deck, carrying his life jacket, before most of the others. There were ineffective attempts to launch the lifeboats and rafts. They all seemed to have jammed, which was odd in a relatively new ship. Then the vessel's bow and stern went up in a V-shape and men were sent scrabbling down to the seething maelstrom in the middle. He held on to a stanchion near the stern, struggling to put on the life jacket. Men were yelling, the younger ones crying; no one knew what to do. He felt the stern rise steeply and realised it would be too high to jump. He managed to get a bit lower, sliding from post to post, then – eyes shut and heart thundering – he rolled under the wire and dropped into the black water.

He lost consciousness immediately.

EIGHT

Lieutenant Babis was sitting in front of the TV, the remains of the handset on the table.

'Interesting?' Mavros asked.

'What?'

'The news on CNN.'

'Not really.'

'You do speak English?'

'Yers, seer, I learn eet from books.'

'Uh-huh. You'll have to pay for that. Ten euros should do it.'

The cop took out his wallet and put a bank note on the table. 'Find out anything that attracts you to the job?'

Colombians certainly don't, Mavros thought. 'I've still got some time. You can go now.'

'I'll be taking the files with me.'

'Be my guest.'

'You'll ring the brigadier when you've made your decision?'

Mavros smiled. 'I'd be working for the Gatsos family, not him.'

'I doubt you'll be able to shake him off. It's an ongoing investigation and we can do things you can't. Collaboration is a good idea.'

'Only a cop would say that.'

The lieutenant went to the door with his heap of files. 'I'll be seeing you again,' he said.

'Not if I see you first.'

There was a noise that could have been a laugh.

The Fat Man appeared a few seconds later. 'Has the tosser gone?'

'He has.' Mavros sat down. 'He pointed out that Kriaras will be expecting me to work with him.'

'Surely you can get the shipowners to keep him off your back. Shit, look at that. Ten euros won't cover a new one.'

'I'll pay the difference, for God's sake. Now let me think.' Mavros took out his notebook and started to draw up a list of pros and cons.

Soon afterwards the bell rang.

'That'll be Nondas. Don't worry, he's not like Anna.'

'He's some kind of money man, isn't he?' Yiorgos said waspishly.

'Just let him in. He's a seriously good cook.'

'Is he, now? It happens I have some pork chops in the fridge.'

Mavros got up when his brother-in-law came in. He hadn't seen him for a month or so. 'What the hell, Nonda? You're not ill, are you?'

'No, I'm on one of those all-meat-but-not-every-day diets. This must be the renowned Fat Man.' The Cretan stuck out his hand.

Yiorgos shook it after a display of comradely reluctance. 'I hear you can cook. Only I've got—'

'Hold on, will you?' Mavros said, taking the CD-ROM from Nondas.

'What have you got?' the Cretan said.

The Fat Man grinned. 'A couple of kilos of pork chops.'

'Right, I'll get them in a marinade. Show me the way.'

'I thought you already made dinner at home.' Mavros followed them, glowering. 'Look, I've got to make an important decision. I want a war council.'

'What's wrong with here?' Yiorgos asked. 'There's enough room.'

'If I sit in the corridor.'

'Well, yes.'

Mavros fetched a chair. Nondas was throwing herbs and pouring oil and wine over the meat.

'The point is, gentlemen, am I being set up?'

They both looked at him, then Nondas started grinding pepper. 'What do you mean?' said the Fat Man.

'If the cops haven't been able to find old Gatsos, how likely is it that I'll pull it off?'

Nondas flattened garlic cloves with the blade of a knife. 'It's not like you to be defeatist, Alex.'

'Think about it. There's a Colombian connection, which Kriaras may or may not know about – but you can be sure he wouldn't fancy taking on an international drug network. There are potential diplomatic issues too.'

'You're a real diplomat,' Yiorgos said, with a grin.

'Piss off. Then there's the Gatsos family. Obviously they know about the Colombian involvement in their business.'

'Which may be wholly legitimate,' Nondas pointed out. 'Got any balsamic vinegar?'

The Fat Man looked at him blankly.

'Maybe, but you've got to be dubious. What's in it for them to employ me at a very high fee?'

'Have your brains slid out of your nose?' Yiorgos said. 'You're the best there is. They want their grandfather back and you hung up your magnifying glass years ago. Only a large inducement would have got you even considering the job.'

'Hm.' Mavros looked at his watch. Half-an-hour to go. 'What do you think, Nonda?'

'I agree there might be some danger, but you've faced that often enough. Christ, even I have that time in Argolidha. Anna still talks about it.'

'We were lucky.'

'You saved us.'

'My hero,' said the Fat Man.

'I seem to remember you almost ended up dead in that case.'

Yiorgos looked chastened. 'That was when I still did what the Party ordered.'

Mavros looked at his notebook. 'The two grandchildren are keen to find Kostas, but some of the other family members look a bit dodgy.'

'What do you expect?' said the Fat Man. 'They're thieving, uber-capitalist—'

'Thank you, comrade. If I take the job, you're going to be interviewing some of them.'

'Hold me back.'

Nondas came over and put his hand on Mavros's shoulder. 'Look, it's work. You can't bury yourself away forever. Your mother's company is dead on its feet.'

'Thanks a lot.'

'No, you've done a great job keeping it going, believe me, but you know what you're best at. Anna feels the same way.'

Mavros bit his tongue. It wasn't unreasonable for his sister to want him to be more fulfilled. 'What about the money?' he said. 'It's far too much. I think I'll ask for less.'

'Don't,' his brother-in-law said. 'They've decided what they want to pay.'

'You could always ask for more.'

Mavros gave the Fat Man a diamond-tipped glare. The truth was, he did feel the pull of what had been his career, the only thing he'd ever loved doing. But he'd failed Niki . . . and Andonis.

'Call them,' Nondas said. 'Make whatever conditions you like.'

In the end, at 11.59, Mavros rang the number he'd been given and told Loukas he'd do it, the only stipulation being that he would work without being watched. He was asked for his bank account details and told the transfer would be made immediately.

'That's it then,' Yiorgos said. 'We've got something to celebrate. I'll get the beers.'

'I'll give you whatever help you need,' Nondas said, shaking Mavros's hand.

'And we've got the chops,' the Fat Man said, handing round bottles of Amstel.

'They need another couple of hours in the marinade,' the Cretan said.

Yiorgos groaned.

It was a long night.

Bastards!

Kostas Gatsos had always been a good hater. Now all his emotions were directed at the people who were trying and torturing him. His right ear – or rather, the place where it had been attached to his head – was horrendously painful. The wound was covered in antiseptic regularly, the dressing changed. When he wasn't seething, he found some hope in that. At least they didn't want him to die of gangrene or the like. His ruined fingers were also being treated. Then he had a thought. Ransom demands were often accompanied by pieces of the prisoner's body – hadn't that Getty heir's ear been sent to his family? Nails would do the job too. Yes, that was it. They were demanding money for him.

But why had they waited so long? It must have been weeks since he was taken. And what was it the man in the balaclava had said after the first trial? Something about full sentence being deferred. Was this how it was going to be? More and more trials until he had no extremities left? Would they take his cock? His balls? He clutched them with his good hand. Anything but that. They might as well shoot him now. Though, given the degree of savagery they'd shown so far, he thought his death would be a lot more protracted and painful than a bullet in the head.

Lying in the dark with his hand on his genitals, Kostas found himself thinking of the women he'd had. He'd never counted, but it must have been hundreds, maybe over a thousand. When he was fifteen, his father had taken him to a whore.

'Turn this boy into a man,' the old man had ordered. God knows when he'd last had sex; he was devoted to his wife and she was slowly coughing her life away.

Kostas wasn't inexperienced in the ways of the flesh. He'd won a scholarship to an English-style boarding school on Spetses. No girls, of course, but no shortage of other boys who were attracted by his mischievous smile and unusually long prick. There were the usual mutual wanks in the toilets and night-time excursions to other dormitories. Kostas was smart though. He didn't go with just anyone. There was one boy with a circumcised member he enjoyed playing with. Otherwise he only gave himself to those who could do things for him – get him off punishments, help him with homework, supply him with luxury foods. As he followed the overweight woman into her chintzy bedroom, it struck him that he'd been a kind of whore himself. He had no problem with that.

'Come on then, my boy, let's see the crown jewels.'

'Show me what you've got first.'

Kostas watched as she – he vaguely remembered that she called herself Gigi in a desperate attempt for a touch of class – opened her dressing gown and let copious breasts fall out of her low-cut nightdress.

'And the rest,' he ordered.

The woman gave him a sharp look and then submitted to his will. She lifted the gown over her head, revealing unshaved armpits, and lay back on the bed. Her thighs were heavy. He leaned forward as she opened them.

He came four times in the next hour.

As far as he had an Achilles' heel, it was sex. Any female was a target – by the time he finished school, he'd had enough of male body parts. The urge took him frequently every day. At Cambridge, to which he'd won a scholarship from a Greek foundation, he screwed his bedder, the cleaner of his rooms at university, who was older than his mother; a librarian; several though not enough students – the late 40s weren't noted for sexual liberation; and plenty of town girls who would do anything for some drinks and a bunch of flowers. But still he was unsatisfied. During one of his final examinations he had to ask for a toilet break so he could relieve himself of a hard-on that refused to detumesce even though he was writing about Keynes's general theory. He got a third-class degree, but that was irrelevant. He already had a job offer from an Athenian bank.

That was only a stepping-off point. After a couple of years he'd managed to raise the money to buy a small tramp steamer. Within five years he was a dollar millionaire and going to parties thrown by the Athenian rich, as well as their counterparts in Monte Carlo, New York, Buenos Aires.

And always the women. He remembered a cleaner at a seaside villa that belonged to an older shipowner. She was on all fours, scrubbing the floor. He flipped up her dress and petticoat, pulled down her voluminous knickers and entered her from behind. An island virgin, she didn't take it well, but he couldn't help himself. The idea that the owners, especially the stuck-up wife, might have found him at it increased his pleasure enormously. He had to pay the girl off, but the sum she accepted was pitiful. The next time he visited, she sucked him off at the breakfast table. The hosts and other guests didn't notice that he bit his lip hard enough to draw blood.

But servants were one thing; the rich always took advantage of them. Other men's wives were a completely different challenge. He enjoyed them more than their daughters, who either threw themselves at him or clamped their thighs together, as unyielding as Swiss bank vaults. One way or another he got all the society wives he wanted; some of them were hideous, although they tended to be the most interested. He took extra delight in fucking the wives of government ministers, the men being no more than marionettes who danced to the tune of the real elite. He remembered Elsa, whose husband had been mayor of Athens and was subsequently minister of trade. She was a screamer. The only place he could safely screw her was at the opera. A large woman was singing an inappropriate Mimi when they got together, her husband having gone off to meet a colleague. He paid off the concierge and they slipped into the women's rest room. He took her against the row of sinks, her evening dress pulled up and her silk knickers ripped open. She almost deafened him in one ear.

Which brought him back to the darkness in which he was lying. Was it the right ear, the one he had lost? Fuck the pathetic cowards who wouldn't reveal their faces. He would cut off the men's cocks and jam them down their throats. As for the woman in the crocodile mask . . . he would have shoes made from her skin.

By five a.m. the Fat Man and Nondas had passed out on the sofa. Beer had been consumed, more by them than by Mavros, who sat with his notebook open at the table among the ruins of the chops. He was constructing a plan of action and had also made a call. Brigadier Kriaras was less than impressed at being woken up, but agreed that copies of the police files would be supplied now that Mavros had taken the case. Lieutenant Babis would act as liaison; not, Mavros insisted, as watchdog.

Before he drew up a work roster for the approaching day, he tried to make sense of what he'd let himself in for. Kriaras apparently wanted him to be involved. After five years that would have included plenty of major cases, he suddenly wanted Mavros in action again. Why? Was the Gatsos family's grip on the government's nuts so tight? Maybe, but Kostas wasn't the first shipowner to have been kidnapped in recent years. Why was Mavros back in favour? The grandchildren were certainly keen to have him, Evi more than Loukas, though the quarter million was the family's, not hers, despite her offer. What did they expect him to find that a major police operation hadn't turned up? Was he to put the wind up other family members? If so, his employers weren't going to be disappointed. And what about the Colombians? He would be talking to Loukas and Evi about their involvement in the group. If they had suspected the South Americans of being behind their grandfather's disappearance, surely they'd have told Kriaras. The strangest aspect of the kidnap was the lack of either a body or a ransom demand. He was sure the old man had plenty of enemies in Greece and globally. A quick look at the background material had shown that he was a hard-nosed operator, who'd put many of his rivals out of business. But the well-executed raid on the villa in Lesvos could easily have led to his shooting as well as his son's. Instead he had been taken. Did someone hate him so much as to spirit him away and lock him up or torture him to death? Had Pavlos been murdered as a demonstration of intent or as a deliberate target? Loukas had agreed he could keep the CD-ROM, so he would ask Nondas to see if Kostas's son had been up to anything suspicious.

Then he had a couple of the flights of fancy that sometimes cracked cases. First, could Kostas, aggrieved at some activity of Pavlos, have set up the hit and his own disappearance? Despite the apparent absence of threats, perhaps he needed to lay low for a while. Second, there was only one man Mavros had encountered who could have organised the attack on the villa and shot Pavlos in cold blood. He doubted the Gatsos grandchildren knew about the

Son, but Kriaras certainly did – in fact he'd sanctioned the killer's employment by a hyper-rich Greek industrialist in the past. Did he suspect or know that the Son was behind the kidnapping?

If so, recommending Mavros to the Gatsos family wasn't anything to do with his abilities. It was to draw the renegade killer into the open; with Mavros, whom the Son had sworn to destroy, as bait.

NINE

Jim Thomson woke up and spat out salt water. He was floating on his back, his clothes sodden, but the life jacket keeping his mouth above the surface of a gentle swell most of the time. There was a line of light low in the sky over the tip of his toes. Was it dawn or nightfall? He heard the call of seabirds and the top of the sun appeared over the far, flat horizon. A new day. Then he remembered the events of the night, the chaos and sudden sinking of the *Homeland*. He looked around, but there was no sign of any crew mates – no debris, only endless water. He didn't have the strength to blow the whistle attached to his jacket. The cork felt heavy and he wondered how long it would keep him afloat. He reached his hands down to his legs and then felt his head. He had no pain and nothing hurt to the touch. If only he could drink something that didn't taste of salt. His mouth and throat were wet, but that gave him no solace. As the sun rose, he had to close his eyes because of its piercing brightness. There wasn't a cloud in the sky. He raised his left wrist but his watch wasn't there. Perhaps he'd taken it off after his shift in the galley. Jesus, what had happened? Thousands of tonnes of steel and coal, seventeen men: was he all that was left? The weather had been good. It was as if the *Homeland* had been torpedoed. Structural failure seemed unlikely as the new class of bulk carriers had been strengthened after earlier models were lost in heavy seas. There had been none of those last night.

He tipped his head back to keep his mouth out of the water and let himself drift. He had no energy to paddle and, besides, there was no land in any direction.

Somehow he survived the day, the sun having burnt his face and hands and, it felt, dried every drop of liquid from his insides. Darkness was a relief of sorts, but he was in agony, every breath seeming to rip his wind pipe. How much longer would he survive?

The next dawn came upon him quickly, the sun up before he had fully regained consciousness. He considered taking off the life jacket and sinking into the cold, dark depths, but he didn't have the will or energy to undo the straps. He rolled on to his front and sucked in water, trying to drown himself. But something in him wouldn't allow capitulation.

At last he heard voices: excited, babbling, high-pitched. He raised his head and saw it – a small craft low in the water, three skinny brown men in shirts and shorts standing up and waving their arms. He tried to raise one of his, but failed. It didn't matter, they had seen him. Soon strong hands gripped and pulled him on board. The sun was low in the west and he caught a glimpse of land. He had survived. As the life jacket was removed, he fainted away . . .

He came round as the boat bumped against a ramshackle wooden jetty. His clothes had been removed and he was in the shade of a tarpaulin, a length of dirty material over his body. A crate of silver fish longer than his forearm lay beside him, their eyes glazed and their mouths open as they had gasped for their last breath. He started to weep, saddened that he had made it while they hadn't. The sea was their element. He was the stranger, he should have been the one to succumb.

People gathered around as he was lifted on to the jetty and carried off like a prize catch. There were scantily clad children, women with long black hair wearing T-shirts and sarongs, old people cackling. He was taken to a wooden hut and laid carefully on a mattress of leaves covered by a brightly coloured sheet. He heard himself croak but, like the fishermen had done, he was given only a sip of water at regular intervals. The woman who shooed all the others out and looked after him was slim and beautiful, her eyes deep brown pools and her fingers soft on his tender skin.

They married and he stayed with her for seven years. The settlement was on the coast of Sulat in the east of the Philippines island of Samar; that much he learned from the local schoolteacher, who knew some English. The people wanted to know where he came from, but he had started another life and wanted the one that had ended on the *Homeland* to fade, as had those with Marigo and before. His childhood and university years were completely gone now. He said he had fallen from a yacht. Nobody showed any surprise when he made it clear he wanted to stay. There was a bus that went to the neighbouring towns, but the village looked towards the sea and its inhabitants had little interest in the land. The heat was that of the tropical rainforest, but he endured it – another way of driving out his previous life. Rebirth by sweat.

He fished with his brother-in-law, Levi, one of the men who had rescued him. When tourists came, they paid little attention to him, his Mediterranean skin having darkened like that of the natives. Pilita had lost her first husband to the sea and couldn't conceal her anxiety every time they went out. He was nervous himself the first time, but once they were beyond the jetty the water didn't frighten him – only on the infrequent occasions that he fell in. Sharks often circled the boat, waiting for the guts from the catch, but he felt strong. Life was good.

Jim still saw Pilita's face as she leaned over to kiss him, her fingers moving slowly over his skin. When the past succeeded in breaking through his carefully constructed defences, he still felt stabs of guilt about leaving her.

'Jesus, is that the time?' Nondas struggled to his feet. 'I've got to get to work.'

'I'm sure our host can provide you with fresh clothes.'

The Cretan looked at the Fat Man. 'Er, no thanks. I've got a spare set in my office.'

'Here,' Mavros said, handing him the CD-ROM. 'See if you can sniff out anything that Pavlos Gatsos might have been up to behind everyone else's backs. And make sure no one catches sight of it.'

'Don't worry, this is worth its weight in platinum. I'll talk to you tonight.'

'Great chops,' Yiorgos called after Nondas, who raised an arm as he left. 'Coffee, Alex? No pastries – that cop ate the last of them.'

'Doesn't matter,' Mavros said distractedly.

When the Fat Man came back from the kitchen, they drank glasses of water before the coffee. After Mavros had sipped his *sketo*, he felt the day fall into shape.

'Right, Yiorgo, I'm going to talk to Evi's mother Eirini and her supposedly sleazy husband Vangelis. You have the pleasure of putting the fear of Lenin into their son, Dinos. Here's his address.'

'Might have known. Kolonaki. I'll have to take a gas mask.'

'Riot central.' The rich area was near Syndagma Square, where there had recently been several anti-austerity demonstrations that ended in tear gas.

'No, fool. Because I don't like the stink of stolen money.'

'You seemed to be pretty keen on the Gatsos family fee.'

'Of course.' The Fat Man glared at him. 'Have you lost your tavli counters? We're relieving them of their ill-gotten gains.'

'Uh-huh. Squeeze Dinos hard. He's a junkie so there might be a connection with the Colombians. Though obviously you aren't going to mention them unless he does.'

'I'm not an idiot.'

Mavros laughed. 'More of a rampaging rhino. Though your hide's getting a bit slack.'

'Eat more chops, that's what I say.'

'But still walk to Kolonaki.'

'What, no expenses for a taxi?'

'Choose life, Yiorgo.' Mavros gave him one of his old business cards and wrote on the back 'As approved by Loukas Gatsos'. He'd considered telling his employer about Yiorgos and the interviews that were about to take place, but decided against it. He didn't want the subjects to receive advance warning.

'Where does the couple you're going after live?' the Fat Man asked, trying unsuccessfully to smooth down his shirt collar.

'Philothei.'

'Ha. No doubt you'll be walking there.'

The unusually green northern suburb was about six kilometres to the north.

'Of course.'

'Liar.'

'See you later. Let me know if anything juicy comes up.'

'Juicy?'

'Interesting, suggestive, I don't know, Yiorgo. Haven't you learnt anything?'

'We've been out of business for five years, remember?'

Mavros stopped at the door. 'True. Look, the son's a junkie and he doesn't live with his parents. There might be some tension you can exploit.'

'Ah, tension. I like it.'

Mavros left the apartment block and picked up a cab on the nearest northbound street. The driver had GPS so there was no problem finding the house. Traffic on Kifissias Avenue was quick-moving in their direction, but gummed up southbound as usual in the morning. They turned off and were almost immediately in a different world, the exhaust fume-ridden air clearer under cover of the tree-lined streets. The taxi dropped him outside an imposing house with high steel rails around it. There were no names on the gate.

Mavros pressed the entry buzzer, aware of the camera above him. A female voice answered.

'Alex Mavros. I need to talk to Mr and Mrs Myronis.'

The buzzer sounded and he pushed open the heavy gate. The marble path that led to the entrance of the house was about thirty metres long and passed through beautifully kept flower beds. Tall pines along the edges of the property prevented it from being over-looked. The house had originally been a neo-classical mansion, but a smartarse architect had been let loose on it. On one side there was an extension with oddly angled walls and a roof that undulated like a wave, and on the other a tower leaning almost as much as that in Pisa, though this one was covered in tiles of numerous – and to Mavros's eye, clashing – colours.

A middle-aged brown-skinned female servant in a black uniform – probably a Filipina – was waiting for him under the columned portico.

'My employers do not receive without appointment,' she said.

'But they will receive me,' Mavros said, smiling. 'Otherwise I wouldn't have been allowed in the gate.'

The woman nodded gravely. 'Follow me, please.' She led him across a wide hall with tiling even crazier than the tower's. In front of him was an elegant staircase that split halfway up.

'His and hers?' he asked.

The Filipina ignored that, heading for a tall wooden door with green panels.

'The breakfast room,' she said, as she knocked and entered.

At the far end of a long table, that Mavros suspected was mahogany, sat a couple in their dressing gowns. He knew he was being put at a disadvantage, but he wasn't going to apologise for the disturbance. Instead he went towards them and stopped by a chair, looking at the puffy-cheeked woman and then the slack-jawed man.

'Very well, sit down,' the latter said gruffly. 'Have you eaten?'

'Yes, thank you.'

'Coffee, then.'

'No, thanks.' Mavros wasn't going to accept any hospitality. He had found that made people uneasy. He felt their eyes on him and occupied himself with his notebook.

'This really isn't a convenient—'

Mavros didn't look up. 'Fine, Mr Myroni. I want to speak to

your wife in private anyway. But if you could make yourself available in, say, an hour?'

'I do have a job, you know.'

Mavros glanced at his watch. 'It's nine thirty. Obviously you don't keep normal business hours.'

Myronis threw down his napkin and stalked away.

His wife put her hand to her mouth. Mavros knew she was in her late fifties, but she looked older. She'd obviously spent a lot of time in the sun and her complexion had suffered. No doubt she would look more presentable with her make-up on – and she'd also be more sure of herself. Things had turned out well so far.

'So, Mr Mavro, Evi told me about you late last night. How can I help?'

He looked into her pale brown eyes. 'Do you in any way benefit from your father's disappearance or death?'

Eirini Myroni's head jerked back as if she'd been slapped. 'How dare you—'

'Please answer the question.'

Her gaze was icy. 'I . . . I have no idea of the contents of my father's will. As you might have noticed, we aren't exactly badly off.'

'Yes. I've been given details of the group and its financial status.'

'You have? What in God's name does Loukas think he's doing?'

'Enabling me to find your father. Surely you must approve of that? Do you know of anyone else who would benefit from his disappearance or death? How about your husband?'

'How . . .' A smile spread slowly across Botoxed lips. 'You're deliberately trying to get under my skin, aren't you?'

'If you could answer the question.'

Her eyes grew cold again. 'Not that I'm aware of. Vangelis is not a Gatsos. He looks after some of the non-family companies I own, but I keep him on a tight leash.'

'How about competitors, enemies?'

'There's no shortage of people who would cheer for business reasons if Father was never found – or found deceased. Some of them are bastards, but I can't see them organising a kidnap.' She paused for thought. 'I don't know, maybe they would. But you can be sure it would be done through layers of intermediaries so they could never be traced.'

'Nobody's publicly declared their hatred?'

'I told the police all this,' Eirini said, pouring herself more coffee.

'Tell me as well. Please.'

'All right. The Svolos family has been at daggers drawn with us for decades. My father takes great joy in outbidding them for shipping contracts every chance he gets. Tefkros Svolos was ten years younger, but Father always claimed he'd driven him to an early death. That was back in the 80s. We and his children ignore each other at functions.' She shook her head. 'I can't see them doing this, I really can't.'

'I'll look into it. Your husband doesn't come from a shipping background.'

'If you know that, why are you saying so?

Mavros caught her eye. 'You know why, Mrs Myro—'

'Please call me by my family name.'

'Mrs Gatsou,' he said, not missing a beat. 'Did he marry you for love?'

She laughed bitterly. 'That wasn't something our kind did back then, though Vangelis was handsome enough when he was young. No, his father was a textile manufacturer. Old money – at least, older than my father's. He had a successful war.'

'You mean he was a collaborator.'

She raised her shoulders. 'Your words. He brought us a degree of respectability in Athenian society. That was about all as the family business collapsed two years after his father died. Vangelis is no captain of industry.'

'Couldn't your father have helped?'

'I imagine so,' she said coolly. 'I didn't ask him. There was no point. He did . . . does what he wants.'

'Wasn't your husband bitter?'

She laughed as she lit a cigarette. 'Not for more than a week. Vangelis has the attention span of an infant.'

Mavros smiled tightly. 'And plenty of other interests.'

'You *have* been doing your homework. Yes, he likes chasing women, drinking, racing cars down the coast road, anything that prevents him using what few brain cells he possesses. We have to pay people to be quiet on occasion, but that makes no difference to our financial well-being.'

'Happy marriage, then.'

'Are you always this insolent? Yes, as a matter of fact it is, at least in the sense that it still functions.'

'Which means you have your own interests.'

Eirini Gatsou stubbed out her cigarette. 'I run several charities, I ride and I sail, as well as being on the boards of several large companies.'

'Any young men?'

She stood up. 'This interview is over, Mr Mavro. What are you doing?'

'Calling Loukas.'

'Mother of God.' She sat down. 'Get it over with.'

Mavros put his phone back on the table. 'I'm not interested in your private life unless it could have any connection with your father's kidnap.'

'You mean, am I screwing Tasos Svolos, aged nineteen?'

'Are you?'

'No. If I was idiotic enough to play games with that family, I'd prefer his sister, Nadia.'

'I see. How about your father?'

'Fortunately incest isn't a family tradition.'

At another time Mavros would have laughed. 'Did your father have sexual relations with the mother, aunt, wife, daughter, sister or any other female relative – or male, for that matter – of anyone who could have taken major offence?'

'You're asking about his girlfriends. No, I don't think so. Recently his tastes have run to blonde young women with long legs and inflated bosoms. He met them at nightclubs. None of them lasted more than a month.'

'You wouldn't happen to know which nightclubs?'

'No. Does it matter?'

Mavros shrugged. 'Dinos,' he said starkly.

Eirini scowled at him. 'Leave my son out of this.'

'Not possible. How does he get on with his grandfather?'

She looked away. 'All right.'

'So he doesn't. What happened?'

'What have you read in those lying scandal sheets?'

'Not much. Tell me more.'

There was a long sigh. 'Dinos has been doing drugs for over ten years; grass at school here, then cocaine and heroin when he was at college in New York. Father gave him a job when he graduated – though he had to make a substantial contribution to the university to get Dinos even the worst class of degree. But my son isn't cut out for office work. He's a film maker.'

'How does he finance that?'

'With difficulty. Father cut him off and told me not to pay him anything. Which, of course, I disregarded.'

'That must have made Dinos hate his grandfather.'

Eirini stared at him. 'Unsurprisingly it did. But he couldn't have organised—'

'A kidnap, let alone the murder of your step-brother.'

'Quite.'

'You don't seem overly concerned about either your father's disappearance or Pavlos's death.'

'You presume too much. I try to keep my emotions to myself.'

'How would you characterise your relationship with Pavlos?'

'Not close. A nice enough man, but weak. Father thought so too.'

'How was he CEO of the group? He must at least have been good at his job.'

She laughed sharply. 'Father ran the company, never mind Pavlos's title.'

'What about his wife, Myrto?'

'In it for the money, pure and simple. Her own people lost everything. All she cares about is art dealing. She bled Pavlos terribly. Father despised her.'

'But it wouldn't have been in her interest to have her husband killed.'

'I don't know. She'll inherit money and property.'

Mavros stood up. 'Thank you, Mrs Gatsou, that's all for now.'

'You mean you'll be back?'

'I'm going to interview your husband. I may have to cross-check information with you.'

Eirini lit another cigarette. 'Whatever you like. The day's ruined anyway.'

Mavros turned away, suppressing a smile. He didn't believe her day was ruined in the least, but her saying so gave him a warm feeling.

TEN

The Fat Man found the street door of the apartment block on Patriarchou Ioakim propped open. He had already scoped the entry phone panel. There was no name on the top space and no Myronis anywhere else, so he reckoned Dinos had the penthouse. Typical spawn of a shipowner. He thought of copying Mavros's old trick of walking up any flight of stairs he found, but dismissed that in a nanosecond. He'd already walked round the Lykavittos ring. That was enough exercise for today.

The lift took him to an unlit hallway and he fumbled for the time switch. When he found it, the light revealed a single door. Again there was no name by the bell. He decided that main force was the way and started pounding on the door. It opened after his hand had begun to hurt.

'Who the fuck are you?' said a skinny guy with rat's tail hair and stubble that designers wouldn't have touched with a jousting lance.

'On behalf of Alex Mavros.'

'Oh, him. What's my sister getting so het up about? The old fucker's been gone for over a month. He's not coming back.'

'Maybe you'd like to take the chain off so we can discuss that.'

'Fuck you.'

Yiorgos took a couple of steps back and rammed his shoulder against the door before it could be closed. The chain was wrenched from its base.

'You can't—'

'Want me to call your step-brother Loukas?'

'You bastard.' Dinos retreated down the dimly lit corridor of his flat, clutching one arm.

The Fat Man closed the door as best he could and walked into what could have been a nice place – if the floor hadn't been covered in bits of charred aluminium foil, pizza boxes, soft drink bottles, souvlaki wrappers and cigarette butts. There were cameras of varying sizes in the corners, as well as a dead cat under a tripod.

'You should get rid of that, Dino. It could give you something you haven't already caught.' Yiorgos picked up the stiff animal by the end of its tail, walked on to the balcony and dropped it over the edge.

Dinos laughed. 'I wish I'd thought of that. The old prick on the ground floor will eat his wig.'

'Sit down, son. We're going to have a heart-to-heart.'

'And if I don't.'

Yiorgos pushed him on to the sofa and, after removing a couple of syringes, sat next to him.

'Your sister told you to be helpful, didn't she?'

Dinos grunted.

'That isn't being helpful.' The Fat Man grabbed the junkie's left arm with both hands and held it over his knee. 'Sorry, this is going to hurt.'

'No!'

'You going to talk now?'

'Yes!'

'That's better.' Yiorgos sat watching, one hand still holding the arm.

'What do you want to know?'

'Who kidnapped your grandfather?'

The young man glared at him. 'How would I know?'

'So you loved the old man.'

'Old fucker, more like.'

'You had a falling out?'

'He thought I was a waster.'

'He obviously isn't senile. Still, you've got this place.'

'My mother bought it for me.'

'Forgot to throw in a cleaner though.'

'There have been a few.' Dinos gave him a hollow grin. 'They don't like it when I get my cock out.'

The Fat Man shook his head. 'Rich young man like you. You have to get your wallet out first.'

Another grin. 'That works too, but only at the beginning of the month.'

'Your allowance? Don't you have any friends?'

'What do you mean?'

'Who might do it for free?'

''Course I've got friends.'

'Names, please.'

'Fuck!' Dinos gasped as a second hand seized his arm and brought it over his interrogator's knee. 'No!'

'Names.'

'Agam . . . Agamemnon Pyrsos, Kirki Houkli – ow! – Jimmy Tzakos, Nadia Svolou.'

'That's your *parea*, is it?'

'Yes.'

'Only there seem to be more males than females.'

'Agam's gay.'

'Who does he – to use your favourite word – fuck? Jimmy or you?'

'Not me! Please . . . let go of my arm.'

Yiorgos obliged. 'So Homer's King of Mycenae takes it up the arse. What a come down. And who do you fuck?'

'Both the girls.' Dinos attempted a smile. 'At the same time, if I'm lucky.'

'I'm impressed. But aren't you mostly stoned?'

'Well . . .'

'There are enough syringes here to get the whole of Kolonaki high. Anyway, you and your grandfather didn't get on.'

'Haven't seen him for over three years,' Dinos mumbled.

'Who pays for your dope? The next time you bullshit me, I'll break that arm.'

'I . . . I deal.'

'At least some of the Gatsos genes made it through to you. But dealers who sample the product usually end up in hospital or dead.'

'My father helps out.'

'How caring of him. Obviously you don't have a job in the family group.'

'No. They even took my shares from me.'

'Who did?'

'The old fucker and Uncle Pavlos.'

'Is that right? Do you own a gun?'

'The cops have already asked me that.'

The Fat Man leaned closer. 'I can hear that arm cracking.'

Dinos's eyes opened wide. 'Yes, yes, I do have a pistol. A SIG Sauer. Most of us do, in case the anarchists come after us. The pigs took it. Anyway, you're pissing up the wrong tree. I was cut off years ago. Why would I go after *Pappous* now?'

'Why indeed? That doesn't let you off the hook though. If you
didn't do it, who did? Come on, suggestions.'

'The old fucker had lots of enemies – other shipowners, people
he let go to the wall, girls he stuck his decrepit prick into . . .'

'Tell me more.'

'I don't know about the business stuff. Loukas and Evi will fill
you in. But I know about some of the girls. He was into Ukrainians,
especially leggy ones with big knockers.'

'And you know this how?'

'Just because I didn't see him doesn't mean I don't know what
he got up to. People talk.'

'Did you tell the cops?'

Dinos dropped his head. 'None of their business.' He glared at
Yiorgos. 'They don't have me down as a suspect.'

'So you say. Keep talking. Where did he find these Ukrainians?'

'Where do you find anyone to fu— ow! Sorry. Nightclubs. I
heard from contacts that he often went to the Paradiso Bianco on
Piraeus Street.'

'He got his Ukrainians from a club with an Italian name.'

'The owners aren't Italian, you—'

'Who are the owners, Dino? Don't go all shy on me. They
wouldn't by any chance have anything to do with the dope you
deal, would they? Thought so. Names?'

'No fucking wa— ah!'

'I promise you, I'll break it.'

'I . . . they're . . . they're Russians, man. You don't . . . you don't
want to mess with them.'

'I can look after myself. Names!'

'Igor . . . Igor and Lavrenti Gogol.'

The Fat Man hoped he concealed his shock. The Gogols had
a big reputation in and beyond the criminal underworld. A Sunday
newspaper had set its investigative team on them. One of them
was blinded with acid, another had both legs broken and the third,
a woman, was repeatedly sodomised. They were found a long
way from the club with nothing to link them to the Russians, too
terrified to talk about what had happened.

Yiorgos got up and smiled at Dinos. 'That'll do for now.'

'That'll do full stop. I'm going to the UK tomorrow.'

'After what you've told me, I very much doubt it. Stick around, Dino.
Otherwise I might let the Gogols know you've been running your mouth.'

Dinos suddenly looked like a vampire had drained every drop of his blood.

Yiorgos made for the remains of the door. He didn't feel a whole lot more sanguine himself.

Jim Thomson looked through the curtains, took in the grey light of early dawn and closed them again. He needed sleep desperately, but every time he dropped off he would be woken by dreams. No, not dreams; the reality of his past lives and the people he had lost, most of them by choice. Like Pilita . . .

He couldn't fathom why he had to move on. It certainly wasn't because he wanted to go home – he had managed to block Greece out completely, it lay deeper than the wreck of the *Homeland* and the skeletons of his crewmates. No, there was something in him that wanted another life. It was as if, having dispensed with his first life – family, friends, the Party – he was now cursed to make new ones for the rest of his life. He didn't know what he wanted, but he had to leave. He didn't even try to explain to Pilita. She wept, but somehow she seemed to understand. Her white man had arrived unexpectedly from the sea and he was destined to leave. They had no children so she was all he had to hold him back. And she, with her great soul, gave him her blessing. She even gave him their savings. But she would not say goodbye, staying in their hut when he left to catch the dawn bus to the local capital.

In Tacloban he found badly paid work in a series of burger bars, eventually graduating to a hotel restaurant. And then fate intervened. He fell in with some Greek seamen whose ship had been towed to the port after losing its propeller. Their cook had either jumped or fallen overboard and there was a job for him. The captain didn't care that he had no papers. He could use the dead man's. Now he was Christos Karras, at thirty-six only two years older than he really was. They resembled each other enough to convince most officials; he grew a moustache to improve the likeness. The ship, a 10,000 tonne refrigerated carrier, was on long-term charter to a British company and sailed mainly from New Zealand to Europe with frozen lamb. Three years passed during which he acquired a reputation for stand-offishness. The truth was, he didn't want to spend his free time with the sailors. He bought books in English every time they were ashore and regained command of the language. He had women in the ports they called at regularly, but he confused their names.

One day, when the *Lutine Star* was in Melbourne awaiting orders, he realised he'd enough of the sea. Taking Karras's passport and seaman's discharge book but leaving behind all but a change of clothes and a few books, he slipped off the ship one evening. He'd saved a fair amount of cash. Within two weeks he had a new identity as Jim Thomson, courtesy of some operators in the local underworld. He bought a bus ticket for the desert, his aim to get as far away from the sea as he could.

'OK, Yiorgo, that's useful. Go back to your place and see what you can dig up on the Russians.'

Mavros ended the call, put away his notebook and asked the solicitous Filipina where he could find her employer. She led him to a door on the other side of the stairway.

'Down there,' she pointed. 'Called den.'

Mavros thanked her and went down well-worn steps. He found Vangelis Myronis bent over a full-sized snooker table. He was now dressed in white jeans and a yellow shirt. He had washed his hair, but he still looked like the over-aged playboy his wife had described.

'Sorry to keep you from your work,' Mavros said.

Myronis looked round. 'Don't get smart.'

Mavros sat in a battered armchair. There was an open bottle of Jim Beam on the table in front of it, but no glasses.

'Have a drink if you like.' There was the clack of balls connecting then his host came over, still holding the cue.

Mavros waited till he had sat down.

'Do you know a nightclub called the Paradiso Bianco?'

That got Myronis's attention. 'I . . . yes, I've heard of it.'

'Ever been?'

There was a long pause 'A few times.' He took a swig from the bottle.

'With your son.'

'What?'

'You help him with his drug dealing.'

Myronis stood up. 'Get the hell out of—'

'Do you want me to invite your wife to join us?'

'I . . .' Myronis sat down again. 'I don't help him. I just give him cash from time to time.'

'Even though Kostas Gatsos forbade that.'

'Dinos is my son, for God's sake. He's got problems. Anyway, what I do is nothing compared with Eirini. She bought him his flat.'

'Do the police know about this little sideline of yours?'

Myronis hung his head. 'No. I'd prefer if it stayed that way.'

'That depends on you answering my questions. Truthfully.'

His host drank more Jim Beam. 'All right,' he mumbled.

'What kind of relationship did you have with the missing man?'

'An obedient one.'

'Meaning he could turn off the cash whenever he wanted.'

'Well, he could tell Eirini to keep me on even more of a pittance.' Myronis's eyes flashed.

'I understand your father-in-law could have saved your family business.'

'Did she tell you that? It was decades ago and I didn't have a clue. You think I still harbour a grudge?'

'Do you?'

'No!'

'Is there anything else you're unhappy about? For instance, the way your son's been treated.'

Myronis lit a cigarette and inhaled deeply. 'Dinos had his chances. The truth is, he never fitted in. The old man doesn't like failures.'

'That must have angered you.'

'It did at the time but Dinos was cut loose years ago.'

'Do you own a firearm?'

'Why, do you? Oh, all right. Yes, I do. A Browning Cynergy shotgun and a Heckler and Koch USP. I do some hunting in the winter, but mainly they're for personal protection. All licensed, of course.'

'Did you get Dinos his SIG Sauer?'

'What? He's been blabbing. Yes, it's an old model. I bought it from a friend years ago.'

Mavros looked at him. For the first time Vangelis Myronis held his gaze.

'What? It's a dangerous world, with terrorists, anarchists, all those scum.'

'How did you get on with your wife's half-brother Pavlos?'

The change of subject surprised Myronis. 'All right, I suppose.'

'There weren't any problems between you?'

'I . . . no, not really. He was a wanker, to be honest. Tried to be the voice of his father, but the old man stomped all over him on a daily basis.'

Mavros leaned forward. 'So you have no idea who's behind the kidnapping and murder?'

'Of course not!'

'Nothing to do with the Gogol brothers?'

'Who?'

'You know who I mean. You didn't tell the police you know them, did you?' Mavros took out his phone. 'I'm calling Brigadier Kriaras.'

'No, please don't. You're right, I know them. But only as a customer.'

'Of overpriced booze and Ukrainian sex-slaves or of drug consignments?'

Myronis was paler than a week-old squid. 'I . . . I've had a drink there occasionally. I don't know anything about drugs. I only give Dinos money. I go elsewhere for girls. Those Ukrainians are too skinny for me.'

'Probably because they're starved. So you see no profit from Dinos's dealing?'

'I don't think he does either.'

'Could this be what this is all about? Your son owes the Gogol brothers so they decide to grab the golden goose?'

'Don't be ridiculous. I mean . . . the old man had bodyguards.'

'Russian bodyguards.'

'Oh, Christ.'

Mavros got up.

'What are you going to do?'

'Talk to my employers.'

'You mean Loukas and Evi? All right, but please don't tell Eirini. She'll have my balls.'

Mavros left the den and the house without further comment. The Russian connection was interesting, but he was wondering about something else. Why had Pavlos Gatsos been shot?

ELEVEN

Despite his rage over the trials and what had been done to him, Kostas Gatsos found himself questioning some of his actions. In the constant dark – he was aware it was a standard disorientation tactic, he'd known members of the security forces during the dictatorship – his past came back to him. He didn't regret anything, but he did wonder whether he could have been less heavy-handed; less vicious, if truth be told. Inevitably his memory settled on Tefkros Svolos. Kostas despised him from the first time they met at a shipowners' function in the mid 50s.

'This is the young wolf who's snapping at our heels,' Svolos said, cigarette holder in the corner of his mouth. 'You're making quite a name for yourself, Mr Gatso.'

Kostas was immediately aware of the latter sentence's real meaning: we've been rich for generations and your family name is shit-stained.

'I don't snap,' he replied haughtily. 'I bite legs off – as with the Australian coal charter.'

Svolos stared at him and then laughed. 'Anyone can make a few good deals, my lad. The question is, have you got the stamina for decades of success?'

Kostas looked at the overweight figure in evening dress. 'The question is, have you?' He smiled and walked away.

From the next day he did everything in his power to stymie the Svolos group's operations. At first he paid brokers and employees to ensure he was always ahead of the game. Then he outbid Svolos for new buildings in the yards in the Far East, meaning the older man had to pay premium prices for European vessels. Then . . . he got nasty. That took two forms.

It was common knowledge that Svolos's third wife, Ariadhni, who was twenty-five years younger, had a wandering eye. Kostas made sure it landed on him. They would meet in discreet hotels and screw each other senseless. As time went by that was no longer enough for him. He wanted them to fuck in Svolos's bed. Ariadhni was reluctant because of the servants, but finally she gave most of them the afternoon off and bribed the few that remained. Kostas still wasn't satisfied. He deliberately arrived an hour late, then took much more time than usual in pleasuring Ariadhni and himself. There was a knock on the door.

'Kyria Ariadhni! Your husband is back!' called the maid.

Kostas smiled, then pinned his lover to the bed.

'Let me go. He'll divorce me.'

'Don't worry, I'll look after you.' Kostas was hard again, excited by the danger. He plunged into her.

'No!' she cried.

'Yes!'

She fell into the rhythm he established and threw her head back. Kostas was hitting her pleasure spot and she was powerless to resist. He held back until the door opened then abandoned himself to the final strokes, bellowing as he came.

'Ariadhni!' Svolos shouted. 'Is he raping you? Gatso?'

'Raping her?' Kostas pulled out and turned so that his naked front was fully visible. 'We've been doing this for months.'

'You filthy gutter-rat!' Svolos said, raising the cane he always carried.

Kostas rushed him, knocking it from his grasp.

'Old man, I can put you on the floor and smash your skull. Is she worth it?' He gathered up his clothes and went into the hall. He heard his lover wail as the cane was brought down on her repeatedly. He let himself out of the house and walked, whistling, to his Oldsmobile.

Tefkros Svolos didn't divorce his wife. She was found that night by the butler at the foot of the marble staircase with her neck broken. The pathologist made no mention of the weals on the dead woman's shoulders, arms and back, ruling that death was accidental. His silence and that of the servants were bought. Kostas was happy. He wouldn't have done anything for Ariadhni anyway. There was gossip in their circle, of course, but he managed to convince Marguerite, his wife at the time, that he was being slandered.

He wasn't finished with Svolos. He wanted his rival's business to go to the wall, no matter how long established it was. He continued his harassment tactics, but there were enough cargoes to go around, though he picked up the most lucrative ones. He needed to cripple the Svolos Group once and for all. He lay in wait for several years, but the opportunity never arose; so he constructed his own. Svolos owned some of the largest tankers in the world. By making large payments to officers and crewmen, he managed to set up two catastrophic 'accidents' within a month. First, the *Svolos Challenger*, carrying over 100,000 tonnes of crude oil, ran aground near Land's End. It was an environmental disaster and the inquiry showed that the ship's steering system was faulty. For good measure, the officer of the watch had made a basic navigational error. Svolos's insurers contested the claim and he was badly hit by the damages awarded the British government.

The second incident amused him even more. He positioned the KEG *Angela*, an old 15,000 tonne bulk carrier, in Le Havre and waited for the right time. After only a week, the perfect combination of heavy fog and a Svolos vessel heading south occurred. His vessel was sent out and suffered a complete engine failure. Warning signals were broadcast, but the wireless operator and bridge officer on the *Svolos Pride*, a fully laden 50,000 tonne bulk carrier, claimed they were never received. The *Pride* ploughed into the *Angela* amidships. The captain, forewarned, got the crew into the lifeboats before the latter sank. The subsequent inquiry found the Svolos group negligent – unaccountably, the *Pride*'s radar had not been in service since she left Rotterdam. Tefkros Svolos's hair was already white, but his heart took the brunt of the stress. He lasted another three years, a broken and ultimately gibbering man.

Kostas stood up, his good hand extended to feel his way through the dark. He needed to piss. Could it be that some spawn of Svolos had arranged the kidnap? Some faithful employee who had dug deeper than the Lloyd's investigators? He shivered.

And then he shouted, 'Fuck you!'

He squatted over the bucket and emptied his bladder. As he went back to the mattress, he had a disturbing thought. Could his son Pavlos have facilitated the kidnap? There were parts of his life that Kostas had never been able to access. But why, then, was he shot? Because he was no longer useful to the kidnappers? Because he knew too much about them?

Kostas Gatsos had always ruled his family with a rod of steel. By doing so, had he scared some of them into acting against him? Fuck family. The only person you could trust was yourself.

Mavros took a taxi to the green building near the sea. A car he recognised was parked by the entrance.

'Lieutenant,' he said. 'How wonderful to see you?'

The policeman scowled. 'You took your time.'

'Did you think I was coming straight here from my breakfast? Sorry. I had this thing called work to do first.'

'Funny. The brigadier wants to see you.'

Mavros took out his notebook. 'I can fit him in a week on Friday at midday.'

'Hear me laughing?'

'You need a bit of practice with that. I'm going to see my employers. You can tell him that. Maybe I'll call him.' Mavros grinned. 'Have you really got nothing better to do with your time?'

'Orders are orders.'

'Of course they are.'

Mavros had been planning to call Kriaras anyway, but not until he'd spoken to Loukas and Evi. The latter was waiting for him at the lift when he emerged from the stair door.

'Good morning, Alex,' she said. 'I hear you've been hard at work.'

'Morning. Oh yes?'

Evi led him into the array of desks. 'We've had my mother on the phone. Dinos too. Who did you send to question him? He says he was pushed around and threatened.'

Mavros smiled. 'Is he a whiner by nature?'

Evi laughed. 'Yes.'

'There you are then. My colleague is firm but fair.'

They went into Loukas's office. He ended a call and got up to shake Mavros's hand.

'My step-mother was appalled that I gave you the group's financial details. I hope you've got them in a safe place.'

'In a safe, literally,' Mavros lied. He was hoping that Nondas would find time to do more digging.

'Good. Are you here to give us an update?'

'Not exactly. I need to run some things past you.'

They sat down around the coffee table. Mavros told them about Dinos's drug dealing and Vangelis's financial involvement.

'He's a fool, that man,' Loukas said.

Evi glared at him. 'But he's my father. Besides, from what Alex said, he's not making any money from it.'

'No, your idiot brother is shooting that all up.'

'Dinos is ill,' Evi said, red-faced. 'He's going for treatment.'

'I think that had better wait,' Mavros put in. 'We may need to talk to him again. There's a problem. The people that supply him are Russian gangsters.'

'What?' the step-siblings said, in unison.

'The Gogol brothers.' Mavros watched carefully to see if they showed any sign of knowing the name. Neither did. 'They own a club called the Paradiso Bianco.'

'Never heard of it,' Loukas said. 'I've no time for such places.'

'Me neither,' said Evi. 'Apart from looking after my donkeys, I go to modern dance classes.'

Mavros tried not to look surprised. Evi wasn't exactly built like a dancer.

'We often wear masks,' she volunteered. 'Our identities are subsumed into the characters.'

'Right.' Mavros turned a page. 'I gather your grandfather had a liking for statuesque Ukrainians.'

Evi turned away.

Loukas glanced at her. 'So I heard. He was . . . is incorrigible. I suppose you have to admire his stamina at over 80.'

'No, you don't,' Evi said, her face flushed. 'It's disgusting, paying to use women's bodies.'

'I agree.' Loukas took her hand. 'I married at 24,' he said to Mavros. 'There's only one woman for me and that's Sandra. She's American. We met at Columbia.'

'Good for you. The thing is, your grandfather may have picked up his Ukrainians at the Paradiso Bianco.'

'Really?' Loukas said, frowning. 'Do you think these Gogols could have kidnapped him?'

'Where did he find his Russian guards?'

'Our lawyer arranges such things. But since one of them was killed, it's hardly likely they worked for the kidnappers.'

'Possibly, but loyalty is always for sale to the highest bidder in that business. Perhaps the other two changed allegiance and he got in the way.' Mavros pushed on. 'Tefkros Svolos. What do you know about him?'

'Not much,' Loukas replied. 'He died years ago.'

'He and Grandfather were fierce rivals,' Evi added.

'Do you know his granddaughter Nadia?'

'Yes, but not very well,' she said. 'Shipping and charity circles.'

'She's closer to your brother.'

Evi stared at him. 'Not that I know of.'

'Apparently she's in his *parea*. Along with Agamemnon Pyrsos, Kirki Houkli, and Jimmy Tzakos.'

Loukas shook his head. 'They're all wasters. Some rich families let their kids get away with anything.'

'They're probably regulars at the Paradiso Bianco too.'

'Are you suggesting one or all of them are involved in the kidnap?' Loukas asked, laughing. 'They can't see beyond their next drink.'

'I was thinking about Nadia Svolou.'

'Svolos Shipping is tiny now,' Loukas said. 'The family is strapped for cash.'

'Even more reason to strike at a hated, much more successful rival.'

Evi and Loukas exchanged glances.

'I suppose anything's possible,' the latter said.

'I'll look into it.' Mavros looked at Loukas. 'Something else. Your father. Why do you think he was killed?'

'I presume because the kidnappers didn't want him.'

'He's worth a lot of money, isn't he?'

'What are you getting at? Maybe he resisted.'

'The autopsy report mentioned no other wounds. Besides, was he the kind of man to resist?'

Loukas bit his lip. 'No.'

'I think he was deliberately killed – the shot to the eye suggests professional skill, which fits in with the rest of the kidnap.'

Evi stifled a sob.

'Sorry.' Mavros poured her a glass of water but kept his eye on Loukas, not wanting to lose momentum. 'Can you think of any reason he should have been targetted?

The young man got up and went to the far side of the desk. 'My father was the CEO of the group. He had the same enemies as my grandfather.' There was tension in his voice.

'Did your father visit the Paradiso Bianco too?'

'Don't you dare speak ill of him!'

'It's a simple question.'

Evi touched Mavros's hand. 'My step-father was a very restrained man. He hardly ever went out in the evening. He spent most of his free time playing chess on the Internet. He could have been a grand master if he hadn't been forced to join the group.'

'Did he hold a grudge about that?'

'Don't be ridiculous,' said Loukas. 'My father understood his responsibilities.'

Mavros kept at it. 'What about female company? I understand your mother is in Paris.'

Loukas looked away. 'They haven't lived together for years. I'm sure he didn't use prostitutes.'

'Was it his idea that the group offer shares to Colombians?'

Both Evi and Loukas seemed genuinely amazed by the question.

'How . . . how did you know about that?' the latter asked.

'From the financial records you gave me.'

'But they're highly complex, as well as enormous in scale.'

Mavros wasn't going to mention Nondas, at least not yet. 'Reading spreadsheets is part of my job. Don't forget, I've been running my mother's company for the last five years.'

Loukas looked at him dubiously. 'That's a small publishing concern, not a global group with hundreds of subsidiaries.'

Mavros went on the offensive. 'You're stonewalling me about the Colombians.' He glanced at his notebook. 'Laura Moreno and Santiago Rojas each hold two per cent of Gatsos group shares.'

'Don't tell me you're making a ludicrous connection between them and Dinos's drug-dealing?' Loukas said.

'I was thinking more of the Gogol brothers.'

Evi turned to him. 'They're serious business people, Alex.'

'I imagine they are. But they run arms and logging companies. How did they end up with Gatsos shares?'

'They wanted to expand into shipping,' Loukas said. 'Careful checks were made and there was no sign of any illegality.'

'And they're lovely people,' Evie added. 'Both visit every year.'

'Presumably your grandfather approved of them.' Mavros looked at Loukas. 'Or was your father the one who brought them on board, so to speak?'

'I don't know,' the young man replied. 'And I doubt it'll be possible to find out for the time being.'

'I know, I'll ask your lawyers. I presume you've told them about me.'

'Of course.'

'Who's the contact person?'

'Mr Siatkas himself.'

Mavros smiled. 'That'll be an honour.' He didn't manage to keep the irony from his voice.

Loukas and Evi failed to respond.

Mavros got up. 'All right, I'll be in touch.' He paused. 'Unless anything else has come to mind that you want to share?'

'I don't think so,' Loukas said.

Evi led Mavros out. There was an array of flags in display cases on the far wall.

'Yellow and purple are the group's colours?'

'Gold and purple,' Evi corrected.

'Very imperial.'

At the lift she looked up at him. 'You don't like us, do you?'

'That's irrelevant.'

'We know your father was a Communist.'

'So's that.' Mavros smiled. 'Besides, who says I don't like *you*? Your step-brother's hard work, though.'

Evi laughed. 'You're telling me. He's already wearing Grandfather's armour. I hate to imagine what'll happen when he comes back.' She clutched his arm, her expression suddenly sombre. 'He will come back, won't he?'

'That's what I'm here to facilitate,' Mavros said in English, as he got into the lift. 'See, I can speak the universal language of business.'

Lieutenant Babis was waiting for him outside.

'Get in. The brigadier's waiting.'

Mavros sighed. 'Just when I was making progress.'

Kostas Gatsos had the feeling more time had passed since the last trial than between it and the first. He hadn't been abandoned – his bread and water was still supplied and the bucket emptied. He asked for his watch but got no response from the balaclava-wearing guard.

What was planned for him? Surely Siatkas would have put the best investigators he could find on the case. The police would be as much use as a supertanker on the rocks. Or maybe the lawyer hadn't. He'd been told so often that the group's affairs were not to be disclosed to an outsider that perhaps he was sitting back and doing nothing. If so, Kostas had only himself to blame.

But he didn't do that. He never allowed himself to accept responsibility for failure. That was why he had executives. Only two or three survived more than a decade. If there was a cock-up, they paid for it with their jobs – unless they were family, of course. That didn't include the useless sponger Myronis; he had no Gatsos blood.

What had Eirini seen in him? It was obvious that Dinos's weaknesses came from Vangelis's pathetic genes. There were rumours that Eirini preferred women now. He couldn't blame her.

Kostas found himself thinking about the women of the family. None of them had submitted to his will, at least not the way he would have liked – meaning *complete* submission. Both his wives had resisted him, Marguerite subtly and Tatiana the opposite, arriving drunk at receptions and pawing the waiters. Pavlos's wife, now widow, spent most of her time in Paris. He'd never understood why his son allowed that. Then again, Myrto was a frigid bitch who looked disparagingly at Kostas and probably Pavlos too. Old money, it was a curse. Her daughter Nana took after her, having decamped to New York as soon as she left school. Shipping meant nothing to her except to finance her art gallery. The only one worth anything was little Evi. She was an ugly dwarf, but she was loyal and loving. Loukas's blonde and freckled wife Sandra openly laughed at Evi. There would be trouble about that when he got home.

If he got home. The unlikelihood of that struck him like a spear cast to the heart. There had been four people at the table, not including the piece of shit who ran things. He'd assumed there would be at least two more trials, but what if there weren't? On the other hand, if they had discovered even a fraction of the scams he'd perpetrated and chopped bits off him for each, there would be nothing left.

Kostas Gatsos wasn't a god-fearing man, but he was beginning to worry about a hell of eternal pain.

TWELVE

'Where are we going?' Mavros asked, as the car sped eastwards along the coastal motorway.

'That's for me to know and—'

'Me not to. Very helpful, Haralambe.'

'Don't call me that.'

'It's your name, isn't it?'

'I prefer "lieutenant".'

'OK.' Two breaths. 'Lambaki.'

'You looking for a punch in the face?'

Mavros opened the passenger window. 'Help! Police brutality!'

Lieutenant Babis pressed the over-ride button and the window went back up. 'What age are you?'

'A lot older than you.'

'That's true.'

'With age comes wisdom. We're going to . . . Glyfadha.'

'Wrong.' The officer took an exit and drove towards the waterfront.

'Long live the Royal Hellenic Navy!' Mavros exclaimed.

The three funnels of the cruiser *Averof* rose up before them. The grey warship that had won command of the Aegean before the First World War was now a floating museum. There had been a scandal a few months earlier when a shipowner's son had held his wedding party on the vessel. The Fat Man had thrown things at the TV.

A dark blue Audi was parked at the corner of the pier. The lieutenant drove close, ensuring the passenger windows were next to each other.

'May I?' Mavros said, raising his forefinger.

Babis grinned. 'Allow me, sir.'

The other car's window was tinted. It lowered to reveal Nikos Kriaras in plain clothes.

'Haralambidhi, you have the copies of the files?'

'Yes, sir.'

'Very well. Give them to him.'

'Yes, sir,' the lieutenant said reluctantly.

'What do you think I'm going to do with them?'

'Show them to your friends in the press,' interjected the brigadier.

'I haven't seen Lambis Bitsos for, oh, at least a week.'

'Eight days.'

'Have you had me followed for the last five years?'

'No. We keep an eye on Bitsos. Do *not* tell him.'

'You think he doesn't know? Anyway, I've signed a confidentiality agreement. No leaks to the media or I lose everything. Even my stubble.'

Kriaras shook his head. 'Is there anything you want to tell me?'

'Drink more Grecian 2000.'

'Haralambidhi, apply a wrist hold.'

'Ow! For fuck's sake . . .'

'Let him go. Well?'

'Actually, I did want to discuss something with you even though I'll be breaking my contract with the Gatsos family.'

'I'm listening.'

Mavros watched as a seagull landed on the wall of the pier beyond the car. It started to eat the remains of a burger from a polystyrene box.

'The Gogol brothers.'

'What about them?'

'You don't fancy arresting them?'

'Why would I do that?'

Mavros told him about the gangsters' connection with Dinos Gatsos and his father.

'Interesting, but what would their motive be for kidnap? They're already supplying dope at inflated prices.'

'I've lived a spotless life recently but unless things have changed an awful lot headbangers like the Gogols don't shy away from kidnaps and professional hits.'

'True. But they usually demand a ransom.'

'Kostas Gatsos had enemies, whatever his grandchildren think.'

'I know that. We've checked several. Oddly, they all had rock solid alibis.'

Mavros watched the brigadier closely.

'You know about the Colombian connection?'

Nikos Kriaras had a good poker face, but the double blink gave him away.

'Haralambidhi?' he called. 'Refresh my memory.'

The lieutenant blushed. 'Sorry, sir. I don't know about any Colombian connection.'

Mavros tut-tutted. 'Shall I enlighten you?'

'If you don't, you'll be taking a bath under the *Averof*'s sewage outlet,' Kriaras said.

Mavros explained, without mentioning his brother-in-law.

'See the benefits of having become a businessman?' he said. 'Obviously no one in the organised crime unit can read spreadsheets.'

'I can,' said Lieutenant Babis.

'Well, it's a lot of material and you've only had a month.'

'That's enough. We'll check these people. Give Haralambidhis their names. Is that it?'

'What about the Paradiso Bianco?' Mavros asked, as the tinted window started to rise.

'We'll let you know.'

'Hold on. There could be consequences if you throw the Russians in the cells.'

'I'll make sure the minister understands that.'

Mavros watched as the window closed. Not for the first time, Kriaras had got more than he'd given. On the other hand, if the Colombians did have drugs gang links Mavros couldn't handle them on his own.

Lieutenant Babis drove him back to his mother's, where Mavros dismissed him and carried away the police files. It was early afternoon. People would be heading home for lunch. Just the time to catch them.

Jim Thomson was sitting in the park in Kensington, a copy of the *Age* across his thighs. The usual disasters both in and beyond Australia. He didn't know why he kept buying Ivy's paper. She'd always had an open mind, that was one of the things that had attracted him to her. That and her magnificent figure. And her sense of humour. And . . .

He was back in Alice Springs in the early 90s. Forty years old, the sea salt long sweated out of him after two years working in a restaurant patronised by personnel from the joint Australian-American satellite tracking base at Pine Gap. What he liked most was being 1200 kilometres from the sea. He had a room in a house owned by an elderly couple who left him to himself. He drank in the bars and, once he could afford an old car, drove into the desert at night. The stars seemed different from the ones he'd seen at sea and in the Philippines, and obviously were not the same as the northern hemisphere constellations he had stared up at from Ikaria. The dry brush reminded him of his homeland, but only in terms of scent and colour. He had cut off his emotions from his senses and no longer felt a connection. Even the heat, worse than an Athenian August, didn't bother him. There wasn't a trace of moisture from the ocean in the air and he liked that.

He first saw Ivy at the camel races. Her white dress was patterned with red flowers that set off her fiery hair. She was with another woman, stern and much thinner. He assumed they were lesbians as the town had a large community. Then Ivy looked back at him, as if his gaze was burning her neck, and their eyes made contact. He went across and slipped her the phone number of the restaurant while her friend was yelling at a beast that had missed its footing. He wasn't normally forward; in fact he hadn't been with a woman since he'd come to Alice. Doing so would have been to disrespect Pilita, even though he was the one who had left. Now he knew that he'd remained faithful because he hadn't met the right woman.

Ivy came to restaurant on her own and waited for him to finish. He took her to a respectable bar and they drank lager. At first she did the talking, slowly drawing him out, but eventually he found his tongue and they conversed on equal terms.

'Who's your friend?' he asked.

'Flo. She's just an acquaintance. I met her on the plane. She's off exploring the lezzer nightlife, good on her.'

'But you . . .'

She laughed and he felt a weight lift. There hadn't been enough laughter in his life.

'No, mate. I like men. Especially since my husband passed away.' She told him about Mick the slaughterman and the fun they'd had; and about the house in Kensington.

'What about you? Where are you from?'

He hesitated. 'Many places.'

'The Mediterranean? You a Greek? Plenty of those in Melbourne.'

He was going to lie but with her that didn't seem right, even then. 'Yes. I had some problems there. I don't like to talk about it.'

Ivy smiled. 'That's all right. We all have our secrets.'

And he never disclosed his, even though she often tried to get him to do so over the years. Hers were minor – a boyfriend she'd two-timed, an affair Mick never found out about. What she really wanted were children, but she was resigned to that never happening.

'I've been in many places,' he said, 'all over the world.'

'So you're either a pilot or a sailor.'

'They have men serving drinks on planes too.'

'You're too much of a hunk for that.'

He smiled. 'You're right. I was a cook on the ships. A useful trade on land too.'

'What brought you to the back of beyond?'

'I could ask you the same question.'

'I'm a tourist, lover. I go to a different place in this magnificent country every year. Come on, why are you out in the desert?'

He raised his shoulders. 'I don't like the sea.'

Her sharp eyes picked up his discomfort. 'More secrets? Don't worry, we're only talking.'

His heart sank. Not only did this stunning, happy woman make him feel alive again, but he desperately wanted to take her clothes off. It was if she read his mind.

'Or maybe we aren't. Let's go.' Ivy got up and pulled him out of the bar.

The clerk at her hotel ignored him as she took him up to her room, hand tight around his wrist.

'I hope you don't think I do this with every man who buys me a beer.'

'I don't care.'

She laughed loudly, then put her hand over her mouth. 'We'll get thrown out.'

He thought of his room with the old people. 'Not a good idea. Here, let me.' He pulled down the zip of her dress and slipped his hands round, having unclipped her lacy bra. She moaned as he touched her nipples. His fingers tingled and he was consumed by curiosity. He had to see her breasts; he'd never felt others like them. In the light from the street he turned her as her dress dropped. He pulled off her bra and examined the hard nipples. The brown circle around them was large and the breasts themselves were heavy, though they stood proud without support.

'Kiss me,' she said, panting.

He did so, on each nipple and then on the lips. They staggered sideways to the bed and she ran a hand over his groin.

'Big man,' she whispered. 'Time you were set free.'

Their lovemaking was relaxed, the passion somehow controlled so that the climax would be all the better. And it was for him. For Ivy, he wasn't sure – until she slammed her hands against the headboard and let out a long shriek.

People started banging on the walls and ceiling, and the clerk phoned up to ask for restraint.

'Too late, mate,' Ivy said, making both of them laugh hysterically.

Four days later Jim gave his car to an Aborigine he used to drink with, packed a single suitcase, dumped the rest of his gear and bought a ticket to Melbourne on the same flight as Ivy. He had hitched his way across the country so seeing it from the air was a revelation. Ivy was right. It was a magnificent country. She was magnificent too. He didn't care any more about going to Melbourne with its large population of Greek descent. He would keep his background to himself. After all, he had a non-Greek name now.

And then, as the plane circled to land, he saw the sea and his heart was pierced. It was his fate to cross water again, he was sure of that – but he would resist it as long as he could.

He worked in restaurants for three years, spending his free time crafting wood, a new-found passion. Ivy knew a picture-framer who took him on and he escaped the tiresome hours of the kitchens.

And all was well until Ivy, who'd kept her own Greek background secret for fear of scaring him off, asked him to take her back to the old country. He'd finally made his mind up. He was leaving the next day.

Mavros was glad to find that his mother had applied the chain and dead bolts.

'Honestly, dear,' she said, rubbing her hands. 'Isn't it time we gave up these precautions?'

'Not until we find the Son.' There was also the small matter of the Gogol brothers. Dinos might tell them about the Fat Man's visit and they wouldn't take long to track Mavros down; but he wasn't going to tell Dorothy about them.

He made himself a sandwich, declining her offer of help, then called Yiorgos.

'Get round to my mother's,' he said 'Sharpish.'

'I'll have to take a cab then.'

'Yes, you will. Get him to wait and ring the bell.'

He went back into the *saloni*. Dorothy was leafing through a pile of typescript in Greek.

'That old academician's treatise on the Byzantine navy? We're not publishing it.'

'It might do as an e-book.'

'If he pays for it to be scanned and set up.'

'You're turning into a capitalist running dog, Alex.'

He laughed. 'It's the company I've been keeping lately.' He had a thought. 'You don't know the Svolos family, do you?'

'I've run into them from time to time. Not so much since old Tefkros died.'

'He was a rival of Kostas Gatsos.'

Dorothy blinked at him. 'That would be putting it mildly. They hated each other. The story is that Kostas had an affair with Tefkros's wife – she was much younger. They were caught in flagrante and the same night the poor woman fell down the stairs and broke her neck.'

'Really?'

'I don't think so. There were rumours that her body showed marks of a bad beating and that her death was no accident.'

'Lovely people. What about the old man's descendants?'

'He had a son, but he died flying his own plane. I think there's a granddaughter.'

'Nadia.'

'That sounds right.'

'Evi Gatsou sent me her address. We're off there now.'

'I can't come, dear. I have to finish this.'

He laughed. 'No, Yiorgos and I.'

'He's working with you again?'

'Yup. So far he's been very effective.'

'Well, if you're sure.' Unlike Anna, Dorothy didn't dislike the Fat Man; she'd known him when he was a trusted comrade of her husband. But she did feel he rather lowered the tone.

'How about the Pyrsos, Houklis and Tzakos families?'

'Theo Houklis is a hairdresser, one of those celebrity types. Awful man. I think there's a sculptor called Dhimitris Pyrsos. And I sat on a charity committee once with Liana Tsakou – she runs one of the private TV channels, I can't remember which. She was widowed when she was quite young. Her husband was an industrialist. Anna will know more.'

The doorbell rang.

Mavros kissed her on the forehead. 'See you later.'

'This Gatsos case,' she called after him. 'It isn't dangerous, is it?'

It was for Pavlos, he thought. 'Not so far. You know shipowners. All . . . urine and wind.'

'Alexander Mavros!'

'Sorry.' He left the flat and ran downstairs. A taxi driven by a well built middle-aged woman with a sweet face was waiting, Yiorgos in the back passenger seat.

'Politeia,' Mavros said.

'Excellent,' responded the driver. 'A decent fare for a change.'

The suburb was at the far northern edge of the city, on the lower western slopes of Mount Pendeli. It had become exclusive from the time that the statesman Konstandinos Karamanlis lived there and there were numerous MPs, business people and artists in the area.

'Who are we going to see?' asked the Fat Man.

'Nadia Svolou.'

Yiorgos grinned. 'Dinos's friend.'

Mavros patted him on the knee. 'Yes, good boy, you did very well.' He rang his sister, watching as they went past the Evangelismos Hospital. Crowds of family and visitors were milling around outside the building. It struck him that their faces were more strained than usual and their clothes less fashionable, even in the upmarket heart of the city. The financial crisis was definitely taking its toll.

He called his sister.

'I'm busy, Alex.'

'Just a couple of things.'

She groaned. 'Now?'

'Please.'

'What did you and Nondas get up to last night?'

'He cooked.'

'That explains his non-appearance, does it? What do you want?'

'What can you tell me about Agamemnon Pyrsos?'

'Son of Dhimitris? Not much. His father was the one in the limelight. I seem to remember stories about Agam – that's what they call him – being gay and a junkie. Dhimitris made a lot of money from his weird sculptures – all sharp points and bulging eyes – but he doesn't feature much these days.'

'OK. What about Kirki Houkli?'

'New money. Her father Theo, the hairdresser, is as camp as it gets, but he must have been married some time in the past since she exists. I've heard it costs at least 200 euros at his salon.'

'You'd never pay that much to get your hair done.'

'I certainly would not. If you're going to be—'

'Only kidding. Jimmy Tzakos?'

'His mother Liana owns Alternative TV. Trash for the masses, but she's surprisingly nice. I think Jimmy's a wannabe actor.'

'You mean he's unemployed.'

'He gets the odd role in sitcoms, not only on ATV, but generally he's a layabout.'

'You're a walking database. One more – Nadia Svolou.'

'Shipping family. There was a feud between her grandfather and Kostas Gatsos, but you probably know about that.'

'I do. Keep going.'

'Doesn't she hang out with Dinos Gatsos?'

'Take another bow.'

'Do you want a Christmas present this year? The only other thing I know is that her mother's an alcoholic. She hasn't been seen in public for a year or more. The family company's almost bankrupt.'

'What's her name?'

'Amelia, known as Meli.'

'A taste of honey,' Mavros said, playing on the meaning of 'meli'.

'I wouldn't recommend applying your tongue to any part of her. Now I've really got to go.'

The taxi was moving up Kifissias Avenue in heavy traffic. There was no shortage of empty shop windows and offices with 'To Rent' signs on them.

'Ordinary people's livelihoods gobbled up by the banks,' the driver said.

'Capitalism eats itself,' said the Fat Man.

'You a Communist?'

'Would that be a problem?' Mavros interjected. Plenty of people were still rabidly anti-Communist because their forebears had been killed or maltreated during the vicious civil war in the late 40s.

'Not particularly,' the woman said. 'I don't love the KKE but I can see it has a purpose.'

'Checks and balances,' Mavros said.

'Someone has to stand up to the big parties in parliament and on the news programmes.'

'Let alone protect workers' rights,' Yiorgos mumbled.

'I don't like the way unions are attached to parties,' the driver said. 'They shouldn't have to be.'

'You wouldn't happen to have studied politics?' Mavros asked.

The woman looked at him in the rear-view mirror. 'As it happens, I did. Married a bastard who left me with two kids and went back to the ships when they were in their teens. Then my father had a heart attack where I'm sitting and I had to take over this heap.'

'It's better than plenty I've been in.'

'That's because I care. But I'm not one of those sharks who overcharge old ladies and tourists, so I could never afford to upgrade. And now earnings are down with the economic crash. If you ask me, we should get rid of the euro and go back to the *dhrachmi*. We've been ripped off in all directions since the change of currency.'

'You've got that right,' said the Fat Man. 'The German banks have sunk their claws into us.'

The conversation continued in that vein until they reached the far northern suburbs, only ending when they pulled up outside a house that was by far the shabbiest in its street.

'Do you want me to wait?' the driver asked.

'Sure.' Mavros handed her a twenty Euro note. 'In case we don't come back.'

She smiled. 'What's in there? A knocking shop?'

'Anything's possible. What's your name?'

'Marianthi. Take your time. I've got the paper to read.' She took a left-of-centre daily from beneath her seat.

'Nice woman,' Mavros said, as he pressed the bell by the rusty gate.

'Think she'll go out with me?' Yiorgos asked.

'No, but you could make a fool of yourself by asking.'

'Thanks.'

'Who is it?' came a scratchy voice.

'Friends of Dinos for Nadia.'

There was pause and then the gate unlocked. They walked up to a door that had once been white. It opened on the chain.

'Hands up!'

The muzzle of a semi-automatic pistol pointed at the Fat Man through the gap.

THIRTEEN

B rigadier Kriaras looked at the officers in the room. Some were in uniform but most wore plain clothes. All were armed. 'Gentlemen.' He paused and looked at the two women, both in their late twenties. 'And ladies. I've just received approval for tonight's operation, helpfully named Hoopoe by the computer. Dim the lights, please.' He pressed keys on his laptop and a building layout appeared on the screen on the far wall. 'Lieutenant Haralambidhi?'

'Yes, sir. This is the nightclub called Paradiso Bianco on Piraeus Street.' He glanced around. 'Anyone been there?'

One of the women raised a hand.

'Identify yourself,' Kriaras ordered.

'Latsou, Elisavet, sergeant, narcotics division.' She had her high-lighted hair pulled back in a knot, emphasising an aquiline nose. 'I went undercover as a regular with one of my colleagues a year ago. We hoped to nail the people who were supplying dealers, but we couldn't get access to the rear of the premises. We picked up a couple of dealers after they left, but both were too scared to talk.'

The databank had already been checked. Dinos Gatsos had no record.

'Very well, sergeant,' he said. 'This is a recent plan. Does it look familiar?'

'Yes, sir.' She stood up and took the pointer from Haralambidhis. 'This internal door is guarded by a couple of gorillas.'

'Other security?'

'On the entrance, obviously, and several big men patrolling the car park, all with earpieces.'

'Outline the plan,' Kriaras said to his sidekick.

'Yes, sir. Groups of three will be in position here, here and here. You'll get your printed dispositions shortly. One group plus the command team will go in the main entrance at approximately 04.00, after the last customers have left. Gunfire is to be kept to a minimum, but defend yourselves if you have to.'

'What about the men on the door?' Sergeant Latsou asked.

'You and Haralambidhis will deal with them,' Kriaras said, looking up from his laptop. 'I see you're a judo and karate expert.' The female cop smiled. 'Sir.'

'Uniformed personnel will form a ring round the outer perimeter and block all potential escape points. We want the Gogol brothers, not dealers.' Kriaras hit the keys and pictures of both came up. 'Memorise these faces. They may have facial hair now. Neither has been seen in public for several weeks.'

'Not even a priest's beard will make them look holy,' Elisavet Latsou said.

Igor had a scar running from the corner of his left eye to his chin, while Lavrenti had a bullet entrance wound on his right cheek and exit wound on his left.

'Lucky for Lavrenti it was a small calibre weapon,' Haralambidhis said. 'It took part of his tongue though, so he can't speak properly.'

'His actions speak for him,' Kriaras put in. 'The Albanian who tried to kill him was found in a dumpster, genitalia in his mouth. He'd died very slowly. So be careful. Most of you will be wearing balaclavas. I won't, but nobody's yet tried to take me out of the game.'

Sergeant Latsou wondered why. The brigadier had achieved some major coups, but she'd heard rumours that he wasn't to be trusted. She didn't care. Catching drug dealers was all that mattered.

Another pair of faces appeared on the wall.

'Alex Mavros and Yiorgos Pandazopoulos, a.k.a. the Fat Man,' said Kriaras. 'They're private operators who might show up. Ensure they're not harmed but equally do not allow them any contact with the Gogol brothers.'

Interesting, the sergeant thought. An unshaven middle-aged man with shoulder-length hair and a slack-skinned pensioner with a bald patch you could skate across. What could their interest in the case be?

'Whoah!' Mavros said, putting himself in the line of fire. He could see a thin woman through the gap. She was holding the pistol unsteadily. 'Mrs Amelia Svolou? We're here on official business.'

'What business?' the woman slurred. 'I told your scumbag boss, I don't have the money.'

'We don't want money,' Mavros said, hands still raised. 'We just want to talk to your daughter.'

'Nadia? What's she done?'

'Nothing. We need some information from her, that's all.'

'You're nothing to do with the Serbs?'

'May I?' Mavros waited for her nod before taking out his wallet and passing her a business card.

'Alex Mavros? Never heard of you.'

'Good.' He smiled. 'Can we put our hands down?'

'I suppose so. Nadia! Two guys to see you.' Amelia Svolou closed the door and undid the chain. 'Come in, then.'

She was wearing a tatty dressing gown and her bare feet slapped across the tiles of what had once been an impressive entrance hall. They followed her into a *saloni* that was large but contained little furniture. There were patches on the walls that had once been covered by picture frames.

'Drink?' the woman asked, pouring herself a tumblerful of vodka – supermarket own brand, Mavros noticed.

He and the Fat Man declined and sat on a sofa whose cover had been shredded by cat claws. A tabby came in and miaowed plaintively. It was followed by a tall young woman in a thigh-length T-shirt. She was almost as thin as her mother, her black hair streaked with blond stripes. A cigarette hung from the corner of her mouth.

'Who're you?' she asked, giving them no more than a glance.

Mavros introduced himself and Yiorgos, calling him his associate. He watched as the older woman tossed the card to Nadia. Late in the day, he realised that Dinos might have told her about the Fat Man's visit. Then again, she looked like she'd only recently woken up, her eyes sticky and ringed in black. 'What can you tell me about Dinos Gatsos?'

'Dinos? He's my friend. We were at school together and . . .' She broke off. 'Why do you want to know?'

Mavros looked across to her mother. She was sprawled in a worn armchair but seemed to be following the conversation.

'There's been a suggestion that Dinos helped the kidnappers of his grandfather.' He hoped that angle would provoke a response despite its shakiness.

It provoked two.

Nadia: 'What? Don't be fucking stupid? Dinos hated his . . . oh . . .'

Amelia: 'Is there any money in this for us?'

'Mama, that's horrible!'

'Do you want new clothes next month? Help these characters out.'

Mavros had cash on him, though he hadn't expected that he'd need to bribe a shipowning family. Still, it would go on expenses and what he heard might be worthwhile.

Meli turned on her daughter, her words definitely not honeyed. 'I told you Dinos was no good but did you listen? The Gatsos family is rotten to the core. How could you befriend someone whose bastard grandfather drove your own *Pappous* to an early grave?'

Nadia glared at her. 'What do you care who I go with? You're permanently pissed.'

'And in charge of your trust fund till you're twenty-one. So talk!'

'What do you want to know?' Nadia asked, in a low voice.

Mavros leaned towards her. 'Did you ever hear Dinos making threats against Kostas Gatsos?'

'All . . . all the time. I mean, not to his face. I never met the old fucker. But D was forever complaining about how he'd been cut off by the family because of his grandfather.'

'If he'd been cut off, how did he live?'

Nadia examined her knees. 'His parents helped.'

'Not *so* cut off then. I've heard he's a dope dealer.'

She stared at him. 'I . . . no . . .'

'That doesn't matter to me. All I'm interested in is if he carried through on any of his threats.'

'You mean did he kidnap the old man? Of course not.'

Mavros smiled sympathetically. 'I'm concerned he may have been used by people who took advantage of him. Can you think of anyone like that?'

It was obvious Nadia could. Her face grew even paler and she started to bite already well chewed nails.

'Please help us,' Mavros said. 'It's worth 500 euros.'

'A thousand,' said Amelia.

They settled on 700.

'There are these Russian guys, they're called Gogol – like the writer.'

At least her years at private school hadn't been a complete waste, Mavros thought.

'They came to our table at the Paradiso once. I think they own

it.' Nadia paused, scratching her calf hard. 'They frightened me.
They've got scars, horrible marks on their faces . . . they talked to
D . . . I couldn't hear all of it, but they definitely mentioned his
grandfather.'

Mavros raised a hand. 'How did they refer to him?'

'"Your grandfather" at first . . . then "the old bastard" . . . and
other terms of abuse.'

'What did Dinos say?'

'He was laughing, going along with it, even though I know he
was scared of them. Then . . . they asked him about the house in
Lesvos. How many people worked there, the rooms, the windows
. . . Oh, and about the dock.'

Mavros wanted to ask her why she hadn't told the police, but he
had another priority.

'And this was before the kidnap?'

'Early summer. Before our *parea* went to Mykonos.'

Mavros considered that. Would Dinos have told the Fat Man
about the Gogols if he was part of the conspiracy?

The bell at the front gate rang.

Amelia Svolou stood up and grabbed her gun.

'No, Mama!' Nadia screamed.

'I'll go,' Mavros said, easing the weapon from her mother's
skeletal hand and going into the hall. He looked out of the narrow
window by the door. A young man was standing beyond the gate,
his head down.

'Well, well,' said Yiorgos from behind, making him jump. 'Just
the idiot we're looking for.'

'Dinos.'

'Bingo.'

Mavros put the gun down on the tiles and went out quickly. 'OK,'
he called back to the Fat Man when he got to the gate. It opened
and Dinos finally raised his head.

'Jesus,' Mavros said, grabbing his arm. 'What happened to you?'
There was a bandage over the young man's nose and tape across
his cheeks.

'Remember that scene in Chinatown?'

'Christ,' said Yiorgos.

Dinos jerked back. 'No, not you again!'

Mavros raised an eyebrow at his friend.

'I never touched him. Well, not much.'

'Who did this?' Mavros asked.

'I . . . I was mugged.'

'Let's take a ride,' Mavros said, deciding he'd got all he was likely to get from Nadia Svolou. He opened the back door of the taxi and bundled Dinos in. The Fat Man got in next to Marianthi.

'Mother of God!' she said, looking in the mirror. 'What happened to you, my boy?'

'Cut myself tidying up my nose hairs,' Dinos mumbled.

Mavros bit his tongue.

'Where to?' the driver asked.

'Where are your friends Agam, Kirki and Jimmy?' Mavros asked Dinos.

'Piss off,' came the reply.

'All right. Let's go and see the family lawyer, Mr Siatkas.'

'No . . .'

'Yes.'

As they drove off, Mavros saw Nadia standing in the open door, one arm across her chest. She looked like a child lost and devoid of hope, but there was one thing he was sure of – neither she nor her alcohol-addled mother had anything to do with the kidnapping of Kostas Gatsos.

Dinos was another kettle of mullet entirely.

Kostas was woken by the guard slamming open the door. Bread and a large bottle of water were deposited on the floor, he could see in the light from the corridor. It was a trial day. He was given time to eat and use the bucket, then tossed a clean but ragged boiler suit.

'What's wrong with you people?' Kostas screamed, as his hands were cuffed. 'Am I an animal?'

The guard grunted but didn't speak.

'It's you who's the animal, you and your idiot friends in their pathetic masks.' The old man looked up at the hooded figure. 'Can you even understand what I'm saying, you cretinous gorilla?'

No reaction. He was led into the large room.

'Fuck you!' Kostas yelled. 'Fuck you and your children!'

The figure in the centre nodded and the guard slapped the prisoner hard on the cheek. 'Your coarseness does you no credit.' He glanced at the person wearing the oversized human skull. 'Though it is a major feature of your character.'

Kostas sat glaring at the judges as he was pushed on to the chair and secured to the floor.

The figure wearing the skull started to speak, a reedy male voice emanating from the gap between the uneven teeth.

'My brother worked for the Gatsos group as an ordinary seaman.'

Kostas glanced at the guard. 'Good for him. He was one of many.'

'To you, no doubt. For me he was my only sibling. He served for nine years on the KEG *Dolphin*. You remember the vessel?'

'Of course. 5,400 tonne tanker that sailed in the Mediterranean and Black Sea.'

'Until she was lost with all hands between Crete and Egypt in July 1983.'

'A tragedy.'

'It certainly was for me. Even though my brother didn't die then.'

'What do you mean?'

'You know very well. You received a letter posted from Mersin in Turkey, documenting the violent regime of Captain Aristeidhis Maniadhakis and the appalling conditions on board.'

'I have no recollection of that.'

The man in the skull held up a piece of paper. 'This is a copy of the page in the mail register dated February 3rd 1983, showing that the letter was received and forwarded to you. It was assigned the serial number 17859/83/KG.'

'Many documents pass my desk every day.' Kostas smiled. 'You don't have the original letter, do you?'

'No.'

'So what's this farce about?'

'My brother sent a copy to one of his closest friends. Unfortunately he'd suffered a severe stroke some months earlier and was no longer able to open his mail. The letter was in the effects passed to his son after his death ten years ago. Only recently did he open it.' Skull looked at the man in the centre. 'Fortunately for us he was amenable to passing it on.'

'No doubt money changed hands.'

'As a matter of fact, it didn't. The individual concerned was so disgusted by the contents that he wanted you to be brought to account.'

Kostas twitched his head. 'You're making this up.'

'Give him this copy of the letter.'

The guard went forward and came back with stapled sheets.

'We have redacted the names as people are currently preparing law suits against the Gatsos group. Page 1: Seaman A beaten unconscious by the captain after knocking against him on the bridge in storm conditions. Further down: seaman B sodomised by captain and locked in cabin for 48 hours without food. Page 2: cook accused of pilfering food and set to scrubbing decks in temperatures between 2 and 5 degrees Celsius. Further down, seaman C forced to paint stern during high winds after complaining of victimisation.' Skull looked up. 'And so the list continues. Do you remember the letter now?'

'No.'

'I didn't hear what you said.'

'No!'

'You're lying. Captain Maniadhakis went on leave a week before the *Dolphin* was lost. Here is a photograph of you with him in the Poseidon's Trident restaurant in Mikrolimani, Piraeus. The date on the newspaper between you is clearly visible. Do you remember that lunch?'

'No. I must have eaten a thousand times at the Trident.'

'Whereas Captain Maniadhakis ate there only rarely. It was too expensive even for a man on his salary and bonuses.'

'How do you know that?'

'We have a signed affidavit from him.'

Kostas Gatsos felt the blood drain from his face. 'He drank himself to death.'

'You may think that, but he talked to me and my lawyer. And before you say the captain is an unreliable witness, here is another affidavit, this one from the doctor who treated him for the last five years of his life. He states that Captain Maniadhakis did not drink alcohol after he was diagnosed with cirrhosis of the liver – which happened two years before his death. He was completely lucid.'

'So what?' Kostas said, unable to disguise that the fight had gone out of him.

'He said you approved of his methods and often told him so. You were particularly impressed by his tight control of shipboard expenses.'

'What's wrong with that?'

'Apart from the fact that he colluded with tame surveyors to hide the true condition of the *Dolphin*'s hull?'

'I had nothing to do with that.'

'On the contrary. The captain stated that you personally told him to handle the matter and paid him to do so. There are syndicates in Lloyd's of London that will be very interested in this information.'

Kostas shrugged.

'You don't care that fifteen men were drowned when the defective vessel went down? You feel no responsibility?'

'I *bear* no responsibility.'

The man in the skull turned to the other judges before continuing.

'The evidence proves that you do. The same applies to the death of my brother, Savvas Yiannopolous. I see you know the name.'

'I do not.'

'Let me refresh your memory. Savvas was reported missing when he failed to appear for the morning watch on February 17th 1983. The *Dolphin* had sailed for the Bosphorus from Sukhumi in what is now Georgia at 7 p.m. on February 15th. According to Captain Maniadhakis, you gave him specific orders by telephone when the ship was in Sukhumi that my brother was to be knocked unconscious, bound in enough anchor chain to weigh him down and thrown overboard when the vessel was in waters nearly 2000 metres deep. This was done with the help of two willing seaman, who were paid for their troubles but subsequently drowned when the ship sank.' Skull looked at Kostas. 'You are a murderer.'

'That's all bullshit. You can't believe a pisshead like Maniadhakis.'

The man in the centre leaned forward. 'Yes, we can, because unlike you he was ashamed of what he had done. He wanted to atone for it.'

'I'm not atoning for anything.'

'Then you are destined for a lonely and lingering death. As is every member of your family. Take him away.'

The guard pulled Kostas to his feet and held him there, giving him a final chance to speak. Then he unlocked the chain and dragged him to the door.

As they got there the presiding judge called, 'Remove the nails from his other hand.'

Kostas Gatsos wet his boiler suit.

FOURTEEN

'You've got no right,' Dinos said. 'Lady, these men are kidnapping me.'

The Fat Man laughed. 'If we were kidnapping you, would we do it in a taxi, bonehead?'

Mavros was talking to Loukas. 'Yes, tell Mr Siatkas we're on our way. I think Dinos wants a lawyer. What? OK, here he is.' He could hear Loukas speaking firmly to his half-brother. 'All right?' he asked, when the connection was cut.

'I suppose so.'

'I'm glad,' Marianthi said. 'Kidnaps are such anxiety-inducing jobs and the bastards usually don't pay us.'

Yiorgos grinned. 'We'll pay. Well, my long-haired friend will.'

'I don't care as long as I get what I'm owed.'

They headed back down Kifissias Avenue, going against the heavy traffic flow, and were back in the centre of Athens in less than half an hour. Siatkas's office was on Omirou Street, near Syndagma Square.

'This is the parting of the ways,' Marianthi said dramatically.

'No, it isn't,' replied the Fat Man. 'I've taken one of your cards.'

She smiled at him, not entirely ironically. 'I'll be waiting for your call with a fluttering heart.'

Mavros got out and held the door for Dinos, who immediately lit a cigarette before walking into the building. The entrance hall was well appointed, pale grey marble on the floors and the walls off-white. To Mavros it said, There's wealth, but most of it's in Swiss banks. They took an unusually spacious lift up to the sixth floor. A stately middle-aged woman rose from the reception desk, nodding respectfully to Dinos and not staring at his nose. She looked at Mavros and Yiorgos as though they were rubbish men.

'Mr Siatkas, please,' Mavros said, giving his name.

The woman led them down a long corridor lined with dark wood. She opened the door and showed them into a large office with a view of the Acropolis. A thin man with close-cut white hair and a thick moustache stood up. The remains of a salad were in a bowl on his desk.

'Welcome,' he said, with a wide smile. 'Take that away, Rina. I've had enough rabbit food for the day. Mr Dino, how good to see you. It's been a long time. What happened to your nose?'

'I was mugged, Theo.' He turned to the others. 'And these men are harassing me. They think I know something about the kidnap. Tell them I'm the last person capable of that.'

The lawyer turned up his hands. 'I'll do what I can. Gentlemen?'

Mavros introduced himself and the Fat Man.

'Alex Mavros in the flesh. I used to follow your career with interest. You certainly had a talent for setting the pussy among the avian rodents. I hear you've been otherwise occupied in recent years.'

'Don't worry, I can still ride my bike.'

Siatkas laughed. 'I imagine you can. Otherwise Mr Loukas, who's nobody's fool, wouldn't have employed you.' He stroked his moustache. 'Though I did advise a substantially lower fee.'

Dinos turned to Mavros. 'How much are you getting?'

He and the lawyer kept silent.

'Enough to buy all the Gogol brothers' stock of narcotics,' the Fat Man hazarded.

Dinos looked outraged.

The lawyer took them to a set of armchairs round a glass table.

'I presume you know of the Gogol brothers, Mr Siatka,' Mavros said, after they'd sat down.

'Water? Coffee? Something stronger?'

'Nothing,' Mavros said firmly. 'Answer the question, please.'

The lawyer continued to stall, pouring each of them a glass of water from a crystal decanter.

'The Gogol brothers,' he said at last. 'I'm aware of their existence. Why do you ask?'

'Like you don't know,' Yiorgos said. 'I suppose you're *un*aware that Dinos is a junkie and dope dealer, who gets his supplies of dope from the Gogols.'

Theo Siatkas's expression was inscrutable.

'You've been instructed to cooperate with me,' Mavros said. 'Please do so or I'm calling your Mr Loukas.'

'There's no need for that,' the lawyer said emolliently. 'You must understand that my primary concern is looking after the Gatsos family's interests.'

'Yiorgo, phone Brigadier Kriaras and tell him about Dinos's link with the Russians.'

Siatkas cracked. 'No, no, that won't be necessary. Of course I know about Dinos – and his father – and their . . . dealings with the Gogols.'

Mavros wasn't letting him off the hook. 'And have *you* had dealings with them?'

'I . . . there are issues of client confidentiality.'

Mavros took out his phone and started pressing buttons.

'Very well.' The lawyer looked at Dinos and raised his shoulders. 'I was authorised by Mrs Eirini Myroni to pay a sum to the Gogols when Mr Dinos was . . . in trouble with them.'

'I thought his father handled that kind of thing.'

Siatkas brushed the lapels of his tailored blue suit as if disposing of dust and the mites in it. 'Mr Vangelis is not always . . . reliable. Nor does he have access to large amounts of cash. He is not a Gatsos, of course.'

'How much was this sum?' the Fat Man demanded.

'300,000 euros.'

Mavros looked at Dinos. 'Do you sell to the whole of Kolonaki?'

'Of course not. The Gogols run high stakes poker nights. I . . . I got in over my head.'

Mavros turned back to the lawyer. 'What happened? Did you deliver the cash?'

'I don't get involved in that kind of activity,' Siatkas said condescendingly. 'A meeting was arranged and one of my juniors attended. The issue was resolved satisfactorily.'

'So you don't know the Gogols personally?'

'Why are you interested in them?'

Mavros stood up. 'I'll tell you why. They got their claws into the Gatsos family via Dinos here – I'm betting they're the ones who did the Polanski number on his proboscis – and they have the professional ability to carry out a high-profile kidnap. We already know Dinos told them about the layout of his grandfather's villa on Lesvos. There's also the question of the bodyguards. I was told you're responsible for the family's security and that you hired the men, who happened to be Russian.'

The lawyer looked at him impassively. 'I didn't hear a question, Mr Mavro.'

'You want a question?' Yiorgos put in. 'How about this? Did the Gogol brothers supply you with the bodyguards?'

Siatkas kept his eyes off the Fat Man. 'I'm struggling to follow.

First you say the Gogols may have kidnapped Mr Kostas; then your elegantly attired associate suggests that the bodyguards came from the brothers. But one of those men was killed by the kidnappers. Surely that wouldn't have been in the Gogols' interests? If the bodyguards were in on the kidnap, why didn't they carry it out themselves?'

It was a reasonable question and Mavros had been waiting for it. 'First, if you think Russian mobsters aren't capable of duping and killing one of their own, you've lived a very sheltered life – which I find unlikely. Second, you haven't answered my associate's question. Did the bodyguards come from the Gogols?'

The lawyer smiled. 'No. One of my people hired them from an agency we've used for years. They have personnel from many countries, usually former special forces men, and it happened that these three were Russian.'

'The name of the agency?' Mavros asked.

'Hightower Executive Security. They're based in London, but I'm sure one of their people will fly down if you want to question them.'

'I'll let you know.'

The discussion moved on to potential motives for the kidnap. Siatkas came up with several business rivals who could have been responsible, but he didn't show much enthusiasm about any.

'How about the Svolos family?'

Dinos perked up, something the lawyer registered.

'They're a busted flush,' Siatkas said. 'I doubt they can afford to upgrade their cars every year, never mind finance a sophisticated kidnap.'

'She and her mother seem to be very frightened of Serbs,' Mavros said.

'Oh, those scumbags,' Dinos said. 'They borrowed money last year and haven't been able to pay it all back. The interest rate's ridiculous.'

Mavros moved over to the window. He could see the large Greek flag flapping on top of the parliament building. Inside they would be arguing about the financial crisis – too late and too ineffectively.

'Perhaps the Svolos family gave information to these Serbs in order to pay off at least part of their debt,' he said, his back still towards the others.

'Nadia would never . . .' Dinos's voice faded.

'I hadn't thought of that,' Theo Siatkas said.

'That's because you're a well-attired type who pimps for rich folk,' the Fat Man said.

'Indeed I am,' said the lawyer, smiling expansively.

Mavros went back to his chair. 'Dino, would you mind waiting outside?'

'What's this?' the young man asked.

'Don't worry, it's not about you.' Mavros waited for him to get up. 'Yiorgo, give him a hand.'

Dinos left, swearing under his breath.

'What's the big secret?' Siatkas asked.

Mavros caught his gaze. 'The Colombians. I hope Dinos isn't involved with them.'

'What Colombians?'

'Don't play the fool. Laura Moreno and Santiago Rojas.'

'Mr Loukas told you about them?'

'As a matter of fact I found out for myself, but he confirmed they're shareholders in the group. What do you know about them?'

'Actually, very little. Mr Kostas brought them in. He handled the background checks himself. I've met them several times, of course.'

'Did either of them strike you as being involved in the cocaine trade?' the Fat Man demanded. 'Or other illegal drugs, for that matter.'

The lawyer's eyes opened wide. 'They're respectable business people. Laura Moreno's father built the company up to one of the country's largest.'

'You can see the reason for our interest,' Mavros said. 'Lots of product in South America and plenty of Gatsos group ships to move it around the world.'

'That insinuation could get you sued.'

'I'm only speculating, Mr Siatka.'

'I recommend you desist.'

'Can we go now, Alex?' Yiorgos said. 'The stench of ox excrement is really getting to me.'

'You'll let me know if you have any further thoughts, Mr Siatka,' Mavros said. 'And I need copies of all the threats received by Kostas Gatsos in the last two years, plus your responses to them. You can courier them to me.' He gave his mother's address, then got up and led the Fat Man out. Dinos went back in. After closing the door behind him, Mavros lingered. Raised voices weren't long in coming.

Jim Thomson fell asleep in his window seat not long after the Qantas jumbo jet took off from Melbourne Airport. When he woke, the plane was well across Australia. He looked down at the great red desert, straining to catch a glimpse of Alice Springs but aware it had already been left behind. He still had an affinity with the dry earth and sand; it was where the sea had finally been drawn out of him. All his years in Melbourne, he had never been in the ocean. Ivy and he went to the beaches and she swam every day she could, completely at home in the water. She never asked why he wouldn't go in but she knew he had painful history. He told her he'd been on the ships, that was all. Marigo still belonged to him in spirit, her parents no doubt long dead and memories of her – and him – on Ikaria faded and few. Would he have stayed with her if she and their child had survived? Deep in his soul he doubted it.

Soon the plane would be over the eastern reaches of the Indian Ocean, heading for Singapore to refuel. They would fly across Indonesia but the Philippines were far to the north east. He wondered about Pilita. He'd never told Ivy about her either. The time he spent with her had been blessed – not that he believed in any deity; at least that had survived from the Party's teachings. The simple life in Eastern Samar had been a necessity for him after the horror of the *Homeland*'s sinking. Suddenly he found himself thinking of that night and the terrible days that followed, as the sun burned away the outer layers of skin from his face and hands. What had happened to the ship? They were in open sea and the weather had been fine. Distant memories resurfaced, rumours about the owner, a sharp operator called Gatsos, Kostas Gatsos, that was it – from time to time he would have his ships scuttled to collect on the insurance. Is that what had happened with the *Homeland*?

He dismissed the thought for consideration later. Now Pilita had returned to him, her smooth dark skin and glossy black hair, her small, exquisite breasts, her delighted abandon . . . Why had he left her? It wasn't that he'd fallen out of love with her, and certainly not vice versa – she was even more devoted, despite their lack of children. No, it had been a feeling that he had to move on, that the village by the sea wasn't his destiny. Not that he knew what his destiny was. He laughed at himself for thinking he should ever have possessed such an epic attribute. His heroic age had lasted a few days in the security police building in Bouboulinas Street. It was rather that, since then, he had some kind of anti-destiny, the lack of a future. The barrenness of the outback had been right for him. It had got rid of his past to the extent that he was able to love another person and even live in a city with many people of Greek ancestry. The time in Samar had served to make him a no one and using the dead cook's name after he left Pilita had been appropriate. The name he once had no longer existed for him.

And then came the irony of Ivy's own Greek heritage. She didn't speak the language because her parents had been killed in a car crash when she was two and she'd been adopted by people of English descent, whence her name. It was only when she got interested in her family heritage a few years before she met Jim that she found out her grandparents had been Greek immigrants to Australia after the Second World War. They had died before she was born and what little remained of their possessions had been sold off to pay for her parents' funerals. But she knew where they came from; the island of Lesvos, where he was going to sprinkle her ashes.

The White Sea, he thought. That was what the Turks had called the Aegean, in contrast to the Black Sea further north. Ahead he could see the bright blue of the Indian Ocean. The water he'd been thrown into from the Greek naval vessel hadn't been white, apart from the foam left by the propeller. The colour he remembered most from Ikaria was a greeny-blue, deepening as days turned to evening. There had been plenty of white-capped waves when the wind got up. Off Samar the Pacific had many hues, but there was never enough white to merit the use of that colour as a description.

And now he was going back to the White Sea. He felt his stomach clench. It would have been better if his shame and guilt had drowned there as had been intended by the torturers. Much of his life had been spent in slow, repetitive voyages between ports that were often little more than heaps of coal or grain silos, glorified fishing harbours or cities that had turned their backs on the uncontrollable, violent element they depended on. The sea was pitiless, unforgiving, bitter. Men who took to it became like it. That was the real root of his decision to leave Pilita. To live in her village, he had to fish. The creatures he brought up were often ferocious, their jaws snapping as they died in the small boat's hold, their glassy eyes contemptuous of mankind's victory over them. The sea was hostile and a myriad killers lived in it.

Jim Thomson was suddenly aware that casting his beloved Ivy's remains into the White Sea that surrounded her ancestral home was the last thing he wanted to do.

'Lieutenant Babi?' Mavros said into his phone, as he and the Fat Man walked away from the lawyer's office.

'What can I do for you?'

'Do you know anything about Russian and Serbian gangsters?'

There was a pause. 'I work for the head of the organised crime division.'

'So that's a yes.'

The policeman grunted.

'Can we meet to discuss them?'

'Sorry, can't do that.'

'What do you mean? Brigadier Kriaras told you to—'

'It's not that. I'm otherwise engaged today.'

'How about tonight?'

'Ditto.'

'Can't you spare half an hour?'

'I'm afraid not.'

'I'll have to call the brigadier.'

'I strongly advise against contacting my superior. He's extremely busy.'

'Is that right? OK, I'll talk to you tomorrow.'

Yiorgos turned to him. 'What's going on?'

'That's what I'm asking myself. I think Kriaras is going to raid the Gogols.'

'Finally the cops do something right.'

'I'm not sure about that.' Mavros called Kriaras's private line and mobile; both rang out and no messaging service was in operation. 'If the Russians are involved in the kidnap they might take very unkindly to being hassled.'

Yiorgos groaned. 'As in, no more Mr Shipowner. And no more second payment of 250 grand.'

'You mercenary tosser.'

'As if you care about Kostas Gatsos.'

'A job's a job for all that, as we half Scots say.'

'What are you going to do? Warn the Gogols?'

Mavros gave that some thought. 'Anonymous call . . . could work. On the other hand, the cops nailing them might get the case moving.'

'You'd better not tell Loukas and Evi Gatsos that.'

'Hm.' Mavros looked at his watch. 'In the meantime, we need to talk to the rest of Dinos's *parea*.'

'Sounds like a job for Marianthi, a driver with great potential.'

'Yiorgo, you've got no chance with her.'

'Says who? When did you last get your end away?'

'That's confidential.'

'I'm guessing three months.'

'You can guess as much as you like.'

'Four months.' The Fat Man made the call. 'She'll be here in ten minutes.'

'Great. Now all we have to do is find Agam, Kirki and Jimmy.'

'Why don't we ask Dinos?'

They were standing in the shade of a tree at the back of the neoclassical Academy of Athens building. Immigrant traders, many African, had laid out arrays of fake big brand handbags, Chinese underwear and pirated DVDs. No one was looking, never mind buying. The traders would go hungry tonight.

'I think he'll tell us to go to hell.' Mavros took out his notebook. 'We know their parents' names. Shouldn't be a problem to find where they live. Hang on . . .'

'Every word, great master?'

'Piss off. No, I'll use this poxy machine's Internet function.' Mavros had finally been talked into getting a smart phone by his sister a couple of months back. He had reached tech overload and restricted his use of the device to phoning and listening to music.

'Facebook?' said Yiorgos. 'Aren't you a bit old for that?'

'I use it to keep in touch with university mates.'

'Mates, eh?'

Mavros shook his head. 'Of the male sex.'

'I knew you were—'

'Shut up. Here we are. Agamemnon Pyrsos. Nice looking guy.'

'If you like skinny guys with bald heads and spots.'

'Let's have a look at his photos.'

'Seems to spend all his time in cafés. Typical rich layabout.'

'Let's check out Kirki Houkli . . . uh-oh, she's more private. No photos. On to Jimmy Tsakos. Plenty of photos.'

'Is that what they call designer stubble? It's much better sculpted than yours.'

'Looks like an insoluble geometry problem.' Mavros went back to Agam's page. 'It's the same place, isn't it?'

'Looks like it. Their favourite haunt?'

'Could be. And there's the name. Martha and Bennie's. Can't be many places with that name. Let's see what the phone directory says.' He called one of the several services whose adverts clogged the TV channels. 'It's in Kifissia.'

'What a surprise.' The northern suburb was one of the richest in the greater Athens area. 'There she is!'

Mavros watched as his friend set off towards the road at a rapid pace. By the time he got there, Yiorgos was in the front passenger seat, talking faster than a smitten teenager.

'If I can interrupt,' Mavros said, giving the destination.

He spent the trip looking out the window with the Stones at full volume through his headphones. The Fat Man on the pull was a fearsome sight, let alone sound.

FIFTEEN

'That's the third trial completed.' The presiding judge was speaking English.

'How was he?'

'Frightened.'

'You had fingernails removed from other hand?'

'Yes. Apparently he screamed like a baby.'

'Good. He's breaking, old bastard. You have decided case for next trial?'

'Not yet. We'll leave him on his own for a week.'

'Thinking about this. Health OK?'

'He's strong for his age. Or at least he was. Now he's cracking, that may change rapidly.'

'Yes. Maybe bring next trial ahead. Other things happen.'

'Such as?'

'You not need know.'

'But our location is safe?'

'You have guards, yes?'

'Of course. I was only wondering if an operation against us was at the planning stage.'

'Maybe. Kriaras is under pressure and you know how he react.'

'With displays of force.'

'Yes. Stand by for change of plan.'

'As ever you can rely on me.'

'As ever? You mean as long as we pay big money.'

'That's the way of the world.'

'Way of your world is pain and death. You do this for free, I think.'

'Whatever you say.'

'Careful I not come.'

'I'd be delighted to see you again.'

The connection was cut.

Marianthi pulled up outside Martha and Bennie's in Kifissia. It was a typical high-end café with buttock-wrenching metal chairs around dark wood tables, coloured tiles on the floor and condescending waitresses.

'There's our pal Agam,' Mavros said, looking at the photo on his phone.

'And the other guy's Jimmy Tzakos, isn't he?' said the Fat Man.

'Which means there's a decent chance the woman is Kirki Houkli.' While the men were well turned out, the female member of the group had fair hair like a bird's nest style and was wearing a crumpled white T-shirt and ripped jeans.

'Stick around if you like,' Mavros said to Marianthi.

'Yes, please do,' added Yiorgos.

'I'll find somewhere to park off the main drag,' the driver said, giving the Fat Man a wink.

Mavros and he went to the table occupied by the three young people.

'Mind if we join you?' the former asked, with a smile.

'Why?' said Agamemnon Pyrsos, his voice nasal.

'Because I want to talk to you.' Mavros took the inner of the two empty chairs and Yiorgos the one that effectively blocked the three in. 'My associate here had a conversation with Dinos Gatsos this morning.'

Agam and Jimmy exchanged glances.

'You won't get us to spill our guts like he did,' the latter said. He had a mole between his carefully shaped eyebrows. 'We're not frightened of you.'

The Fat Man gave him a slack smile.

'I'm working for the Gatsos family,' Mavros said, introducing himself. 'On the kidnapping of the old man.'

'What's that got to do with us?' Kirki said, putting down her milky frappé.

'You tell me.'

'Nothing, obviously,' said Agam. 'We're Dinos's friends. I've never even met his grandfather.'

'I did once,' said Jimmy. 'Not a pleasant man.'

Mavros looked at the young woman.

'Me? My father's a society hairdresser. He isn't the kind of man Kostas Gatsos has any time for.'

'You're the kind of young woman he might have time for,' Yiorgos said, leering.

'You're disgusting. I've never even seen him in the flesh.'

Mavros looked at his notebook. 'Agam, your father Dhimitris sold several sculptures to Mr Gatsos.'

'That was when I was in short trousers.'

'Like these ones?' Mavros held up his phone. He had accessed a photo from the Gatsos archives. Kostas was standing with a curly-haired man in front of an art work that looked like it had recently exploded. There was a small boy in front of them. 'That's you, isn't it?'

Agamemnon Pyrsos hung his head while Kirki and Jimmy laughed.

'You're very fetching,' the young woman said.

'Leave off.'

'The point being,' Mavros said, 'don't lie to me. I do this for a living.'

Yiorgos nodded vigorously, the five-year hiatus completely forgotten.

'Here's a question for all of you. What does Nadia Svolou feel about Kostas Gatsos?'

'Where is Nadia?' Jimmy said, glancing at his showy watch.

'Answer the question, please,' Mavros said.

'If you're so smart, you'll know about the feud between the Svolos and Gatsos families,' Agam said disdainfully.

Mavros's gaze was icy. 'If you're so smart, you'll tell us why she hangs out with Dinos Gatsos.'

'Because she likes him,' Kirki intervened, stretching across the table for a sachet of sugar and revealing much of her chest. 'Anyway, the old bastard cut Dinos off. There's no love lost there.'

'Which is why I've been wondering if Nadia and Dinos played a part in Kostas Gatsos's kidnapping,' Mavros said.

The three young people laughed loudly.

'That's insane,' Jimmy said, running ring-laden fingers through his hair. 'Nadia wouldn't hurt a fly and Dinos is a . . .' He broke off and looked away.

'Dope dealer?' supplied Mavros. 'I know. Which makes him vulnerable to pressure, especially from the people who supply him.' He looked around the table. 'You know who they are, of course.'

Silence, apart from the café's pounding music.

'The Gogol brothers, Igor and Lavrenti, own the Paradiso Bianco, a club your *parea* often visits. They're easy to recognise – there are scars all over their faces.'

More silence.

'All right,' Mavros said, 'here's how this works. I finger you to the cops as Dinos's fellow dealers . . .'

Eyes sprang wide.

'Or you come clean. Yiorgo, count down from ten.'

Jimmy Tzakos crumbled at six. 'All right, all right. Dinos did blab to those Russian headbangers about his grandfather's villa in Lesvos. He was drunk and stoned, we tried to stop him.'

Kirki Houkli's bare foot was heading up Mavros's thigh. 'Please, give us a break.' She inhaled sharply as he caught her ankle between his knees and squeezed hard. 'All right, I'll tell you what you want to know.'

Mavros relaxed the pressure but held the ankle where it was.

'There's this Colombian guy,' Kirki said.

Agam and Jimmy tried to look surprised, but neither was convincing.

'Santiago something . . .'

'Anyone else know his surname? No? Go on.'

'We met him in the Paradiso – when was it? – early in the summer, I think. He came in with Dinos and Nadia. They'd been out to dinner at L'Abreuvoir.'

The Fat Man pursed his lips. It was one of Athens' most exclusive French restaurants, patronised by the rich and their hangers-on.

'Did this Santiago meet the Gogols?' Mavros pressed.

'He already knew them. They greeted him like he was a brother.'

'Kirki!' hissed Agam.

'What's the harm? Anything to get these idiots off our backs.'

'Idiots?' Yiorgos said. 'Which makes you what?'

'Quiet,' Mavros said. 'Go on.'

'The Colombian went through to the back with the Russians and Dinos. They were away for at least an hour. That's all I know. Can I have my foot back now?'

'Not yet. Did you ever see Santiago again?'

'No.'

The men also answered in the negative.

'Did Dinos – or Nadia, for that matter – say anything about him?'

'Not a word,' Kirki said. 'We wondered about that because they usually tell us everything, especially Dinos.'

'So the word "kidnap" was notable by its absence.'

'Definitely.'

'Have any of you been foolish enough to cultivate the Gogols?'

'No!' said Kirki. 'They scare me. I only go to the club because of Dinos and Nadia. They get us cheap drinks.'

'Gentlemen?'

'Same here,' said Jimmy.

'And here,' said Agam.

'Not to mention the not so cheap drugs.' Mavros glanced at Yiorgos then stood up. 'That'll do for now.'

'For now?' Kirki said. 'I've told you everything I know.'

Mavros looked at her and the others, then followed the Fat Man out.

'What do you think?' he asked, as they walked down the street.

'I need to call Marianthi.'

'"Athens, and a wood nearby." I'm going to start calling her Titania and you Bottom. I meant about Dinos's friends' story.'

Yiorgos shrugged. 'Spoilt rich kids in over their heads. I can't see any of them as kidnappers.'

'Or instigators. No, neither can I. But Nadia Svolou's link to the Colombian – who I'm assuming is Santiago Rojas, the Gatsos group shareholder – puts her back in the frame. Maybe she's less of the lost girl than she looks. Dinos still strikes me as a waster and not much else.'

The Fat Man was talking volubly on his phone.

Mavros looked at the newspapers pinned up around a kiosk. They all had headlines about the financial crisis and the government's attempts to curtail tax evasion. There wasn't any mention of Kostas Gatsos who, he was sure, had steered many millions away from the tax authorities over the years.

Marianthi took them back to the centre. Yiorgos started winking theatrically as they approached the end of Kifissias Avenue and Mavros decided to let him have the evening off. He asked the driver to take him to his mother's flat.

'Be good,' he said, as he got out of the yellow cab.

'We won't,' the Fat Man said.

Marianthi laughed. 'Is he always like this?'

'Oddly, no. It's your fault.' Mavros watched the car turn off Kleomenous and then ran up the stairs. The case – or perhaps his friend's rare success with a woman – had energised him.

'Hello, dear,' Dorothy said falteringly, after she let him in. She lay down on the sofa, her face grey.

He went over. 'Are you all right, Mother?'

'I think so. I just felt a little faint.'

'I'll call the doctor.'

'Don't be silly. I'll be fine in a few minutes.'

There had been an increasing number of these spells in recent months. Dorothy had been taken to hospital and sent home after tests. Her neurologist had told him and Anna that she was healthy enough for an eighty-five year old, especially one with her medical history.

Mavros brought her a pot of her favourite tea, a concoction of fruit and herbs, and a plate of shortbread. As she'd said, she was soon sitting up and looking better.

'Don't worry, Alex,' his mother said, her eyes moving to the photos of Spyros and Andonis on the sideboard. 'You know I'll soon be going wherever they are. It's nothing to be sad about.'

'That's easy for you to say,' Mavros said, his voice nearly breaking.

She laughed softly. 'I know, I know. For years I've been telling you to put your father and brother behind you and get on with your own life. I've been backsliding, haven't I?'

'You have. I'm going to put rocks behind your rear wheels.'

His mother took his hand and he felt her fingers tremble. 'It was good advice for you, but I never really took it myself. Spyros's death was one thing – he lived a good and courageous life, though he deserved another decade. But Andonis . . . he was so young . . . and we never found him, despite your best efforts . . . imagine if I die and he's still alive. If I could only see him in the flesh before I go . . .'

Mavros blinked back tears. He wished he could see Andonis too. His elder brother had been his hero when they were young, as well as his best friend and example. But it was too late now. Andonis had been gone for nearly four decades.

'What are you doing this evening?' said Dorothy, returning to her usual self.

'Anna's not going to be happy. I need to see Nondas.' He called his brother-in-law, who agreed to come round when he finished work.

Mavros spent the time trying to speak to Nikos Kriaras and

Lieutenant Babis. Neither responded. Something was definitely about to happen and that worried him. He tried to distract himself by accessing articles about the Svolos family's business activities. There was no doubt that the holding company was an expiring duck.

Nondas arrived with a bunch of flowers for Dorothy. They'd always got on well, not least because he had blunted many of Anna's sharp edges.

'Svolos?' Nondas said, over Mavros's shoulder. 'I give them till Christmas.'

'Generous. Anything more on the Gatsos group?'

Nondas took out the CD-ROM and inserted it into the disk drive. 'Look here.' His fingers darted over the keys until a page came up.

'The Greenland Reefer Company,' Mavros read. 'Not marijuana.'

'Sadly, no. Reefer, as you must know by now, means refrigerated ship.'

'Of which the Gatsos group has several.'

'And this company, based in Panama, owns one ship, the *Greenland Reefer*.'

'What's the interest?'

Nondas had pulled up a chair. 'Two things. First, the ship's been under arrest in Ulsan, South Korea, since last May, on suspicion of breaking trade sanctions with North Korea. And, second, the Greenland Reefer Company used to be owned by a Colombian who had a small share in the Gatsos group, but who was shot to death in a roadside ambush in August. It's now owned by Santiago Rojas, who bought it from the victim's relatives at what seems to be a bargain price.'

Mavros raised an eyebrow. 'His name's been coming up a lot recently.'

'According to the English-language Colombian press, the murder has the mark of professional criminals. Rojas may have been behind them. If he can organise a shooting in Colombia, he can probably manage a kidnapping in Greece.'

'Not least since he was here in the early summer.'

'Was he indeed? A sanctions-breaker and a murderer.'

'And quite possibly a drug baron. I'll explain later.'

Nondas sat back and undid his tie. 'The thing is, this Rojas doesn't manage the ship or arrange its cargoes.'

'Let me guess. That's done by one or other Gatsos.'

'Kostas, as far as I can tell.'

'Could Rojas be trying to edge the old man out, first by nailing him for going up against the UN – which failed because of Gatsos's influence over much of the media here and abroad – and then by disappearing him?'

Nondas slapped him on the shoulder. 'You've solved the case, Alex.'

'Hardly. We still have no idea of Kostas Gatsos's whereabouts.'

'True.'

'Are you boys staying to eat?' Dorothy called.

'No, thanks,' Mavros said. 'We've got dinner at L'Abreuvoir.'

Nondas grinned.

'Hardly your kind of place, dear. Very expensive.'

'Don't worry, Mother, we're not paying.'

Mavros called Loukas Gatsos and arranged to meet him and Evi at the restaurant in an hour. The conversation Nondas had with Anna was less straightforward. Another late night at the office didn't really cut it.

Laura Moreno was nervous. It was a rare sensation and one she didn't like. She hadn't felt this way since her father died when she was only two years out of Harvard Business School. In the twelve years since then she had not only consolidated Colarmco as one of the world's most highly rated arms companies, but had increased profits by over 150%. It was still a family business but her brothers, two older and two younger, realised her capabilities early on and did not contest their father's stipulation in his will that she become CEO. It helped that she'd made them all board members. She'd also done things that had been beyond her father: she'd not only made the company profitable internationally, but had given it a patina of respectability. Weapons were not sold to anyone with large amounts of cash; potential customers were vetted and the nature of their need for arms investigated by in-house experts.

But none of that was the source of Laura's discomfort. She stood at the open French windows in the drawing room of the old house on the hill and looked down at Bogotá. The breeze tugged at her black evening dress and made her draw her lace shawl tighter around her shoulders. She felt her nipples harden in the flimsy bra and stepped back. That was the last thing she wanted her guest to notice.

'Ah, señorita, you are beautiful tonight,' said Conchita, her long-serving maid. 'You are beautiful every night, but that dress . . . Your hair is all right? The gold is wonderful against the black. Such skin – you are a true South American princess.'

'Stop it, Conchita. Half the country is *mestizo*.'

'But not many pay the attention you do to their Amerindian roots.'

'I don't ignore my European heritage.'

'No, but you feel closer to your ancestors in the high lands.'

It was true. Her father had traced the family back two hundred years. One of their Spanish ancestors had married a princess from a chiefdom in the Andean highlands. She had been to the area several times and was learning the dialect.

'Such a shame you never found the right man, my child,' Conchita continued. 'But maybe your fortune will change. Maybe even tonight.'

Laura waved her away in mock annoyance. With customary acuity, her maid had identified the reason for her nerves – the man who was expected. She looked up at the portraits on the walls, men and women in their finery with unnaturally perfect skin and features. But the visitor was not coming to make love to her in the way her ancestors would have been familiar with. No, he was coming to exert power over her, to force his way on to the board of Colarmco and to steal the family's wealth. But he had made a serious mistake. She fought harder than any man and she never lost; although being hardnosed in business had made a mess of her love life.

The butler opened the door to her rear and ushered in the visitor.

'Señor Santiago Rojas, señorita.'

The logging tycoon walked across the Persian carpet, his chest almost bursting from his frilled evening shirt.

SIXTEEN

Mavros and his brother-in-law found Loukas and Evi Gatsos sitting outside the restaurant. Both were in the clothes they'd been wearing earlier.

After introducing Nondas, Mavros said, 'Long day at the office.'

'They always are,' said Loukas.

'Must be worse since your grandfather was kidnapped,' Nondas offered.

Loukas eyed him dubiously. 'We have more responsibilities, yes. What do you do, Mr Chaniotaki?'

'Investment banking. No shipping, though.'

'Ah.' Loukas turned to Mavros.

'Nondas is also my associate. He's been looking through the Gatsos group financial data. I've sworn him to secrecy, of course.'

Loukas and Evi looked at each other.

'You should have asked us, Alex,' the young woman said, more disappointed than angry.

'I told you I would be using trusted associates.'

'Very well,' Loukas said. 'I'm sure Mr Chaniotakis will be aware of the consequences of classified information getting into the public domain. It will be obvious where it came from.'

Nondas smiled, untroubled by the implicit threat. 'You can trust me. I'm a Cretan.'

That made even Loukas laugh.

'Let's order,' he said.

Mavros and Nondas decided on chateaubriand, while the others went for fish. They all had consommé to start. Loukas ordered bottles of Bourgogne Aligoté and Clos de Tart.

'I take it this is an update,' Evi said, picking at a piece of bread.

'Of sorts,' said Mavros. 'More an exchange of information, I hope.'

'Oh yes?' said Loukas.

Mavros took a sip of wine. 'The Greenland Reefer Company.'

'What?'

'You're insulting our intelligence,' Mavros said.

'What do you need to know?' Evi put in, glaring at her step-brother.

'I need to know what you know.'

'Very well,' said Loukas testily. 'The vessel is under arrest in South Korea on suspicion of breaking trade sanctions with North Korea.'

Mavros looked at him. 'Who sent the ship to the North?'

'That I don't know, but I imagine my grandfather was involved.'

'There's more.' Mavros nodded to Nondas.

'The former owner of the company was killed in an ambush in Colombia a few months ago. Are you aware who now owns it?'

Loukas hesitated. 'I can't know everything about the group.'

Nondas turned to Evi.

'I have no idea,' she said.

'Even though there are so few Colombians with shares in the group,' the Cretan pondered. 'No matter. The current owner is Santiago Rojas.'

'Ah,' said Loukas.

'There's something else I've discovered about him,' Nondas said. He'd told Mavros as they walked to the restaurant. 'He's suspected of having links with FARC, the Marxist-Leninist revolutionary army. His logging company operates near areas under FARC control and the Colombian authorities have tried unsuccessfully to remove his workers.' He paused. 'But there's more.'

Loukas had stopped eating. 'There always is.'

'FARC – which has a record of kidnapping high-profile individuals – has been involved in cocaine production for years, getting much of the financing for its activities from selling the drug. Of course, what they need most of all is weapons.' Nondas stopped again, this time to cut off a piece of steak and put it in his mouth.

Mavros watched, impressed by his brother-in-law's ability to hold an audience. He'd only seen that during family recitals of Cretan banditry and World War Two heroism.

'Weapons,' Nondas repeated.

'Oh my God,' said Evi. 'Laura Moreno's Colarmco.'

'Indeed. But I haven't been able to find anything linking her company and Rojas's.' Nondas wiped his mouth. 'Apart from the fact that both are shareholders in the Gatsos group.'

'Our grandfather was responsible for involving Laura and

Santiago,' Loukas said. 'My father may have known something about it, but I have seen no files. Anyway, what could one Colombian company selling arms to another which then supplies the guerillas have to do with us?'

'Now you really are showing disrespect,' Nondas said mildly. 'Your grandfather may have managed to keep news of the *Greenland Reefer* out of most of the media, but *Lloyd's List* reported that North Korean-made rifles and light artillery were found on the ship.'

'We knew about that,' Evi said, 'but *Pappous* said it was South Korean propaganda.'

'Despite these photos,' Mavros said, holding up his phone.

'Yes,' said Loukas firmly. 'I've spoken to the captain and seen copies of the manifests. The ship did discharge in North Korea, but sailed in ballast.'

'That's still an infringement of UN sanctions,' Mavros said. 'But I don't care about that. What bothers me is that you've been less than frank. I'm beginning to wonder if you'd ever have told me about the Colombians if Nondas here hadn't spotted their names.'

Loukas took a sip of water – he hadn't touched his wine. 'What is it you're saying?'

'Look, nothing's written in stone, especially this early in an investigation,' Mavros replied. 'But Dinos's links with the Gogol brothers, the Colombians' potential involvement in both gun-running and the drugs trade, and your grandfather's close ties to Santiago and Moreno can't be overlooked.'

'You think the Colombians are behind the kidnapping?' Evi said, her voice soft.

Mavros shrugged. 'They could be, as could the Russian gangsters.' He turned to Loukas. 'You are being straight with me when you say there's been no ransom demand – of any kind? No attempts by the Colombians to increase their shareholdings in the group?'

'None at all. Come, Evi, I think we've heard enough idle speculation.' Loukas got up.

'Please call me later,' Evi said, before she followed her step-brother. She looked shell-shocked.

'Touched a nerve there, didn't we?' Nondas said, reaching across the table for Loukas's half-eaten fish. 'I don't suppose they'll mind if we drink their wine too.'

'Feel free,' said Mavros. 'I'm the one who's been left with the bill.'

'Put it on expenses, fool.'

'Why didn't I think of that?'

'Purple Leader to Red Team,' Lieutenant Haralambidhis said.

'Receiving. In position.'

'Green Team?'

'Receiving. In position in 30, repeat 30 seconds.'

'Blue Team.'

'Receiving. Perimeter secured.'

'Yellow Team?'

'Receiving.' The last voice was Elisavet Latsou's.

'Is she up to this?' Brigadier Kriaras asked. He was sitting in an armoured Land-Rover, wearing combat fatigues and body armour. The rest of the team that would go in the front of the Paradiso Bianco was in a similar vehicle close behind.

'I'm sure of it.' Lieutenant Babis was in the same garb, his helmet already on and a pump action shotgun across his knees.

'You'd better be. Are all the customers out?'

Haralambidhis made a call on his phone and spoke briefly. 'Yes, sir, our man inside confirms it's clear.'

'Let's do it then.' Kriaras put on his helmet.

'All teams, move forward in three, two, one – GO.'

The driver took the Land-Rover down the road that had been blocked by traffic police a minute earlier. Immediately after it got to the front of the nightclub, Yellow Team ran forward and used a ram to smash open the heavy doors.

'Stay here, sir,' Babis said, opening his door.

'Yes, sir,' Kriaras replied, his service pistol drawn.

There were shots from inside the building, then shouts from the rear. Green Team was covering the back, while the larger Red and Blue teams were spread out along the sides of the car park.

Babis ran in, stepping over the motionless body of a man in a suit – one of the bouncers. He headed for the door at the side of the stage. It had already been broken down. There were more shots.

'Two of ours down,' he heard in his earpiece. It was Elisavet. 'And one other, unidentified.'

He ducked as machine-pistol fire sprayed above him. Through the haze he saw four bodies on the floor, two of them moving. The rear door was pushed open and cold air rushed in. Babis saw two men break out, firing machine pistols at the unprotected faces of the Green Team officers. Two of them went down. The men kept running.

'Red, Blue Teams,' he said into his mouthpiece, 'redeploy to rear of building immediately.' He raised the shotgun but, before he could fire it, was hit by several shots when one of the men turned. He crashed to the ground, stunned by the impact to his Kevlar vest.

From there he saw Sergeant Latsou drop to one knee, raise her pistol and get off three shots. The man who'd hit him dropped with a cry. The other turned and let out an agonised yell. He tried to drag the other man with him, but was forced to make evasive moves when Elisavet continued to shoot. He ran ahead on his own, replacing the machine pistol's clip. Again he fired at face height, officers diving to the ground.

Babis hauled the shotgun to his shoulder and fired four times, the recoil making his chest hurt even more, but the runner was out of range. He was at the fence, then over it. Sergeant Latsou screamed in frustration as she fired on the run. Then he was gone.

'After him!' Babis shouted. He watched as Elisavet rallied the unwounded officers and got them over the fence, then his head slumped to the ground.

He couldn't have been out for long. When he came round, his body armour had been removed and he was in the recovery position. Brigadier Kriaras's boots were a metre away.

'How do you feel?'

'Like a horse rode over me.'

'Metaphorically it did.'

'What, sir?'

'I'm talking about your career in the organised crime division.'

Babis remembered. 'One of them got away.'

'Igor Gogol. Lavrenti's taken shots to the legs and lower back, but he'll live. He bit the hand of the officer who tried to give him first aid.'

'Animal.'

'His brother and he killed three men and left another four with serious facial injuries. Some may lose their sight. He also shot two uniformed men on the other side of the fence, fortunately only in the arm and leg.'

'Fuck.'

'The only positive note was struck by Sergeant Latsou.'

'She shot Lavrenti.'

'And she's leading the search for Igor, though I don't have much hope of apprehending him. He's bound to have a car stashed nearby.'

'At least we've got the other one for resisting arrest.'

'Don't worry on that score. There's a large consignment of cocaine in the basement. People were measuring it out and putting it in sachets.'

'Maybe we can get him to talk. They might have old Gatsos.'

'We'll try, of course, lieutenant, but I'm not optimistic. Our only chance was to take them both. If anything, the situation's worse now.'

Babis groaned as he sat up. 'How's that, sir?'

'You know Igor has a reputation for extreme violence. That might be very bad news for Kostas Gatsos if they were the ones who took him.'

Babis heard Elisavet's voice in his earpiece. 'Yellow Team. Request permission to terminate search.' He relayed the message to Kriaras.

'Yes, bring them back. I already have uniformed officers looking for suspicious pedestrians or vehicles in the area.'

A paramedic came over and asked Babis to bare his chest. There were three red marks where bullets had been stopped by the vest.

'You'll need an X-ray to make sure no ribs are broken.'

Babis touched the marks gingerly. 'Later. Go and check on the others.' He got up and watched as Sergeant Latsou jogged across the car park, her team behind her.

'Good shooting,' he said, when she stopped in front of them.

'Indeed,' said the brigadier. 'You're one of the few success stories of this chaotic operation.'

'We weren't expecting such a violent response,' Babis said.

'Always anticipate the worst, isn't that what you were taught at the academy?'

Babis watched as Kriaras stalked off. When he turned back, the sergeant had taken off her helmet and untied her hair.

'SWAT Barbie,' he said, taking a chance.

'My weapon's still loaded, lieutenant,' she said, looking at the shotgun on the ground. 'As well as being centimetres from my hand.'

Babis raised his hands. 'Ceasefire in effect.'

'No such condition for women in the Greek police.' Elisavet Latsou went to her people, one of whom had been knocked flat by gunfire.

'Shit,' said Babis.

'Another one!' yelled an officer from behind a desk that had been overturned. He ducked down, then reappeared. 'Deceased male, shots to the chest and head. Wearing a suit.'

Sergeant Latsou crossed the room. 'Lieutenant, you'd better get over here.'

Babis got to his feet with difficulty and went towards her, almost doubled up in pain.

'Fuck,' he said, when he saw the middle-aged man sprawled on the floor. His photograph was on the operations board. It was Vangelis Myronis.

It was now officially the worst night of his life and the rest of it would be spent writing his report. Would he still have a job with Kriaras by dawn? If he did, he wouldn't be surprised if the brigadier sent him to tell Kostas Gatsos's daughter what had happened to her husband.

'I am become a name,' Kostas Gatsos recited.

'For always roaming with a hungry heart
Much have I seen and known; cities of men
And manners, climates, councils, governments,
Myself not least, but honour'd of them all.'

Tennyson's *Ulysses* had been his favourite short poem since he was in his late teens. Now he was old he identified even more with Ulysses, who had finally come home after ten years fighting the Trojans and another ten on the return voyage. The long poem that had always meant most to him since he was at primary school – he'd been a precocious and voracious reader – was Homer's *Odyssey*, whose hero the Romans knew as Ulysses. He thought it was why he'd become a shipowner; the endless movement of the waves, sometimes welcoming, at others tempestuous; the monsters to be overcome; the loss of comrades. All those were echoed in his business life. He had used people – bankers, brokers, traders, politicians, industrialists, shipbuilders. When he needed them he was their friend, showering gifts and hospitality; but when they no longer mattered, he cut them loose like fatally holed vessels. He had used the people who worked for him, inspiring them to sacrifice all for the group and then getting rid of them before they learned too much to gain a hold on him. He had treated his wives like chattels, dressing them in the finest fashions and jewellery to improve his own image; he had abused them in numerous ways in the bedroom, in front of the children and in public. But still his huge and ravenous ego wanted more of everything – money, power, influence, sex . . .

He thought of Ulysses, leaving 'the sceptre and the isle' to his son before setting out on a final voyage, 'To follow knowledge, like a sinking star, Beyond the utmost bound of human thought'. But what was the knowledge Kostas wanted, what new experiences could he expect? Was lying in a darkened room with antiseptic on his mutilated head and fingers going to provide a deeper understanding?

That was it. He would discover more about how his devious mind worked, he would go through his life and examine what he had done in a different light. 'Old age hath yet his honour and his toil' – for him that would be to rationalise his deeds. Why had he broken the South Africans sanctions and done away with the whistleblower? Why had he fucked Tefkros Svolos's wife and driven the older man's company to the wall? Why had he sunk the *Homeland* and had the complainer from the *Dolphin* thrown overboard? For personal gain and the profit of the group, of course, but there was more to it than that. Something in him wanted to triumph in every situation, even now, with his fingers and head stinging and aching. But why? Was it the hardship he had suffered as a child? His parents had been through much worse during their escape from Turkey. Was it in his genes? Neither his father nor his mother had been fighters, let alone visionaries. It was all they could do to put food on the table every day – a battle in itself, he accepted. Fortunately his brains had got him out of poverty at an early age.

Destiny. That was what it was. He had always felt he was better than others and that he would do great things. So it had proved, but he wasn't finished yet. It wasn't his fate to die in this hole after being mutilated over and over again. 'Death closes all: but something ere the end, Some work of noble note, may yet be done.' In the first instance that work meant staying alive until he was rescued – he was sure Loukas and Evi would be doing everything they could. He would survive and he would know himself better.

Then the world would really have to look out.

'Police have captured one of the Gogols.'
'Which?' asked the presiding judge.

'Lavrenti. He not talk.'

'You hope.'

'Is more. Myronis killed in shooting.'

'He wasn't a Gatsos by blood, but his death may make them try harder to find the old man.'

'This happens already.'

'What?'

'Man name of Alex Mavros. Loukas hired him.'

'That *is* interesting. I thought he'd retired from missing persons work.'

'Big money paid.'

'I know Mavros.'

'You tried kill him, yes?'

'No, I've been making him hide behind steel doors for years. I was the reason he gave up missing persons work.'

'You want kill him now?'

'Why not?'

'No. Direct order. Only if Mavros find you. Understand?'

'Yes.'

'Work quick with Gatsos now.'

'I thought the point was to make him suffer as long as possible.'

'Do next trial soon. More orders after.'

'Yes, sir.' The connection was cut. 'And fuck you.'

SEVENTEEN

Mavros went back to his mother's and crashed out. He slept badly, plagued by dreams of Niki and, unusually, of his brother Andonis. The latter, rather than smiling at him as he had in the past, was a shadow of himself, his hair white and his face heavily lined. Mavros woke, feeling nauseous, to the sound of his phone at 6.30 a.m.

'It's me.'

'Shit, what do you want so early, Lambi?'

'It's not what I want, my friend. Didn't you ask me to let you know if anything went down at the Paradiso Bianco?'

Mavros sat up, his mind clearing fast. Lambis Bitsos was crime editor on one of the daily papers and on a private TV channel.

'What's happened?'

'Kriaras's lot raided the place around 4 a.m. They took heavy casualties. Lavrenti Gogol was shot and is in hospital. His wounds aren't life-threatening. His brother got away. The police took a large haul of drugs, mainly coke. Hello? Have you died?'

'I'm thinking.'

'It better be about what you're going to give me in return.'

'Now isn't the time.'

'I hoped that five years being a publisher might have made you more appreciative of the services people provide.'

'You'll get a story sooner or later.'

'How about a sniff?'

Mavros considered that. The brigadier had acted without dropping him a hint, so he didn't feel obliged to keep his mouth shut.

'Try this: "A source has revealed that the raid is linked to the investigation into the disappearance of leading shipowner, Kostas Gatsos." Juicy enough for you?'

'Juicier than the choicest footballer's wife. Are you serious?'

'Yes.'

'Out of interest, how much did the family cough up to get you out of retirement?'

'Don't worry, you'll get some of it if your services continue in this vein.'

'Right you are. I'll be on air in half-an-hour.'

'Breakfast with Bitsos: crime, sex and deep fried aubergines.' The journalist was an inveterate consumer of pornography and, despite his lean build, a major gourmand.

'Not a bad idea. May your cock always swing loose.' The call was terminated.

'Wanker,' Mavros said, aware that he wouldn't go back to sleep.

He got up and pottered around the kitchen. Years of living alone meant that he could fend for himself, but today he couldn't be bothered. Besides, he wanted to see what had gone down at the Fat Man's.

Half an hour later he was at the door, leaning on the bell push.

'Who is it?'

'Mr Marianthi.'

'Get lost.'

'Come on, Yiorgo. I haven't had breakfast.'

The chain rattled and the door opened. Mavros went in like a sniffer dog.

'She's not here,' the Fat Man said. He was wearing only a sagging pair of underpants. 'But she was until four-thirty.'

'I thought she had kids.'

'Babysitter stayed over.'

'So you—'

'Yes, we did. Twice.' Yiorgos started to dance, but soon stopped. 'Need to conserve my energy. She's coming back later.'

'I'm very happy for you. Now can you make the coffee?'

'Your wish is my command. Hope you don't want any *galakto-boureko*. I didn't have time to make it.'

'This gets better and better.'

'Don't worry, I've got some toast-bread. Should be honey too.'

Mavros followed him to the kitchen and told him about the raid on the nightclub. Kriaras and Lieutenant Babis still weren't answering their phones.

'Might shake things up,' the Fat Man said.

'Might do worse than that.'

'How did your meeting with the Gatsos siblings go last night?'

'Step-siblings. Nondas hit them with some stuff he'd dug up on the Colombians. They claimed ignorance.'

'Where does that leave us?'

Mavros breathed in the scent of coffee as the Fat Man stirred the

contents of the *briki*. 'We still have two things to do. First, talk to
the surviving bodyguards from the villa on Lesvos. I got their address
from Siatkas. Apparently one of them speaks reasonable Greek.'

Yiorgos slid a plate of toast and honey towards him. 'And second,
check out Kostas Gatsos's recent girlfriends.'

'Well spotted. Evi knows some names. To be honest, I doubt
they'll talk. Their pimps will have them under pressure after what's
happened to the Gogols.'

'Do you want to split up?'

'No. The Russians might turn nasty and there's no way I'm letting
you loose on young women in your current state.'

'What state?' Yiorgos looked down. 'I'm not engorged.'

'Good to know. Are you sure you aren't going to strain your
heart with Marianthi?'

'As sure as toast is toast,' the Fat Man said, taking the last piece.
'I'll have a shower, change clothes—'

'What, on the same day?'

'And call our delectable driver.'

'Old love,' said Mavros. 'It's so touching.'

'You're just jealous.'

Yiorgos was right.

The jumbo jet was in the final stages of its approach to Athens
airport. Jim Thomson looked down at the roads and fields. He
recognised nothing. The new airport was to the east of Athens and
he had never been familiar with the area. He recognised the summit
ridge of Mount Imittos, even though it was the wrong way round.
There were many more TV and radio transmitters than when he'd
been a student. The terminal buildings were the standard modern
style and could have been anywhere. His stomach was churning,
not because he was home but because he seemed at the same time
to be in a foreign country. The wheels touched the runway and the
big plane started to slow. A few Greeks of the older generation
applauded the pilot.

He let people stream past him and was the last passenger to get
his hand luggage down. The stewardesses waited for him patiently,
though their smiles were strained by the time he wished them good
day. Then he went along sterile passages with advertising in English.
He felt utterly disconnected from the images of the Acropolis and
other ancient sites. This is your heritage, he told himself. Why aren't

you moved? He knew the answer. It was too late. He should either
have come back when he was still young or stayed away forever.
The latter had been his intention, but he had to fulfil Ivy's last wish.

He presented his Australian passport. It was stamped without
question. Then he collected the suitcase that contained the urn and
went through customs without being stopped. There were five hours
till his flight to Lesvos and he had planned to wait in the airport,
but he found the place so soulless that he decided to put his bags
in left luggage and take a taxi into the city. He would have time to
see the place that he now couldn't keep out of his mind, even though
he'd suppressed it for decades. He owed it to his mutilated and
murdered comrades.

The driver was morose. Jim spoke only English and the other
man had little. They moved swiftly along wide highways, rising to
the flank of Imittos from where the city, much bigger than he
remembered, spread across the enclosed plain as if all the grey-white
building bricks in the world had been thrown about by a particularly
active child. The sea spread out southwards, pale blue between the
island of Aegina and the peaks of the Peloponnese. Still nothing
stirred in him. They drove down into the crowded streets and he
read the signs and placards in the language he had tried unsuccessfully to forget. But the computer and phone shops and the multiplicity
of banks caught his eye more than the buildings that had been there
when he was a resident. They headed down Alexandhras Avenue
past the ragged old Panathanaikos stadium. He'd never been interested in football. His priorities back then had been much more
high-minded – or so he thought.

And finally they were there, on the corner of the street that ran
parallel to Bouboulinas. He paid the driver, struggling with the new
currency. Then he walked down to the road that ran past the rear
of the Polytechnic and the National Archaeological Museum. There
were so many wonders in the latter – the gold masks of Mycenae,
the marble youths and maidens, the bronze figures of Poseidon and
the little jockey – but they meant nothing to him. Instead he was
consumed by the horror he had experienced in number 18, the
headquarters of the Security Police during the dictatorship. He found
he couldn't approach the building, his ears suddenly filled by his
screams and those of others, and the revving of motorbikes that
drowned the noise; the tapping on the walls of the cells that some
prisoners used to communicate – he had never done that. After his

failure to keep silent, after the agony of the fish hooks that had been inserted into his arms, sides and legs before the lines were stretched by a pulley till his body was raised into the air, after he had talked and talked, betraying everyone he knew, giving names, addresses, everything he was asked . . . after that he was broken, no longer himself, a different creature. And he himself had been betrayed. Instead of being sent to a camp, he was thrown into the night sea to drown.

He stepped backwards and knocked into someone.

'Careful,' said an old woman in black. 'You nearly sent me flying.'

'Sorry,' he replied, in Greek. 'I . . . I don't feel very well.'

She looked at him curiously, her clothes dirty and shopping basket full of what appeared to be balls of old newspapers.

'Are you one of them?' she asked. 'You're the right age.'

'One of them?' he mumbled.

'The wretched people who were tortured.'

Suddenly he couldn't stand to be there. He ran along the back of the Polytechnic, where the dictators had sent tanks against unarmed students, and turned left into Exarcheia Square. Although one side was lined with trendy cafés, there was still graffiti on the walls and a palpable air of resistance. That cleared his mind.

He had to find them, the ones he'd deserted. Not his former comrades, he could never face them, but his family. Was his mother still alive? His brother and sister should be. Then he looked at his watch. There wasn't time before his flight. But he swore he would look for them on his return from Lesvos. He owed them at least a short visit. Anything else was beyond him.

In the taxi Jim Thomson asked himself what the hell he was doing. He was in Greece to dispose of Ivy's ashes, not to dig up the rotting remains of his past. When he came back from the island, he would stay in the airport until his connection to Singapore.

Athens was as dead as his father had been for decades.

'What are these gorillas called?' the Fat Man asked from the front passenger seat.

'Vadim and Gleb,' Mavros replied.

'Wasn't there someone in Hollywood called Vadim?' Marianthi asked, as she turned on to Mesoyeion Avenue and headed for Ayia Paraskevi.

'You're thinking of Roger Vadim,' Mavros said. 'I think he might have been of Russian descent, but he lived in France. He was the husband of Brigitte Bardot and Jane Fonda – not at the same time – and director of such young man's classics as *And God Created Women* and *Barbarella*.'

'I remember both of those,' Yiorgos said, nudging Marianthi. 'Plenty of flesh on display.'

The driver laughed and leaned over to kiss the Fat Man. The vehicle swerved, almost hitting another before she got it under control.

Mavros was gripping the back of the seat. 'Bad time to display my inner movie geek.'

'I don't know,' said Yiorgos. 'So, Vadim and Gleb. What are we going to ask them?'

'The usual stuff – what's their favourite breakfast cereal, do they take sugar in their coffee, were they bribed to give the kidnappers safe passage . . .?'

'Ha ha.' The Fat Man looked over his shoulder. 'Really?'

'Possibly with a bit more subtlety regarding the latter.'

Marianthi found the backstreet in the suburb without using her satnav. 'I had an aunt who lived in this neighbourhood,' she said. 'We used to stay with her in the summer. It's cooler up here.'

Mavros looked at the wall of Mount Imittos, the vegetation having already turned green after the rains of late September. The street was narrow and the apartment buildings scruffier than much of the area. He looked at the panel by the door. There was a button with no name and that was the one he pressed.

'Who is?' said a man.

'From Siatkas,' Mavros said, hoping the lawyer's name would carry more weight than his own. There was a pause, then he was buzzed in.

'I'm going for a coffee in the square,' Marianthi said. 'Call when you need me.'

Yiorgos waved her off.

'Come on, you love-sick lump, we've got work to do.'

They took the lift to the fifth floor.

'Do you want me to do the talking?' the Fat Man asked.

'I don't think you'll scare these guys like you did Dinos.'

'Suit yourself.'

Mavros thumped on the only door without a name next to it. He saw the spyhole darken on the other side.

'Come on, I told you – we're from Siatkas.'

The door was opened by a large man with a shaved head and biceps bursting out of his T-shirt. There was a pistol in his right hand.

'Got a licence for that?' Mavros asked.

'You police?'

'No, I private investigator. Maybe English is better?'

'Nyet.'

Mavros shrugged and went in. After the door was closed behind them, they were led down a dark corridor.

'This Vadim,' the Russian said, nodding to the similarly muscle-bound hulk on the sofa. The room was cramped even though there was little furniture.

'And you're Gleb.' Mavros introduced himself and Yiorgos.

'Why you here? We talk to Mr Siatkas and police.'

Mavros remembered the sparse police file. 'You didn't say much. I was hoping you could be more expansive with us.'

'What?'

'Tell us more,' the Fat Man said. 'Like were you bribed to let the kidnappers in and out without a fight?'

Mavros groaned as Gleb raised the pistol.

'You no talk us like this!' the Russian shouted. 'Friend Boris killed in villa.'

'Put the gun down,' Mavros said, moving his arm slowly towards it. 'My friend wasn't serious. Please forgive him.'

The Russians glared at Yiorgos and eventually Gleb put the pistol on the table.

'Siatkas say we must talk you so OK. You only.' He pointed at Mavros. 'You friend fuck off.'

'Go and find you know who,' Mavros said, sighing with relief as the Fat Man headed down the corridor. 'All right, Gleb and Vadim, tell me what happened at the villa.' He raised a finger. 'Before the kidnap.'

'Before?' said Gleb. 'What mean?'

'For a start, was it the first time you three went to Lesvos?'

'No. We go last year. Mr Kostas, he friend us. He say we nasty, he nasty too.'

Mavros had looked at his notebook in the taxi and remembered the salient points of the police report.

'You were assigned to Mr Gatsos in June last year, yes?'

'True. We work him full time. Go Lesvos, Mykonos on Gatsos boat. London, New York, many places in Europe. Not always us three, sometime more.'

'But you three at the villa.'

Gleb nodded. 'And at Athens houses.'

Kostas Gatsos had properties in Dhionysos to the north of the city, Vouliagmeni to the southeast and in central Piraeus, as well as weekend homes on Aegina and Evia.

'Going back to my first question, what happened at the villa before the kidnap?'

'Nothing,' Gleb said, glancing at his unconcerned colleague.

'No strange people spying on the villa, taking photographs, coming close in boats, that kind of thing?'

'Course not. We very careful.'

'What about the town of Molyvos? Did Mr Kostas have friends there?'

'Friends? Mr Kostas no have friends Lesvos.'

Mavros laughed. The bodyguard had a down-to-earth charm.

'People they lick arse, they want money, but they hate him. I see this easy.'

The question and answer was going better than Mavros had imagined.

'So Mr Kostas had enemies in Molyvos.'

'No only Molyvos, Lesvos town too. Rich people feel small because he very more rich. He laugh their face.'

'Names?'

'I no know names. No my work.'

'You got a computer here?'

'Course. How else Vadim get porn?'

'How else indeed?' Mavros went over to the laptop that Gleb had taken from beneath his chair. He'd have liked to clean the keyboard and screen, but thought that wouldn't go down well. He found the official Lesvos website and clicked on the link to 'Notable Citizens'. There were various dead writers and artists, and then a list of prominent businessmen. He brought up their photos one by one and showed them to the Russians. By the end of the process, he had three names: Thanasis Gritsis, Makis Theotokis and Stelios Xenos.

'You didn't tell the police this?'

'No, but send report employer Hightower. They give Siatkas, yes?'

'They give Siatkas, maybe. He give me, no. Tell me about them.'
'Nothing for tell. Mr Kostas shout them in business conference year ago. They say he not welcome Lesvos.'
'Do you think they could be behind the kidnap?'
Gleb laughed. 'Fat men, small balls. Gritsis most angry. He have house Molyvos.'
'Did you see him this summer?'
'Yes, one time in taverna. Mr Kostas order lobster for friends, Gritsis say he steal tax. Mr Kostas throw wine over Gritsis. He leave shouting.'
Mavros thought about that. Could a small-time island money businessman have been involved in the kidnap?
'No,' Gleb said, ahead of him. 'Gritsis nothing. He no have kidnap money.' He leaned forward. 'You know, men who shoot Mr Pavlos and Boris professional. Why me and Vadim hit ground. People hire them have much money. If they check villa, we not see.'
That made sense. Reconnaissance would have been undertaken before the villa was occupied to confirm the information Dinos had blabbed to the Gogols.
'Anything else you want to tell me? If I catch them, Boris's killers will go to prison for a long time.'
Gleb grinned, showing uneven yellow teeth. 'You no catch them. You get close, they catch you. Then . . .' He drew his hand across his throat.
Mavros got up. 'Thanks for that.'
'Hey, you tell Gatsos family give us other job or let us go. We bored.'
'I'll mention it.' He had no intention of doing so – the Russians were staying where they were until he found Gatsos.
'What?'
'I tell them, OK?'
'OK, friend.'
On their way down the stairs, Mavros called the Fat Man.
'Where are you? I want some lunch.'
'That's what we're eating. There's a taverna on the far side of the square.'
Yiorgos might have lost weight, but he was doing all he could to pile it back on. Of course, as of last night, he was getting a lot more exercise.

EIGHTEEN

Kostas Gatsos sat facing the masked judges, the guard by his side.

'I want to make a statement,' he said, his voice unwavering.

'Really?' The presiding judge glanced left and right. 'Very well, but be aware that any display of truculence will be summarily punished.'

'I am guilty of all the crimes you have so far outlined and of whatever Mr Octopus is about to hit me with. I am also guilty of numerous others you don't know about, though most of those are less serious than what you've accused me of. You hear? I'm guilty of everything. Now what are you going to do?'

The person in the octopus mask stood up. 'Let us be clear about this.' The voice was that of a woman, speaking heavily accented English. 'You admit that you brought the Colombians Laura Moreno and Santiago Rojas into the Gatsos group in order to get into the South American drugs and arms businesses?'

Kostas stared at her. 'I don't know what you're talking about.'

'And that the *Greenland Reefer*, currently under arrest in South Korea, was carrying arms for the FARC guerillas in Colombia.'

'My . . . my son Pavlos supervised day-to-day business.'

'The arrest of a vessel caught breaking UN sanctions is hardly day-to-day business, Mr Gatsos.'

'Well, I know nothing about it.'

The octopus tentacles swung as she turned to the other judges. 'He's lying, of course. It's one of the things he does very well.'

'Who are you?' Kostas shouted, immediately feeling the heavy hand of the guard on his shoulder. 'How do you know all this? Show yourself, coward. All of you, show yourselves!'

'You do not give us orders,' said the man in the centre. 'Consider this. These trials have been recorded and the transcripts will soon be published around the world.'

'So what? These so-called trials are illegal. You kidnapped me. I'm saying anything to get better treatment, to be freed. You pulled out my fingernails, you cut off my ear. How's that going to make you look?'

'You're an intelligent man. You can imagine that skilful editing will emphasise your criminality, as well as avoiding your wounds.'

'Bastards! They'll catch you, you know they will!' Kostas fell silent after he was slapped hard on the cheek by the guard.

'I doubt it,' said the man in the balaclava. 'But even if they do, your wickedness will be ample justification.'

'What are you going to do to me now? Cut off my other ear? Pull out my toe nails.'

'Both those options have been considered, but we have decided on a far more excruciating punishment, one that applies to all your crimes and not just this latest one.'

Kostas was silent. He was trying to imagine what could be worse than the agonies he had suffered. Then the lights were dimmed and an image flashed up on the screen behind the judges.

'Do you recognise that?' the presiding judge asked. 'Does it mean anything to you?'

'I . . . no, it doesn't. What is it?'

'Lying again. It really is second nature to you. Surely you remember the late, unlamented Stratos Chiotis, Athenian underworld boss from the 60s to the early years of the new millennium.'

'I . . . I met him from time to time at receptions. He had legitimate business interests.'

'Some of which you invested in, although blackmailing popular singers who were gay and forcing girls from mountain villages and islands into prostitution are hardly legal. Anyway, as you know very well, during the dictatorship Stratos Chiotis was introduced to an unusually savage Security Police torturer.' The man in the centre stood up, walked to the end of the table and stepped down from the dais. He came up to Kostas and grabbed his chin. 'You had extensive contacts with Papadhopoulos and his gang of fools, of course. They provided you with numerous business opportunities and you weren't shy to bolster their bank accounts and property portfolios.'

'So?' Kostas said, his eyes blazing.

'You met the torturer in question and used him on some of the people that got in your way – union representatives, whistleblowers, even, I understand, a mistress whose mouth was bigger than was good for her. I have just one question. What was the individual in question known as?'

Sweat poured down Kostas's face, but still the grip on his chin
tightened like a vice.

'I'm sorry, I couldn't make that out.'

'The . . . the Father,' Kostas gasped.

'That's right.' The man let go and stepped to the side. 'And he
was the designer of the method illustrated on the wall, correct?'

'Yes,' Kostas said weakly.

'Which involves?'

'Fish . . . fish hooks and . . . and lines.'

'Correct. You'll be glad to hear that the Father didn't have your
constitution and has been walking the realm of the shades for some
years now.'

'Good,' muttered Kostas.

'But never fear. Or rather, always fear.' The man pulled off his
balaclava, revealing a thin face and crew-cut hair. His eyes were
closer to black than dark brown. 'I am the Son.'

Kostas Gatsos closed his eyes. He knew that nothing would save
him from the offspring of the persecutor he had paid so well.

Mavros, the Fat Man and Marianthi had finished eating when the
call came.

'Evi and I, her mother and Dinos have all received them. It's
disgusting, you have to do something . . .'

'Slow down, Louka, what's happened?'

'Nails, my grandfather's nails. Two each. What shall we do?'

'How do you know they're the old man's?'

'I . . . whose else would they be?'

'It could be a hoax. Contact Brigadier Kriaras and ask him to
send them for DNA testing as soon as possible.'

'Yes, yes, I'll do that. But they must be his, surely.'

'Let's hold off on that. How did they arrive?'

'By courier. We all got them in the last half-hour with personal
signature required. I called my mother in Paris and my sister in
New York. They didn't get anything.'

'Kriaras's people will follow up the courier angle – give them
the documents and wrapping when they pick up the nails. Wear
gloves.'

'Right. God, Alex, it was disgusting . . . dried blood and . . .
they're crushed at the ends, I guess from pliers or something
similar . . . it must have hurt him terribly.'

For the first time Mavros heard something approaching empathy from Kostas Gatsos's grandson. That angered him, but not as much as Kriaras's botched raid on the Gogol brothers' club. He was sure there was a connection. He assured Loukas he'd be at the office as soon as he could.

'There's something else,' the young man said. 'Evi's father. He went out last night to meet some friends and he hasn't come back.'

'Is that unusual?'

'Apparently so. He always returns by dawn.'

'Tell Kriaras about that too.' Mavros rang off and filled Yiorgos in on what had happened.

'We got too close?'

'We may have nudged the kidnappers into action, or rather Kriaras has. Come on, we need to get down to Phalero.'

'More kilometres for you, Marianthi,' the Fat Man said.

She smiled. 'I could get to like you even more than I do already.'

'Same here.'

Mavros batted the back of Yiorgos's head and called Dinos.

'I hear something nasty was delivered.'

'I almost threw up.'

'Are you at home?'

'Went back to bed.'

'All right, we'll pick you up in about 20 minutes. Bring the nails and the packaging with you. Pick them up with a plastic bag on your hand and put them into another one.'

'Why?'

'Just do as I say. Come down when I ring the bell.'

Mavros then called Eirini Myroni. 'About the nails.'

'Oh, God. Loukas told me to wait for the police to pick them and the package up.'

'Good. To clarify, there was a package for you alone?'

'Yes. My poor father. Bloody sadists.'

'We're dealing with professionals.'

'Have you heard my husband's gone missing?'

'You've no idea where he might be?'

'Asleep after some all-night poker game, probably. Though he makes a rule of coming home.'

'Talk to the police when they come – they've been advised.' Mavros cut the connection.

A few minutes later his mother called.

'Hello, dear. How are you?'

'Fine.' Mavros always tried to retain a degree of calm with Dorothy. 'You?'

'All right. You might like to know that a courier delivered a package for you about half-an-hour ago.'

'Jesus. What size and shape is it?'

'It's in a padded envelope but I can feel a small box inside. It's not a bomb, is it?'

Since the threat of the Son years ago, Mavros's family had lived too close to potential danger.

'No, I don't think so, but stay away from it all the same.' He had a thought. 'Didn't the courier ask for a personal signature?'

'He did, but I forged it.'

'What?'

'I didn't want him coming back later. I've got work to do.'

'I've never known you do anything like that.'

'Shows how little you know me, dear.'

'All right, I'll be round shortly.' He rang off. 'Fuck!'

Marianthi glanced at him in the mirror. 'That's hardly feasible now.'

'I don't know,' said the Fat Man.

'Shut up! Something's been couriered to me at the old dear's.'

'Ah,' Yiorgos said, his grin disappearing.

Mavros called Loukas and asked him to tell the police that he was bringing Dinos and his package. He didn't mention his own delivery. It was conceivable it wasn't related to the case.

Dinos appeared with a supermarket carrier bag, his face grey.

'This isn't my idea of Christmas,' he said.

'You want to complain,' said Mavros. 'At least you've opened yours.'

It was only a couple of minutes to his mother's. He ran up the stairs and waited to be let in. Dorothy pointed to the package in the corner. Mavros went into the kitchen and picked up a plastic bag and a pair of latex gloves.

'See you later,' he said, kissing his mother on the cheek.

'Is everything all right, dear. You seem a bit—'

He was out of the door before she finished. When he got to the stairwell, he pulled on the gloves and opened the envelope, which had only a standard shipping note on it, the sender's name Ioannidhis – hardly uncommon, but it was also the name of the most hard line member of the military junta from 1967-74. Was that significant? He took out his penknife and ran it along the tape that secured the cardboard box. It was from a cake shop with numerous branches. Mavros knew full well he should have taken it to police HQ and had it X-rayed, but he didn't think it was dangerous.

He tugged open the box, his breathing rapid. A bundle wrapped in paper napkins. He pulled them apart and his head shot back.

The human ear was damp, having presumably been frozen. It looked like a blue and red bird that had crumpled up and died. A pair of damaged fingernails lay alongside it.

The plane crossed over southern Evia and then there was only the Aegean below, the pale blue dotted by white. Jim Thomson looked down and shivered. There it was, the element that had almost done for him all those years ago; the blood-chilling, heart-stopping sea that he had ridden to Ikaria and Marigo. But now he was headed west rather than southwest. His wife's bones would have long since been exhumed and placed in a tin box in the ossuary.

As the aircraft started to lose height, he took in Lesvos to the left. There were a couple of large, narrow-necked bays and in the far distance a mountain massif. Lepetymnos was its name, according to the guidebook he'd picked up at the airport. The wind buffeted the plane as it turned north for the final approach. As they got lower, Jim saw that the coast was fringed by white, as if the island had put on lace for the arrival of Ivy's ashes. The urn was in bubble-wrap in his suitcase. It struck him that he would soon have to make his last farewells to the woman who had loved him and whom he had cherished – though his ability to love had never fully recovered from what had been done to him by the torturers. He had a girlfriend back then, her name escaped him. Was she still alive? Did she ever think of him? He had blocked her from his memory and the thought of the pain he must have caused by disappearing made him bow his head.

He had hired a car online and found the small blue Citroen in the airport car park. His intention was to spend the night in Mytiline, the capital, before driving to the place where Ivy's family had come from. Across the water to the east was the dim outline of the Turkish coast. He had been to the country several times on the ships and found the people welcoming, even in the harbour dives. The music sounded too much like that in Greece for comfort and he confined himself to eating places that echoed only to the sound of customers' voices. Turkey had its own problems with military governments and the mistreatment of political prisoners, but he'd never allowed himself to think about that. Politics had meant nothing to him from the moment he hit the White Sea.

He had booked a room at a hotel on the seafront. After checking in, he walked around the town. Nearby was a church – Ayios Therapon, according to his book – on which one large breast-like dome looked down on multiple smaller ones. Further round the bay were the remains of a fortress that was originally Byzantine, but he didn't have the energy to walk there. Then it occurred to him that he could easily dispose of Ivy's remains beyond the port. No one would know and they would go into the same sea. But he quickly dismissed the thought. He had promised Ivy he would carry out her wishes and he had enough honour left to do so.

Tomorrow he would go to Molyvos.

'Finally you answer your phone.'

'I've been busy,' Nikos Kriaras said brusquely.

'Me too. I've just received a package containing a human ear and two fingernails.'

'You too?'

'Maybe raiding the Gogols' place wasn't such a good idea.'

The brigadier grunted.

'Why do I get the feeling there's something you aren't telling me?'

'I don't answer to you. I gather you're heading to the Gatsos building.'

'With Dinos, yes.'

'Lucky you. I'm on my way to his mother's.'

'I spoke to her a few minutes ago.'

'Her floor's about to disappear from beneath her.'

'Meaning?'

There was a pause. 'I may as well tell you. The rest of the family will soon find out. Vangelis Myronis was killed during our operation last night.'

'What?'

'You heard me. He was at the Paradiso Bianco, we're not sure why. The other customers had all left.'

Mavros glanced at Dinos. 'Who was responsible?'

'The ballistics show that Lavrenti Gogol shot him. He had an unusual pistol, a Desert Eagle chambered for .44 Magnum cartridges.'

'Lucky it wasn't one of your people. It suggests the victim knew something they didn't want to come out.'

'Correct. I'll bring Mrs Myroni down to the shipping office if she's up to it.'

'What about—'

'Put him on.'

Mavros watched as Dinos listened to Kriaras. His forehead furrowed and he squeezed his eyes tightly shut. It seemed that he was more attached to his father than he'd let on. When the conversation was over, he handed the phone back and put his hands over his face.

'I'm very sorry,' Mavros said quietly.

The Fat Man turned round, then looked to the front when he saw his friend's expression.

'I . . . I don't . . . understand,' Dinos said, his voice suddenly that of a little boy. 'Dad . . . didn't . . . didn't . . .'

Mavros waited for him to the finish the sentence, but instead he began to sob.

Marianthi looked in the mirror and then steered towards the pavement. She got out and opened the back door, squeezing in beside the young man and putting her arm round him. They sat that way for several minutes, then she returned to the driver's seat and continued down Leoforos Syngrou.

Dinos cried heartrendingly all the way to the Gatsos building.

NINETEEN

aura Moreno had managed to put two rows of seats between herself and Santiago Rojas on the flight from Madrid to Athens; from Bogota, first class had been full and she'd been forced to sit next to him. Although she'd made clear to him at dinner back home that she wasn't interested in joining with him to buy out or suborn Gatsos group shareholders, he'd taken that as only a preliminary rebuttal. He spent several hours on the first flight reiterating his points and he'd have had his hand on her thigh for that time and longer if she hadn't made it very clear that she objected to his advances. He'd given her a loose smile and kept on talking.

She looked out of the window and took in pale blue water and mountains that looked like they'd been scourged by an angry god. In the half-hour before they landed at Athens, she constructed a plan. Becoming a shareholder in the Gatsos group had been an invitation she couldn't turn down. Although Kostas was an old goat, his long career had shown that he could make money with his eyes shut. She hadn't known that Santiago was approached at the same time – if she had, she'd have declined. There was a lot of talk about Rojas in Colombia and he was exactly the kind of operator she didn't want Colarmco to be tainted by. While having access to Gatsos vessels was a benefit, competition was such that she could have covered her shipping needs with other companies at reasonable costs. The easy thing would have been to sell her shares, even to Santiago, but Colarmco needed every dollar it had for the development of new products and she was damned if she was going to give up a reliable source of income. Of course, Rojas was offering her a way to make even more money.

Although Laura had done her best to forget the evening when Santiago had come to the house, she was still plagued by the memory of it . . .

'My dear, you are magnificent,' he'd said, as he was ushered into the ornate drawing room. His evening suit was exquisitely cut, disguising the bulge of his abdomen. He was in his early fifties, his swept-back hair suspiciously black and his heavy face marked by scars from a logging accident when he was young.

'Santiago,' she said, turning away. 'Is this evening really necessary?' She handed him a glass of the bourbon he favoured.

'You know it is. There are people we must impress, investors who can help us grow.'

'Us?'

'Don't be coy, Laura,' he said, his voice hardening. 'Our common interest in the Gatsos group is only the beginning. We can become the biggest company in the country, one of South America's biggest.' He sipped his whisky and smiled. 'Of course, it would be enormously beneficial if we came together as a couple as well.'

It wasn't the first time he'd proposed to her in such a profoundly unromantic way – business first, private lives way behind. She'd refused him before and had no intention of changing her position now. She bit her tongue and allowed him to escort her to one of Bogotá's most exclusive restaurants, where they met a group of well-dressed but rapacious businessmen and bankers. Some she knew, but she liked none of them. They were buzzards, carrion creatures who cared nothing for natural justice and the toil of the workers. Her father had often told her that the root of the family's wealth was its employees. Their interests had to be protected if a profit worth having was to be harvested.

The dinner was bad enough – false courtesy, off-colour comments, downright unpleasantness. Worse was to come in Rojas's huge American limo on the way home. The chauffeur raised the partition and Santiago moved close to her. Before she could react, his hand was on her breast and his lips on hers. They stayed there, tongue pushing against her teeth, until she managed to get the small pistol she always carried out of her clutch bag. His eyes sprang open and he pulled away.

'Don't tempt me,' she said icily. 'You're gross and vulgar. No one would mourn you.'

He licked his lips. 'I like a strong woman. Together we can—'

'Do very little. I'll sell you my holding in the Gatsos group.'

'You're bluffing, my dear. I know the state of Colarmco's finances.'

Laura glared at him. 'I'll let you have them at a discount.'

'No,' Rojas said, his face hardening. 'You'll do as we agreed:

come with me to Greece and put our proposition to the other investors. You need the money.'

She couldn't argue with that. With the concrete mass of Athens to
the left of the plane, she was confused about what she was going
to do. But Santiago Rojas could go straight to hell.

The atmosphere in the board room in the Gatsos building was tense
but, to Mavros, surprisingly controlled. Eirini Myroni had arrived
with Nikos Kriaras, Lieutenant Babis in tow. The widow's eyes were
red, but her expression showed defiance more than shock. Evi ran
to her and was embraced with a modicum of maternal love, while
Dinos hung back, his face now dry but his head hung. Eirini put
an arm round him and whispered some words. Then Loukas came
up, bent to kiss her on both cheeks and gave his condolences. Mavros
waited and then added his own words.

'I've had enough of this,' Eirini said firmly. 'Find my father.'

'That is primarily the responsibility of the police,' Kriaras said.

The widow turned her gaze on him. 'My husband would still be
alive if you people hadn't stormed the nightclub.'

The brigadier looked past her. 'Our information was that there
were no customers inside. Are you sure you have no idea why Mr
Myronis was there?'

'Leave her alone!' Dinos shouted. His mother took him to a
corner with Evi.

Mavros moved towards Kriaras. 'It was about drugs, obviously.
What I want to know is why Gogol shot him. He must have known
something the brothers didn't want to come out.'

The brigadier nodded. 'Since you're so well connected with
the family, see if you can discover what.' He turned and told the
lieutenant to collect the ear and nails for DNA testing. While they
and the packaging were being put into sterile bags, Loukas took
Mavros's arm.

'This is a warning to us, I presume,' he said.

Mavros shrugged. 'It's likely that it was prompted by the raid on
the Paradiso Bianco. Whether that means the Gogol brothers are
behind the kidnap of your grandfather, I'm not sure.' He turned to
Kriaras. 'I don't suppose Lavrenti is talking.'

'Literally not a word. And he's got a flashy lawyer on his
case.'

'No sign of Igor?'

'No. He knows how to look after himself.'

Loukas Gatsos bit his lip. 'What do we do now?'

Kriaras scowled. 'I'd like to give your half-brother Dinos the third degree, but Siatkas has already warned me off.'

'Aunt Eirini's protective of him,' Loukas said. 'You can hardly blame her at this juncture.'

'What about the couriers who delivered the body parts?' Mavros asked.

Kriaras looked even more disgruntled. 'The packages were handed in at different offices around Athens. We're interviewing the clerks, but I suspect that, even if they remember the people who brought them in, they'll have been wearing dark glasses and baseball caps. The names – all of them members of the Junta – and the contact numbers on the documentation are bound to be fake.'

'You might strike lucky,' Mavros said.

'And you might find Kostas Gatsos.'

'Why members of the dictatorship?' Mavros said.

'They're probably far-left tossers covering their tracks,' the brigadier said dismissively.

'Or colonels' sympathisers.'

Kriaras's expression hardened. 'I suppose it was you who talked to that shitsucker Bitsos.'

'What?' Mavros said, playing as innocent as he could.

The brigadier shook his head and went over to his subordinate.

'So?' Loukas said.

'I have some angles I need to follow up,' Mavros replied. 'I'll talk to you later. In the meantime, I'm going to try to talk to Mrs Myroni.'

'Good luck with that. Better call her Gatsou, especially now.'

Mavros went over to the huddle in the corner.

Evi came towards him. 'My mother's taking it worryingly well. They haven't got on well for years, but I expected at least a few tears.'

'Don't be too hard on her. People react in different ways. She'll probably fall apart when she gets home. Will you go with her?'

'Yes.' Evi waited. 'Was there something else?'

'Your Uncle Pavlos. Vangelis's death has made me wonder more about the shooting in Lesvos. Could they have been up to something together?'

Evi's eyes flashed. 'What do you mean?'

Mavros held her gaze. 'I mean, was there some project they were engaged in without your grandfather's knowledge?'

'Not that I know of. I'm sure Loukas would have heard of it.'

Mavros looked at her thoughtfully and then went for broke. 'Could they have been behind the kidnap?'

Evi's head jerked back as if he'd slapped her. 'You can't think that,' she said, her voice low and unsteady.

'I have to consider it. They may have been used by people who subsequently wanted them silenced. Can you check your father's mobile phone and computer?'

'The police told us his phone was destroyed in the raid. They didn't find any suspicious calls on the list from his service provider. As for his laptop, it was still with him. The police have it. Apparently it's damaged.' She let out a single sob.

Mavros put his arm around her shoulders. 'See if he left any notes or the like. It'll be better if you do that rather than me or the cops disturbing your mother.'

'She told them they could search the house tomorrow and not before.'

'There's your opportunity then.'

'What are you going to do?'

'Better I keep that to myself.' Mavros patted her back and then headed for the exit.

Light flooded into Kostas Gatsos's place of imprisonment.

'Come!' yelled the guard in the balaclava. 'Quick!'

Kostas got up, then insisted on emptying his bladder into the bucket. He had only small ways of resisting now but they helped him keep hold of his sanity.

'Another trial?' he asked, as his hands were cuffed behind his back.

The guard laughed.

The shipowner was pushed down the corridor, for the first time beyond the door he'd gone through before. There was another one about five metres further on. It opened as he approached.

'Welcome to hell,' said the Son, his head and face uncovered.

Kostas's stomach clenched. He made himself look unconcerned, his eyes on the torturer's grinning offspring. He'd seen his photograph in the media after a series of violent murders and had never forgotten it. Then he took in the apparatus in the centre of the room.

The familiar masked people stood to the rear, Skull making a florid bow.

As he got closer Kostas made out the lines of nylon and wire hanging from metal bars above a stainless steel table. At the end of each one was a fishing hook, some small, others disguised by plastic worms. The largest were slightly above the corners of the table.

'Only cowards would put an old man through such . . .' Kostas struggled for the word. '. . . such abuse.'

The Son smiled. 'Abuse is the story of your life – abuse of people, abuse of laws, abuse of institutions, abuse of power.'

'A torturer lecturing me on ethics.'

The Son grabbed his chin. 'I'm not lecturing, you piece of shit. As you know very well, I'm telling the truth.' He kept hold and walked Kostas to the horizontal surface. 'Look at the instruments of your agony. The small hooks will be attached to parts of your body where the nerves are particularly sensitive – lips, nipples, cock, inner thighs. The big ones go through your shoulders, wrists and ankles.' He pointed up to the bars. 'Then you'll be lifted and suspended in the air, all your weight on the hooks.'

Kostas pulled away and spat at the other man. 'Fuck you and all the others. They're too scared to take off their pathetic masks.'

'There's a reason for that,' the Son said, taking hold of the old man's chin again. 'Would you like to hear it?'

Kostas took a deep breath and pushed the younger man against the table. There was a grunt.

'You're a tough bastard,' the Son said, twisting the small hook Kostas had stuck into the fabric of his jacket. 'But that will just make things worse for you.'

'How much fucking worse can they get?'

The Son grinned. 'There are always choices. For instance, if you hadn't been so recalcitrant, we'd have offered you a way out – a way to return unharmed to the ugly green building in Phalero Bay.'

'You're lying. You can't wait to string me up.'

'You're a good judge of character, old man. But my desires aren't paramount here.' He shrugged. 'Still, since you don't want to hear our proposition, I'll just have to fulfil them.' He turned to the guard. 'Hold him tight.'

Kostas watched as the lines on the near side were pulled aside. His clothes were ripped off, then he was lifted on to the steel surface and his arms and legs secured with leather straps.

'Come closer, my friends,' the Son said. 'You've been waiting for this for a long time.'

He took hold of one of the hooks and, after pinching the flesh on Kostas's right forearm, skilfully inserted it in the skin.

'No screams? Very good. Let's go for one of the big hooks.'

'Please,' Kostas gasped. 'I want to hear your proposition. Please.'

The Son put down the large hook reluctantly, looking round at his colleagues. 'Who would like the privilege?'

'It's mine,' said the woman wearing the crocodile head. 'Kindly remove that hook. Carefully.'

The Son complied, provoking only a low moan from his victim.

'Kosta Gatso,' the woman began, 'I am authorised to—'

'Who authorised you?' the old man demanded.

'I advise you to be silent,' Crocodile said. 'Your next outburst will lead to the termination of the offer.' She turned to the Son. 'And to a long and agonising death. Nod if you understand.'

Kostas did so.

'Very well. I am authorised to offer you your life on the following conditions: one, that you liquidate all of your personal holdings in the Gatsos group.'

There was no response, but Kostas's eyes were suddenly glazed.

'Two, that you establish a not-for-profit foundation with a budget of one billion euros, dedicated to the improvement of the lives of Greece's poor including immigrants and the Roma. Three, that you pay a sum of three billion euros to the Greek government in lieu of the taxes you have evaded throughout your life. Four, that you set up a fund of one billion euros to compensate those employees of Gatsos companies and their families who have genuine grievances. And five, that you withdraw from all business and social activities, and confine yourself to your property on the island of Anydhros. That is our proposition. You have twenty-four hours to consider it. Light, a clock, paper and pencil, and a table and chair will be provided so that you can make whatever basic calculations may be necessary.' The woman stepped back.

'But remember,' the Son said, leaning over the confined man. 'It's either agree to all those conditions or you're handed over to me.'

Kostas waited as the restraints were loosed and then sat up stiffly. He did not speak as his hands were cuffed behind his back and he was pushed towards the door. He heard the words of Tennyson's

'Ulysses' over and over again – 'To strive, to seek, to find, and not to yield'.

For the first time he didn't think he was going to be able to live up to them.

Mavros called Nondas as soon as he was back in the taxi with the Fat Man and Marianthi.

'Have you got anything on Pavlos Gatsos?'

'No smoking gun,' his brother-in-law replied, 'but he was definitely hiding things.'

'Money.'

'Of course, but not only that. He and Vangelis Myronis—'

'Now deceased.'

'Right. They set up a couple of companies that I'm checking out. Should have more by tonight.'

'OK, call me when you do.'

'Where to?' asked Marianthi.

'Kastella, Piraeus.'

'So close,' she said mournfully.

'Come off it,' said Yiorgos. 'You've had the meter running.'

'That's one way of putting it.'

Mavros had his fingers in his ears. 'Get your motor running, head out on the highway . . .'

'Is that some decadent American band?' the Fat Man demanded.

'You know it is.'

'Well, I don't,' said the driver.

'Steppenwolf, "Born to Be Wild",' Mavros said. 'Never seen *Easy Rider*?'

'No,' Marianthi replied. 'I've done it though.'

Yiorgos guffawed while Mavros shook his head.

A few minutes later they were winding up a narrow street leading to the top of the small hill that overlooked the yacht harbours. Apart from the open air theatre and some park land, the area was as packed with apartment buildings as everywhere else in the port city. But the street they stopped on, near the small church on the summit, was definitely a cut above the others.

'Come on,' Mavros said to the Fat Man. 'Marianthi, you'd better make yourself scarce. We'll call you when we need you.' He held his friend back. 'No touching farewells, please. We shouldn't be that long.'

Yiorgos blew a kiss at the driver as she pulled away. 'That wasn't very nice, sending her away.'

'Needs must. What we're about to do isn't strictly legal.'

'Strictly?'

'It isn't legal at all. See that block over there, the extremely luxurious one.'

'In grey marble? So what?'

'Pavlos Gatsos owned it. We're going to break in.'

'There's police tape all over the street door. Why didn't you get Lieutenant Baboulas to let us in?'

'Because I don't want him or his boss knowing what we're up to.'

'So how are we going to get in?'

'The Party taught you how to get into the homes of the bourgeoisie, didn't it?'

'Yes, but that involved steel bars and we didn't care about leaving prints or traces.'

Mavros handed him a pair of latex gloves and pulled on his own.

'I happen to have with me a set of jemmies.'

'How long is it since you last used them? Let me guess. Five and a bit years.'

'Correct. You're going to stand behind me, providing cover.'

'This is crazy.'

'Don't worry, I've got my motor running.'

In the event, it took Mavros seven minutes to open the locks on the reinforced steel door. By that time the Fat Man had gushed litres of sweat.

TWENTY

'Where are we going?' Laura Moreno asked, as Santiago Rojas led her from the large hotel to a taxi.

'To meet a very useful man.'

'Is my presence essential?'

'Certainly, my dear.'

'Don't call me that.'

Santiago gave her one of his patronising smiles, as if she were a skittish young woman who had to be given her head rather than the CEO of a major company.

'I mean it. I'm not your dear and I never will be.'

Rojas gave a destination she didn't catch to the driver, who looked puzzled but got going anyway.

'A pleasant early evening drive, that's all, Laura. And a profitable meeting, followed by drinks on the Grande Bretagne roof garden.'

Laura had stayed at the city's finest central hotel before and enjoyed the glorious view of the Acropolis. She wasn't sure why they'd been booked into the luxurious but anonymous American chain hotel, but couldn't be bothered to ask. She looked out of the tinted windows at the rush of traffic on the wide avenue that led up from the sea. On the pavements people were walking slowly, the sun still beating down. She realised their clothing was less smart than she remembered and their expressions harried.

To her annoyance Santiago had read her mind.

'The Greeks are suffering,' he said, pointing at a beggar in rags. 'They overspent and now they have to pay the price.'

Laura had read more discerning reports. 'They should never have joined the Euro zone. Their leaders sold them out and let the foreign banks flood the country with cheap loans. Now ordinary working people are paying the price for the corruption of the politicians and the tax evasion of the rich.'

'I never had you down as a socialist.'

'I never had you down as a FARC supporter.'

Rojas's face darkened. 'Surely you don't believe those idiotic rumours. My company works in areas near the guerillas' stronghold.

Sometimes accommodations have to be made. That doesn't make me a supporter of revolution.'

'Maybe not,' Laura said, as the taxi turned right and headed towards the slope of the city's eastern mountain. 'But they hardly make you the kind of man I want to do business with.'

There was silence as they drove upwards along narrow streets with apartment blocks on each side. Eventually they reached an open area covered in grass. Rojas told the driver to wait.

'Come, we can walk here.'

Laura was wearing flat shoes and a mid-calf skirt. 'What is this place?'

'Behind that wall was a shooting range used by the Nazis during the Second World War. Apparently many Communists and resistance fighters were executed there.'

'Charming place for a stroll.'

'It wasn't chosen by me. There's our man.'

A burly figure had stepped out from behind a lamp post twenty metres ahead. He wore jeans and a green sweatshirt with the hood pulled up.

'Not a banker then,' Laura said.

'Not exactly.' Santiago strode ahead and shook the man's hand. They watched as she approached. Laura introduced herself.

'This is Igor,' Rojas said. 'You don't need to know his surname.'

'I don't think I want to,' she said, taking in the man's scarred features. 'Why are we here?'

'Igor is in business like us,' Santiago said, in English.

'Can't he speak for himself?'

'I speak, lady, but maybe you no like what I say.'

'Really?' Laura tried to conceal her unease. She glanced at Rojas.

'Igor has a sum of money he would like to invest in Colarmco. He has already taken a two per cent share in Maderera Jaguar and is very happy with the results.'

Laura twitched her head. 'Why can't Mr Igor make his offer for shares via the usual channels?'

'Ah,' said Santiago, smiling broadly. 'He doesn't like such channels. In fact, he avoids them completely.'

'I'm going back to the taxi,' she said. 'This isn't how I do business.'

The man called Igor took her arm and squeezed it. 'Ms Moreno, you no have choice. But I honest with you. Greek police want me

for murder after raid my nightclub. I also big drug dealer.' He raised
his other hand and pointed to a figure on the other side of the park,
who had a camera raised. 'You photographed with me so police
think we work together. Now you do business?' He let go of her
and she stumbled back.

'What is this, Santiago?' she gasped.

Her companion raised his shoulders. 'Sometimes it's best to go
with the flow, my dear. Igor can confer many blessings on us.'

'Screw you!' she said and turned away.

'Hey lady!' Igor called. He was holding his hand like a pistol.
'Bang bang.'

Laura Moreno strode back to the taxi, her heart pounding. When
she reached it, she told the driver to take her to the Athens police
headquarters, leaving Santiago where he belonged: with his gangster
friend beside the old place of execution.

'What if there's an alarm?' the Fat Man asked as Mavros ripped
away the police tape and pushed the door open.

They cocked their heads.

'As I suspected,' Mavros said. 'The cops turned it off.'

'You might have mentioned that earlier. Christ, will you look at
this place?'

The block had not been subdivided into separate apartments. The
open-plan ground floor was filled with high-quality furniture.
Paintings by well-known Greek artists covered the walls.

'It's going to take days to search the whole building,' Yiorgos
said.

'Maybe.'

'Definitely.'

Mavros smiled. 'On the other hand, we can use our brains.'

'Meaning?'

'Where's the least likely place someone would look for secrets?'

The Fat Man looked around. 'I don't know . . . behind the
paintings?'

'Bit of a crime movie staple.'

'No, I mean between the canvas and the backing panel.'

'That's not a bad thought. Go ahead, hack open those valuable
works of art.'

'Maybe we should get permission from Loukas Gatsos.'

'I'd rather he didn't know what we're up to.' Mavros went over to a large desk. 'Ever read an Edgar Allan Poe story called "The Purloined Letter"?'

'It wasn't on the Party's approved list.'

'And you were such an obedient member. Doesn't matter; the point is, a compromising letter is stolen and then hidden in plain sight, so to speak.'

'You think Pavlos Gatsos was a Poe fan and the information we want – whatever that might be – is somewhere obvious?'

Mavros laughed. 'Not necessarily the former, but the latter's worth a shot. You take this floor and I'll go upstairs. When you've finished, take the second floor. Check the magazines on the coffee table, the books on those shelves and so on. If we're lucky, he'll have backed up his files on a CD-ROM – check that pile of CDs and DVDs. Otherwise there might be a memory stick, which could be anywhere, or a paper folder. Follow your nose, and I don't mean to the kitchen. Though maybe that's as good a place as any.'

Yiorgos groaned and then got started.

Mavros went up the solid wooden staircase, deciding against the lift to the right of it. He found himself in another open space, this time with a large dining table. There was an imposing wooden dresser full of glasses, plates and bowls. He opened it and ran his hand around the contents, finding nothing out of place. From what he'd heard, Pavlos Gatsos was a dull man, but that didn't mean he hadn't possessed a secret sense of humour. So he felt the cushions on each of the dining chairs in case the dead man found it amusing to have his guests' backsides on his secrets. He didn't.

The Fat Man didn't come up so Mavros took the second floor. This time there were separate rooms. Guest bedrooms, he surmised, after opening each door. The Poe method seemed overstretched here; it was unlikely Gatsos would have risked his secrets being discovered by the people he had to stay. Still, he checked the few books on each bedside table and ran an eye around the well-appointed en suite bathrooms. The third floor was again open plan, the walls lined with steel filing cabinets. The leads from computers lay beneath several desks, while three TV screens were suspended from the ceiling. There was a row of clocks on the right wall, showing the time in eight global cities. The desk was piled with yellow cardboard folders. He opened each one, but found nothing that was suggestive. There were budgets, vessel statistics, voyage reports and copies of charter parties. He took the budget folders to show Nondas.

The fifth floor, the penthouse, was the dead man's bedroom. There was a walk-in wardrobe full of suits and other clothing, a large en suite bath and shower room, and a dressing room with ceiling-high mirrors on every wall. Mavros stuck his tongue out at the four reflections of himself, the thrill of the hunt fading fast. He went over to the bed, an emperor-sized explosion of multi-coloured quilt, sheets and pillows. The view from the windows was superb, down the Attic coast to Cape Sounion and the shadowy islands beyond. He sat on the bed and considered the rich man's house. Where would he have secreted his most private documents?

Then it struck him that there were no photos of Loukas or his sister Nana on any of the floors he'd been on. He had been told that Pavlos's wife Myrto was estranged from him, living in Paris, but surely he had feelings for his children. He called the Fat Man's mobile.

'Anything?'

'Just a lot of dirty DVDs. The hyper-rich, eh?'

'Wondered what was delaying you. Any family photos?'

There was a pause.

'Oddly, no.'

'What about in the kitchen?'

'Hang on.' There was the sound of heavy footsteps. 'No, I don't see any.'

'Not even on the fridge?'

'I don't even know where the fridge is. All the fittings look the same.'

'Hold on.' Mavros cut the connection and took the lift down.

'Found it,' Yiorgos said, holding open a wide door. He closed it. There was nothing on the outside.

Mavros started opening the cupboards both above and below the work surfaces, the Fat Man following suit. There were plates, cups, pans and food supplies, most of the latter unopened.

'What about those?' Yiorgos said.

Mavros looked up and saw a line of blue and white hooped storage jars with 'Flour', 'Tea', 'Sugar' and the like, on the top of the cupboards.

'Cornishware,' he said. 'My mother has some like that.'

'You don't suppose . . .'

Mavros grabbed a chair from the breakfast bar and clambered up.

'Here,' he said, handing the first one to the Fat Man.

In a few minutes all were on the bar. Mavros got down and went over, his heart beginning to pound.

'What have we got?' He looked along the row, taking in the names. 'Bollocks, we'll have to check them all.' He took the lid off the Meal jar, but it was empty.

Yiorgos stuck his hand into kidney beans.

'Nothing,' he said.

The tea and sugar jars were empty. Mavros opened the Flour jar, which was nearly full of the white powder. His stomach flipped. Could this be a link to the cocaine dealt by the Gogols and Dinos? He examined the rim of the jar. There was a dusting of white dust on it. He tasted it gingerly; it was flour.

'What are you doing?' the Fat Man asked, as Mavros cleared the other jars away with one arm.

'Stand by to become a ghost.' He upended the jar and enveloped them in a cloud of flour. There was a muffled click as something heavier hit the surface of the breakfast bar.

Waving his hands, Mavros looked at the object in a clear plastic bag partially covered by flour. It was a dark blue memory stick.

'Well, well,' he said. 'Edgar Allan was right.'

'That was hardly in plain sight,' Yiorgos said, coughing.

'It'll do for me. Let's get out of here.'

They left the house and walked quickly down the hill, brushing flour off as they went. The Fat Man called Marianthi and asked her to meet them on the front at Pasalimani.

'You won't miss us,' he said. 'We've become albinos.'

Mavros kept on slapping away the white powder, wondering why there hadn't been any family photos. Had Pavlos's children turned against him as his wife had?

Jim Thomson drove to Molyvos the next morning. It was a fine day, the blue sky broken only by scattered high cloud. Lesvos was fertile, animals on either side of the road, even horses in some fields. There were olive trees and chimneys from the pressing factories, many of them disused. Inland from the Gulf of Kalloni the road turned north and the mountain massif on the east grew more imposing. At Petra a thin volcanic outcrop rose behind the modern village and then the Genoese castle above Molyvos became visible, a stone shout of defiance to the Ottomans who eventually captured the island.

He left the car outside the old town and walked round the cobbled alleyways, looking for somewhere to stay. He was still struggling with the idea of casting Ivy's remains to the waves and needed time to prepare himself. Eventually he found an old merchant's house that was still taking guests. He pretended he spoke no Greek and let the elderly black-clothed owner, Kyria Stella, practice her hit-and-miss English on him. She showed him to a large room on the first floor, the windows providing a fine view of the lower town and the sea beyond. She told him there was a good taverna at the harbour, pointing out the small sea wall and an old warehouse. Then she left him alone. His bag was in the car but he needed to lie down for a while. When he woke it was nearly dark. He hadn't dreamed, which was a relief. He was still uneasy at being back in Greece, even though he'd never been to the island before. Perhaps his familiar ghosts – his family, the friends he had deserted – would stay away from this eastern outpost of the country. He had noticed people who were obviously illegal immigrants being herded into a bus in Mytiline as he was leaving. The proximity to Turkey meant that Lesvos was first stop in Europe for many of the Middle and Far East's unfortunates. It was a transition point, just as it would be for Ivy to the next world she had believed in and he most definitely did not.

After carrying his bag up to the house in the last of the light, he headed to the harbour. Lights were strung outside a taverna and it was still warm enough to sit outside. He kept up the tourist image, allowing an eager young waiter to talk him into ordering a grilled fish and mountain greens, as well as a carafe of local wine. Beside him a table of local worthies was downing *ouzo* – he remembered Lesvos was famous for the aperitif – and swallowing *mezedhes*. Their voices were loud and he couldn't avoid hearing what they were saying.

'It was Gatsos's own fault,' said one. 'He always was a stingy bastard. He should have had a small army of guards. Everyone knows how well-off he is.' The rotund man laughed. 'Or was.'

'Come on, Thanasi, that's not right. The man might be suffering in a hole in the ground.'

'Which is where he belongs, Maki.'

'You're too hard,' said another man, this one unusually small, but with a huge drooping moustache. 'Just because you had a dispute over land with him . . .'

'He robbed me, Stelio, and bribed every judge on the island. I'm supposed to care he's been kidnapped? He'd have been better off sailing the seven seas on one of his many ships.'

Jim gradually realised that he knew who they were talking about. He had seen stories in the *Melbourne Age* about a Greek shipowner who had been abducted, but for some reason he hadn't noticed it was Kostas Gatsos – or perhaps his subconscious had blanked that out. One of the Gatsos group companies was the owner of the *Homeland*, the ship that had gone down off the Philippines and cast him into the waters of the Pacific. He had been suspicious about the sinking and what had caused it but, along with so much of his previous lives, he had blotted that out when he left the sea. Now, as he'd already realised, coming back to Greece meant facing a succession of nightmares.

'Maybe the family will sell the villa now the old bastard's gone,' Thanasis said. 'I might even buy it.'

His companions laughed.

'Where would you get the money?' asked the one called Stelios.

'The Gritsis businesses aren't doing that well,' added Makis.

'Just you wait.' Thanasis called for the bill. 'Come on, the suckling pig should be ready. If it isn't, the wife'll be sorry.'

Jim Thomson watched them go, a trio of grizzled old men in expensive leisure clothes. Thanasis Gritsis was even wearing a gold chain.

After he'd eaten, he asked if there was an internet café in the town. He went to the nearest one and did a search for Kostas Gatsos. Half-an-hour later he was much better informed. The man who had been the ultimate owner of the *Homeland* – each ship was the property of a different company – had been kidnapped from his villa a few kilometres east of Molyvos nearly five weeks ago and nothing had been heard of him since. It was the most recent newspaper story, under the byline of Lambis Bitsos, that attracted his attention most:

> The Gatsos family has hired experienced missing persons specialist, Alex Mavros, to assist in the search for the patriarch. Mavros, who has kept himself out of the limelight for the last five years, was involved in several high profile cases, including those of the terrorist Iraklis and the Chiotis organised crime family. He was unavailable for comment as we went to press. It is safe to say that if Alex Mavros cannot find Kostas Gatsos,

then no one can. Brigadier Nikos Kriaras, who heads the police enquiry into the kidnap is unlikely to be happy about the family's decision. He would not return the *Free News*'s calls.

Jim Thomson sat back and rubbed his eyes. Alex Mavros: another ghost from the past. The sooner he disposed of Ivy's ashes and got back to Australia the better.

TWENTY-ONE

Mavros and Nondas were sitting on the Fat Man's sofa. The latter was in the bedroom with Marianthi, though he claimed they were only having a lie-down.

'What did you tell Anna?' Mavros asked.

'The truth,' the Cretan said, with a grin. 'Well, a version of it.'

'Late night with the figures?'

'You owe me. I couldn't find anything particularly dubious in the budgets, but it's hard to be sure without in-depth knowledge of the group's complexities.'

'All right, let's see what's on Pavlos's memory stick.' Mavros put the device into one of his laptop's USB ports.

An icon opened on the screen. It led to a single file. Mavros clicked on it.

They looked in silence at the document that appeared.

'Shit,' Nondas said, scrolling down. 'You know what this is, Alex?'

'I can see it isn't good.'

'You've got that right. This is an agreement, dated August 13th this year, between Pavlos Gatsos, Vangelis Myronis and Santiago Rojas, outlining how they intend to wrest control of the Gatsos group from Kostas. They've already got a lot of shareholders' preliminary agreement on the grounds that the old man's lost his grip.'

Nondas continued to scroll down. 'There are several mentions of a "timber residue" to be shipped from Colombia to Europe. Is that what I think it is?'

'I presume you're thinking of stuff that looks like this,' Mavros said, shaking white powder from his shirt pocket.

Nondas licked a finger, put it on the powder and licked it. 'It's flour.'

'I noticed. You think this is a glorified dope deal?'

'Hardly. Have you any idea what the Gatsos group is worth?'

'Billions?'

'Plenty of billions. I've only begun to discover what they're into. They've invested heavily in China over the last decade.'

There was a shriek from the bedroom.

Mavros shook his head. 'A lie-down.'

'Good luck to them,' Nondas said, laughing. 'See what happens when you lose weight?' He slapped his own belly. 'Maybe I should do more exercise.'

'I'm surprised Anna doesn't have you giving her fifty on a daily basis.'

'Who says she doesn't? I just put it all back on again at lunch.'

Mavros sat back. 'Where does this get us?'

'It might explain why Pavlos and Vangelis were killed.'

Mavros looked at his brother-in-law. 'I don't know. The former was shot during the kidnap and the latter during a police raid on Russian mobsters.'

'Who were into drug-dealing.'

Mavros did a search for 'Gogol' in the document.

'You didn't really think they'd be mentioned.'

'No, but something doesn't add up. Pavlos' and Vangelis' plan to take over the group seems to have been moving ahead. I'd been wondering if they were behind the kidnap, especially since the Gogols appeared. But in fact the absence or death of Kostas wouldn't be to their advantage.'

'It would if Pavlos hadn't been killed,' Nondas said, drinking beer that he'd taken from the Fat Man's fridge. 'He'd have been in pole position to take control.'

'It seems unnecessarily risky and Pavlos didn't have a reputation for taking chances.'

'I agree. The shareholders they tapped will have gone into their shells until the situation's resolved.'

Mavros emptied his Amstel. 'Someone else is behind the kidnap.'

There was a loud crash from the bedroom.

'For God's sake, Yiorgo!' he yelled.

Nondas laughed like a fifteen-year-old. 'Santiago Rojas,' he said, when he caught his breath. 'Maybe he was playing a different game. Maybe he's the one who's really in with the Gogols.'

'Could well be.'

The doorbell rang.

Mavros got up and went to the entry phone. No one answered his demand that they identify themselves.

'Bloody delivery boys.'

He was on his way back to the sofa when the bell rang again, this time the one on the flat door. He looked through the spyhole and shook his head in surprise before opening up.

The moment a statuesque dark-haired woman in a calf-length skirt swept in, the Fat Man appeared from the bedroom with a towel stretched around his waist. Marianthi's head came out from behind his.

'Get back in here immediately!' she ordered.

The door closed behind them.

The woman took in Mavros and Nondas, unabashed by the farcical episode she had just witnessed.

'Is one of you Alex Mavros?' she asked, in English.

'I am.'

'Laura Moreno,' she said, extending a hand. 'I badly need your help.'

The feeling's mutual, Mavros thought.

In his office on the ninth floor of police headquarters Brigadier Kriaras was glaring at Lieutenant Haralambidhis.

'The tests confirm that the ear and nails are from Kostas Gatsos.'

'Sir.'

'And the forensics evidence from the packaging is a dead end.'

'No prints in the database. One of the clerks said she remembered the customer wearing gloves. And a hood and dark glasses.'

'They probably all were. What about Lavrenti Gogol? Is he still as hermetically sealed as a mussel in a hurricane?'

The lieutenant raised an eyebrow. 'Sir. His lawyer's claiming we used excessive force and that the Russian shot Vangelis Myronis by accident because our entry gave him a shock.'

'Fuck the smartarse's mother. I take it there have been no sightings of Igor Gogol.'

'No, sir.'

'Have you got *any* good news for me?'

The lieutenant lowered his head.

'Mavros,' Kriaras said. 'What's he up to?'

'I don't know, sir.'

'Not good enough.' The brigadier picked up his phone and made a call. 'The bastard's not answering his phone, at least not to me. Find him and find out what angles he's investigating.'

'Yes, sir,' the lieutenant said gloomily. Then he had a thought. He could order Elisavet Latsou to come with him.

'I'll be waiting for your call.'

'Sir.' Babis left the office and immediately rang the sergeant.

'Sure,' she said. 'Where are we going?'

'Neapolis.'

'That won't take long. I'll meet you in the car park.'

'Done. Uniform not required.'

'You want me in my underwear?'

'Pardon?' The lieutenant was so surprised that the response came out quicker than that of a teenager whose grandmother had caught him in front of a porn film.

'See you shortly, sir,' she said, then cut the connection.

Lieutenant Babis strode to the lift like Hermes with a message from Zeus. It was only as the contraption juddered into action that he remembered one of Hermes' duties was accompanying the dead to the underworld. Not the best of omens for a night on duty.

'How did you find me?' Mavros asked.

'I didn't want to use the telephone,' Laura said, her English unaccented. 'Loukas Gatsos sent me to your mother's apartment. She was kind enough to give me this address.' She looked around the Fat Man's place. 'You live here?'

'No,' Mavros said quickly. 'With my mother.' He realised how feeble that sounded. 'She hasn't been well.'

'It's nothing to be ashamed of. The native tribes in Colombia look after their old people with great devotion.'

Nondas nudged Mavros.

'I'm sorry, this is my brother-in-law, Nondas Chaniotakis.'

'You're a shareholder in the Gatsos group,' Nondas said.

Laura's dark eyes opened wide. 'How do you know this?'

'Don't mind him,' Mavros said, taking her arm and leading her to the sofa. 'He's been helping me with certain financial aspects of the kidnapping.'

'I hope you don't think I had anything to do with it,' she said, as she sat down.

'Of course not. You said you needed my help.'

A high-pitched cry came from the bedroom.

Laura smiled. 'I take it that is Mr Pandazopoulos – do I say it right?'

'Yiorgos, yes,' Mavros said, rubbing his forehead. 'He's . . .'

'Checking a taxi driver's suspension,' Nondas supplied.

Mavros gave him a stony stare. 'Anyway, you were saying, Ms Moreno.'

'Please call me Laura. I wasn't saying, but now I will. Since you know I'm a Gatsos group shareholder, I presume you are also aware of Santiago Rojas.'

'We are,' Mavros said noncommittally.

'I . . .' She dropped her gaze. 'I was going to the police about this, but I changed my mind after speaking to Loukas – not that I went into detail about what happened.'

Mavros saw she was frightened though doing her best to conceal it. 'Relax, Laura. Between us we'll find a way to handle your problem.'

The Colombian laughed sharply. 'If only . . . The fact is, I made a mistake in getting too close to Santiago regarding business. He talked me into taking ownership of one of the Gatsos companies, as Kostas did himself. They were very convincing. I had no idea that such profits could be made from shipping. Having an in-house transportation company is useful for Colarmco too.'

Mavros nodded. 'But?'

'But I've just been threatened by Santiago and a Russian called—'

'Igor Gogol?'

Laura Moreno stared at Mavros. 'How did you know?'

'He's on the run after the police raided the nightclub he and his brother own.'

'So he said.' She told them what had happened at Kaisariani.

'The shooting range?' said Nondas. 'Lovely.'

'That's what I thought.'

'So Rojas and Gogol are partners in crime,' Mavros said. 'You should take a look at this.' He handed her the laptop, having refreshed the document.

Laura read it, scrolling down, then turned to him. 'I know nothing about this, but it squares with Santiago's attempts to get me to help him take over the Gatsos group. He's approached a lot of shareholders.'

Mavros looked at Nondas. 'Surely the family will have enough shares to see anyone off.'

'You'd think so,' his brother-in-law said. 'It's become clear that the CD-ROM Loukas supplied doesn't tell the whole story, not least about the holdings he and his relatives have. In any case, Pavlos Gatsos would have had a substantial percentage of the shares and perhaps Myronis was planning on getting hold of his wife's one way or another.'

'I heard about Pavlos's death, of course,' Laura said. 'I was shocked but I can't say Santiago was.'

Mavros was studying her face. He looked away when she met his eyes.

'Why did you both come to Greece?' he asked.

'That was something else Santiago persuaded me to do. He wants to use me as a figurehead for his machinations with the group. My plan was to take a few days away from home so I could convince him I would have no part of what he's doing. I never imagined he would try to press a Russian thug on my company.'

'What exactly do you want from me?' Mavros asked.

Laura bowed her head. 'Protect me?'

Nondas raised an eyebrow.

'That isn't what I do,' Mavros said, wondering why a high-flying and wealthy businesswoman would be so needy. 'I'm a missing persons specialist.'

She gave him a piercing look. 'You're trying to find Kostas Gatsos. I'm part of that case.'

'You are,' he conceded. 'And you must know a lot about Rojas.'

'I do,' she said, with a smile.

Suddenly there was activity at both the bedroom door and the flat entrance. The Fat Man and Marianthi, fully clothed, came out of the former, while the bell at the street door rang.

Mavros left Nondas to do the introductions and answered the entry phone.

'Come on up,' he said, putting the receiver back on the wall. 'It's Lieutenant Babis,' he reported to the others. 'Marianthi, can you take our guest into the bedroom? I don't want the police to know she's with us.' He explained to Laura in English.

If the South American had any reluctance about entering Yiorgos's boudoir, she didn't show it.

The flat bell rang.

'Be a good host, Yiorgo,' Mavros said.

The Fat Man glowered at him then opened up.

The policeman was followed by a muscle-bound young woman, both of them in plain clothes.

'Evening, all,' he said. 'This is Sergeant Elisavet Latsou.' He introduced the three men, getting their names right.

The sergeant sniffed the air. 'Expensive perfume. I can't quite place it.'

'My other half's,' Yiorgos said. 'Only the best for her.'

'Really?' Disbelief dripped from her lips like honey in a ravaged hive.

'Refreshments?' Mavros interjected.

'No, thanks. We won't be staying long.' The lieutenant went over to the open laptop. Just before he got there, Nondas closed it.

'What can we do for you?' Mavros asked.

'I need to talk to you in private,' Babis said. 'How about in there?' He pointed to the bedroom door.

'Er, no,' the Fat Man said. 'It's in a hell of a mess.'

'Follow me.' Mavros led the lieutenant to the bathroom. 'Shall I turn on the taps like in the spy films?'

'That won't be necessary. The brigadier's wondering if you've come across anything we should know about.'

Mavros grinned. 'Sweet. What do I get in return?'

'Sorry?'

'I made it clear that I wouldn't work under surveillance. If you want something from me, I want something back.'

'But we don't have anything. Lavrenti Gogol isn't talking, his brother's gone to ground, and there's nothing on the people who sent the packages.'

'But the ear and nails have been confirmed as belonging to Kostas Gatsos.'

'Yes . . . how did you know that?'

'A not very difficult guess.'

Babis shrugged. 'There, I've given you something. Now it's your turn.'

'What makes you think I have anything?'

'Well, the brigadier—'

'Has a suspicious mind. Look, you lot have been working on the case for a month and you've got nowhere. I've been around for a couple of days and suddenly there's progress. What more does he want?'

The lieutenant gave him the eye. 'Are you pulling a fast one?'

'My speed is limited these days.'

They went back to the *saloni*, where Nondas and the Fat Man were on either side of the female officer on the sofa.

'Come on, sergeant,' Babis said. 'We're finished here.'

'You've got that right,' Yiorgos muttered.

'Are you sure we can't help you with anything?' the lieutenant asked desperately.

'Quite sure, thanks,' Mavros replied. 'Have a good night.'

Elisavet Latsou gave him a fierce look then followed her superior to the door.

'Actually, she could have stayed,' the Fat Man said.

Mavros and Nondas feigned shock.

'How could you?' the former said. 'Your newly acquired other half is only metres away.'

'Piss off.' Yiorgos opened the bedroom door. 'You can come out now. What on earth are you doing?'

The others joined him. Laura Moreno was lying face-up on the bed, Marianthi massaging her feet.

'Reflexology,' she said, looking up. 'I've got a certificate.'

'Why didn't you do that on me?' the Fat Man said.

'All finish,' Marianthi said in English, before turning back to her lover. 'As if you gave me a chance,' she added, in Greek.

Laura sat up and put on her shoes.

'Had me worried there for a moment,' Yiorgos said.

'Right,' said Mavros, 'who wants to come to Lesvos tomorrow?'

Kostas Gatsos was in what he now saw was a room with an arched roof. Curved wooden boards had been fixed over the bricks about a metre above the floor. Where was he? A hole in the ground? There were some islands where houses were built into the side of cliffs. Was he on Santorini?

A wooden chair and table had been brought in, as well as a note pad and a pocket calculator. The clock ticked so loudly that he'd smothered it under his blanket. He could still hear it. He had been in the light for over six hours and he was still in shock. They wanted his money. Everything always came down to that; he of all people should have known.

'Aaaaah!' he shouted.

The balaclava-wearing guard opened the door and looked in. 'You die?'

'That would put paid to your proposition, wouldn't it?'

The door slammed behind him.

Kostas thought about that. If he were to die, his captors wouldn't be able to bring about what they wanted. The problem was, he didn't have it in him to commit suicide. He could have throttled himself with the blanket or stabbed himself with the pen he'd been given, but he was too fond of his life to throw it away. That made him brave. Or did it? He thought of the ancient Greeks who had sacrificed themselves – Leonidas and his Spartans, the Theban Sacred Band, even Socrates, who could have escaped prison before he was forced to drink hemlock. They were real heroes; he'd read about them throughout his life, looking for lessons. But in the final analysis, he was just a pirate with animal cunning and a mind for figures. He threw the calculator against the wall.

Would he give them what they wanted? The sums were huge and would leave him with little to live on, though the family would help. Or would they? He thought of Eirini, his only child now– she had little love for him, particularly because he ignored the useless Vangelis; Loukas was sharp, even Evi had a hard core, and Dinos hated his guts. Then there were the relations by marriage. Although his wives were dead, Pavlos's wife Myrto disliked Kostas so much she had moved to Paris – or so she'd told him. He wasn't sure if Pavlos was aware of that. He suspected Nana, their daughter, far away in New York, cared little for her grandfather.

Fuck the Son and his cronies! He wasn't giving away his billions. They'd have to earn it! They could string him up by hooks, but he didn't think they had the guts. Then he remembered the iron glint in the Son's eyes. He was even more vicious than the Father had been. He would take pleasure in seeing Kostas suffer, the longer the better.

The Son. He gave the impression that he was in charge, but someone else had to be behind him. The stone-hearted torturer would never want money to be wasted on a foundation for the poor and on tax; he would want it for himself. So who had organised the kidnap? Could a member of the family be involved? Was Loukas as daring as that? The little schemer might be. It had been hard to know what he was thinking even when he was a boy – his greatest interest had been drawing maps of imaginary countries, islands with great mountain ranges amid dolphin-haunted seas. That made Kostas think of Anydhros, Waterless, the remote Cycladic island he had bought a decade back and done very little work on. The house there was small and a generator was needed to provide electricity. Boats could approach only in the calmest seas and water had to be brought in by tankers.

With no businesses to run and surrounded by the white crests of the Aegean, Kostas Gatsos knew he would go stark staring mad within a month. His stomach somersaulted as he realised that the Son and the judges would be fully aware of that.

TWENTY-TWO

Mavros sent Nondas off, telling him to check if Babis and his sidekick were keeping watch in the street. He called a few minutes later to say he hadn't seen them.

'What now?' the Fat Man asked.

'I'm sure Laura's had enough of your bedroom. We'll go to my mother's.'

'And tomorrow?'

'I'll let you know about the flight.'

'Not first thing in the morning.'

'Why, have you got something better to do?'

Yiorgos grinned. 'You know, we should take Marianthi to Lesvos. It's a big island and we'll have to hire a car.'

'I'll think about that. Good night.'

Laura waved to Marianthi, who was on the phone to her sitter.

Mavros and Laura walked down the stairs.

'They're a charming couple,' she said.

'That's the first time I've heard that word used about Yiorgos, even in part.'

'I've seen plenty of liars and cheats. He's a good man.'

'He is. And he hasn't had a female friend since I was in my twenties.'

'You know him so long?'

'All my life,' he said, looking around cautiously and leading her on to the street. 'All right, I think it's clear.' He hailed a taxi.

'You're sure it will be all right for me to stay?' Laura asked, drawing her shawl around her shoulders after they'd got in.

'Of course. You've already made friends with Mother, it seems.'

'She is very sympathetic. What is her name?'

'Dorothy.'

'Like the girl in *The Wizard of Oz*.'

'Unlike her in every sense apart from the name. It's Greek, you know, even though my mother's Scottish. It means "Gift of God".'

'You have brothers, sisters?'

'Just Anna, Nondas's wife. She's younger than me though she thinks she isn't.'

There was a pause.

'You are troubled, Alex.'

'I had a brother too. Andonis. He was eleven years older than me and he disappeared when I was ten. During the dictatorship.'

'You never heard what happened?'

'No.' Mavros suddenly remembered the Son's words on a dusty hillside near Delphi six years ago. 'Your brother's alive.' For years he'd hoped the bastard had been telling the truth, but now he was sure it was nothing but a cruel taunt.

The taxi was approaching Kleomenous.

'What about you?' Mavros asked.

'There are five of us. The family's so close I've never felt the need of marrying. Though men keep trying to grab me.' Laura put her hand to her mouth. 'I'm sorry, I don't know why I said that.'

'You had a shock in Kaisariani,' he said, paying the driver. Or was she toying with him?

On the sixth floor Mavros fiddled with the locks. One of the problems of the heavy-duty system they'd applied after the Son's threats was that his mother couldn't apply the chain if he was out after she'd gone to bed. It was a risk, but nothing had ever happened.

He led Laura inside.

'Nice place,' she said, looking around the *saloni*. 'Did you grow up here?'

'No. The family house was near the Fat Man's – Yiorgos's – place. My mother moved here in the late 70s.'

'After your brother had gone. Does that make him seem even more distant?'

Mavros caught her eye and nodded. 'You have more empathy than most.'

She laughed softly. 'People are always telling me I know more about how they feel than they do themselves. I've been called a witch more than once.'

'Well, Circe, let me show you the guestroom.'

'Circe from the *Odyssey*, yes? I read it at school.'

'Good for you. You'll find everything you need, I think. There's an en suite bathroom.'

'Thank you, Alex. I mean for this, but also for taking me under your wing. I will pay, of course.'

'Forget it. The Gatsos family is covering all my expenses as well as remunerating me ridiculously well. What I need to know is if you want to come with us to Lesvos tomorrow.'

'You're going to Kostas's villa?'

'Among other places. Do you know it?'

'I stayed there in the summer.'

'Really? Who was with you?'

'Pavlos, Santiago, Eirini Myroni – without her unpleasant husband, rest his soul – Loukas, Evi and several business contacts of the family.'

Mavros wondered why neither Loukas nor Evi had mentioned that. Then again, he hadn't asked.

'I like the island so, yes, I will accompany you, if I may. Maybe I can help in the villa. I presume that's where we're going?'

Mavros nodded. 'We shouldn't be there for long. I'll organise the tickets.'

'Goodnight,' Laura said, kissing him on the check.

As he walked away, Mavros breathed in her scent. It was unfamiliar, exotic, even wild. The woman had a powerful presence.

On the desk he found a large envelope with a courier's logo. The lawyer Siatkas had done as he'd asked and sent over the threats made to Kostas Gatsos and the responses to them. After he'd booked seats for himself, Laura, the Fat Man and Marianthi on a plane that left in the middle of the afternoon, he ran though the lawyer's print-outs. Most of the messages were from people letting off crisis-inspired steam – 'king of thieves', 'fucking tax-dodger', 'louse on the back of the people' and so on. They had desisted after Siatkas threatened them with libel. He isolated two that seemed more serious. One was a series of densely printed political statements from a group called The Red Terror. He ran an internet check and found a few references in the newspapers. The feeling was that the rants, which had been received by several politicians and businessmen, had been written by disaffected students. They had not been linked to any acts of violence.

The other was a single email addressed to Kostas Gatsos via the group's information address. Dated July 29th of that year, it read:

> You have murdered people, sunk your own ships, broken international embargoes, treated your crews like slaves and defrauded Lloyd's of London, as well as hidden your ill-gotten

gains from the tax authorities. If you hadn't paid off the press and used your influence, your sexual misconduct would have brought you universal opprobrium. Kosta Gatso, you will pay the price for those sins. God the Father and Christ the Son will extract every drop of blood from your veins.

Siatkas had responded to that with his standard threat of legal action, but that was toothless as the sender was called NoMan666 and the email account doubtless untraceable. Mavros considered the content. Had the old man really done all those things? He knew that some shipowners committed criminal acts and he had heard of ships being sunk for the insurance money. But had NoMan666 any grounds for what he – or she, the name could easily be a blind, just as the use of the devil's number was no evidence of Satanism – had written? If so, where had such information originated?

Mavros went down the corridor to his room, passing Laura's door. He was discomfited and he wasn't sure why. The South American attracted him, but he didn't fully trust her. Could she be a plant by Rojas, her experience by the shooting range nothing but a fairy-tale? She seemed genuinely frightened. Then again, people who ran large companies were equipped with titanium backbones. They also knew how to dissemble.

It was only as he lay down on his bed that it struck him. 'God the Father and Christ the Son'. Was the assassin who had threatened him and his family six years ago involved in the kidnap? Why would the Son have advertised that by sending a message in advance? Because he was a megalomaniac and psychotic sociopath who couldn't resist playing games, even when he was the only one who understood them.

Sleep did not come easily that night for Mavros.

The dawn breeze woke Jim Thomson and he got up to open the shutters. To the south the sea was calm beyond the town, a low moon casting the last of its light on the surface. He got dressed and quietly made his way out of the house. The sun was behind the mountains and the day was brightening only slowly. He stood on the ridge looking down at the red-tiled roofs and the fishing boats in the small harbour, then turned the other way. Across the straits Turkey ended in a rocky knuckle. Closer to hand a path led to a cemetery surrounded by cypress trees and he decided to walk to it.

He hadn't taken Ivy's ashes with him, but the rocks beyond the trees struck him as a potential place to consign them to the Aegean.

Against a lightening sky Thomson walked down the concrete track. The cemetery was preternaturally serene, the birds only beginning to chirp and the water ahead washing smoothly over the rocks. He went down there and found a niche to sit in. He was wearing only a T-shirt and the temperature hadn't risen much yet. He watched the sea take colour, grey gradually becoming pale blue, then reached forward to put his hand in the shallows. The water was cold and he shivered at the idea of Ivy entering it for the last time after so many swims in the warm southern ocean. But he decided this was the place. Tomorrow he would do what he'd promised.

As he was walking back, he saw a line of trees leading to a large house on a crest of rock above the sea's edge. It had to be the Gatsos villa – he had checked its location when he was on the internet. This was as good a time as any to have a look, before the staff arrived for work. Something more than curiosity was driving him – it was as if the rich man's house was a magnet attracting the man who had narrowly escaped death on the Gatsos-owned *Homeland*, for some as yet unclear purpose.

As he got closer, he made out a two-metre high fence outside the line of trees. Old Gatsos had taken his privacy seriously, not that the security measures had saved him. The fence went down the angle of rocks towards the sea. Without questioning what he was doing Jim headed in that direction, suddenly desperate to get inside the place. When he reached the point where fence met water, he saw that it continued along the breakwater and then went beneath the surface. He was in a dilemma. The only way of getting to the shipowner's house was by entering the element he had avoided for decades. Was it worth it? He looked through the lines of razor wire and saw another fence with a gate between the flat concrete of the dock area and the steps leading up from it. Although there was police tape across the steel barrier, the door itself was slightly open. He decided to brave the water and stripped down to his underpants. Why now, he asked himself. To get a feeling for where Ivy's going? Without warning, he threw up. That did it. He needed to clean himself.

At first the chill waves that were getting up hampered his movements, but he soon found the strokes he had long forgotten and his breathing became more regular. He swam beyond the breakwater and made a wide turn, moving slowly in case he encountered under-water wire. When he was sure he was safe, he headed towards the jetty and climbed up a row of steel rungs in the concrete. He caught his breath and wrung out his pants. What the hell was he doing? He couldn't answer the question, but the act of entering the sea had made him fearless. He went up the first steps, tore away the police tape and pushed open the gate.

The steps went up in a series of switchbacks to the low wall surrounding a wide terrace. Thomson moved slowly, unsure if there were guards still on the premises. A large bougainvillea covered a blue pergola, under which wooden loungers lay in disarray. Some of the cushions were on the tiles. He went up to the full-height sliding windows and looked inside. A space had been cleared to his left, the furniture removed to show a deep red stain on the floor tiles and a large splash of similar colour on the far white wall. This was where the old man's son had been shot. Thomson shivered, and not from the cold. He tried to shift the windows but they were all locked.

Glancing around, he saw an unfenced stair built against the wall on his right. He went up it, poking his head over the top of a parapet. It was protected by a wooden roof and had presumably been a guard post. The rough stone was smooth where sleeves and arms had moved against it. There was a 360 degree view, the roofs on the upper ridge of Molyvos and the castle walls higher up outlined in the brighter blue of the morning.

Thomson blinked and turned towards the mountain to the east. The sun was above its lower slopes now, rays glinting on the radio mast and satellite dish on top of the tiles. He put his hand against his forehead and squinted. Something green and oval was lying in the drain pipe beneath the roof. There was a metallic handle leading from its top with a thin ring a little below. Three letters and a number, the former in what he thought was Cyrillic script, had been stencilled on the bulging side.

He was no expert but it looked very like a hand grenade.

Mavros's mother showed no surprise when Laura came into the *saloni* in mid-morning. 'Ah, Ms . . .'

'Moreno, but please call me Laura. Alex invited me to stay, I hope that's all right. I'm sorry, I never oversleep.'

'As you can see, my son almost always does so. Help yourself to his breakfast.' The old woman smiled encouragingly.

'He has a sweet tooth, I see.'

The table was covered with croissants, cake and several jams.

'Oddly, he takes his coffee without sugar. The rest is his Scottish genes. My country is notorious for its sugary diet.'

Laura poured herself orange juice and tore apart a croissant before dipping the pieces in strawberry jam.

'That's home-made,' Dorothy said, 'but not by me. I used to until I had a stroke. I still work though.'

'Alex told me about your publishing company.'

'He's been a great help. And you? What brings you to the Edinburgh of the south? My Greek friends hate me calling it that.'

Laura laughed. 'I've been to Edinburgh. It's a beautiful city.'

'In the centre, yes. Some of the poor areas on the outskirts are as bad as any in Europe.'

'Everywhere it's the same – certainly in Bogotá.'

'My, you're a long way from home.'

'I run a family company, though it's rather larger than yours.'

'And what do you produce?'

'Weapons. We supply several national armies.'

Dorothy failed to hide her surprise. 'You're an arms dealer?'

'No, no, we manufacture and I make sure we work directly with end-users. Dealers in what we make are . . . unpleasant people.'

'Ah. You're here on business?'

'Of a sort.'

'Only I don't think the Greek armed forces are going to be in the market for new weapon supplies in the near future.'

Laura finished her juice. 'I've read of the economic situation. No, I have a small interest in shipping.'

Mavros appeared, his hair wrapped in a towel. 'You're up,' he said to the guest.

'As you see. Good morning.'

Mavros returned the greeting and then kissed his mother on the cheek.

'Laura makes guns,' Dorothy said.

'I know. I'm keeping my head down.'

'Idiot.' Dorothy raised an eyebrow, her curiosity unspoken but clear enough.

'Laura knows Kostas Gatsos,' Mavros said. 'We're going to Lesvos to check some leads out.'

'Are you? Let me see, I'm sure we have friends on the island. Kiki
. . . no, her husband died last year and she's back in Athens . . .'
'It's all right, Mother. We don't need somewhere to stay. I've
booked rooms.'
There was a short silence.
'How about some Greek coffee?' Mavros said to Laura. 'Though
I can't promise it'll be as good as you've had from Kostas Gatsos.'
'Yes, please. Like you I take no sugar.'
'Except in pastries and jam.'
She smiled. 'Your standard breakfast, I gather.'
'Oh no. The Fat Man's *galaktoboureko* – custard pie – is what
I go for when I have the chance. Which is at least three times a
week. Back in a few minutes.'
Laura watched him go and turned to Dorothy. She had noticed
the photographs on the dresser.
'Alex told me about your older son.'
Dorothy's eyes widened. 'Did he? It's unusual for him to open
up to a stranger. Andonis . . . Andonis is the mystery in our family,
the gap, the silence. We've got on with our lives, but deep down he
still defines us all.' She smiled sadly. 'We're incomplete, craving
even the worst sign of what happened to him. He's why Alex became
a missing persons specialist, of course.'
Laura went over and sat by her, then took her wrinkled hand. 'In
my country people disappear all the time. It is a ruinous situation.
Did I say that right?'
Dorothy leaned against her. 'You did, my dear. In truth, we are
ruined.'
Mavros reappeared with a tray on which he had put two small
cups. He peered at them dubiously then went to the table. Laura
joined him shortly afterwards and they began to speak about Santiago
Rojas and the Gatsos group.
When they left an hour later, Dorothy held her son back at the
door and whispered to him, 'She's a good one. Don't let her go.'
Mavros gave her an infuriated look, before kissing her on the
cheek and reminding her to apply the bolts and chain. As he followed
the Colombian to the lift he shook his head. Trust his mother. He
hadn't even laid lips on Laura Moreno and there was Dorothy
envisaging them as a couple.
She was usually a good judge of character, though.

TWENTY-THREE

Nikos Kriaras tossed the print-out on to his desk. 'Well done, lieutenant – at last. Now what are you going to do about it?'

'Follow them. I've booked two seats on the same flight.'

'Two? I'm not going back to that lesbian-overrun island.'

Babis looked above the brigadier's head. 'I didn't think you were, sir. Permission to take Sergeant Latsou.'

'On the grounds that you and she did such a sterling job finding nothing out from your meeting with Mavros at his obese companion's shit hole last night?'

'It was her idea to run Mavros's name through today's flight manifests.'

'Was it now?' Kriaras grinned. 'Maybe she's in line for promotion.'

Lieutenant Haralambidhis stood to attention, his face impassive but his mind roiling.

'Very well, take her with you. Need I remind you about the regulations concerning fraternisation?'

'No, sir.' Babis was innocent of any infraction. When he'd tried to take Elisavet's hand last night she'd pulled it away, though her smile gave him grounds for hope. 'Something else, sir. You notice the highlighted name Moreno, Laura?'

The brigadier stretched forward, examined the list and nodded impatiently.

'She's one of the Colombians who's a shareholder in the Gatsos group. A further check of flight manifests showed that she arrived from Bogotá via Madrid yesterday. Another Colombian, Santiago Rojas, was on the same plane.'

'Where is he?'

'Not going to Lesvos.'

Kriaras twitched his head. 'So what, Haralambidhi? Is this man of interest to us?'

'Potentially. He's also a shareholder in the Gatsos group and he owns a ship, the *Greenland Reefer*, that's under arrest in

South Korea for breaking the embargo on trading with the North.'

'Did you find that out or was it another of the thrusting Sergeant Latsou's contributions?

'I did, sir.'

'What course of action do you propose?'

'We could find out where he's staying, put a tail on him.'

'Why? Because he owns a ship that's been arrested on the other side of the world? That isn't a crime under Greek law.'

'Perhaps you could ask Loukas Gatsos about him, sir.'

'Perhaps I could.' The brigadier frowned. 'Why?'

'Because he might be involved in the kidnapping – there are suspicions that he's a drug supplier, as well as in league with the revolutionary FARC guerillas.'

'Whose are these suspicions?'

'The FBI's. I spoke to their man here.'

'You did what?'

'You were in the management meeting, sir. I decided it couldn't wait.'

Nikos Kriaras damped down the volcano that was threatening to blow inside him – inter-agency liaison was his domain. 'I'd rather you didn't go tripping off to Lesvos, but I can see the virtues of keeping an eye on Mavros. Make sure he doesn't spot you.'

'No, sir, I mean, yes, sir. We've come up with a good cover.'

The brigadier eyed him doubtfully. 'All right, but keep in regular contact. Don't turn your mobile off for a second. And minimise expenses.'

Lieutenant Babis saluted and left the office. The expenses might not be a problem. He was going to suggest to Elisavet that they share a room – for the benefit of the Greek tax payer, of course.

Mavros and Laura sat together on the plane, which was only half full. The Fat Man and Marianthi – who had managed to talk her mother into looking after her kids – had started off immediately behind them, but had moved to a more secluded area.

'Touching, aren't they?' said Mavros.

Laura laughed. 'You're very cynical, Alex Mavros.'

'With Yiorgos for a best friend, I have to be.'

'I told you, he's a good man. So are you.'

'That's Latin American candor, is it?'

'Maybe.' She looked out of the window. 'When I was at Yale, my room mates laughed at me because I always said what I thought. I learned from that. In Colombia I have a reputation for being reserved. Steely, even.'

Mavros smiled. 'I'd have difficulties with the man or woman in the Bogotá street then.'

'I'm not always like this. I'm relieved to get away from Santiago.' Her tone was suddenly less confident. 'And from Athens. I don't want to see the Gatsos family at this time.'

'Why not?'

Laura was staring out of the window. 'The sea is white.'

Mavros moved his head. 'Little white goats, they're called here. White horses in English. At this time of year the blue isn't as bright as you'll have seen in summer.'

'The Gatsos family – I don't know what I'd say to them, not least because I know Santiago is scheming against them.'

'You could tell them.'

She turned to him. 'Yes, but that would make Santiago my enemy, which would not be good for Colarmco. His company is big and he has many politicians in his pocket. I fear for my family as well as myself.' Her face hardened. 'But I don't take well to being threatened.'

Mavros took in the mixture of emotions. 'Why do you think Rojas got into shipping? If he's a drugs kingpin, he'll be using small aircraft and boats rather than ocean-going vessels to move his product, won't he?'

Laura nodded. 'It's true. I think he is power-mad. Kostas Gatsos is one of the world's best-known tycoons. What better target for Santiago to take on and beat?'

'But does that include kidnapping?'

'After he turned that Russian on me yesterday, I think anything's possible.'

'Just as well you came to me.'

She smiled. 'I think so.'

The plane landed shortly afterwards. The Fat Man and Marianthi followed them off. None of them noticed the couple in flowered shirts and unseasonal shorts that hung back until they'd all disembarked.

The hire car that Mavros had booked – a Japanese 4x4 – was

waiting outside the airport. Marianthi got in the driver's door and Yiorgos joined her in the front.

'Where to?' she asked

'Molyvos,' Mavros replied. 'I want to see the Gatsos villa and there's a local businessman who might be able to help us. For a start.'

'Two hours at most,' Marianthi said, handing the map to the Fat Man.

'Have you been here before?' Mavros asked.

'No. But with the bull bars on this thing, nobody's going to slow us down.'

'Great,' Mavros mumbled.

They drove across the island as the sun began to fail. The hills were verdant after the first rains and the olive trees strained against the wind that had got up from the north.

'It's beautiful,' Laura said. 'But not like my country.'

'Tell me,' Mavros said.

'We are high, nearer the clouds – not just in Bogotá but in the mountains where my people originated. Well, some of my people – I am of mixed descent, native and Spanish.'

That explains the unusual looks, Mavros thought.

'For me the sea is a foreign element, while it's in your veins. My spirit resides in the high places, where the peaks point to heaven and the condors hang on the thin air like messengers from another realm.'

'You're a poet.'

She laughed. 'I used to do well with writing at school and university, but my father always made it clear that my future would be in the business, despite my brothers and the fact that they are more westernised. They have never been to our mother's tribal region.'

Mavros was beginning to realise that he had a seriously exotic creature next to him. Or was that just a card she was playing to disorient him, to make him spill his thoughts? If she was Rojas's spy she was a hell of an actress, but he couldn't rule out the possibility.

The sun was setting over the choppy sea as the lights of Molyvos appeared in the distance.

'See?' said Marianthi, looking at the dashboard. 'One hour and forty-three minutes.'

'My heroine,' said Yiorgos.

'Yeah, yeah,' said Mavros.

*   *   *

Santiago Rojas had been unimpressed to find that Laura hadn't returned to the hotel in the evening, but he assumed she'd gone to dinner with Loukas and Evi Gatsos. When she failed to show in the morning, he began to worry. Had his use of Igor Gogol been a step too far? The stupid bitch. If she talked to anyone, she'd be sorry. In the meantime, he had Greek investors to meet and would have to come up with an excuse for her absence. Illness was the easiest solution. He'd tell them she had a weak constitution, making it even more obvious that he was the main man. On the other hand, he knew how tough Laura was when it came to business.

His suite was large but characterless, not that he cared. He spent more than a quarter of each year in similar places across the Americas and the wider world. They served his needs adequately. The provision of high-class tarts was easily arranged, but the one he'd had last night – Moldovan, she'd said, which was a first for him – had been too eager to please. That was what drove him crazy about Laura. She wouldn't give in to him, she sometimes looked at him as if he was a piece of shit. Which he was, of course, he had no illusions about that. But he was soon going to be exceptionally rich and influential. Surely even she couldn't resist that. If she did he would ruin Colarmco's operations with strikes and attacks on shipments, then buy the company on the cheap. That would teach her how worthless her self-regard was. She could go to a hut in the mountains and chew coca like her ancestors.

His mobile rang and he answered it, bending forward as he listened.

'No, Loukas,' he said, after the irate young man had finished, 'I'm sorry I didn't contact you when I arrived yesterday, but a labour dispute flared up in one of our largest mills. My company involved with FARC and drug production? I can't imagine where you heard such a thing. Not all Colombians dip their hands in the white stuff. The FBI don't know their dicks from their fingers. What was that? You haven't seen Laura? No, she was quite distracted when I last saw her. Bad news from home, I think. The arms trade is a difficult one the way the global economy's heading. I'm busy all day, but hope to see you for dinner tomorrow.'

So much for Laura. If she turned up he would treat her like a fractious teenager and if she didn't it would be her loss.

His phone rang again. This time he bent over even further,

straining to catch every word. The news was interesting, very interesting indeed.

Mavros and company had checked into a guest house near the harbour at Molyvos. They met up half an hour later and repaired to a taverna that their host had recommended. The place was almost empty, a white-haired man in the corner with his head bent over his food and a trio of old loudmouths near the door. The north wind ensured that no one was sitting outside.

The Fat Man went to the kitchen and did his thing.

'Spaghetti with lobster for five and a large salad, all right?' he said on his return. 'Oh, and some *mezedhes*.'

The selection of appetizers – pieces of octopus with oregano, small cheese pies, small fish in vinegar – arrived with a litre of white wine. Glasses were filled and chinked before the food was attacked. No one had eaten since the early afternoon.

The only person who wasn't concentrating on what was on the table was Mavros. He was looking at his phone, trying to find a photograph. When he did, he compared it with one of the men at the front of the taverna.

'That's Thanasis Gritsis,' he said to Yiorgos quietly. 'The one with the gold chain.'

'I've seen him before,' Laura said. 'He had an argument with Kostas here in the summer.' She smiled. 'The old man threw wine over him.'

'So I heard. Excuse me.' Mavros got up and went over to the table. 'Mr Gritsi? Could I have a word?'

'Speak, hippy.'

The portly man's companions laughed.

'In private would be better for both of us.'

Gritsis glared at him and then turned his gaze on the table to the rear. It looked like he recognised Laura.

'Is this about that fucker Gatsos?'

'Why don't we step outside? We'll stay in sight of your friends if you're worried.'

Gritsis reacted as expected. 'Worried by a washed out long-hair? Do you know who I am?'

Mavros nodded respectfully and opened the door. Thanasis Gritsis heaved himself from the table and followed him. They stood on the taverna's deserted terrace.

'What's this about? Who the hell are you?'

Mavros gave him a card. 'As you surmised, I'm working on the kidnapping. I was wondering if there was anything you could tell me about it.'

'Me? What would I know? Anyway, I've spoken to the police.'

'I've seen the file. You were less than frank.'

Gritsis took a step towards him. 'What the fuck does that mean?' Mavros hadn't moved and their faces were now only a few centimetres apart. 'You omitted to mention that you had a longstanding feud with Kostas Gatsos.'

'What are you saying? That I had him kidnapped?'

'I'd say that was beyond your capabilities. Gritsis Industries no longer produce olive oil, soap or ouzo. You're living on your savings, which I have no doubt are substantial but not sufficient to hire professional operators.'

Gritsis' chest had deflated. 'How do you know this?'

'When you have the Gatsos wealth behind you, nothing remains secret.'

'Except where the decrepit pirate is right now.'

Mavros smiled. 'True. Tell me about the feud. To put your mind at rest, I don't think you know anything about the kidnap.'

'Thanks,' Gritsis said sarcastically.

'On the other hand, if I later find out that you've concealed information from me, I'll make sure the tax authorities run a very exhaustive audit on your finances and those of your friends.'

Gritsis glanced inside, turning away when Makis Theotokis and Stelios Xenos gave him questioning looks.

'I need to sit down,' he said, staggering slightly.

Mavros took his arm and helped him to a chair, then sat next to him.

'Are you all right?'

'My heart's not so good and this isn't helping.'

'Talk and it'll soon be over.'

'There isn't much to it, believe me. Gatsos bought a piece of land I'd had my eye on for decades and built his ugly pile there. An outsider, for God's sake. He claims he's a local, but he was only on Lesvos for a few months when he was a kid. I argued with him more than once and he told me to fuck off. When I set my lawyers on him, he got his people to burn down one of my factories.'

'Can you prove that?'

'Of course not, but I'm sure of it. That was the beginning of my company's decline.'

'So you had a strong motive to dispose of him one way or another.'

Gritsis's face whitened. 'What do you mean?'

Mavros ignored that. 'You live here, don't you?'

'I have a house in Mytilene, but I've always spent the weekends and holidays in Molyvos. Now I stay here most of the time.'

'That means you'll have picked up plenty of gossip about what goes on at the villa.'

'I don't deal in gossip.'

'Let me ask some specific questions. Did you hear about anyone taking an interest in the villa in the weeks and months before the kidnap?'

Gritsis stared at him. 'You mean like they were casing the joint?'

'Could be.'

'He had guards, you know – big Russian brutes.'

Thanasis Gritsis looked around. 'Listen, I haven't told anyone this and I don't want it getting back to me.'

'It won't – as long as we aren't seen together for longer than it takes.'

'All right, all right. There was a fisherman who used to work off the Gatsos place, Pipinos was his name. He told me that one of those gin palaces was often in the vicinity – not close, but definitely a presence.'

'A motor yacht?'

'Yes, those things show-off Athenians drive around in during the summer – like sea-going 4x4s.'

'Did Pipinos see who was on it?'

'That was the thing. The people weren't the usual clueless city-types. They were all burly men in black T-shirts and shorts. Some of them would go diving, even though the water there's too deep for spear-fishing.'

'Are you sure they weren't guests of Gatsos or more guards?'

'Yes. Pipinos saw them head off at full speed one time the Gatsos boat came out.'

Mavros studied his interlocutor's expression and decided he was telling the truth.

'Where is this Pipinos?'

'That's the thing. His *kaïki* was found one day in late August near the Turkish side. Pipinos wasn't on board and there's been no sign of him since. But I'll tell you what makes me suspicious. The forward anchor was missing.'

'Accident? Suicide?'

'Pipinos was very experienced. As for suicide, his only daughter was getting married a few weeks later. Besides, he wasn't that sort.'

'Who do you think murdered him then? Why didn't you tell the police?'

Gritsis's jowled chin sank to his thick neck. 'I'm a coward like everyone else, you fucker. After Gatsos was kidnapped, I didn't want the people who shot his son and his guards coming after me. Besides, where's the proof?'

Mavros leaned closer. 'You've got insurance, haven't you? What is it, a photograph?'

'Yes, of the boat. I told Pipinos to take one for his own safety.'

'That was smart of you. It didn't occur to you that telling Kostas Gatsos about these people might have prevented his kidnap?'

'Like I care. What am I, his guardian angel?'

'Give me it. Now.'

'My lawyer has the original. I've got a copy at home.'

'I'll come with you. Tell your friends you'll be back shortly.'

Gritsis did so. The others watched uneasily as he and Mavros disappeared round the corner of the old warehouse.

Ten minutes later they returned, though the trio of old men departed almost immediately.

'I kept you some lobster,' Laura said, giving the Fat Man a triumphant look. 'And some pasta.'

'What was that all about?' Yiorgos asked.

'I'll tell you later.'

As Mavros started to eat, he caught a glimpse of the man in the corner. Their eyes met briefly and then a copy of the *International Herald Tribune* was moved sideways to break contact.

TWENTY-FOUR

Kostas Gatsos was led into the judging chamber and sat on the chair in front of the table, his ankles chained to the floor. The people in the crocodile, bird of prey, skull and octopus masks were there again. The Son was sitting in the centre, his head and face uncovered.

'Time's up,' he said. 'Will you do as required?'

Kostas sat still, his favourite line of Tennyson running continuously through his mind – 'To strive, to seek, to find, and not to yield'.

'Mr Gatso, your time is up,' the Son repeated.

There was no reply.

The five heads clustered together.

'Very well,' the Son said, after they had separated, 'you leave us no choice.'

Kostas waited until he'd been unchained. 'Fuck you and fuck your children, your mothers and your grandmothers!' he yelled.

The guard backhanded him across the cheek and he fell sideways.

'You can't take my money!' Kostas said, his voice shrill. 'Loukas will stop you, the shareholders will stop you.'

The Son stood up. 'You think so, old man? Would it interest you to know that many of the shareholders are ready to remove you from your position as president of the Gatsos group?'

'Liar!'

The Son started reading from a list of names.

Kostas listened carefully until the recital ended. 'Their shares come to no more than 30% of total holdings.'

'True,' the Son said mildly. 'To get over 50% several of the close family would have to side with the rebels'

Kostas was pulled to his feet. 'That will never happen,' he said, shaking off the guard's hand.

'Are you sure of that?'

'Of course.'

The Son nodded to the figure in the crocodile mask. It was removed to reveal Kostas's daughter Eirini. Before he could react, the octopus head came off. His son Pavlos's wife Myrto sat smiling at him. Then the bird of prey's head was lifted from that of her daughter Nana.

'Unbelievable!' Kostas gasped.

'But true,' said the Son.

'What are you crazy women doing?' the old man screamed. 'You'd be on the street without me!'

Eirini gave him a sharp smile. 'Everything is about you, isn't it, *Baba*? You've spent years despising my husband and son. Did you really think that wouldn't hurt me?'

'The same with Pavlos,' said Myrto. 'You treated him like a slave and Nana like a deserter when she went to New York.'

Her daughter nodded. 'We think it's time you retired, *Pappou*. I'm sure you'll be able to find a Ukrainian hooker to keep you warm.'

'You all happily took the money provided by the group,' Kostas said, his tone was less assured. 'You're really selling me out?'

The women looked down on him, making no attempt to hide their contempt.

'You realise, of course,' said the Son, 'that your family members only came for today's judgement. The earlier judges were who they said they were – people whose lives you ruined.' He turned to his left. 'Would you like to see who's concealed by the remaining mask?'

'To hell with all of you,' the old man said, but he couldn't resist looking. 'You!'

Santiago Rojas stared at him as if he was a scab-ridden dog. 'Your time is over,' he said, turning to the others exultantly.

Kostas's four traitors left the room without a further glance at him.

'I imagine you'll be looking forward to getting out of this place,' the Son said, stepping down from the dais.

'Fuck you,' Kostas muttered.

'But first there's a formality we have to go through.'

'What do you mean?'

The Son smiled. 'Your punishment has still not been carried out. Bring him to the torture chamber.'

Kostas watched as the muscular figure strode ahead. He could understand Myrto and Nana caring nothing for him, let alone the drug-dealing piece of shit Rojas – they weren't Gatsos blood; but his own daughter Eirini? What had happened to turn her against him?

Not long afterwards, when the first hooks had been applied, the Son told him about Vangelis Myronis's death. He should have known his useless son-in-law would extract a price, even from the after life.

Kostas Gatsos wished he'd already crossed the bar, as Tennyson had put it, but his passage was going to be a very arduous one. The tape over his mouth meant he couldn't even scream.

After dinner Mavros and the others went to a bar for a night cap and then headed back to the guest house. He had already sent the photograph of the boat to Loukas and asked him to run a check: its name, *Meltemi Rider 7*, was visible at the bow.

'What are we doing tomorrow?' the Fat Man asked, one arm round Marianthi.

'We'll check the villa. You never know what the police might have missed.'

'Right,' said Yiorgos. 'Breakfast at 9?'

'I suppose so,' Mavros said unenthusiastically.

'I'll have done fifty laps of the pool by then,' Laura said.

'It isn't very long,' he pointed out.

'All right, a hundred. Actually I think I'll find a beach. I want to taste the sea.'

The Fat Man and Marianthi had already gone upstairs.

'I have a bottle of aguardiente,' Laura said.

'Should I be frightened?'

'No,' she laughed. 'It's only 30% proof. Although sugar cane's the main ingredient, it has an aniseed taste.'

'Colombian ouzo?'

'Sort of.'

'All right, I'll try anything once.'

She led him into her room. It was larger than his, with a four-poster bed draped by a mosquito net.

'Huh,' he said. 'I've only got an electric repellent.'

'Ladies need pampering,' Laura said, handing him a glass. 'Salud!'

They drank and the top of his head remained on, just.

'Not bad.' He followed her to a sofa by the window. The shutters were still open and the lights of the town pulsed in the gusty night.

'You have no woman, Alex Mavros?' she said, crossing her legs.
'Not so you'd notice.'
'Pardon?'
Mavros took a deep breath and told her about Niki, then about
the threat to Gatsos that could have come from the Son.
'That's awful,' she said, clutching his forearm. 'You think this
man killed your Niki and took Kostas?'
'There isn't much evidence in either case, but I'm sure he has
some involvement in the former. As for Gatsos, I can't tell. Whoever
took him has covered their steps very well. What I don't understand
is why Pavlos was shot. If his father was taken to facilitate the
take-over of the group, something he was working on, then why is
he dead? I'm beginning to wonder if there's more than one set of
kidnappers, or at least people with different aims.'
Laura looked at him. 'You're taking a risk telling me such things.
How can you be sure I'm not a – what is the word – plant?'
'You don't look like a geranium.'
She slapped his hand lightly. 'You know what I mean.'
'I do and I can't be sure. But in my business, even though I've
been out of it for five years, you get a sense for people who aren't
what they seem.'
'And I am not one of those?'
'Everyone dissembles. The question is, how much?'
She drank again and smiled. 'So am I dissembling now?'
Mavros felt a warm wave flood across his body. It was a long
time since that had happened. He became reckless.
'You're trying not to let your desire for me become obvious.'
Laura Moreno wasn't shocked. She moved her face closer to his
and held his gaze.
'And you?' she said, her voice low.
'I'm failing abysmally to do the same.'
They kissed, aniseed on their lips and tongues. Then their hands
began to move across each other's bodies, parting clothing and
slipping on to burning flesh.
At some point Mavros detached his mouth. 'I think . . . I think
we should move to the bed. I'm sure I heard a mosquito.'
Laura laughed. 'I can hear hundreds.'
Soon the net was closed around the bed and clothes were removed.
In their cocoon the lovers inhabited a private paradise.

*   *   *

Again Jim Thomson woke early. He had slept very little, rolling about for hours before he slipped into unconsciousness. He was going to dispose of Ivy's ashes that morning, but that thought wasn't what kept him awake – it was the long-haired man with the stubbled face in the taverna who'd done that. He'd looked him up on the internet after he'd been in Athens and found photos of him in online newspaper archives. His hair was greyer and his face more lined, but it was unquestionably him: Alex, little Alex. He remembered playing with him when he was a boy, even though he himself had been much older. That came from the time he had repressed for so long and the memory was hazy. Smiles and laughter, joy when he saw his brother, those came back to him. Alex Mavros. He was presumably following some lead on the Gatsos kidnap. He had considered talking to him in the taverna but he hadn't been able to – not with other people there. Alex had gone outside with the loud-mouth called Gritsis for some time. What had he discovered?

Thomson remembered the eyes – blue, but with a splash of brown in the left one. The boy had been shy about the flaw but he seemed to have got over it. It was obvious there was chemistry between him and the pale brown-skinned woman. She was stunning, a South American he guessed. There had been times in Brazilian and Venezuelan ports that he'd never wanted to suppress, even after he was with Ivy.

The time had finally arrived. He got up and washed his face, then put on the clean clothes he had ironed the night before. He wasn't wearing a suit or tie, but he wanted to look his best. Ivy always smiled when she saw him in the new clothes she'd bought. 'My handsome man,' she'd say. 'It was a happy chance that brought us together.'

But now to part for the final time. He picked up the urn and left the house. On his way down the cobbled lane that led to the northern edge of the town, he picked a few bougainvillea blooms, stabbing his fingertips on the thorns. He walked down the road to the cemetery into the northerly. The sea was heaving, waves dashing against the rocks below. He'd be lucky to get away without a soaking, not that he was bothered by that prospect after his swim to the Gatsos place. He'd been going to take a small branch of cypress as he passed along the enclosure of the dead, but that wasn't right for Ivy. She had been for life and was now destined for eternal movement. The earthbound tree was inappropriate. Blossom that faded quickly was better, though the sea was what she had wanted as her last home; she understood her own nature better than anyone.

Thomson scrambled over the wet rocks, the urn under his arm like a rugby ball – he had watched many games on the TV without understanding what the players got out of the violent contact sport. They were lucky; they hadn't been through what he had at their age. He found the spot he'd decided on and kneeled down on the rough stone. Spray came over him and he looked out at the sea. In the early morning light it was grey, but there were white crests and curls as the wind beat down. He struggled to get the top of the urn off and then leaned forward, his hand over the gritty contents.

'Go, Ivy,' he said, his words torn away by a strong gust. 'Go to your ancestral element. I hope I'll be able to join you. Go, my Ivy. You're free.'

He let the ashes sprinkle over the water, watching as they disappeared almost immediately in the surf. When the urn was empty he sent it in after her. It was gone in an instant as well. Then the white sea splashed him from head to toe. He stood up and stepped away, content to have the last of Ivy on clothes he would never wash again.

At breakfast the Fat Man gave Mavros a look that showed he'd understood immediately what had happened between him and Laura. Their faces must have given them away. Marianthi was more discreet, concentrating on the fresh bread and jam.

'Morning,' Mavros said, reaching for a jug of juice.

'It certainly is from where I'm sitting,' said Yiorgos. He smiled at Laura, who caught his eye with no sign of embarrassment.

'Right,' replied Mavros. 'Here's the plan. We drive over to the Gatsos villa and see if we can get in. If we're lucky there won't be a police presence any more.'

'You're going to break in again?' the Fat Man said.

'Again?' repeated Marianthi.

'He's always doing it,' Yiorgos said, putting his head down. His plate was filled with cheese, bread and biscuits.

'What's he saying?' Laura asked.

'Nothing. I was just outlining what we'll do today. First we'll go over to the villa. Maybe you'll notice if there's anything different.'

'All right.' Her hand disappeared beneath the table and squeezed his thigh. 'But I need to show you something first.' She got up, leaving a half-eaten roll, and walked elegantly to the staircase.

'And I need to check if Loukas has sent back anything on the boat,' Mavros said, leaving at speed.

Laura's door was ajar. He knocked and went in. She was naked on the bed, her skin glowing against the white sheet.

'I've seen that before,' he said, closing and locking the door, then struggling out of his trousers.

'Not in daylight,' she said, putting a hand between her legs.

Their pleasure was quick and torrid, a need that both had to satisfy without delay.

After catching his breath, Mavros booted up his laptop. There was a message from Loukas:

> *Meltemi Rider 7* – Manhattan 66 model, built Gibraltar 2006, length 22.10 metres, breadth 5.20 m, draft 1.50 m, top speed 31 knots, sleeps eight comfortably, value around one million euros, chartered from August 1st to September 30th to company owned by Pyotr Alenov, suspected front man of Russian oligarch Sergei Potemkin, redelivered on latter date to Alimos marina. Potemkin has interests in Black Sea and global shipping and trade; he is also suspected of drug dealing by Interpol and Europol, but no charges have been brought. He is close to Russian leadership. Why interest in boat? Where are you?

Mavros felt Laura's warm breath on his shoulder.

'Sergei Potemkin? I've met him. He's a friend of Santiago's. Kostas Gatsos knows him too. I've never heard of the other man.'

'I'm not surprised. Loukas probably had to pay a lot for the link to Potemkin. Oligarchs keep their operatives at arm's length in public.' Mavros sat back and ran his hand over his stubble.

'What is it?'

'I'm thinking about whether to tell Loukas we're here. I think I will. There's no point in lying to my—' He broke off.

Laura leaned closer. 'Worrying if you can trust me? Don't worry, I won't tell anyone.' She laughed softly. 'Especially not Santiago.'

'That would be a very bad idea. I'm now wondering if his playmate Igor Gogol is involved with this Potemkin as well.'

'That might explain why Santiago has been so successful in persuading shareholders – he has the Russian's capital behind him.' She shivered. 'Sergei Potemkin is a very cold man.'

'Nice. If he had Kostas Gastos kidnapped, that would explain why there's been no ransom demand.'

Laura stepped away. 'You think he's dead, don't you?'

'Every day that passes it becomes more likely.'

'Poor Kostas. He wasn't the monster people make him out to be. Well, not entirely.'

'I'll take your word for it. Evi feels that way too, but not many others do.'

Laura nodded. 'She's sweet, but there is fire in her.'

Mavros replied to Loukas, saying that he was in Lesvos and would report back later in the day.

'Right,' he said, 'we'd better get going. What? Again?'

They left after they'd briefly gone back to the Happy Isles where the ancient heroes took their post-mortem leisure, although there was no sign of the great Achilles.

Lieutenant Haralambidhis and Sergeant Latsou were in a guest house a hundred metres down the cobbled track from the one Mavros and his group occupied. They had split up the previous evening, Elisavet watching the taverna from across the harbour while Babis kept an eye on the car Mavros had hired. They met up after the targets had returned to their guest house.

'She fancies him,' Elisavet said. 'Can't you see?'

'I wonder if they spent the night together,' he said wistfully. 'Unlike us.' The sergeant had accepted the need for them to share a room, but had wrapped herself up in a sheet and gone straight to sleep.

'What did you expect?' she demanded. 'You're my senior officer.'

'So what?'

Elisavet Latsou sighed. 'God, you're thick, sir. Haven't you noticed? I only have eyes for women.'

Babis groaned. 'Well, you're on the right island.'

'I know,' she said, smiling. 'Molyvos has quite a reputation.'

They were sitting on the terrace, which provided a view up the road to the other guest house.

'They're not exactly making an early start,' the sergeant said, adjusting her sunglasses.

'Maybe they're . . .'

'Maybe. I think we should go and talk to Mr Gritsis. How do you know he didn't tell Mavros more than he told our colleagues last month?'

'Because he's a slimebag. The local people told me he has a grudge against old Gatsos, but he hasn't the wherewithal to do anything about it.'

'We should grill him. Maybe he shot him and dumped his body in a sea cave.'

'What, having also shot the guard and Pavlos Gatsos with his old pals wearing balaclavas? Not very likely.'

'I still think he knows something.' Elisavet Latsou watched as a white-haired man with a deeply lined face walked down the cobbles. 'He was in the taverna last night. Do you think he made contact with Mavros?'

'Do you want to grill him too?' Babis asked ironically. 'He's a tourist, for God's sake.'

The sergeant watched the man with the damp shirt and trousers go by. 'He omitted to take his clothes off when he had his morning swim,' she said.

'Forget him. There's movement up there.'

They watched the two couples emerge from the guest house's gate.

'What do you think?' Babis said. 'Off to the villa?'

'I wish I was a detective.'

'That can be arranged. Or could have been.'

They picked up their bags, put on the baseball caps they'd bought at Athens airport and headed out.

TWENTY-FIVE

Marianthi followed the road round the eastern part of Molyvos, the Genoese castle rising above them like a stone wave, then drove towards Eftalou. Three kilometres later there was an imposing arch on the left. Police tape was wound through both halves of the steel gate, but there didn't seem to be any locks or chains.

'Surely it can't have been left open,' Laura said.

'It's not impossible,' Mavros said, getting out. 'The local police would have been the last ones here. They probably assumed the family would send someone to lock up.'

Laura had joined him at the side of the road. 'It's unlike Loukas to have forgotten such an important thing.'

'He is running a multi-billion-dollar business.'

'There is another possibility,' the Fat Man said across the vehicle's bonnet.

'Someone's broken in.'

'Smartarse,' he said, glowering at Mavros.

'It isn't hugely likely as a burglar wouldn't bother to wind the tape between the bars so diligently.'

'Not impossible,' Yiorgos said grumpily.

'True. You go first.'

'Thanks a lot.'

'Your hands.'

There was a box of rubber gloves in the boot. The Fat Man handed them around.

Marianthi declined. 'I'm not touching anything. I'm the driver, remember?'

'Among other things,' said Yiorgos, moving swiftly away. He started to undo the strips of blue-and-white tape. Mavros helped him and soon the gate was clear.

'Here goes,' the Fat Man said and put his shoulder to the left side.

It opened without difficulty. Mavros did the same with the other half. They stepped through and looked down the long drive. It was lined with oleanders, alternately pink and white. There were taller trees, some of them palms, in the background. The driveway had been asphalted.

'You get back in,' Mavros said to the others. 'I'll close up and drape the tape around.'

Marianthi drove through, waited for Laura and Yiorgos to get in and then floored the accelerator.

'Hey!' Mavros shouted.

The brakes were applied heavily, then the 4x4 reversed towards him.

'Very funny,' he said.

'It was his idea,' the driver said, angling her head towards the Fat Man.

'What a surprise.'

'He has a mental age of nine,' Marianthi said. 'It's sad.'

Laura was still laughing.

'Can we get on, please?' Mavros said testily.

They passed flower beds and a wide lawn, before the house came into view. The architect had clearly been given a free hand.

'Corbusier meets Frank Lloyd Wright,' Laura said. 'That's what Kostas told me.'

'I've seen more attractive bus stations,' Yiorgos said. 'Whoah!'

Marianthi braked hard, stopping a few centimetres in front of a bearded old man holding a garden fork towards them as if it were a weapon. It is a weapon, Mavros thought.

'Who are you?' the local demanded. 'Arsehole press?'

Mavros got out but kept his distance. He identified himself and explained that he worked for the family.

'*Yeia sas*,' Laura said, smiling at the old man.

'*Ach, Kyria Laura*,' he said, launching into a string of Greek.

'He says he's very pleased to see you again and he's very sorry about what happened to Mr Kostas and if he'd been on duty that day he'd have sent the coward kidnappers on their way with spades up their . . . rear ends, and—' Mavros held up a hand and asked the speaker to stop.

'His name is Yannis,' Laura said. 'He showed me the flowers in the summer, not that I could understand their names.'

'Yannis Kipouros,' the old man said, hearing his first name. 'And I don't need any comments about my surname.'

'Yannis the gardener, in name and deed,' the Fat Man said.

'I said, no comments!'

'Kyrie Yanni,' Mavros said, 'did you know the main gate is unlocked?'

'Since the guards left there are no keys. I've told the estate manager, but he's in Athens now. I come in through a side gate – which I keep locked, understand?'

'I'm sure you do,' Mavros said emolliently. 'Can you show us around the place? If you like, I can call Kyrios Loukas.'

'Not necessary. Kyria Laura is all the authority I need. What do you want to see?'

'Inside the villa. Do you have keys?'

'Of course. I water the plants inside too. Follow me.'

Marianthi stayed in the car while the others went up the wide marble steps to the main entrance. The doors were steel, the light streaming in through palm-sized pieces of diamond-shaped glass.

'How did the kidnappers get in?' Mavros asked.

'From what I heard,' said Yiannis, 'one of the doors was left ajar. The police interviewed the staff and one of the maids admitted she'd been outside for a cigarette. I know her, Gogo, she's a good girl. I don't think she was lying.'

'You don't think she'd been bribed?'

The old man turned to Mavros and thought about that. 'I don't know. I haven't noticed her wearing expensive clothes or anything. This was where the guard was shot,' he said, pointing to a red-black stain on the white marble floor. 'I asked if I could clean it – none of the other staff will come in – but the police said no.'

Mavros looked to both sides and then ahead to an ornate stone staircase.

'Left to the library and sunroom,' Laura said, 'and right is the formal drawing room. But Kostas didn't like this floor. He spent all his time on the first and second levels.'

'Notice anything different?'

She turned her head. 'I don't think so.'

'What's upstairs?'

'Bedrooms on the next floor, and on the top the dining room and terrace. We usually ate outside in the evenings. It's beautiful.'

'Did Kyrios Kostas sleep on this floor?' Mavros asked Yiannis.

'No, he had the only bedroom up top.'

'Take us there, please.'

The old man hesitated. 'I don't know if the master would like that.'

Mavros held out his phone. 'Call Kyrios Loukas.'

There was a pause.

'No, it's all right. Kyria Laura knows the way. I have things to do.'

'You've been in Kostas's bedroom?' Mavros asked, after the gardener had gone downstairs.

She laughed. 'He wasn't shy about showing it off. He even told me some of the famous women he'd had in there. My lips are zipped.'

He followed her through a partly open door. The room was huge, even the large bed dwarfed. The windows looked west and north, bougainvillea hanging from pergolas on the terrace.

'What did he do in here? Hold a polo championship?'

'More like show jumping,' Laura said, pointing at the antique furniture that was dotted about.

'I suppose you ride.'

'Of course. Don't you?'

'Not even a motorbike.'

'You don't know what you're missing. You should come to Colombia. There are places you need a horse. Oh.'

Mavros stepped closer. 'What is it?'

She pointed to a gilded escritoire against the wall to their right and went over.

'There was a painting up here.'

'I can see the outline.'

'It was a naïf painting by a local, I forget his name . . .'

'Theophilos?'

'Yes.'

'He's well known. We passed the museum of his work near the airport.'

Laura's fingers were on her smart phone. 'I thought I'd snapped it. Here it is.'

She held up the device and Mavros took in a colourful landscape against which people were dancing. There was a large brown building in the rear, a tall chimney rising from its left side.

'You know him?' she asked.

'I'm not an art expert, but he's the foremost Greek traditional painter. He died before the Second World War.'

Laura was ahead of him. 'Read this.'

Mavros ran down the online encyclopedia page, which told him that Theophilos Hatzimichail or Kephalas had lived between 1870 and 1934, had been mocked for wearing the traditional kilt and had spent much of his life in Volos on the mainland. He worked for food and wine, and it was only after his death that his paintings ended up in the Louvre and other major galleries.

'I took the photo because I liked the figures in old-fashioned costume,' Laura said. 'They reminded me of my own people in the mountains.'

'Did the kidnappers take it?' Mavros said. 'And if so, why?'

'Maybe we can help with that.'

They turned quickly. Lieutenant Haralambidhis and Sergeant Latsou were standing a few metres inside the capacious room. The latter was taking a laptop from her backpack.

'Have you been following us?' Mavros asked.

'Have you been crossing police tape without authority?' was Babis's riposte.

'Here it is,' the sergeant said. 'The housekeeper stated that a Theophilos painting had been taken from the master bedroom. She definitely saw it the morning of the kidnap because she dusted the frame.'

'I wondered when you were going to get your files on computer,' Mavros said, though he was annoyed that he hadn't noticed the report about the missing art work himself.

'Laura Moreno,' Babis said, nodding at the Colombian.

'Impressive,' Mavros said. 'The airline manifest?'

'Correct.'

'You're the least convincing pair of tourists I've ever seen.' Mavros looked away when he heard the Fat Man's voice on the stairs. Shortly afterwards he and Marianthi appeared.

'Great,' said Yiorgos. 'Undercover cops who wouldn't fool a five-year-old.'

The sergeant scowled but her superior ignored the gibe.

'Can I see?' he asked.

Mavros nodded and Laura captured the image again.

'I can't make out the writing along the top.'

'Me neither,' said Mavros. 'Maybe there's a photo shop in Molyvos that can blow it up.'

'We'll come with you,' the lieutenant said.

The group moved downstairs. As Mavros reached the 4x4 the old gardener came up to him, waving his arm.

'I forgot,' he said. 'Someone was here yesterday.'

Babis identified himself.

'Haven't found the master yet, have you?' Yiannis said, spitting on the gravel.

'Who did you see?' the lieutenant said impassively.

'A man with white hair. He swam round the wire and went up the stairs from the jetty. I was on the far side of the garden and he'd gone by the time I came across. I don't think he took anything. Probably just a nosy bastard.'

Elisavet looked meaningfully at Babis, while Mavros, Laura and the Fat Man watched.

'We'll follow you,' Babis said.

Mavros shrugged. 'It's a free country.'

'Unless your name's Kostas Gatsos,' said Sergeant Latsou.

Igor Gogol eased down the throttles of the speedboat as he approached the breakwater at Plomari on the southern coast of Lesvos. The town had a pleasing look, rising up a hill with trees covering the top. At this time of year it was settling down to the quiet days of winter, those who had work in the surviving distilleries and olive-presses thankful for their good fortune. Not that Igor cared. He had flown in on the early morning flight, his fake Greek ID card arousing no suspicions. The rental boat was perhaps a touch attention-seeking, but he had learned that it paid to impress the super-rich and Sergei Potemkin was in the premier league of oligarchs. He hoped he would finally get to meet him. Alenov was a fixer who didn't like to get his hands dirty. That was why he'd hired the Greek psycho to run the kidnap. The Son scared even Igor.

He saw one of the Russian's hard men on the quay, or rather, one of the men who thought they were hard. Putting the engines in neutral, he tossed a mooring rope to the gorilla and completed the docking procedure.

'The boss was expecting you by car, Gogol.'

Igor seized his wrist and pulled him close. 'As I'll tell the Greek, you can never have too many modes of escape. Know what "mode" means?'

The big man's face had turned red.

'Thought not. Know how many bones there are in your wrist? No? The answer's eight. Then there are the ends of the radius and ulna, plus the beginnings of the five metacarpals. Making a total of fifteen.' He caught his captive's eye. 'The real question is, how many do you want me to break?'

'None,' the big man squeaked.

'None, what?'

'None, Mr Gogol.'

'Your wrist survives. For now. Where's the fucking car?'

On the drive inland, the heavy Jeep bouncing over potholes, Igor ran through how he was going to play things again. The Son – what kind of idiotic handle was that? – was supposed to have softened up old Gatsos. The shipowner was to think he would be signing papers to set up his foundation and pay tax and compensation, but in reality he'd be handing over his shares to Potemkin via the Colombian Rojas. After that, there were loose ends to be tied – lines had been overstepped and excesses perpetrated. The Son himself would soon be a target.

Igor sat back and touched the marks on his face. He saw the driver glance at him uneasily, which was the point. He considered stripping off his shirt and giving the foot soldier the full show – his back had not only been tattooed in the prison outside Moscow, but heavily scarred by the beatings he'd taken when he was in his early twenties. They had turned him into a man, they and the reading he had done. The experienced 'thief-in-law' who had taken him under his wing recommended spending as much time as he could with the classics – not just the Russians, though Tolstoy and Dostoyevsky were essential, but the ancient writer Homer. He taught you about physical courage and endurance, although more important were perspicacity, caution, daring and cunning. Igor's hero was Odysseus. Not only had he led his men through ten years of vicious fighting and in-fighting – the Greek kings were like gang bosses, greedy and quick to violence – but he had designed the Wooden Horse that brought down the Trojans. Then he had spent ten years getting home, although many of them were spent with females hungry for him, the witch Circe and the immortal Calypso. Igor thought about the women in his life: a succession of whores, in his early days drug-addicts with addled minds and more recently the pick of the girls conned into leaving home for jobs in the west. But Greece didn't count as a western country. It was Middle Eastern in its levels of graft and corruption – which had suited Igor and Lavrenty fine. He briefly wondered how his brother was getting on in the police cells or prison. He'd have to find a way of getting him out. A helicopter would do it.

Then, as they pulled up behind the dilapidated building, Igor Gogol remembered the woman he'd met by the old execution ground. Laura Moreno. She was one sweet piece of half-breed Colombian ass. And, best of all, Santiago Rojas said he could have her when everything was finished. Rojas wanted her taught a lesson, her and that cocksucker of a private investigator Mavros.

'What's your name?' Igor demanded, as the driver turned off the engine.

'Lev,' came the muted reply.

'You know what it means?'

'Yes.'

'Well, try to be more of a lion then.' Igor opened the door. 'But not when I'm around.'

The photographer in Molyvos hadn't needed to blow up Laura's image of the Theophilos painting. Instead he downloaded it and zoomed in on the writing along the top.

'Feast of St George at the Theotokis factory,' Mavros read.

'Bloody Christians,' muttered the Fat Man, when they got outside, 'taking my name in vain.'

'Theotokis,' Mavros repeated. 'He's one of Gritsis's friends.' He flicked through his notebook. 'Yes, Makis Theotokis.'

Elisavet Latsou was already accessing the police files. 'Here he is. Thomas Theotokis, son of Ion, aged sixty-two, landowner and farmer.'

'Where does he live?' Mavros asked.

'There's an address in Mytilene and one in Plomari.'

'Lot of ouzo-making there,' Yiorgos said, licking his lips.

'Thank you for that contribution,' Mavros said. 'What is it, Babi?'

The lieutenant was looking at him pensively. 'You don't suppose . . .?'

'Kostas Gatsos could be there?' Mavros completed. 'I was just thinking that. Maybe that's why the painting was taken. Although all that's done is make us suspicious.'

'Bit of a long shot,' Yiorgos said. 'There must be dozens of old factories on this island.'

'Then we'll search them all,' said Elisavet firmly.

'We should get hold of Theotokis first,' Mavros said. 'I'm heading to Gritsis's place. Perhaps the pair of them did some kind of deal to get at Kostas Gatsos. The rest of you, go back to the guest house and get ready for a rapid departure.'

'I'm coming with you,' Babis said. 'That's not negotiable.'

Mavros shrugged.

'Me too,' added the sergeant.

Mavros led the way to the well-appointed house halfway up the hill. He looked at his watch. 'It's about lunch time.'

'Hungry?' Babis asked.

'Not particularly, but it increases the possibility he'll be home.'

When they got there Babis applied a heavy hand to the pale blue door.

'Mr Gritsis, please,' he said to the wizened woman who answered after some time.

'We're eating.'

'Never mind that.'

They pushed past her and found Gritsis with a napkin round his neck and a plate of stuffed tomatoes in front of him.

'Take his mobile,' Mavros suggested.

Sergeant Latsou held out her hand.

'What is this?' Gritsis demanded.

'You're under arrest for withholding information pertaining to the Gatsos kidnapping case.' Elisavet turned to the seated man's wife. 'And so are you. No phone calls.'

'What?'

'Where's Makis Theotokis?' the lieutenant asked.

'He left this morning. Back home in Mytilene by now, I should think. How dare you—'

The sergeant deftly handcuffed him and his wife.

'You're coming with us,' Elisavet said.

They went out into the sun, Gritsis's napkin still covering his chest.

'Meet you in a quarter of an hour at the parking place,' Mavros said. 'And don't let him talk to anyone.'

'Yes, sir,' Babis said, under his breath.

The pain still racked him, even though the hooks had been removed some time before. Kostas Gatsos was back in his cell, in the dark. Although his skin hadn't been pierced by all the sharp instruments, he'd let out muffled screams despite the tape over his mouth. He hadn't been lifted up on the terrible apparatus either, but that was only a small mercy.

Still he wouldn't give up. They'd put papers in front of him before he was pierced, but he refused even to look at them, never mind add his signature. He told them to suck their cocks. The Son laughed at that, then told him that his punishment would be spread out over several days.

Could he take it, Kostas asked himself. Yes, he could. That might have been in question before he'd seen his ungrateful cow of a daughter and the two gold diggers on the platform. There had been times he'd been beaten by men, though not many, but he would never allow women to get the better of him. He'd rather die.

Suddenly he started to cry, though he made sure no sound passed his lips.

TWENTY-SIX

Mavros and the others headed down the cobbled lanes to the parking place at the bottom of the town. Laura slipped and he put out a hand quickly.

'Thank you, kind sir,' she said.

'I'm a knight in shining armour.'

'Your hair's long enough.'

'That makes you Queen Guinevere.'

She looked around. 'Doesn't look much like Camelot here. I liked it though.'

'Better than the Villa Gatsos?'

'Actually, yes. The nights were dull there.'

'And you raise your eyebrows about us,' the Fat Man said, from behind.

They found the lieutenant on the phone outside the unmarked car, while Sergeant Latsou kept an eye on the elderly couple in the back seat.

'Does he know anything about Theotokis's properties?' Mavros asked Elisavet.

'Claims he only owns the two we have on file.'

'Maybe he sold one or more others.'

She nodded. 'It would be helpful if this country had a digital land register.'

'Among other things.'

Babis finished his call. 'The brigadier says we're not to involve the Lesvos police. He thinks the kidnappers may have got at someone in a senior position. He's bringing a team over as soon as possible.'

'Meaning?'

'By late evening.'

'Are you prepared to wait that long? Kostas Gatsos is over eighty. He might be close to death.'

The lieutenant glanced at his companion. 'What do you suggest?'

'You pick up Theotokis in Mytilene and squeeze him as hard as you can,' Mavros said. 'If he sold the place to outsiders we may have cracked the case. We'll go to Plomari and wait for you to confirm that.'

'No way.'

'We can hardly go barging into a private citizen's house and drag him out, can we? That's your job.'

'I don't like it. This operation is under police control.'

Mavros glared at him. 'Is that right? What's its name? Operation Screw-Up? Because that's what you people did at the Gogol brothers' place. Besides, I'm not taking control. You told me Kriaras said the locals have to be kept out of the loop. I'm making the best use of the available man- and woman-power.'

'All right,' Babis said. 'But I want your word you won't do anything until we get down there.'

'Done,' Mavros said, turning away.

'No. Give me your word.'

'For God's sake.' Mavros did as he was told.

Shortly afterwards they left in convoy, Elisavet driving the front car. They stayed together until the junction beyond the Gulf of Kalloni, where Marianthi turned south.

'Look at those olive trees,' Laura said. 'I love the grey-green glints from them.'

'So do I,' Mavros said.

'Do you have any Lesbian blood?' she asked.

Mavros laughed and translated for the others.

'No,' he replied. 'Not a drop.'

'What's so fun . . . oh, I see. You realise that's horribly narrow-minded and bigoted?'

'Forgive me.'

'I'll think about it.'

She did, but not for long.

The clatter of feet down the narrow street hadn't escaped Jim Thomson's attention. He had returned to the villa across the fields that morning, stopping short when he saw cars outside the building and people going in and out. The old man he'd seen at the far side of the garden the day before was present again, talking to the long-haired Alex Mavros, as well as to a solid man dressed as a tourist who was obviously a cop.

Thomson's time in Molyvos was over and he was ready to go. He'd been thinking of driving down to the strange rock pinnacle at

Petra, but when he heard the commotion he decided to tag along. Something was obviously happening. If Kostas Gatsos was to be found, he wanted to be there. He didn't rationalise why, it just felt right. The old bastard had done away with the *Homeland* and he wanted to confront him about that. No, he said, under his breath, as he reached the hire car. There's more to it than that. You want to see what Alex Mavros will do. He's haunting you . . .

He put his suitcase in the boot, but kept his hand luggage in the passenger's side footwell. The Russian grenade was wrapped in a T-shirt, along with a small stone he'd found between the rocks where he parted from Ivy.

Marianthi stopped outside a café on the sea front in Plomari. Mavros looked round as he stretched his back.

'Pretty place.'

'Yes,' said Laura. 'Maybe we could come back when this is all over.'

'Don't you have to get back to Colombia?'

'Business brings me to Europe every few months.'

'Good. Wish I could say the same about Colombia.'

'Plenty of missing people there.'

'Not much Spanish in here,' he said, tapping his head.

'Languages can be learned.'

Mavros led her and the others inside, disturbed by the turn the conversation had taken. They'd only spent one night together and Laura was already building a future for them?

The Fat Man went to the bar and started dictating how he wanted the coffee to be made.

'Thanks for asking what we wanted,' Mavros said, when his friend came to the table they'd chosen.

'Yes,' said Laura. 'I'd like a Manhattan.'

'You're getting unsweetened Greek coffee, end of conversation.'

'But I like sugar in mine,' Marianthi protested.

'Traitor. Besides, sugar's bad for you.' Yiorgos pointed at Mavros. 'He told me that.'

Mavros raised his hands. 'Guilty, but only as regards him. You should have seen him when he really was the Fat Man.'

'I wish I had,' Marianthi said, with a sweet smile.

Yiorgos kissed her on the cheek. 'Don't worry, yours has got sugar.'

Mavros shook his head. When the waiter arrived with the coffees, he asked the young man with the shaven head if there were any disused factories in the vicinity.

He laughed. 'Dozens. Why are you interested?'

'We're researching a location for a film,' the Fat Man put in. 'We need somewhere with a chimney on one end.'

'That doesn't narrow it down much.'

'We heard something about a place owned by the Theotokis family.'

'Ah, now you're talking. Old Thomas sold it about a year ago. It was an olive pressing plant. My father used to work there. Apparently someone was going to fix it up, but nothing's happened. I think it has a chimney on the right as it comes into view.'

Mavros tried to disguise his interest. 'Is that so? Whereabouts is it?'

'Go east past Playia and a couple of kilometres further on there's a turn off on the left. It's pretty overgrown but the place is under a kilometre inland.'

Mavros gave him a large tip. 'We have competitors, so I'd be glad if you didn't mention to anyone that you sent us there.'

'No problem,' the young man said, pocketing the cash.

'What do we do?' Yiorgos asked. 'Wait for the cops or check it out ourselves?'

Mavros glanced at Laura. She could scarcely contain her excitement. Marianthi looked more circumspect.

'Consider this,' he said. 'If Kostas Gatsos really is there he'll be under guard, armed guard. Remember what happened to Pavlos and the Russian at the villa.'

'All right,' said the Fat Man. 'We can just find the factory and keep an eye on it till the cops turn up.'

'Let's do that,' Laura said, draining her coffee cup overenthusiastically and spitting grounds into a paper napkin.

Mavros's belly somersaulted as he remembered his suspicions about her. Could Santiago Rojas have planted her as a spy? Would they be walking into a trap? He hadn't seen her make any calls, but that didn't mean she wasn't equipped with a tracking device. No, he couldn't believe it. Her fear on the evening she showed up at Yiorgos's had been genuine enough. Which brought someone else to mind – Igor Gogol: was he involved with the kidnap or even on Lesvos now? Mavros sincerely hoped not. Then again if the Russians

were behind the kidnap, Pyotr Alenov would probably have plenty
of hard men of his own. Gogol might even be one of them.

'All right,' he said. 'We'll go. Marianthi, you can drop us off at
the junction.'

'No chance. I'm going with my man.'

Yiorgos beamed.

'Me too,' said Laura.

'Wouldn't it be nicer if we just had a double dinner date?' Mavros
asked.

Laura looked hurt. 'There's no need to be ironic.'

'I think you'll find there is, but never mind.'

Marianthi drove along the coast and then followed the road to
the village of Playia. She missed the left turn and had to reverse
when Mavros yelled. The bushes on either side were thick, but the
branches nearest the pitted asphalt showed signs of having been
brushed by vehicles recently.

'Slowly,' Mavros cautioned.

The road widened after the first fifty metres, olive trees planted
at regular intervals in the fields on either side.

'There!' Laura cried.

The top of a chimney was visible above the leaves.

'Pull in here,' Mavros said.

Marianthi took the 4x4 deep into the olives where it wouldn't be
visible from the road, then switched off the engine.

'Right then,' said the Fat Man, opening his door.

'No,' Mavros said firmly. 'I'm calling Lieutenant Babis.' He did
so and listened to the policeman, asking some questions. Then he
rang off.

'So?' Yiorgos asked.

'Jesus, what's got into you?' Mavros demanded. 'Trying to be a
hero in front of Marianthi?'

The Fat Man frowned. 'Just trying to help.'

'Getting yourself killed is decidedly not helpful.'

Laura touched his hand. 'What did he say?'

'Theotokis told them he sold the olive press via an estate agent
to an unknown buyer. Babis and the sergeant are on their way. They
should be here in about an hour. But Brigadier Kriaras has ordered
that no action is to be taken until his team arrives later tonight.'

'Great,' Yiorgos said. 'What if old Gatsos dies in the next few
hours?'

'Old Gatsos might have died weeks ago,' Mavros replied. 'There's no hard evidence he's here.'

The Fat Man sighed. 'OK, how about this? If any vehicle goes up or down the road to the factory, we go and have a look.'

'Leaving the women behind.'

'No!' Laura and Marianthi exclaimed with one voice.

'We'll be safer with our heroes,' Marianthi said.

Mavros smacked his forehead. He thought wistfully of the old days when he hadn't even involved Yiorgos in his cases. Although they hadn't always worked out so well.

The thin man with the hooked nose and bright blue eyes stepped off the boat from Ayvalik and passed through Greek customs and immigration without any delay; he had a Turkish passport and spoke the language fluently. He did not reveal that he also spoke fluent Greek. He was wearing a worn black coat and carrying a battered suitcase. Within ten minutes he had disappeared into the back streets of Mytiline and, after going back on himself several times to ensure no one was following, went into a dilapidated apartment block. The small flat on the top floor had been booked by a travel company in Istanbul and paid for in cash. He went straight to the cupboard in the bedroom and, standing on a chair, felt for the bag he knew would be at the back of the highest compartment. He pulled it down and opened it on the bed. All the clothing and equipment he'd arranged for was present, as was a Greek ID card in the name of Christos Beratis. There were also five mobile phones fully charged and each with 20 euros credit. He used one to call his contact in the Greek police, then took out the battery and SIM card and crushed the device beneath his heavy boot. He would drop the pieces in separate waste bins.

As he'd suspected, time was short. His man at the old olive press had kept him up to date with what had been done to Kostas Gatsos. It was clear that the end game had begun. The old man was so belligerent that it was possible the Son would kill him rather than set him loose. That had to be prevented.

He went down to the harbour front and picked up the hire car, a medium-sized Jeep, that had been reserved online.

'There you are, Mr Berati,' said the smiling young female clerk, handing over the keys. 'You'll find a map in the glove compartment. Enjoy your time on Lesvos.'

He nodded then picked up his bag. He had carefully wrapped the weapons with clothes to prevent unwanted metallic sounds. He was also wearing the same fedora that he'd kept on during the crossing. In his considerable experience people struggled to remember the facial features of those wearing hats. Not that it mattered. He had several exit routes arranged.

At first the main road west out of Mytiline was busy with people leaving the town, but soon the traffic thinned. He went round the Gulf of Yera and headed south. He calculated that he'd be at the old factory in under an hour. The fact that he was both outnumbered and outgunned did not bother him in the least.

The afternoon light was fading and the birds were singing their last songs as they settled on the branches.

'What's that?' the Fat Man said, his voice low.

Mavros strained forwards. Lights appeared in the gloom and a large black 4x4 moved down the road to the factory.

'Shit,' he said, under his breath. 'Looks like there's some kind of action here.'

'Time to go,' Yiorgos said.

Laura and Marianthi got out, closing their doors quietly. Both were wearing jackets.

'We go in single file,' Mavros said, 'me at the front and Yiorgos at the back. No talking, even though we don't know for sure yet that old Gatsos is here. When I move my hand downwards, hit the dirt. Make sure your phones are on "vibrate".'

He waited till everyone complied and then led the way through the olive trees. The pressing plant was about several hundred metres ahead and they managed to get within thirty by keeping to the trees. Around the building was a clear space, dotted by broken-down lorries and rusting wagons.

The car that had passed was parked by a heavy steel door. Two men in dark clothes were standing together. They were heavily built and their heads were shaved.

'How the hell are we going to get past them?' Mavros whispered.

'Who says we want to get past them?' Yiorgos said, having joined him at the tree line.

'You've suddenly seen reason, have you?'

'Those two are armed, even I can see that.'

The pistols in the guards' belts became more visible when one of them lit a cigarette.

'We could split up,' Mavros said. 'You and Marianthi go left and see what you can find, Laura and I go right.'

'That means you'll have to cross the road.'

Mavros nodded. 'We'll backtrack to the bend.'

'All right.'

'But no heroics. Call me if you see anything interesting.'

'Same to you.' The Fat Man patted him on the back. 'Look after your woman,' he said, backing away.

My woman, Mavros thought, unable to block out a vision of Niki hanging from the ceiling. What am I doing, bringing Laura here?

As if to justify her presence, she tugged his sleeve and pointed to the door.

He watched as Santiago Rojas and Igor Gogol came out of the factory.

'Those bastards,' she hissed. 'Let's get them.'

Mavros led her away, wondering exactly how they were to achieve that without weapons, even though she seemed ready to rip their throats out. He looked at his watch. Babis and his sidekick would be here soon. They should wait.

Then there came the muffled but unmistakable sound of a shot from the factory. It was followed by eight more.

Jesus, Mavros thought. Have we just stood by as Kostas Gatsos was blown to pieces?

Jim Thomson heard the shots too. He'd parked his hire car on the main road after he saw Mavros's vehicle turn left, then cut across the olive plantation till he was within sight of the group. With him he had his rucksack, the Russian grenade still wrapped up with the stone from Ivy's committal. He had no idea why he'd brought it, but it was beginning to look like a good idea. He saw the big 4x4 arrive and two men get out. The distance was such that he couldn't make out their features. They were both wearing dark clothes. They spoke briefly to the pair that seemed to be on guard duty and went inside.

Jim lay down and looked up at the darkening sky, the first stars beginning to appear. They reminded him of his time on Ikaria with Marigo. Here he was, only a few kilometres from the white sea that had nearly swallowed him after his disgrace. Instead it washed him clean, healed his wounds and carried him to the other side of the world, despite Kostas Gatsos's plans. What was he doing on this Greek island, part of a homeland that was no longer his?

Jim Thomson couldn't answer that question, but he watched the foursome as they split up, then followed the long-haired Alex Mavros and the woman before the shooting started.

After that it was every man for himself, never mind women and children first.

TWENTY-SEVEN

'What do we do?' Laura asked, her fingers trembling against Mavros's hand.

His phone vibrated.

'Did you hear that?' the Fat Man whispered, in agitation.

'Yes. What can you see?'

'Not a lot. There are more vehicles round the back but the only light's coming from a window on the ground floor. Curtains or the like must be over it because it's faint. Hang on, two people have just come out. The door to one of the car's being opened. Fuck! It's him. It's Kostas Gatsos!'

'Is he alive?'

'Yes, he's walking but with difficulty. They're putting him in the back seat. What do we do? Marianthi? Christ, where's she gone?'

'Stay put. She's probably just lying low. This must all be a shock. I'm going to get round the back on this side. Out.'

'Stay here,' he said to Laura. 'Kostas Gatsos is alive.'

'Forget it, Alex. I'm coming with you.'

'Shit. All right.'

They moved forward, hands extended to make their way through the trees.

Then there was the roar of an engine. Lights appeared to their left and a car drove quickly through the trees and on to the road, heading away from the factory. Then it screeched to a halt at the narrowest section after the olive trees and was manouevred until it blocked the road.

'Marianthi,' Mavros said. He watched as the driver got out, leaving the lights on, and ran for cover.

A shot rang out, then another.

'Go and see if you can find her,' Mavros said. 'She might have been hit.'

'No, I want—'

'Do as I say, Laura. Please. This is getting bloody.'

She kissed him on the lips and headed to the lights, before swerving away towards the main road.

'Nicely done,' Mavros muttered. His phone vibrated again.

'What happened?' the Fat Man said, his voice strained.

'Marianthi's blocked the road. Laura's gone to find her.'

'Were the fuckers shooting at her?'

'Probably. Stay where you are. I'm coming.'

But before Mavros got far, a voice rang out.

'Mavro! Alex Mavro! Are you there?'

Mavros's stomach clenched. The Son. Even though he hadn't heard the killer's voice for six years, he recognised it immediately.

'We have unfinished business, you and I. Don't you want to know what happened to your Niki? Come over and I'll tell you. That way you'll also be saving the life of Kostas Gatsos. Surely you don't want to be responsible for his death just as he was on the point of being set free? You know I'll kill him in a heartbeat.'

Mavros's phone went off again.

'Don't do it!' Yiorgos said, speaking at normal volume. 'It's a trick.'

'Can you see Gatsos?'

'They're taking him back inside. There's . . . there's a pistol to his head.'

'That's it, I haven't got a choice. I'm going in.'

'No, don't do—'

Mavros turned off his phone and went forward with his head down. There were several lights on around the pressing plant now. When he came out of the trees, he stood up straight and raised his hands high.

'There he is,' the Son said cheerfully. 'Move forward.' He held no weapon, but two of the guards had pistols aimed at him. 'I told you we'd meet again.'

'Fuck you,' Mavros said, blinking away flashes of Niki's dangling body.

'You knew I was behind this, didn't you?' The Son watched as the guards searched Mavros, then nodded.

'I saw the threat about the Father and Son. A pretty stupid communication.'

'Why? No one but you cottoned on and you only found us by luck.' The assassin stared at him. 'How did you find us, by the way?'

'The Theophilos painting.'

The Son laughed. 'I knew we shouldn't have taken it, but I was under orders. It's a collector's piece.' He turned on his heel. 'Bring him in. And get that car off the road.'

Mavros was pushed through the door and taken to a wooden staircase that led downwards. He caught glimpses of rusty cauldrons and machinery, the bitter smell of crushed olive stones filling his nostrils – and something else: the reek of human waste and the metallic tang of blood.

'Here we are,' said the Son, ushering him into a room.

Gagging with horror and fear, Mavros took in the apparatus. There was blood on the hooks and table.

A man with a badly scarred face joined them.

'What is this?' he asked the Son, in English. 'We must go now. Police are coming.'

'Fuck the police!' the Son screamed suddenly, eyeballs bulging. 'I've been waiting for years to deal with this piece of shit!'

'Igor Gogol,' Mavros said to the other man. 'You realise what this animal's capable of, don't you? He'll ruin everything for the sake of an old gru—' He collapsed, fighting for breath after the Son buried a fist in his abdomen.

'Wait for me,' the assassin ordered. 'I won't be long.' He grabbed Mavros by the shoulders and wrestled him into the torture chamber.

'You . . . you killed . . . Niki.'

The Son smiled. 'Is that what you think? What you've been thinking for years? Well, I'm sorry to disappoint you.'

'The photo . . . of me and . . . Rachel Samuel?'

'I slipped that under the door all right, but you can't hold me responsible for how your mad lover reacted.'

'Want . . . a bet?'

'Lie down on the table or the first hook will be in your eye.'

Mavros did as he was told, still struggling to catch his breath.

'Good,' said the Son. 'I'm sorry I haven't had time to sterilise the hooks. Still, Kostas Gatsos's blood is very rich.' He laughed harshly.

Mavros looked into the killer's eyes and saw the emptiness in them. Then he realised the Son was so far from normal emotions that he had a fatal character flaw. In his arrogance he thought no one would resist when confronted by the awful instruments of pain. Mavros knew what he had to do.

The Fat Man was caught in two minds. Should he go back to the vehicle and find Marianthi or try to help Mavros? He was about to

start towards the factory on a hopeless charge against the odds when
he heard a rustle behind him.

'Need help?' said a voice, the Greek pronunciation slightly off
kilter.

Yiorgos turned and in the dim light made out a white-haired
figure that he recognised.

'You were in the taverna last night,' he said, in a loud whisper.
'Who are you?'

'Jim Thomson.'

'Australian?'

'You could say that. You're Yiorgos Pandazopoulos, aren't you?'

'How do you know that?'

'Alex Mavros's sidekick. I've read about you in the newspaper
archives.'

The Fat Man stared at him. There was something about the well-
preserved man that rang more distant bells.

'Anyway, he's in trouble.'

'Yes,' Yiorgos said. 'Russian mobsters and a shithead torturer
called the Son.'

'Better get moving then.'

'What's that?'

'A hand grenade.'

'Ah.'

'Pay close attention to what I'm going to say.'

'Certainly. What have I got to lose?'

Mavros moved his right hand quickly and grabbed the Son's balls.
Then he took one of the larger hooks and forced the barbed end
into the killer's neck as he bent down in agony.

The man in black at the door raised his pistol and then looked
over his shoulder. There was a commotion behind him, voices raised
and then silenced. One continued to speak loudly, in English.

'This is the pin from the grenade in my other hand. As you can
see, I'm keeping the lever depressed. If I'm shot, you can imagine
what will happen. I'm not familiar with Russian models, but I'm
pretty sure everyone in here will be cut to pieces by fragments. So
give your weapons to my comrade and sit down with your hands
behind your backs.'

'Do something, you fools!'

Mavros picked up what he thought was a Spanish accent. Then

there was a gun shot, the noise very loud in the enclosed basement. Groans could then be heard.

'Give me that,' Mavros said, pointing the Son's pistol at the man by the door, who glanced at the writhing figure of the Son and complied. 'This is Alex Mavros, coming out.'

He did so and was confronted by a row of black-clad men sitting against the wall, their eyes wide.

'Yiorgo?'

'Present. I shot the fucker.'

Mavros glanced at Igor Gogol, who was rolling across the floor, clutching his thigh.

'Who's your friend?'

The Fat Man turned to the man with the grenade. 'I don't know.'

'Yes, you do. You've forgotten.'

Mavros stared at the white-haired man, his heart pounding. Could it really be?

Then there was a dull crump and the basement filled with smoke. Fingers scrabbled in the dark as the disarmed men tried to reclaim their weapons.

Laura and Marianthi had moved closer to the factory after the black 4x4 had bulldozed theirs from the road. The two men in it reversed at speed, then got out and ran into the building.

'What's going on in there?'

'No good,' Marianthi replied, in her limited English. 'Yiorgos and Alex, where they?'

'They must be inside.'

'We go.'

A figure with a hat pulled low stepped in front of them. He had a machine pistol in each hand and was wearing black leather gloves.

'Not a good idea,' he said, first in English and then in Greek. 'Stay here, off the road. Did I understand you to say that Alex Mavros and Yiorgos Pandazopoulos are in the building?'

Laura and Marianthi were nodding.

'Don't worry, I'll look after them.'

'Who are you?' Laura called after him, but there was no response.

They watched as he approached the door cautiously, then slipped inside.

'James Bond?' Marianthi asked, then laughed nervously. 'Police?'

'Too old for 007,' said Laura, leading her into the cover of the trees. 'How did he know their names?'

'They famous,' Marianthi said. 'Big heroes.'

Laura looked dubious.

'At last,' Santiago Rojas said, as the smoke from the smoke grenades cleared. 'I was beginning to think you were all idiots.'

Two black-clad men stood at the foot of the staircase, pistols in their hands. One of the men who had been sitting down was holding another semi-automatic against the head of the man with the grenade, his other hand gripping the captive's arm.

'Give me grenade,' he said, in guttural English. 'Or I put your brains on wall.'

The white-haired man complied and was immediately punched hard in the stomach by another guard. The Fat Man received the same treatment. The first man painstakingly replaced the pin.

'Where's Mavros?' the Son shouted, blood pumping through the fingers of the hand he was holding to his neck. 'Find the fucker!'

Men spread out across the basement, throwing open doors.

'And Gatsos?' Rojas asked.

'Screw Gatsos! He's in the cupboard in the torture chamber. Find Mavros!'

There was a burst of fire, then another, and the men at the bottom of the stairs collapsed, heads shattered. A figure in black wearing a hat moved quickly past them

One of the Russians shouted and then went down, his head haloed in crimson.

Rojas turned and ran, while the Son grabbed a pistol and emptied the clip at the attacker.

There were more bursts from the far end of the basement. Men started screaming.

The Son walked forward painfully, picking up another pistol, and dropped to his knees by the Fat Man and the white-haired man.

'They die if you don't throw down your weapons,' he said, jamming the weapon's muzzle into Yiorgos's neck.

'Take me,' Mavros said, stepping from the room next to the torture chamber and putting down the pistol he had grabbed. 'Let them go.'

The Son looked round and grinned. 'I know, I'll take you *and* them.'

The shots came before he could pull the trigger. They hit him in the back and head. He fell forward over the men who had been his potential victims, his legs twitching briefly.

Mavros had turned round.

The man in the Homburg came towards him slowly, looking into each room. Then he smiled crookedly.

'Hello, little brother,' he said.

Mavros dropped to his knees as the hat was removed to reveal Andonis's still dark hair and weathered but instantly recognisable features. His blue eyes shone above the hook of his nose as they had done a lifetime ago. Then Mavros's vision was obscured by tears.

TWENTY-EIGHT

W hen the shooting started in earnest, Laura started to run to the factory. Marianthi wasn't far behind. They found no one on the ground floor, but could hear voices from the basement.

'Alex?' Laura shouted, oblivious to danger.

'Yiorgo?' followed Marianthi.

They went down the stairs, stepping round the bodies at the foot. The Fat Man was standing with a white-haired man beside a sprawling corpse. Marianthi ran to him.

'Careful,' he gasped, as she ran into him. 'I got hit.'

'Shot?' she screamed.

'No, punched in the gut.'

'Who's this?'

'I don't know.'

Laura ran along, looking into rooms. She stopped when she saw Mavros and the man they had met outside, his hat now in his hand and the machine pistols in his coat pockets.

'Alex?' she said. 'Are you all right?'

'Yes,' he answered hoarsely.

Laura could see his eyes were damp.

'Who's this?'

'My . . . my brother.'

'What?'

'Come,' the other man said. 'We have to get out of here before the police arrive.' He smiled at Laura. 'Don't worry, you'll have him back shortly, Ms Moreno.'

'How . . .?' She watched as they moved past her and approached the stairs. Mavros's brother spoke to Yiorgos and handed him the machine pistols. He also talked to the white-haired man, who followed them after shaking the Fat Man's hand.

Then Laura looked to her left and saw a sickening framework of hooks and lines above a table. She went towards it, unable to stop herself. Then she heard a faint knocking from inside a heavy cupboard. The key was in the door. She turned it and stepped back

as a short, naked figure tumbled out. The ends of his fingers were
stained brown and his right ear was missing.

'Kostas.'

'Laura,' the old man said. 'I'm glad to see your glorious
anatomy.'

She took his arm, seeing the wounds on his wrist and across his
body.

'What did they do to you?'

'Never mind that. Where's my bitch of a daughter?'

She let him go as he hobbled towards the door, this time keeping
her eyes off the torture device. It was no longer clear to her that
Greece was the cradle of western civilisation.

'Stephanos Hatzis, of all people,' Andonis Mavros said, as the trio
walked towards the olive trees. 'What brought you here?'

'It's a long story,' said the white-haired man. 'And no one's called
me that for over three decades. I'm Jim Thomson now.'

'Stephanos?' Mavros said. 'I remember you.'

'And I you. Andonis brought me to your family house once. We
were in the same Youth Party group.'

'I . . . I can't believe this,' Mavros said, staring at his brother in
the last of the light from the factory. 'You disappear for thirty-eight
years and turn up as I'm about to be killed? What the fuck's that
about?'

Andonis drew closer. 'Listen, Alex, I don't have much time. I—'
He broke off and looked down, then took off the glove from his
right hand and reached for Mavros's. 'You have to understand. I
was . . . broken in Bouboulinas Street. They made me betray . . .
everyone.'

'The same happened to me,' said Jim Thomson. 'You can't live
with the shame. This is the first time I've set foot on Greek soil
since 1975.'

Andonis nodded slowly. 'That's how it is, little brother. I could
never face Mother or Anna or you. I wasn't just a traitor to the
Party and my comrades, but I disgraced our father's good name. I
couldn't stay, I couldn't get in touch . . .'

'Bullshit!' Mavros shouted. 'You think Mother would have cared
about that? You were tortured, for God's sake. No one could stand
that. Fuck you, Andoni. No calls, no letters, no contact for all this
time. It's obvious you don't give a damn about us.'

'That isn't true,' his brother said, reaching out to the hand that had been snatched away. 'I got involved in work that I'm not . . . I'm not proud of.'

'What are you talking about?'

'The Soviets?' said Jim.

Andonis looked at him briefly. 'Them and their successors.'

'What were you?' Mavros demanded. 'A KGB hit man?'

'A fixer, more like. But I gave that up five years ago. Now I right wrongs that others can't. You can be sure I've been following your career closely, Alex. I'm very sorry about Niki.'

Mavros stared at him. 'You've been following my career? You fucking arsehole, we could have worked together. Do you know how much time I've spent looking for you? Instead you got involved with the Son, didn't you? That's why you made sure he couldn't talk back there.'

Andonis looked puzzled. 'Why do you say that?'

'Back in 2004 he told me you were alive.'

'He must have picked that up from the people he worked for. Some are ex-KGB. As is Pyotr Alenov, who set the kidnap up at Sergei Potemkin's behest.'

'I know he did,' Mavros snapped. 'And Santiago Rojas was their mole on the Gatsos group board.' He paused and tried to get a grip on his breathing. 'So what am I supposed to say? "Thanks for saving my life, big brother, and goodbye"?'

'I have to go, Alex. You know the police will be here soon. But I promise I'll be in touch again.'

'Maybe you could do that before Mother dies. She's eighty-five, you know.'

'I think of her every day.'

'I'll bet you do. Do I let her know you've been hiding from her and the rest of us all these years? No, I don't think so. Let's see if you have the balls to do it yourself.'

Jim Thomson came closer. 'Don't be so hard on him, Alex. You don't know what failing your friends does to you.'

'Go to hell. You're both cowards. Where's the honour in hiding from the people who love you?'

Andonis smiled sadly. 'You saw what went on in the basement back there, Alex. Where was the honour in that?'

A vehicle came racing down the access road, lights blazing. The two older men stepped deeper into the trees.

'Here come Greece's finest,' Andonis said. 'I'd be grateful if you kept my name out of this, Alex, but I'll understand if you don't.'

'Ditto,' said Thomson.

'There's also a man in there with a sword tattoo on his neck,' Andonis continued. 'He was my contact. I asked Yiorgos to let him go, but if you could check . . .'

'Where are you going?' Mavros said. 'How can I get in touch with you?'

'Leave that to me.' His brother looked at the white-haired man. 'Come with me, Stephane. We have things to talk about.'

Thomson looked at him. 'I wanted to tell that old bastard Gatsos I was on a ship he had sunk, but what's the point? There's nothing else to keep me here.'

Andonis approached Mavros and opened his arms. 'I'll tell you about my life when we next meet, Alex.'

'What makes you think I give a shit?'

Another soft smile. 'It's in your eyes, my brother. And under that grizzled stubble.'

Mavros walked into the embrace and felt his sibling's thin frame. In his youth Andonis had been muscular and solid.

'Are you ill?' he asked, swallowing a sob.

'Not that I know of. Just approaching sixty after too many hard years.'

'Stay alive, Andoni. There are people who need to see you again, soon.'

'I hear you.'

They kissed each other on the cheeks, then Mavros watched as Andonis and his old comrade disappeared into the darkness. He stood there for a time, taking in the calls of the night birds and the rustling of the leaves in the wind.

Lieutenant Babis and Sergeant Elisavet got out of their hire car, pistols at the ready.

'Over here,' Mavros called. 'Don't worry, everything's under control.' His voice was level, but the emotional turmoil almost made him throw up.

When they got to the basement, Mavros managed to get across to the Fat Man, Laura and Marianthi that *he* would tell the officers what had happened. Andonis hadn't killed all the Russians, only three who had gone for their weapons, and the Son. The others had serious but non-lethal wounds. They weren't in the mood to talk and probably never would be. There was no sign of any man with a sword tattoo. Igor Gogol had passed out from loss of blood and Elisavet Latsou tied a tourniquet around his upper thigh. Ambulances were on the way.

Mavros said that a firefight had started when he brandished a grenade that he found – he made sure he picked it up so his fingerprints were on it. Kostas Gatsos had been calmed down by Laura and was hunched in a blanket, his eyes wild but his mouth closed. He looked physically frail. Santiago Rojas's gabbled accusations were ignored by Babis after Mavros told him that the Colombian was involved in the kidnap. When the lieutenant saw the torture table he was even less inclined to pay Rojas any heed.

No one was allowed to leave the old pressing plant, although Mavros, Yiorgos, Laura and Marianthi, along with Kostas Gatsos, were taken upstairs by Sergeant Latsou. She had found a makeshift kitchen, and Marianthi volunteered to make coffee and sandwiches.

It was nearly eleven o'clock when Nikos Kriaras arrived with his team. He gave Mavros a steely glare and went downstairs. Ten minutes later he appeared at the top of the steps and beckoned to him.

'What the fuck went on here? Who gave you permission to start a battle? Kostas Gatsos could have been killed.'

'Unlikely. He was locked in a cupboard until the shooting finished.'

'And the rest?'

Mavros told him his version of events, saying they'd decided not to wait when they heard shots.

'Where were they taking him?'

'You'd better ask Rojas that.'

'He's clammed up. Wants a lawyer.'

'He'll need a good one. He was working with Igor Gogol, but I think you'll find the plot goes much higher than them.'

'Greeks?'

'Not primarily.'

'Thank God for that.'

'Let's you off the hook a bit, yes. But I doubt you'll be able to stop Kostas Gatsos telling his story to the world's media.'

Kriaras smiled tightly. 'That's all to the good, considering the Greek police was responsible for his discovery.'

'So that's how it's going to be.'

'What do you care? You've got the family's half million euros.'

'I suppose. If the old man doesn't renege.'

The brigadier grabbed his arm. 'What happened to the Son?'

'He lost his head or at least the functioning parts of it. Aren't you pleased? He could have come out with some pretty tales about how you used him over the years.'

'Do you want me to arrest you?'

'On what charge? Telling the truth? And something else – the Son knew I was coming. How do you explain that?'

'I don't have to.'

'Really? If I find the slightest evidence that you were in contact with him, your career will turn into a mushroom cloud.'

Nikos Kriaras stalked away.

'Can we go now?' Mavros called after him.

'Yes, but I want you all at police headquarters in Athens tomorrow afternoon at the latest.'

'Please.'

The brigadier kept walking.

Mavros thought about what he'd said. Why would Kriaras have been in cahoots with the Son? To ensure he got credit for the case while letting the killer escape? Anything was possible in the policeman's world of graft and services rendered, but that was a stretch. There was probably a lower ranked informer.

'What did you say to him?' Lieutenant Babis asked.

'The usual pleasantries.' Mavros looked at Sergeant Latsou, who was supervising the photographing of the Son's corpse. 'Some body,' he said.

'Yes, he had muscles like . . .' He saw where Mavros was looking. 'Careful. We don't tolerate comments about fellow officers.'

'Especially not when they're female.'

'Exactly.'

Elisavet looked round. She might even have smiled.

Marianthi drove them to Mytiline, where they found rooms in a harbour front hotel. Mavros organised e-tickets on the morning flight. They only had a few hours to sleep, but none of them wanted to go straight to bed. Laura and Marianthi sat together in one of the rooms, not as shell-shocked as they might have been, while Mavros and the Fat Man shared small bottles of Plomari ouzo from their mini-bars.

'What did Andonis tell you?' Yiorgos asked.

Mavros filled him in.

'I never thought we'd see him again,' the Fat Man said, when he'd finished. 'Let alone when we were staring death in the face.'

'We'd better see him again soon or I'll go looking for him.'

'Like you've been doing all your adult life.'

'Except during this case. And the last five years.'

'Which goes to show that patience is a virtue.'

'Thanks for that, Aristotle.'

Later, in bed, Laura gave Mavros a serious look.

'You're taking it badly, aren't you?'

'Thirty-eight years,' Mavros said bitterly. 'Why didn't he call? Once would have been enough.'

Laura kissed him on the cheek. 'No, it wouldn't. I can see that. It was either full contact or nothing.'

'That's your considered opinion, is it?'

'Are we having our first fight?' she said, eyes flashing.

The tension left Mavros's body. 'No. I'm sorry. It would have been much worse having to handle this without you.'

She kissed him again.

'I mean, I'd have had to cry on the Fat Man's shoulder.'

Laura nudged him in the ribs.

'Ow! My abdomen's a restricted zone.'

'Really? I'll have to see if I can find somewhere else that'll respond to my advances.'

She succeeded. Neither of them got much sleep.

The wind was gusting hard when they left the hotel, the water in the port churning.

'This is going to be a hell of a flight,' Yiorgos said.

'If it isn't cancelled,' Mavros said. He was hoping it would be because he hated turbulence.

They drove past signs to the Theophilos Museum at Vareia.

'I'd have liked to visit that,' Laura said. 'His work's very unusual. I wonder where the painting from the bedroom is.'

'I doubt it'll ever surface. Greed, that was what let the Russians down. If they'd left the painting where it was, we'd never have found the old olive press in time. I wonder what they were going to do with Kostas. Still, he probably owns other Theophilos works. Maybe he'll ask you back next summer to see its replacement.'

She looked at Mavros. 'If he does, it'll have to be an invitation for two.'

'Four,' the Fat Man grunted. 'We risked our skins for him as well.'

'Maybe he'll give us a reward' said Marianthi.

'Don't worry, I'll cover it,' Mavros said.

'You can say that again,' Yiorgos declared.

The driver smiled when Mavros pointedly didn't.

On the plane Laura looked down at the wind-blasted sea.

'It's even whiter today,' she said. 'Like a huge llama coat.'

Mavros was holding on tightly to the arm rests.

'Of course,' Laura continued, 'llamas can be grey, reddish-brown and black too.'

The plane dropped suddenly and Mavros used the paper bag that he'd put between his knees.

'Goats,' he said, wiping his mouth with a tissue.

'What?'

'I told you on the way over. Little white goats.'

'Oh yes.' She paused. 'But llamas are much sweeter than goats.'

'Will you stop talking about long-haired quadrupeds?'

Laura gave him a cold and studied look. 'Is *this* our first fight?'

'No,' he sighed. 'Call the bloody sea what you like.'

They hit more turbulence and he used the bag again.

Laura sniffed. 'How much ouzo did you drink last night?'

That provoked another bout of vomiting. Mavros's stomach only calmed down when the plane came to a halt at Athens airport. Then it struck him like the edge of a broadsword that his challenge to Andonis meant he was going to have to dissemble to Dorothy and Anna. Would he be able to pull that off?

EPILOGUE

'So these are the heroes who found me,' Kostas Gatsos said. He was sitting in the leather chair behind the desk in his office. Loukas was on his left, while Evi had ushered Mavros, the Fat Man and Marianthi in. She introduced them, having been given the last two's details by Mavros over the phone. They had come straight from police HQ, where they'd given statements. Laura was still there, but had insisted she'd come down to the green office building on her own.

The three nodded to him, shaking his bandaged hands being out of the question. There was also a dressing over the wound where his ear had been.

'Idiot doctors,' he said. 'I told them they were wasting their time. Now I look like Vincent van Gogh after the piano lid crashed down.' He glanced at Evi. 'Did van Gogh play the piano?'

'Oh, *Pappou*,' she said, laughing.

'Anyway, these envelopes are for you. You deserve them, though my initial thought was that young Loukas had been seriously over-generous.'

Mavros found a cheque for a quarter of a million more than he'd been promised. The looks on the faces of Yiorgos and Marianthi suggested they'd been well rewarded too. They all gave thanks, the Fat Man and taxi-driver signing confidentiality agreements.

'Enough of that,' Kostas Gatsos said, waving his arms. 'Now we must get on with running this business. Fortunately all our shareholders are staying on board, except Santiago Rojas. And Eirini, Myrto and Nana, the treacherous bi . . .' He looked at Loukas and Evi. 'I'm sorry, but they went against the interests of the family. And now they've all left the country. Good riddance.'

Evi blinked back tears, while Loukas's chin was set firm. Soon afterwards, Evi took them to the lift.

'I'm glad he's back, but he seems even more driven than before. And he's agreed to set up a charitable foundation with ten million of his own money. He said something about compensation too, I don't know who for. It's been a day of surprises.'

'Life's full of them,' Mavros said, kissing her on the cheek.

The young woman blushed.

Out on the street a taxi pulled up and Laura got out.

'Have you finished?'

'In a big way,' the Fat Man said. 'Can we give you a lift?'

'I'm sure Marianthi needs to get back to her kids,' Mavros said, catching Yiorgos's eye.

'His place is on the way back to mine,' the driver said, with a wink a pantomime dame would have been proud of.

Laura kissed them both and waved as the taxi departed.

'What now?' Mavros asked. 'I hope you didn't say anything out of turn to the cops.'

'I stuck to your story,' Laura said solemnly. 'I'll talk to Kostas on the phone later. Come on, show me the sights.'

'There's a fish restaurant not far away that's normally way above my pay grade.'

'Don't worry,' she said, taking his hand after they'd got into a taxi. 'I'll pay.'

'You will not.'

Laura smiled. 'OK, but when you come to Colombia everything's on me.'

'Including the llamas?'

'Of course.'

That evening they had the dinner of their lives. Then they took a room in the best hotel in Piraeus and made love for most of the night.

The next day Laura flew to Madrid and on to Bogotá.

'You let her go,' Dorothy said.

Mavros handed her another cup of tea.

'She isn't mine to let go, Mother. But we'll be seeing each other again.'

'I'm glad,' she said softly.

Mavros looked at her. 'Are you all right?'

'Yes, dear. Decrepitude and departing vitality, that's all.'

The photographs of Andonis were behind her head. Mavros felt a strong urge to tell her that her elder son was alive, but the doorbell rang and the moment was lost. He went to undo the chain, realising that excessive security measures were no longer necessary. For the first time he felt relief at the Son's death, though it meant he would never find out the extent of Kriaras's knowledge of the kidnap. Perhaps it was minimal – after all, he had put Mavros in contact with the Gatsos family. But the brigadier may have had his strings pulled by shadowy establishment figures – such as shareholders – interested in the old man's kidnap and ousting from the chairmanship of the group.

'What happened?' Anna said, as she kissed him. 'Kostas Gatsos is free, but there's no mention of you in the media.'

Mavros put his finger to his mouth. 'Confidential.'

'Come on,' said Nondas. 'I already know more about the Gatsos group than anyone except the old pirate himself.'

'Maybe I can be persuaded to drop a few nuggets. You'd better not follow suit, you Cretan lunatic.'

Dorothy got up to greet them. She suddenly looked better.

Mavros watched as she kissed her daughter and son-in-law. Dorothy lived for her family, even though she pretended publishing was her main interest. She hadn't been particularly enthusiastic when he told her he could pump a lot of money into the business – and it was hers alone now, as he was going back to missing persons work. The financial crisis meant that bankrupt people were disappearing in droves. Not only that, his curiosity had been re-engaged by his brother's reappearance. He desperately wanted to know the details of Andonis's life.

Mother cares so much for her children, Mavros thought. I have to tell her about Andonis. I have to tell Anna.

He stepped forward, mouth half-open, then glimpsed a photo of his brother as a twenty-one-year-old – so inspiring, so much energy, such subtle intelligence. The thin figure he had embraced on Lesvos was very different, worn down by his experiences, saddened, the vitality sapped despite his decisive intervention. Would Andonis do as he'd said and get in touch?

Mavros made up his mind. He would keep silent for a month. If Andonis didn't make contact, he would tell his mother and Anna about him.

He sat on the sofa next to Nondas and listened to the conversation. Then he remembered Laura's almost forbidding beauty on the plane, her dark hair set against the white sea through the window, and felt more alive than he had done for years.

AFTERWORD

The usual warm thanks and raised glasses to the people who keep Mavros a going concern:

Edwin Buckhalter, Kate Lyall Grant and all the team at Crème de la Crime; Broo Doherty, most diligent of agents; my esteemed mentor Dr J. Wallis Martin; my readers and social media friends, you happy band of brothers and sisters; my real sister Claire for hospitality and much else; my real brother Alan for raunchy rhythms – check out the Dark Rays; and, last but not least in the least, my beloved nuclear family, who rock, roll, jump and jive, each in their inimitable way – Roula, there would be nothing without you; Maggie, where's Kevin Lip? Alexander, put the Tooth Fairy down NOW!